DRUNK ON THE JOB

THE MISADVENTURES OF A DRUNK IN
PARADISE: BOOK 4

ZANE MITCHELL

Drunk on the Job
The Misadventures of a Drunk in Paradise: Book #4

by
Zane Mitchell

Copyright © 2019 by Zane Mitchell

ISBN: 9781070388823
VS: 70182020.02
ASIN: B07S7Q7L62

To my children.
You are the reasons I push myself harder every day.

"DON'T DO IT, ARTIE. JUST—DON'T FUCKING DO IT."

The truth of the matter was, I wanted nothing more than to support my friend and boss, but I just couldn't help but feel like the decision he was making was one of those instantly regrettable ones—sort of like telling a woman the truth when she asked if the jeans she was wearing made her ass look big. *Why, yes, as a matter of fact, honey, your ass does look huge in those jeans.* Never mind the fact that you had good intentions when saying it. Personally, I appreciated a big ass on a woman. But that didn't change the fact that getting punched hurts.

And *there* it was, folks.

The key to the issue at hand.

I didn't want my buddy getting hurt. We'd become too good of friends for me to just let that happen without even *trying* to stop the train wreck.

So when Al Becker chimed in, taking my side, I was grateful. "Look, Artie. The kid's right. I've supported every other decision you've made for all the years we've been friends, but this one, I—I just don't think I can support."

With both of his meaty arms resting on the poker table in front of him, Artie Balladares peeled his thumbs up off the green felt in somewhat of a muted protest. "Aww, come on, fellas. I don't see what the problem is here."

I looked around the table. None of the rest of the guys were brave enough to say what they were thinking. I could see it on their lily-livered, liver-spotted faces. Here's the deal with that —each and every one of them had been taught as a child that honesty is always the best policy, but they were also taught that if you don't have anything nice to say, you don't say anything at all.

So let me ask you a real question. What happens when those two proverbs collide? What do you do? Do you keep silent and let your best friend make the biggest mistake of his life because the truth isn't very nice? Or do you man up and slap some truth on him?

So before I continue with my story and you deem me an asshole, realize that my inner Drunk *requires* me to do the latter. I mean, do any of you even know me? Sparing a friend's feelings comes secondary to preventing them from making a life-altering mistake.

Because after all, you know how the saying goes—*friends don't let friends marry hookers.*

And as I looked around the poker table that afternoon, it nearly blew my mind that none of the old codgers surrounding me had the cojones left to speak up. It was literal insanity. So if I had to be the bad guy, once again, so be it.

I leaned across the poker table to look Artie squarely in the eye. "I don't get it, Artie. Why you gonna buy the milk when you get the whole goddamned hooker for free?"

Al looked over at me and shook his head. "I don't think you got that expression right, kid."

"Seriously, Al? You wanna split hairs about a fucking *expression*? Artie wants to marry a hooker!"

Al's hands flailed up into the air. "I just told him it's a bad idea. What're you yelling at *me* for? I'm on your side."

I looked around the table again. "Well, how about the rest

of you guys? It can't just be me and Al that think this idea's dumber than the idiot who thought getting a mustache tattooed on the inside of their index finger was a good idea."

Putting his cards down on the table, Gary "The Gunslinger" Wheelan sighed, leaned back in his seat, and crossed his arms over his protruding beer belly. "Fine. If we're being honest, I gotta say I agree with Drunk and Al, Artie. Maybe marrying a hooker's not really the best idea you've ever had."

An annoyed groan rumbled from the depths of Artie's oversized innards, and his cheeks pinkened up. "For one thing, men, let's get something straight." He stabbed one stubby sausage finger into the table. "She's a professional escort. Not a hooker. Okay? So can we stop calling her that? She and I find the term offensive."

I rolled my eyes. "Oh my God. She's a fucking hooker, Artie. Calling her a professional escort is like calling a car thief a professional automobile relocator. It's all bullshit!"

Artie looked around the table, scanning the faces of Big Eddie, Ralph the Weasel, Bob Hope, Elton John, and Tony Soprano, but no one else dared to make eye contact with him. "Seriously, guys? *None* of you are on my side?"

Ralph tossed a pair of poker chips into the center pot. "I mean, I get *why* you wanna marry her. She's one tasty-looking potato chip."

"Oh, come on, Ralph." Artie winced. "Don't talk about my girlfriend like—like she's a piece of meat or something."

"Hey, hey, hey!" Ralph's hands went up defensively. "I didn't say she was a piece of meat. I said she was a potato chip. But you gotta be real, Artie. Lotsa men on this island—well, lotsa men on this island got a taste of her salt on their lips, if you know what I'm sayin'."

Big Eddie's twiglike arm staggered hesitantly up into the air. "I—I don't," he stammered.

I rolled my eyes. "Well, we know *you* don't, Eddie."

"What about you, Drunk?" asked Artie.

My head lolled back on my slackened shoulders. "Ugh, Artie."

"I'm serious. You, uh—and Val ever get, uh"—he swallowed hard—"salty together?"

Lifting my head, I chuckled. "You can't even say it, can you, Artie?"

Artie lifted one of his big beefy shoulders, and his eyes glanced around the table uncomfortably. "I was trying to be discreet."

"You just told us you want to propose marriage to a hooker. You really think your life is gonna be discreet from here on out?"

Artie mopped up the sweat that poured from his brow with a bar rag. "Fine. You met her before I did. Did you and Val ever, uh, have sex?"

"No!" I leaned forward and slammed two flattened palms down on the table. "But lots of guys have! And if I had been one of them, would that make you change your mind?"

Artie shook his head as his eyes swung down to the table. "No, that's in the past."

"Then I guess it doesn't matter that she *tried* to sleep with me."

"It really doesn't. We're starting off with a clean slate. She's a changed woman."

Frowning, I mulled that over for a second. "Look, Artie. Val's a sweet gal. And she's hot. I'll give her that much. And *maybe* beneath those ginormous fake boobs of hers she's got a big heart. You know? She could definitely be a hooker with a heart of gold. And it was one thing when you were just having sex with her. Because I get that. We're men and we have needs. But, Artie, a minute before she met you, she was sleeping with anyone that paid her. You really wanna marry someone who's had more balls in her mouth than the Hungry Hippo?"

"Drunk!" Al's objection came out more forcefully than usual.

The guys all chuckled, except for Artie. His face was redder than I'd ever seen it. He slammed two meaty fists down on the table and roared at me. "That's enough! I told you, she's starting off with a clean slate. I trust her."

I shrugged and sat back in my seat. "She's gonna take you for all you're worth, Artie. Mark my words."

The clubhouse's back porch fell into an awkward silence then. It was midweek, and just past lunchtime. Behind us, the Beachgoer, the Seacoast Majestic's fancy poolside restaurant, sat mostly empty. Only busboys, dishwashers, and cooks remained, cleaning up the tables and preparing the restaurant for dinner. Silverware, glasses, and plates clinked like wind chimes in the distance, and overhead, the frond-shaped ceiling fans made nearly silent whooshing sounds, providing gentle relief from the heat of the day.

Behind us, a table full of elderly women playing bridge had even fallen silent. I was sure they were listening in—getting the scoop. After all, the resort owner marrying a "professional escort" would be fodder for the gossip hounds for weeks to come.

Al stared at me like he couldn't believe the things that had just come out of my mouth. Like I was supposed to feel bad or something. But if I had anything to feel bad about, it was that I'd made Artie mad. That hadn't been my intention. It was just that he'd caught me off guard with his announcement.

I honestly had nothing against Valentina Carrizo. She seemed like a nice woman. But not only was she less than half Artie's age, I also knew she consorted with some less-than-stellar people. I'd met her at a seedy bar in the District a few weeks back, and upon meeting, she'd been so brazen as to grab my junk and then she'd offered to sleep with me for half price. Later I'd hired her as a singing hookergram as a distraction for a guy I'd been investigating, and it had become clear that she'd do just about anything for a buck. So to think that Artie wanted to *marry* her, well, it just sort of blew my mind.

Surprisingly enough, Big Eddie, the quietest guy of all the old-timers I hung out with, was the first one to break the silence. His sunken-in eyes, hidden behind a pair of browline reading glasses, swung over to look at Artie. "Uh, Artie. You're planning to have her sign a prenup, right?"

All eyes turned to Artie.

He drew his eyes off Eddie before shifting uneasily around the table. "Well, I did bring it up to her when the subject of marriage came up. But Val—uh, well, she really didn't seem to like that idea."

Shaking my head, I chuckled to myself. I had no idea that a pair of fake breasts and a round ass could turn a smart man like Artie Balladares into such a schmuck. But I kept my lips pressed together and only tossed both hands up into the air. I'd said my piece. If Artie wanted to lose everything to a hooker, that was his choice. I was no more his accountant than I was his mother.

But Al hadn't liked that answer. He lifted his bushy white brows high on his otherwise bald forehead. "Artie. Eddie's got a valid point. Come on. Tell me you're not seriously gonna marry Val without a prenup."

Throwing his hands up in an exaggerated shrug, Artie grunted. "Well, I don't know. Nothing's settled. Obviously, I haven't popped the question yet. But when the subject came up the other day and I mentioned a prenup, she sort of balked at the idea. Like I'd hurt her feelings."

Tony, usually a very loud, opinionated man, had been sitting idly by in his motorized scooter listening to the conversation. It was at this point that he finally decided to chime in. "Look, Artie. I'm probably one of the few men here who's actually *not* opposed to you making it official with Val. I like the woman. And I'm not gonna lie. If you marry her, then she's gonna be laying around the pool a lot more often and that's not exactly offensive to me. But the guys are right. If you marry her, you gotta have a prenup. You've got too much to lose. The resort. Everything you've worked for your whole life. Shit, Artie, your pride is worth something, isn't it?"

Artie sighed. "I'll think about it, fellas. Okay? I'll think about it. Now I hope you'll all get on board with this. Val's a good woman. She'll make a good wife, and, well—I love her."

"We just want what's best for you, Artie," said Gary.

"Val *is* what's best for me. I want you all to know that. She's brought excitement and energy back into my life. I haven't had that in—in years. You guys probably can't tell, but hell, I've lost twenty pounds since we started dating."

Al reached a hand out to his old friend and squeezed his shoulder. "What would Jennie say about you marrying Val?"

Artie massaged his forehead with his fingers and was quiet for a few long seconds. Finally, he looked over at Al. "Jennie's gone," he said quietly. "While she wouldn't necessarily be thrilled with my choice in women, I know she'd want me to be happy. And Val makes me happy."

I sighed. I felt Artie's loneliness to my core. While I'd dated around a lot over the years, it wasn't until I'd met Pam that I'd felt that feeling of loneliness dissipate. Of course it had been short-lived, but the truth was, I knew how great it had felt to be in love and to *feel* loved. How could I wish anything less for my friend? Was it really *my place* to pass judgment on Artie's love life? He *deserved* happiness. And what kind of friend would I be if I stood in the way of that happiness?

"Look, Artie. If Val makes you happy, I'll try and get on board. For you, all right?"

Artie looked at me in surprise. "You're serious, Drunk?"

"I'm serious. It's not like I have anything against Val, personally. I'm just worried about you. But I agree with the rest of the guys. If you're gonna go down this path, the least you should do is have a prenup drafted by a good lawyer."

"I'll look into it. Okay?"

"That's all we're asking, Artie," said Al.

A smile curved the edges of Artie's mouth. He clapped his hands together as if the topic of his engagement had been settled. "Great. Now we can talk about the proposal I have planned. I'm trying to work out all the details at the moment, but I might need a little help from my friends."

"Want me to spell out 'Will You Marry Me' on the beach in one-dollar bills?" I asked with a shrug.

All the guys shot me evil stares.

"What?!" I shrugged. "That's not funny?"

Artie ignored me and continued. "The island's annual Carnival festival kicks off on Friday. Now I know all the big events are off resort property, but I've hired some live entertainment for the resort, and I think after the big fireworks display, I'm gonna pop the question on the beach under the stars."

"I guess that's as good of time as any to do it," said Al.

Even though I wanted to try and get on board, I still wasn't quite there yet. I grimaced. "You sure you wanna do it so *soon*, Artie?"

All the guys' heads bobbed around the table.

Artie glanced around the room, making eye contact with everyone. "Look. This isn't up for group discussion. I'll think about the prenup, but other than that, it's settled. I'm proposing to Val this Friday night. And that's that."

2

An hour later and after finishing our poker game with the guys, Al and I left the clubhouse's back porch and wandered into the sports bar on the other side of the building. With little else to do, we sat at the bar and caught the tail end of a Royals game and asked the bartender to make each of us a margarita.

For those in the room that have never had the pleasure to meet me before, let me take this quiet moment to introduce myself. My name is Daniel Terrence Drunk, Jr., and I live on Paradise Isle, a small island in the middle of the Caribbean Sea. I'm Terrence to my mother and my friend Al's wife, Evie, T or T-Bone to some of my friends back in the States, Danny to one woman in particular, whom you'll meet eventually, and Drunk to almost everyone else.

I'm a "gangly fellow," as my mother would call me. At six-foot-four, I'm mostly legs and arms, and I'm top-heavy, with an oversized nose, a thick pile of dark Grecian hair—which I usually keep safely tucked under a black fedora, and a larger-than-life ego. I consider myself a good-looking fellow, hence the larger-than-life ego, but I'm quite aware that I'm not every-one's brand of oatmeal and I'm fine with that, because if *everyone* liked me, I think I'd be doing something wrong at life.

As it stood, I had a handful of close friends, Al Becker being one of the closest, I had a cushy job, and I lived on a fucking tropical island.

I was currently winning at life.

When the Royals game was over, Al hopped off his barstool and walked to the end of the bar while I attempted to suck down my strawberry margarita without incurring brain freeze.

"Fuck," I muttered, pinching the bridge of my nose. "I need to stop ordering these blended."

"You say that every time," said Al as he hobbled back over to his stool with a rolled-up newspaper in his hand.

"Every time I'm right. But I like 'em blended."

Once Al was properly situated, he unrolled the Paradise Isle newspaper. While I struggled to unthaw my brain, Al scanned the front page. Less than a second later, his breath caught in the back of his throat. "Well, I'll be!"

"You'll be what? A monkey's uncle? You know, I never understood that expression. What's that really mean—a monkey's uncle? Why couldn't it be a horse's ass or a bull-frog's dick or something a little more catchy?"

Al tipped the paper sideways to give me a look at the front page. "Well ain't *this* a bullfrog's dick," he said out of the side of his mouth.

A quick glance made my eyes nearly burst out of my skull. There was a huge picture of *me* on the front page. "What the—"

"You made the Sunday paper. You're a *celebrity*, kid!"

I plucked the paper out of Al's hands and read the head-line. *Newest Islander Takes Down the PGC.* "Holy shit."

"Can I get your autograph, Officer Drunk?" asked Al with a chuckle, sliding a pulpboard coaster across the polished wood bar top to me.

"Ah, piss off." I groaned as I scanned the article. *Officer Drunk of the Kansas City, Missouri Police Department...* "These fuckers. They just told the whole goddamned island I'm a police officer."

"Well, you *are*. Or at least you *were*," said Al.

"*Were*, Al, were. *That's* the operative word." I shook my head. I *hated* being called Officer Drunk.

"You know, if I remember correctly, you said you wanted to be the island's next eligible bachelor after Ziggy Thomas bit the tarmac. From your lips to God's ears."

I slumped forward against the bar top. Al spoke the truth. For a moment, I'd liked the idea of women on the island throwing themselves at me. But that was before Frankie Cruz and I had had our *moment*. Ever since then, I'd been dying to take her up on the offer of bringing me back to her place. I'd tried making that happen a few times since everything had gone down, but lately, it seemed, Frankie had been a hard woman to get ahold of.

"Yeah. I know, but maybe that was childish of me."

Al quirked a grin. "Ya think?"

"Shut it."

He chuckled. "Ah well. What's done is done. I can't imagine this article will cause you any harm or anything."

"I don't know. Frankie might not like it. I didn't see *her* name in there. Chicks get freaked out about shit like that. She might be a little sore at me, like somehow I tried to take all the credit."

Al swatted the air with his gnarled eighty-seven-year-old hand. "Ah, give her some credit. Frankie's smarter than that. She knows you didn't write the article."

And then out of nowhere, a blood-curdling scream ripped through the air, piercing my eardrums and quickening my pulse. "AHHHH!"

My head turned just as it sounded again.

"Ahhhhh!"

And then someone else's scream chimed in. "Get away from me!"

Dropping the newspaper onto the bar, I lurched off my barstool and sprinted outside. I burst out the clubhouse doors and instantly froze, unable to believe what I saw.

What the fuck?!

When Al caught up to me, we glanced at each other.

"Holy sweet potatoes," he breathed.

The concrete pad in front of the clubhouse was now swarming with chickens. Two hundred or more chickens had invaded the pool, swim-up bar, and miniature golf course. I stared blankly as I watched the wild band of rust-colored chickens chasing after the resort guests, wondering how in the hell this was even happening.

"What the—?"

"Ahhhhh!" went the scream again.

I looked to my right to see a short elderly woman on the miniature golf course, shaking a putter at a particularly aggressive rooster who was asserting his dominance by flapping his wings at her.

"You get away from me!" she yelled at it.

I raced over in her direction and flapped my arms, hollering at the bird. "Shoo. Shoo! Get outta here!"

The bird got spooked and ran, but I could hear screams and shouts from every different part of the area. Even though I had no idea how this was happening or why, as head of resort security, this was go time for me. I had to take control of the situation.

"Okay, just stay calm, everyone," I hollered, cupping my hands around my mouth. "My name is Danny Drunk. I'm the head of resort security here. I'm going to need everyone to clear the area for the time being. I'll get these chickens rounded up and removed in a jiffy. So if I could have you all make your way up to the lobby or to your rooms, that would be great." I waved my arms in a forward motion, indicating everyone should move towards the golf cart parking area.

People around me groaned. I could tell they were pissed

about having to load up all their stuff, but thankfully, I supposed, the resort had settled into what Artie referred to as a "slow patch." As it was finally warmer in the States, business was down slightly, so our guest count was relatively low. The pool and beach area were far from full, but there were still guests that I needed to keep safe.

"Golf cart attendants, please take full loads and return immediately until we've escorted all guests up to the resort."

As guests began evacuating the area, I rushed back over to the clubhouse to find Al standing on the staircase, his mouth gaping open. "Where in tarnation did all these chickens come from?"

"I have no idea. But, Al, I need you to call Artie. Tell him to get down here right away. And then do me a favor and close up all the clubhouse doors so the chickens can't find their way into the restaurant and bar."

Al nodded and turned around to head back up the stairs, pulling his phone from his back pocket. "I'm on it."

I hollered across the pool to Manny Velázquez, the stocky Puerto Rican swim-up bartender that I now considered a personal friend, "Hey, Manny! Gimme a hand?"

"Sure thing, Drunk."

Manny and I spent the next ten minutes evacuating guests from the pool area. Every time we made a move, it seemed, we stepped on a chicken, making them squawk louder than a hormonal woman with a bone to pick. Every way we turned, there were more chickens. They just kept coming, like someone had turned on a chicken faucet and had forgotten to turn it off. I'd never seen anything like it.

When all the guests were finally gone, I turned to Manny. "Where'd they all come from, Manny?"

"I don't know, man. They came from the beach, I guess. First there were just a few of them, and then they were coming a dozen at a time. I literally blinked and the next thing I knew the beach was swarming with them."

I scratched my head. It was possible I'd overslept on the day they'd taught chicken wrangling at the academy, but that didn't change the fact that I had to figure something out fast. "Well, let's see if we can't get them to go back to wherever they came from."

Manny looked skeptical but shrugged. "We can try."

Together, we began by chasing the chickens off towards the ocean, hoping they'd just follow their original route and go home. Wherever *home* happened to be. Just as long as it wasn't on our beach and pool area. But the chickens didn't seem to like that idea. We'd herd them one direction and they'd skirt around us or between us and race right back in the direction we'd just chased them off from. It was ridiculous.

By the time Artie got down to the pool area, Manny and I had done little in the way of chicken evacuation and instead had only managed to wear ourselves out by running around and flapping our arms up and down. For his part, Al was seated at a table on the clubhouse's wraparound porch, getting a kick out of watching Manny and me look like a bunch of fucking idiots.

"What the hell? Drunk!" hollered Artie from across the pool. "Where did all these chickens come from?"

"Like I know, Artie? They just—showed up. But they won't leave!" At my feet, a chicken pecked the top of my big toe. "Gah!" I screamed, nearly jumping out of my flip-flops. I shot out a leg, sending the thing skittering out of reach. "Get outta here, you feathery mother-clucker!"

"Drunk!" Artie screamed.

"What?!"

"Quit playin' around, for Pete's sake!"

My mouth gaped. *Quit playing around?!* "You think this is *fun*? Little clucker just yanked a toe hair."

"Come on. Get 'em rounded up and out of here. The guests up there are steaming mad."

"I'm trying to round them up, Artie. But there's gotta be a

couple hundred of them. What am I supposed to do with them?"

"I don't know. Get some of the maintenance vans over here and load them up."

Was he serious? Not a single one of the chickens could've passed a walk-and-turn sobriety test, let *alone* walk in the direction I wanted them to. Did he really think I'd be able to convince them to get in a fucking van?!

"Hey, Drunk," hollered Manny, walking through a flock of chickens to stand next to me. "You want me to call my cousin?"

"Your cousin? Why would I want you to call your cousin?"

"He's an exterminator."

"Does he have any experience with chickens?"

"I don't think so, but maybe he could spray them with something."

I looked at Manny sideways. "Manny. Are you fucking insane? I don't think we wanna do a mass murder here. We just wanna relocate the bastards."

"I guess we could call my other cousin," he offered with a shrug.

"What's he do? Work for KFC?"

"Nah, man. He works for animal control."

I stared at him blankly. "Yeah. How about we fucking do that instead."

Manny pulled his cell phone out of his pocket. "Yeah, okay. I'll call him."

"Sweet. Thanks. Great idea." I turned to walk away and then stopped short. "Well. The second idea was a great idea. The first idea was just fucking psychotic."

With the phone to his ear, he laughed. "Hey, man. All ideas can't be winners."

3

THREE AND A HALF HOURS LATER, AL AND I SAT IN FRONT OF Artie's desk. My shirt was drenched with sweat from all the running around down at the pool. I was exhausted, and my body was still working to come down off the adrenaline high.

"Man, that was some shit," I said, laughing after taking a swig from the bottle of Dr Pepper I'd grabbed on the way in to refuel. "Thank God for animal control."

"What are they going to do with all those chickens?" asked Al.

"The animal control guy said there's a chicken farm not too far away. He's going to give them a call and see if somehow we wound up with their chickens by mistake," said Artie.

I shook my head as I screwed the lid back on my soda. "What I don't understand is how the hell an entire flock of chickens escapes from a chicken farm and just *happens* to make their way onto our beach?"

"Maybe they were scheduled for a trip to the butcher's and they *chickened* out?" said Al with a shrug and a half-smile.

I rolled my eyes. "Oh my God. There's that German humor again."

"Well, you know, I wondered that same thing," said Artie,

wagging a finger. "So while you were getting them all rounded up, I drove down to the guard shack and spoke with Wilson. They didn't just *happen* to make their way onto our beach. According to him, a delivery truck came through earlier with a poultry shipment. He assumed it was meant for the kitchen and let them through, but he had no idea they were live chickens."

Dumbfounded, my jaw dropped. "You're joking?" I couldn't believe that someone had actually dropped them off intentionally!

Artie shook his head. "We're not exactly sure what happened. Wilson didn't get the name of the company the driver worked for, so we don't know if the shipment was meant for the chicken farm down the road or if someone else got their wires crossed." He threw his hands up. "We may never know exactly what happened."

"That's crazy," I said, with a bewildered smile. "You know, it's gonna take us a week to get all the bird shit cleaned up down there. And of all weeks for this to happen, we've got Carnival happening this weekend."

"Yeah, I already call—" Before Artie could finish his sentence, the phone buzzed and a woman's voice spilled out. "Mr. Balladares, Sylvester Smallwood is on line two for you."

Artie's shoulders went slack and his whole demeanor visibly changed right in front of us. "Did he say what he wanted?"

"No, sir. He just asked to speak with you."

Artie sighed. "Alright. Thank you, Alicia." The phone clicked and he glanced up at Al and me. "Ugh. I *hate* this guy."

"Yeah, we noticed. Who's Sylvester Smallwood?"

"He runs the Crystal Point Resort next door," said Al.

"You've heard me talk about him before. Everybody just calls him Sly."

My eyes widened. "Oh, Sly? Yeah. I've heard you mention him before. Sly's last name is Smallwood? Well, ain't that a kick in the nuts to be named Smallwood." I laughed. "No wonder he just goes by Sly."

Artie sighed. "Yeah, well, he's certainly got a chip on his shoulder to go with the unusual name. I actually went to high school with him. He's a real jerk."

I stared incredulously. "You went to high school with the guy who owns the resort next door? How the hell did things shake out like that?"

Al chuckled. "Artie opened his big mouth, that's how it shook out."

Artie let out a heavy sigh. "It was at a class reunion about ten years ago. Sly was there and I happened to mention how great Paradise Isle was and how my dream was to buy a resort on the island one day."

"Sly beat Artie to it," said Al knowingly.

My mouth went slack. "You're kidding? He *stole* your dream? Who *does* that?"

Artie's face flushed redder than usual. He pursed his lips. "Sly Smallwood. That's who." He looked down at his desk and shook his head sadly. "It was my own fault. Sly always was a bully in school, and I admit I wanted to impress him a little and prove that I'd actually done something with my life. I bragged a bit about my tales of travel and my Case IH dealership. And then I mentioned that when I retired, I'd love to buy a resort here and live out my days in paradise." Artie shrugged. "How was I to know he'd *buy* a resort here before I did?"

"So he was here first?"

"Yup. He bought the Crystal Point literally that same year I mentioned it. Of course I had no idea until after I'd already bought the Seacoast Majestic. And then it was too late." Frowning, Artie held a finger to his lips to shush me. "Now, I better take this and see what he wants. Just hang on a second, fellas."

I leaned back in my seat, stretching out my long legs while Artie put the call on speakerphone.

"Sly, it's Artie. You need something?"

"Artie Fartie!" boomed the voice through the speaker. "What the hell took you so long? Have a heart attack on the way to the phone?"

Artie's eyes skipped up to glance at me uncomfortably. "Now's not a very good time, Sly."

"From what I've heard it's *never* a good time at the Seacoast Pathetic!" Sly chuckled through the speaker. "Seriously, though, I only called to offer my condolences. I heard you had a bit of a pest infestation problem today. Did you call the police? Is anyone suspecting *fowl* play?"

Sucking in his breath, Artie stared wide-eyed at the phone. "This was you, Smallwood?"

The question was met with only laughter on the other end of the line.

Artie's eyes narrowed into angry slits. "I should've known it was you, you sonuvabitch!"

I sat up in my seat and turned an ear to the phone. Were these two implying that this *wasn't* an accident after all?! This jerk was actually claiming responsibility for it? Who *did* shit like that?

"You know, from what I've heard, it was a real *eggs*-citing day over on your side of the beach." More evil chuckling.

"I'm gonna get you for this, Smallwood!" shouted Artie.

The blood in my veins began to simmer. Not only because he'd been responsible for the chickens, but because of how he was speaking to Artie!

"Oh, Balladares, you know I didn't mean to *ruffle any feathers*, but go ahead, do your worst. I promise you, revenge isn't all it's *cracked* up to be."

I wanted to lurch forward and share a few choice words with the asshat on the other end, but Artie, seeing the look on my face, shot me a warning look. When he held up a finger at me, I pressed my lips together, and instead of exploding, I seethed inside.

Artie's finger sliced the air determinedly as he barked into the phone. "I've had enough of your pranks, Smallwood. This is where it ends!"

My eyes widened. Was I understanding this correctly? There'd been *more* pranks? And Artie was just gonna let this guy off with some lame warning?

"Oh, you're absolutely right, Artie. This *is* where it ends. Shall we call a truce?"

My head shook wildly from side to side, silently demanding that Artie do *anything* but agree to a truce with the man.

But Artie shrank in his seat, like Sly had him beat. "You're the one doing all of this, not me. But lemme tell you. It ends today, Smallwood. *It ends today.*" With that, he hung up the phone.

"Artie!" I bellowed the second the call ended. "What the fuck, man? You're just gonna let that guy off like that? It ends today? Like that's supposed to scare him? He unleashed two hundred and fifty chickens onto your resort today! There's enough bird shit out there to feed a small army!"

Al shot me a quizzical look.

"Yeah, well, it's over. It's done. He won't do it again," Artie grumbled.

"Bullshit, he won't do it again. What else has he done?"

Artie glanced up at Al, causing me to look at Al too.

"He messed with a shipment of lobsters a few weeks ago," said Al.

"What do you mean *messed* with?"

Artie sighed. "Well, do you remember a couple weeks back, we were supposed to have that lobster feed?"

"Yeah. Vaguely."

"You were busy helping Giselle Marrero out, so you probably didn't hear what happened."

I frowned. "No, I don't recall hearing anything. What's the story?"

Artie sighed. "Well, apparently the delivery truck went to the wrong address. I don't really know what happened. The address number was transposed over the phone somehow. I don't know if that was their fault or ours, but they went over to Sly's resort, instead of our place."

"Okay?"

"Well, apparently, the Crystal Point's receiving department just saw the address, but didn't notice it was marked for us and since they weren't expecting the lobster shipment, they called Sly down to deal with the delivery driver. When he realized it was actually *our* shipment, he had it returned to sender instead of just sending it over to us."

"You're kidding? The driver never realized he'd gone to the wrong resort?"

"No. He was a new driver, and according to his paperwork, he was at the right address. And since it was a resort, he thought he was at the right place." Artie shook his head. "And I'd placed the order kind of last-minute, so I'd already paid a surcharge for the expedited delivery. And when Sly had it sent back, I lost the surcharge I paid for shipping, plus I had to pay a second time if I wanted them to reattempt delivery."

"Well, that's bullshit! It wasn't *your* fault their asinine driver went to the wrong fucking resort."

Artie threw up his hands. "That's what I argued too, but because I couldn't prove that it was their error, they said the best they could do for me was not to charge me for the lobsters I had sent back."

"Oh, how fucking nice of them."

"And then on top of everything, they said there was absolutely no way they could get the lobster to me in time for the lobster feed. So we ended up having to cancel it and we had a lot of pissed-off guests."

I stared hard at Artie. "I can't believe you didn't tell me any of this. You're supposed to keep me in the loop, Artie."

"Like I said, you were busy helping Giselle Marrero, and I didn't want to bother you."

"Artie! I would've handled it!"

"I know you would've, Drunk."

My blood was really heated now. Sly Smallwood deserved to be pecker-punched for what he'd done. "This is all bullshit!" I rose to my feet and began to pace the room, letting out some of the energy that was building inside my muscles. "Who does stuff like that?"

"Sylvester Smallwood does that," said Artie.

Al looked uncomfortable. "He's been a pain in our ass since Artie bought the place."

"The guy's ruthless," Artie agreed.

I looked back and forth between Al and Artie. I could tell by the looks on their faces that they hadn't told me everything. There was *more*?! "Yeah? What else has he done?"

Al and Artie exchanged uneasy glances, like they didn't know if they wanted to reveal all of the gory details of their encounters with Sly.

"Oh, come on. Just tell me."

Artie cleared his throat. "Well, the first week I took owner-ship of the resort, he had his gardeners come over and cut all the hedges to look like—" He glanced over at Al again.

My wide-eyed stare ping-ponged back and forth between the two old men again. "To look like what?"

"He cut 'em to look like male genitalia," finished Al.

My eyes widened, but an unintentional smile crept onto my face. "He trimmed your bushes to look like *penises*?! That's pretty cocky coming from a guy named Smallwood." Despite myself, I had to chuckle. If I were being honest, it *was* a little funny.

Artie slammed his hand down on his desk. "It's not funny,

Drunk. I had to have the whole row of hedges cut back to practically nothing."

"They're bushes, Artie. They'll grow back."

Artie frowned. "That's what Smallwood said. That damn man. He's so infuriating. He was like this in high school. Always pulling pranks on people. He especially liked to pick on me for some reason. That was one thing then, when we were kids, you know? But now these pranks of his are driving away business, and business is already down. I can't afford for him to keep up with this ridiculousness. We're men, not children, after all."

Thinking about the chickens and the lobsters he sent back made me angry too. "Maybe we need to reciprocate and teach them you don't mess with the Seacoast Majestic!"

"No, no, no. That's not the way to settle this. It'll only encourage him to keep going. I think we just need to have a talk with them. Face-to-face. Man-to-man."

"I'd rather get revenge," I grumbled.

"That's not the way you do it, Drunk," said Al. "You're supposed to turn the other cheek."

"You guys can turn the other cheek all you want, but that's not my MO. I'd rather *punch* the other cheek." I stopped pacing and looked down at Artie.

"Look, Drunk. This is what I want you to do. Tomorrow I want you to go over there and have a talk with Sly. Tell him to knock off the shenanigans or we'll have to get the authorities involved."

"You mean you want me to go over there and tell him if he doesn't stop bullying us I'm gonna tell the principal on him? Why don't we just get my mother involved too? I know. I'll tell him if he doesn't shape up, I'm telling my mommy on him. That oughta set him straight." Anger burned the pit of my stomach as I defiantly backhanded the air. "I just can't do it, Artie. That makes us sound so—so *wimpy*."

Artie threw his hands up. "That's how we're handling this,

Drunk. Now, call and set up a meeting, and I want you over there first thing tomorrow. When you're done, report back to me. I want to know what he says."

Annoyed, I pointed at him. "Fine. But only because you're my boss and I don't have seven million dollars of 'fuck you money' anymore."

"I can appreciate that," said Artie with a nod.

I stormed the door. "Come on, Al. Let's go get dinner. All that chicken wrangling made me hungry."

4

LATER THAT EVENING, I SAT OUT ON THE FRONT PORCH OF MY private cottage, located between the back side of the Seacoast Majestic Resort and a patch of rainforest, and further yet, the ocean. With my long legs extended out in front of me on my porch railing, I quietly nursed a bottle of warm Corona while listening to the sounds of the island. It seemed the tree frogs, crickets, and coquis all had tea to spill and were unabashedly spilling it out into the world. The night air was very still and humid and almost suffocatingly hot. Even so, the windows in my cottage were all wide open as they always were, mostly because I preferred the smell of fresh island air and I hated frigid air conditioning just slightly more than I hated having sweaty balls.

I think it was the excessive humidity in my room that had me tossing and turning that night, despite the long day I'd had. But it could've also been the fact that suddenly, it seemed, I had a lot on my mind. So I'd gotten up, grabbed a beer from the fridge, and decided to take in a little nature. And now, sitting all alone on my porch, I thought about Sly Smallwood and the pranks he'd been pulling on Artie, unbeknownst to me.

If Artie had his way, I'd go over there tomorrow, wag my finger in the guy's face, and look like a fucking chump. That ate at me. I was no fucking chump, and acting like one, even at my boss's request, irked me to no end. I felt like now was the time for retribution, not unbridled admonishment. Convincing Artie, though, would take some work. I just hadn't quite figured out the right angle.

I wondered what Val would say about Artie acting like a pussy. In her line of work, Val was used to strong, tough men. How long would she last with a guy like Artie? A guy who ruled his resort with a spongy fist and an even spongier heart. How long would it be before she took advantage of him or hurt him?

I had to force myself to think of the bright side when it came to Val and Artie. Even if she did hurt him eventually, like we were all predicting, would it be worth it if Artie managed to get a few good years out of her? At least he'd have memories to keep him warm at night. I wondered if that was all a person needed in life. Fond memories.

That was when my mind wandered over to Francesca Cruz. I finished my warm beer, then got up and went inside to grab another. I came back out and got comfortable again in my chair.

Frankie Cruz.

She'd been on my mind quite a bit ever since that kiss we'd shared when I'd been in the hospital a couple weeks prior. We'd both made it obvious that we were into each other. I was just itching to pick up where we'd left off. But it seemed that suddenly, she was constantly unavailable. I'd left her several messages on her voicemail. She returned my call once, but she'd only had a minute to talk. Texts were the better way to get ahold of her, but still, those went hours and sometimes even days unanswered.

Even though we were having problems connecting, at least I knew *why*. She was busy with her new job. After our PGC bust, she'd been promoted to inspector. I was thrilled for her, but that didn't change the fact that I was a little hurt that she didn't have time for me anymore. She'd told me I just needed to be patient with her; she was still trying to figure out her new life and her new schedule.

So patient I'd agreed to be. Frankie was worth it, after all. I'd even stopped messing around with other women. But on nights like tonight, when I was wide awake and lonely, it was especially hard being patient. I just wanted someone to share my day with. I wanted someone I could tell about the chickens I'd wrangled and Artie's ridiculous plan to propose to Val and how Sly Smallwood had cut Artie's bush to look like a fucking penis.

The more I thought about it, the more I missed Frankie. The more I wanted to talk to her and hear her voice.

"Fuck it," I muttered to myself. I reached into my back pocket and pulled out my phone. It was almost two in the morning, but I dialed Frankie's number anyway.

It rang six times before she answered.

"Hello?" she whispered into the phone.

"Hey, Frankie."

"Danny? Is that you? What time is it?"

"Mmm, just about two."

"Two?! Is everything all right?"

"Yeah, everything's fine," I said in a low, smooth tone. "I just missed you. I wanted to hear your voice."

"I miss you too, but it's two in the morning, Danny. Call me when it's not dark out, 'kay?"

I got the sense that she was just about to hang up on me. "Frankie, wait!"

"What?"

"You'll never guess what happened today." I grinned as I said it.

"What happened?" she mumbled into the phone.

"Our resort neighbor pulled a prank on us and released two hundred fifty chickens onto our beach."

"Oh yeah?"

Her *oh yeah* sounded like the kind of *oh yeah*s I gave to my mother when I wasn't really paying attention. "Yeah. You would've gotten a charge out of seeing me running all over the place looking like an idiot."

"Mmm. That's nice."

"Yeah." I inhaled deeply and pulled my lips off to the side. I let it out in a big sigh. "How was your day?"

"Danny, I was sleeping. I have to get up early tomorrow. I have a meeting."

"Oh. Right. Sorry I woke you up."

"Is okay," she mumbled. "I'll talk to you later."

"Wait, Frankie! You wanna hang out s—" The line went dead before I could finish my sentence.

I stared at my phone. "Shit."

My head rolled back on my shoulders, and I stared up at the wooden rafters covering my porch, my mouth gaping wide open. What was I doing? How had worrying about Artie Balladares's love life and sweating over a woman become my *life*?

I sat up straight and chugged my beer. My priorities were messed up or something.

Something *had* to change. This couldn't be my life forever.

I was just about to get up and grab another beer from the fridge when, out of the darkness, I noticed a set of headlights coming up the narrow road towards the cottages. I frowned, wondering who in the hell was back here on this private road at two in the morning. The dead-end road behind the Seacoast Majestic led to only three cottages: Artie's, mine, and the empty one next to mine. I couldn't imagine Artie out and about at two a.m.

About halfway up the road, the driver cut the headlights. The dark car crept along the gravel road, passing the empty house to my right, then passing my place, before stopping in front of Artie's place. Lo and behold, a pair of soaring chrome wings in the front grille caught a shred of moonlight, telling me the vehicle was a Chrysler. Black. If I had to guess by the body style, I'd suppose it was a Chrysler 300. The windows were darkly tinted, and in the darkness, the car was little more than a shadow. If I'd been drinking longer, I would've easily written it off as a figment of my imagination.

I stared long and hard at that car, wondering like hell who was in there and what they were doing over at Artie's this late at night. As the possible scenarios ran through my head, I wished I had my gun on me. But my gun was inside my place, unloaded on the nightstand. I was scared to move, afraid that if I left my post, I'd miss something of importance. But after several long, quiet seconds of nothing happening, I decided to dash inside and grab it. Then suddenly, as if on cue, the passenger door opened. I froze in my tracks. A thin sliver of ambient light spilled out of the car.

That was when I saw her.

Valentina Carrizo.

Wearing a minidress, hardly a bandage really, she leaned over and said something to the driver, then closed her door gently, being careful not to slam it. She waited until the car drove away before sneaking up the front steps to Artie's place and slipping inside.

When she was gone, I stood up.

"I fucking knew it," I whispered. "You can take the rooster outta the henhouse, but you can't take the cock outta the hen."

5

IT TOOK ME A REALLY LONG TIME TO GET TO SLEEP THAT EVENING. I tossed and turned for hours before finally drifting off. I couldn't help but to think about Val, wondering what she'd been up to getting out of a strange car and sneaking back into Artie's place at two in the morning. I debated what I'd say when I saw her next, and what, if anything, I should say to Artie.

Then my thoughts had turned to Frankie and our short conversation. It was probably all the Dr Pepper I'd had so close to bedtime that had fucked with my mind. So when Earnestine, my parrot, woke me at the crack of dawn, I was not a happy camper.

"Rawck! No morning kisses, no morning kisses. Rawck!"

With my eyes closed, I seethed at the bird undoubtedly standing in my window. Like I needed to be reminded I was waking up without a woman in my bed, *again*.

Kick a guy when he's down, why don'tcha, Earnestine?

Her little nails clicked on the wooden windowsill. I knew she was doing her morning dance. I pulled a pillow over my head and tried to fall back asleep. I didn't have to be ready until nine, when Al had agreed to pick me up. Somehow, I managed to doze for another hour, but as if I'd ordered an eight a.m. wakeup call, Earnestine woke me up again, singing in my window.

"Rawck! No morning kisses, no morning kisses. Rawck!"

I grimaced. I was going to have to work on giving the bird some new morning material. "Shuush!" I grunted.

"Wake up, wake up, wake up, wake up!" she chanted, jumping up and down in the window box.

"Ugh." But when I looked at the alarm clock and saw that it was eight, I knew that was the end of snoozing. I threw the covers off and launched the pillow at Earnestine. She ducked as she always did and the pillow flew out the window. I'd have to remember to go grab it, along with the other three that were surely still out there.

Trying to chase the sleep away, I took an extra-long shower and then dressed in what I considered to be fancy, professional clothes. A pair of navy Bermuda shorts, a white tank top under a pink button-down shirt printed with hula dancers, and my navy canvas boat shoes. In the bathroom, I smoothed on a little hair wax and put on my fedora and shades and then went to the kitchen. I grabbed a bottle of Dr Pepper from the fridge and a king-sized Twix bar and went outside to sit on the porch to eat my breakfast and to wait for Al to pick me up.

As usual, it was a beautiful morning on Paradise Isle. The temperature was a perfect seventy-eight degrees. The air smelled sweet and fresh, like a combination of jungle flora and rain. In the forest behind my cottage, birds went about their morning business, chittering up a storm, and I could hear the faraway sounds of the resort already bustling with energy.

I sat on the low porch railing with my long legs dangling next to the bright red blooms of the ixora plant stationed in front of my cottage. I'd literally been sitting for all of two minutes, sipping my morning dose of caffeine and noshing on some chocolate and caramel deliciousness, when Artie's front door opened and Valentina Carrizo emerged onto the porch, wearing some shoelaces tied strategically around her body.

Alright, fine. Perhaps it was slightly more than just shoelaces. *Slightly.* I think it was supposed to be a bikini —*thing*.

Two hot pink triangles were suspended around her neck by a lime-green string. The little bits of cloth barely served to cover her nipples and provided absolutely *zero* coverage for her sideboob, underboob, nor cleavage. And let me be completely frank with you.

The woman had *a lot* of the aforementioned.

A slightly larger lime-green triangle tied with pink string covered her lower lady bits, and she wore neck-breakingly-high hot pink heels that clicked on the porch as moved about, tying a sheer pink sarong around her hips.

I debated for a moment if I should take the opportunity to ask about the late-night rendezvous I'd witnessed the night before. "Hey, Val," I hollered over at her.

"Ohhh, hellooo, Drunk," she crooned in her thick Colombian accent from across the yard. Her hips and breasts jiggled as she leaned forward to flutter her long manicured fingers at me.

The sound of my name on Val's lips bristled the hair on my arms. The combination of her flirty nature, barely-there outfits, and accent made everything that came out of her mouth sound like a horny owl's mating call to my ears. Oddly enough, she seemed to be one of the few women I'd ever met who unnerved me quite so much.

I had to act casual.

"Where you headed?"

"To the pool. Where else would I go like *thees*?" She held her arms out and gyrated her hips.

I pointed to the back of Artie's place. "Artie has a pool. A private one."

"Yes. I know. But I don't like to be all alone. I like to see all the people."

Why did that not surprise me? "It's kind of early for the pool."

"No. Is good to go before it get too hot." She pulled her long dark braid over one shoulder, gave a little wiggle to tighten her sarong and then navigated the stairs in her heels. "Would you like to join me?"

"Oh. Thanks, but nah. Artie's got me on an assignment already this morning."

"Oh, that's too bad." She plumped out her bottom lip and gave me puppy dog eyes. "I *deedn't* want to go all by myself."

I wondered how in the hell Artie was going to keep that little dame occupied for the rest of her life. It sounded like a helluva lot more trouble than a little bit of sex was worth. "You have any girlfriends on the island you could invite over?" I wanted to add, *or that drive a black Chrysler 300*, but I bit my lip. I'd sneak it out of her somehow.

She lifted a shoulder noncommittally. "I don't have too many girlfriends here. I *jused* to have a lot of girlfriends back in Colombia, but they don't come with me to here."

"Ah. Well. There's a lot of permanent female residents here at the resort. Maybe you're gonna have to get to know a few of them."

She frowned. "They are all very old women. I don't *theenk* they will want to be my friend."

"Well, you won't know if you don't try."

"The men here are *very* friendly, though," she said, shrugging.

"Yeah. I'll bet," I said. "Are you enjoying living here with Artie?"

"Ohhhh yes!" She threw me a bright-eyed smile. "I love it here. *Ees* so beautiful."

"Yeah, it's very beautiful all right. But I'm sure you miss your old life. There was probably way more excitement. It can get pretty boring around here."

"I not really miss it," she said, her face animatedly changing to a frown.

I was just about to press on and see how I could steer the conversation to ask what I really wanted to know when Al pulled up in the sleek six-seater Black Panther golf cart he'd purchased a few months back. He came to a screeching halt at the bottom of my porch stairs, nearly colliding with the extended lip of the last riser. "You ready, kid?"

I stood up, crinkled my Twix wrapper and stuck it in my pocket. "Yeah, I'm ready. I was just saying hello to Val."

Al looked over at the woman who was just climbing into the Barbie pink golf cart Artie had bought just for her to drive around the resort. "Oh, I didn't see you there, Val," he said, lifting his fuzzy white brows.

I coughed out the word "bullshit," but neither Val nor Al seemed to catch it.

"Beautiful morning, isn't it?" said Al.

"Yes, it is. Very beautiful. Well, I better go before it get too hot." She gave us both a wave. "Bye-bye."

"Bye, Val," I said.

"See you later, Val," echoed Al.

When she'd backed out of her parking spot and driven away, I climbed in next to Al. "You didn't see her there, huh?" I teased with my brows lifted skeptically. "The prescription on those glasses need to be punched up a little?"

He stared at me blankly. "What? I didn't see her."

"You're full of shit, you know that? Val sticks out like a dick on a fucking donkey."

Al smiled at me. "Well, unlike you, kid, I'm not one for checking out donkey dicks." He chuckled over his misdirection.

I pursed my lips. "I mean it, *Al*. Artie's gonna have a real problem on his hands if he marries that one. She's already given every geriatric man here a cure for their erectile dysfunction. How long's it gonna be before some guest catches her eye and she cheats on Artie?"

Al put the Black Panther in motion and sent us cruising down the road behind the Seacoast Majestic, heading for the main entrance. "I'll have you know I never had that problem."

I frowned. "Evie never cheated?"

"Erectile dysfunction."

I stared over at him. "And *why*, pray tell, would I need to know that? You think I really care whether or not you can still pitch a tent?"

"You're the one that brought it up!"

"I was trying to make a point, Al. Not get intimate details about your schlong." I poked my little finger in my ear and gave it a wiggle. "Now how am I supposed to unhear that?"

Al frowned. "Oh. Well, what was your point?"

"Val! And Artie! He's gonna marry her, for crying out loud."

"I thought you said you were gonna support him."

I sighed and leaned back in my seat. "Ugh. I *am* gonna support him. Just like I know *you're* gonna support him. I just —" I took a pause, wondering if I should tell Al what I'd seen the night before. Just because she'd been out at two in the morning didn't exactly mean she'd reverted to her old ways, and without concrete proof, I'd only come off looking like a jackass if I was wrong. "I just don't trust her."

"Well, I don't exactly trust her either, but I don't think there's much we can do about it, Drunk. Artie's in love."

"I know." Sighing, I shook my head. "Fucking Artie. Had to go get himself a hooker for a wife. Why couldn't he just fall in love with one of the single widows that stay here or something?"

"Well, you're the one that introduced them. I think we can safely blame you for this."

I swiveled in my seat and pressed my fingers to my chest. "You're saying it's *my* fault?!"

"I didn't say it was your fault. I said I was *blaming* you."

"That's the same thing! I don't think *me* introducing them makes me the responsible party here."

"Well, if you hadn't introduced them, would Artie even know her right now?"

I opened my mouth to argue with him, but then promptly snapped my mouth closed again. As much as I hated it, Al had a point.

He nodded and wagged a finger in the air. "Ahh. See?"

"Whatever. So it's my fault. Fine. Then I guess I'll have to make it my personal mission to make sure Artie doesn't get hurt." And if that meant tracking down whoever drove that black Chrysler, then I guessed that's what I'd have to do.

"Look. You can't bubble wrap him, kid. He's a grown man."

I chuckled. "Al, even if I *wanted* to, I wouldn't be able to. There ain't enough bubble wrap on this *island* to bubble wrap Artie."

"So how about we focus on what you *can* help him out with? His Sly Smallwood problem."

That was all it took. My mind immediately jumped off the Valentina Carrizo soapbox and hopped onto the Sly Smallwood one.

"Fucking Sly Smallwood. I can't believe Artie never told me about any of the problems he's been having." I gave a wave to the guard shack attendant and then gripped the bar holding up the golf cart's roof as Al made a sharp right onto the main road. I wasn't a hundred percent confident we'd made the turn with all four wheels on the pavement, and my whole body rocked from side to side until we evened out.

With both hands firmly grasping the steering wheel at ten and two and his eyes barely above the steering wheel, but laser focused, Al didn't seem to notice the bumps and just kept talking. "Like he said, you were busy. He didn't wanna bother you."

"I'm his head of resort security, Al. It's my job for him to bother me. Otherwise, what am I doing here?"

"Look. He finally told you, didn't he?"

"Well, yeah. *After* Sly unleashed war on our resort. And now my hands are tied because Artie wants me to *use my words* instead of handling it like a man."

"Look, kid, maybe you weren't aware, but men *can* handle problems without using their fists."

With my mouth agape and my brows knitted together, I held a hand to my chest as if I'd just been stabbed through the heart and stared at Al. "*Et tu, Brute?*"

Al rolled his eyes. "Have you always been this dramatic?"

I smiled. "It's one of my finer qualities, I think."

"Your mother tell you that?"

Al took the next right turn into the Crystal Point Resort driveway, once again taking it on two wheels.

I stared at him when we landed. "Your mother teach you to drive?"

"Don't talk about my mother. My mother was a saint."

"Anyone who raised you had to be a saint, Al."

Al pulled the cart up to a stop in front of the Crystal Point Resort lobby. "Here we are. Do me a favor? Try and be serious in there? And keep your fists to yourself."

"No promises."

"I'm not joking, kid. For once. Just do what you're supposed to do. For Artie, okay?"

"Alright, I'll do my best." I started walking away, giving him a little wave of my fingers over my shoulder.

"Good. I'll just be over here waiting for you," Al hollered after me. "Take your time. I'm in no hurry. I've got a paper to read."

That made me smile. I stopped walking and turned around. "Are you *ever* in a hurry, Al?"

"I'm sure when I get old I'll be in a hurry to die, but as of right now, not really."

Turning back around, I chuckled to myself. *News flash, Al, eighty-seven ain't exactly on the young end of the age spectrum.*

6

WHEN THE HUGE WOODEN DOORS TO THE CRYSTAL POINT RESORT slid open and I took my first step inside, I felt like I'd walked into another world. I was so used to what I referred to as the Seacoast Majestic's "Golden Girls Chic" styling that I'd never pictured Caribbean resorts looking differently. I was first struck by the sheer immensity of the lobby. Carefully inlaid tiles formed artwork on the sprawling floor. Palm trees and beaches, tiki huts at sunset—I didn't consider myself much of an art connoisseur, but even *I* had to admit the panoramic scenes were breathtaking. A steeply pitched roof with exposed rustic beams in the vaulted ceiling added more awe to the stunning architecture. Modern square pieces of furniture were arranged in little groupings around the lobby. Their check-in counter was twice as long as ours and fronted by stone pillars with marble counters.

Lively music played over speakers, lending a hip modern vibe. The strong scent of orange blossom and mint, with a hint of cinnamon, enveloped me and provided a bit of coziness amid the larger-than-life surroundings.

But despite the obvious differences in design, layout, and

stylistic choices, the *biggest* difference between the Crystal Point and the Seacoast Majestic was the people.

If I were being completely honest, the Seacoast Majestic was your grandparents' resort. In fact, Artie *prided* himself on the fact that his resort catered to those of advanced years. There was no overly loud music. No rap. No rock. Only easy listening, the steel drum bands of the Caribbean, and, of course, *lots* of Jimmy Buffett. He served early buffet dinners with an array of denture-friendly foods. For entertainment, he featured putt-putt golf and merengue lessons with Freddy Garcia after nap time on Tuesdays and Thursdays. And whether he did it intentionally or not, one of the *biggest* selling points of the Seacoast Majestic was that there were very few twenty-year-olds. Even thirty- and forty-year-olds were a rare commodity. It was almost as if life began at forty-five at the Seacoast Majestic.

In fact, when you Googled spring break resort destinations on Paradise Isle, the Seacoast Majestic didn't even show up on a single blogger's list. But the Crystal Point Resort did. And now I understood why.

For every old person at the Seacoast Majestic, there was a young person in their place here. I couldn't believe it. Beautiful bikini-clad women strolled about, drinks in hands, all with plastic bracelets displaying their ability, or inability, to drink alcohol. Men in swim trunks with bulky chests and bronzed skin double-fisted the drinks and chatted with pals in loud, booming voices.

My mouth gaped as I wandered through the lobby, drinking in everything the resort had to offer. How in the hell had this place been unknown to me all this time? Artie and Al had been holding out! *Manny* had been holding out. Surely *he* should've known what was just down the beach from the Seacoast Majestic. Shit, we shared Angel's Bay with these people! How had some of them never wandered onto our beaches?

"You look lost. May I help you, sir?" asked a short young woman with dark hair that cascaded down her shoulders in perfect waves. She wore a pair of khaki shorts and a red polo shirt with the Crystal Point Resort logo embroidered on the breast.

Shit. Even their *employees* were younger and hotter than our employees! Taking everything in, I struggled to pick my chin up off the floor so I could respond. "Umm, yeah. I, uh—have an appointment with Mr. Smallwood at nine thirty."

She smiled at me. "Oh. Well, why don't you have a seat in one of our massage chairs, and I'll let someone know you're waiting." She gestured towards a row of oversized brown leather chairs lined up against a wall just beside their check-in counter.

I smiled dumbly. "Okay."

She walked me over to the chairs. "Can I get you a drink while you're waiting, Mister—?"

"Oh, Drunk. Just Drunk, no mister. And yeah, sure." I glanced around the room at the fancy inlaid tile floor and the marble counters and bobbed my head. *When in Rome.* "I'll take a mimosa if you've got one handy."

She smiled at me. "Of course. I'll be right back."

I took a seat in one of the chairs and fiddled with the controls until I felt a roller ball pulsate against the small of my back while the leg massagers kneaded my calves. I closed my eyes and leaned my head back to discover a ball running across my shoulders and neck. Had I just found heaven? Why hadn't Pam booked us a room *here*?!

I'd been seated for a few minutes when the lovely dark-haired woman returned with a champagne flute. "Here you are, sir."

I opened my eyes and smiled at her pleasantly. "Oh. Thank you."

"I let the office know that you're here. Unfortunately, I was informed that something came up and Mr. Smallwood is not here right now."

I frowned. Suddenly I was less disappointed that I wasn't going to get to see Sly Smallwood and more disappointed that I had to leave paradise so soon. "Oh."

"But he did have someone else prepared to take your appointment. Our head of resort security will be meeting with you instead. I hope that's all right?"

While I'd really wanted to meet Mr. Smallwood, maybe this was better. Maybe my Crystal Point counterpart and I would be able to find some kind of common ground, and I would be able to convince *him* to talk some sense into his boss.

I nodded at the girl. "Yes. That should be fine."

She shot me a winning smile. "Very good. I'll let the office know." She glanced down at her watch. "It should only be another few minutes."

"No hurry at all." I grinned as I sipped my mimosa. I closed my eyes and leaned my head back. I'd just get lost in relaxation while I waited.

Minutes passed and I'd *almost* dozed off when I heard someone in front of me clear their throat. The second time I heard it, it was louder, making me whole body flinch. I felt the cold wetness of my orange juice spilling onto my shorts and down my leg.

I looked up to see a very tall, slender woman in a fitted grey suit and pointy-toed black high heels standing in front of me. She had exotically tanned skin, in such a way that I suspected perhaps she was a mashup of nationalities rather than simply suntanned, and she had long, wavy almost-black hair. Her eyes were green and looked down at me with a vague amount of annoyance, something I'd come to expect from certain women, but usually not before we'd even spoken. She wore red lipstick, and the front of her blazer opened to expose the black satin camisole she wore underneath and just a *hint* of cleavage.

Sexy was an understatement.

Holy shit.

"Are you Drunk?" she asked.

I gave her a dastardly grin. "Not yet, but I could be. Care to join me at the bar?"

She sighed and crossed her arms over her chest. "From the Seacoast Majestic?"

And just like that, I was reminded I was here on business. "Oh. Yeah." I stood up, feeling lighter on my feet after my massage and calmer than I'd been when I'd walked in. I held a hand out to her, but it was wet and sticky from the mimosa I'd spilled down the front of my shorts, so I gave it a flick in the air before wiping it on the back of my pants. Then I extended it to her again. "Danny Drunk. I've got an appointment with the head of resort security. Is he ready for me?"

Ignoring my hand, she let out an annoyed sigh and then promptly spun on her heel and took off. "Follow me."

I tried to sidle up next to her so we could talk, but when she noticed me gaining on her, her high heels clicked faster on the tile floor. Chasing after her, I felt like a kid being led to detention by the school principal or something. She slid between a couple of oversized meatheads engaged in a conversation, forcing me to have to excuse myself to get between them.

"Hey, fellas. Sorry. Excuse me. I'm trying to follow her."

One of them nodded and clapped me on the back. "Attaboy, mate."

"Go get her, champ," said the other.

I bristled. I hated it when people called me champ. What was I? A fucking eight-year-old? I wanted to say "I ain't your champ," but I had bigger fish to fry. The feeling of annoyance came flooding back, and I was reminded that these people were the enemies. I wasn't supposed to be in love with their fucking mimosas or their massage chairs and hot women. Their supreme ruler had done Artie dirty! And just like that, I was *thankful* that the douche canoe reminded me I was in a shitty mood.

So I stuffed down the fact that some dipshit had called me champ and I chased after the woman in the suit. She turned a corner down a corridor and then stopped and waited for me in front of a door marked Security. Opening it, she swept her hand in front of herself as if to say *go on in*.

"Thanks. It was, uh, nice to meet you." After giving her a stiff bow, I walked inside. Feeling somewhat nervous to meet my counterpart, I was surprised to find the office empty.

The woman followed me in and closed the door behind us before strolling around to the opposite side of the desk. She gestured towards a chair in front of the desk. "Have a seat, Mr. Drunk. My name is Erika Wild. I'm the head of resort security here at the Crystal Point Resort. What can I do for you?"

7

I stood in front of her, blinking owlishly. *She* was head of resort security? I wondered if my stiff posture gave away what I was thinking.

Yes, all right. I'll admit it. I'd been expecting a man. Stupid insensitive stereotype, yes. But what can I say? She'd caught me off guard. That happens occasionally. Like when you forget what you're drinking and take a slug from your bottle thinking the fizzy spiced-cherry deliciousness of Dr Pepper is going to flood your mouth, and instead you're met with the sweet, citrusy taste of Mountain Dew and you're like, *what the fuck*? It's not that you dislike Mountain Dew—not in the least. It's just that your brain was expecting one thing and it got another. It takes a second to adjust. You know what I'm saying?

I swallowed hard, trying to inconspicuously conceal the adjustment my brain was having to make. "Oh. Yeah, uh—you can just call me Drunk."

"Mr. Drunk will suffice." The curt response came out in a distinctively British accent.

"Uh, okay." Frowning, I gave a glance over my shoulder.

"So, uh—where's Sly? I thought I had an appointment with him today."

"Something unexpected popped up and he had to step out. He sends his apologies."

I pursed my lips. "Sure he does."

Erika leaned forward slightly and folded her hands on her desk. If she noticed the blatant sarcasm in my voice, she didn't let on. "So. What can I help you with today."

"Well, I'm not sure exactly. I'd have preferred to speak with Sly directly."

"Because he's a man?" she asked, lifting a brow.

"Because he's a—? No. No." I frowned at her, shaking my head. "This has nothing to do with him being a man and you being a—" I pointed my finger in the air and squiggled it around sort of tracing her feminine outline with it.

When my voice trailed off, she filled in the blank for me. "Woman?"

"Yeah," I exhaled.

She gave me a sad patronizing face, like she was looking at a little boy who'd lost his mother at the zoo. "Mr. Drunk, I have a lot of things going on today. If you could get to the point?"

Sensing she was about to kick me out if I didn't get on with it, I blurted it out. "I'm here because of the chickens."

"The chickens," she repeated blandly.

"Yeah. The ones Sly let loose on our beach yesterday."

"You had a chicken mishap on your beach yesterday? I see. And are you here to cry party fowl?"

I stared at her hard then. Despite her pun, her face hadn't lost its steely glare, and yet something didn't sit quite right with me. She looked a little too unsurprised. A little too *aware*. A little too *guilty*.

I narrowed my eyes. "You know about that, don't you?"

"I might have *heard* about an incident with some chickens. You are, after all, just down the beach from us."

But I shook my head. There was more to it. I wagged my finger at her. "No, no, no. You didn't just *hear* about the incident. You had something to do with it. Didn't you?"

She looked annoyed with me. "Look, Mr. Drunk—"

"Drunk," I asserted firmly. "Just Drunk."

Her expression changed then from annoyance to disdain. She pressed her lips together in a tight line and looked at me hard like she was sizing me up.

"Drunk. Look. I don't know about the security department you're running over at the Seacoast Majestic, but over here at the Crystal Point, I run a very tight ship. There is little that happens on my beach that I'm unaware of."

"That's not what I asked you. I asked if you had something to do with it."

She lifted a shoulder noncommittally. "Look. Nothing gets done at this resort without Mr. Smallwood's approval."

"You're skirting the question, Ms. Wild."

She sighed. "Fine. What would you like to know?"

"Did you or did you not having something to do with the two hundred and fifty chickens released on our beach yesterday?"

With her lips tight, she bobbed her head. "I did."

My jaw dropped. I couldn't believe that was all it took for her to be so forthcoming.

"Is there anything else?" She stood up.

But I remained seated. "Anything else?!" I looked up at her, stunned disbelief making my head spin a little.

"Yes. Anything else I can help you with?"

I could feel the heat on my temper rising. "Yes, as a matter of fact. And you can start by sitting your skinny ass down. We're not done here!"

Erika Wild rolled her eyes and sighed. Putting her knuckles on the desk, she leaned forward, giving me a look straight down the front of her blouse. "Look. It was just a little tomfoolery between old school chums. You were aware that our bosses were schoolmates, weren't you?"

"Yes, I heard, but—"

"The chickens thing was only done in good fun. I'm not sure what else you need to know."

"Good fun?!" I bellowed, sliding forward on my chair at her admission. "That was a horribly evil prank. Do you know how much chicken shit we have to clean up now before we can let our guests back down to the pool or on the beach?"

That caused a little smile to play around the corners of her mouth, and her body relaxed slightly. She sat back down.

"Oh, come now. Don't tell me you're wound so tight over at the Seacoast Majestic that you can't take a little joke."

I frowned at her. "Oh, we can take a joke. But *that* little stunt wasn't a joke. Do you have any idea how *hard* it is to corral chickens? I spent hours trying to round them all up."

She plumped out her bottom lip and knitted her brows together in an irritating show of fake pity. "Oh. Poor Drunk. Get a little exercise, did you?"

Annoyed at her cavalier attitude, I stared at her hard. She might be a glimmering diamond on the outside, but I was beginning to think that she was pure coal on the inside.

"Did Smallwood even order that? Or was it all you?"

She leaned forward in her chair and put her elbows on her desk, resting her chin on her interlocked fingers. "Must we *really* point fingers?"

"Yes! Yes. Let's point fingers!"

"You disappoint me, Drunk."

I balked. "*I* disappoint *you*? I don't even know you, lady."

She rolled her eyes. "When Artie hired someone like you as head of resort security, I thought we'd get a little better showing. Clearly I was mistaken."

"Someone like myself? What's that supposed to mean?"

She gave a tiny shrug. "I don't know. You've earned a bit of a reputation already. We've heard you're a bit of a badass. A charmer. A jokester. You're cavalier." Shaking her head, she sighed. "You know, that last kid in charge of security, Ozzy—was that his name? Ugh, he was scared of his own shadow. Pulling pranks on him was like frightening a two-year-old. But I must say, you've yet to live up to the hype. You seem very *plain* to me."

I frowned at her. I'd never been called plain a day in my life. "Well, fuck you very much. Explain to me why you need to pull pranks on *anyone* anyway."

"I told you already," she said flippantly. "It was simply old chums having a bit of fun."

"No, it's really not. When you hurt our business, it's not in good fun. We've had guests checking out because of your little prank. We got a Carnival festival coming up this weekend, and there's bird shit all over our beach!"

"Ugh," she groaned, leaning back in her seat and letting her head fall back slightly. "See what I mean? Where's this cavalier badass we've all heard about? Look. No one got hurt, did they? Grow a pair, why don't you."

I stared at her in shock. *"Grow a pair?!"* Feeling my blood begin to simmer on a low boil, I stood up and looked down at her. "You didn't seriously just tell me to *grow a pair*, did you, lady?"

Shaking her head, she chuckled. "Wow. I had no idea Artie hired such a sensitive she-man over there. How *does* he pick his heads of security anyway? At a *men*-struation support group?" She made a condescendingly sad face. "Aww, lemme guess. Do you cry at greeting card commercials as well?"

Offended, I frowned. I mean, don't get me wrong, I appreciated a good Hallmark commercial as much as the next guy, but dang, she was cutting deep. "As far as I'm aware, you and Smallwood have been low-key vandalizing the Seacoast Majestic since Artie took ownership. I'm here today to put a stop to it."

She stood up then and looked at me firmly. "Look. If you

and Balladares can't handle a little friendly ribbing from time to time, then perhaps you're not as prepared to be in this business as you think."

"You think unleashing two hundred fifty chickens on our beach and cutting our hedges to look like phallic symbols is friendly ribbing?"

"Yes, as a matter of fact, I do." She slammed a file closed on her desk. "Now. If you'll excuse me. I have *real* business to attend to today. I assume you can see yourself out."

I wasn't sure how I'd thought the meeting today would go. I guess I thought I'd hear a lot of apologizing and promises that the pranks would end. I'd never thought for a second that I'd walk into a woman's office to be insulted and practically goaded into retaliation. I stared at the evil woman in front of me. I wanted to call her names—tell her what I really thought of her, but I was too stunned to clap back.

I walked to the door and pulled it open, stopping just in the doorway. "Yeah. I can see myself out. Just know that you and Smallwood haven't heard the last of the Seacoast Majestic." I punctuated my threat by slamming the door shut behind me.

8

"THE WOMAN WAS A COMPLETE MONSTER, ARTIE. I DON'T KNOW A thing about Sly Smallwood, but I can't imagine he could be worse than Erika Wild." Adrenaline had my limbs wired, and I paced around Artie's office trying to let out some of the aggression that had only continued to build after I'd left her office.

"Well, I've really only seen the woman in passing. I've never actually *met* her before," said Artie, seated behind the desk in his office.

I stopped pacing and whipped around. "When I complained about the pranks they've been pulling, you know what she told me?"

Al's face puckered. He'd already heard it all on the way back to the Seacoast Majestic.

"She told *me* to grow a pair. Me! And she called me a fucking she-man, Artie! She said you find your heads of security at menstruation conferences. I didn't even know women had those! She's ruthless, I'm telling you!"

Artie quirked a grin. "I mean, the she-man thing, that's kind of funny."

"Artie!" I bellowed. "The woman was a complete and utter nutjob! It's not funny!"

"I—err, uh, uh-hum." He cleared his throat. "Yes, I know it's not funny, Drunk. Sorry. You're absolutely right. Well, what now? What do we do?"

"Well, for starters, I'll tell you this. I played by your rules, Artie. I went over there to have a civilized conversation, and it got me *laughed* at. If I'd done things the way I wanted to do them, we'd be on top right now, not the laughingstock of Angel's Bay." I wasn't exactly sure what our next move was—I was too amped up to think—but I knew one thing for sure. We were retaliating!

"First of all, kid, you need to calm down," said Al, watching me pace the room.

"You don't think that's what I'm *trying* to do, Al?"

"Not really. I think you're working yourself up even more. Maybe you should have a seat. Take a few deep breaths."

Every nerve ending in my body tingled with anger. "Oh-ho-ho-ho-no. You won't get me with that *female* stuff. This isn't yoga class, Al. This is war. You don't have a seat when you're at war." I did stop walking, though, and I looked at Artie. "Artie, we can't back down. We gotta retaliate. Tell me you're in."

Artie sighed. He stared at me for a really long moment and then finally, I saw his face relax slightly. He was conceding. We had to take action or look like fools. "Fine. I'm in."

I screwed my face up and fisted the air. *Victory!* "Good. Then we need to come up with a plan. We need to *destroy* that children's resort over there. Were you aware that it was all just a bunch of goddamned kids over there? Seriously. The median age's gotta be max twenty-three."

"Oh yes. I'm keenly aware of the makeup of their clientele," said Artie.

"I can't believe that I've been here all this time and *no one* has said a word to me about all the hot women over there."

"Well, for starters, they're the competition. Why would I tell you about the competition? I thought if I *told* you, I'd never see you again. You'd spend all your time over there. And *second*, if twenty-three is the median age, then they're far too young for you."

I rolled my eyes. "I said twenty-three was the *median* age, not the max. I'm only thirty-five. There were *some* women more my age over there."

"Like who? Erika Wild?" teased Artie.

My eyes widened. "Don't even kid around about her. That woman's a praying fucking mantis. You couldn't sleep with her without updating your will." I shook my head. "And have you *seen* the place over there? It's fucking amazing with their little tile artwork and their massage chairs. They put the little nautical schtick we got going on over here to shame."

"Yeah, yeah. I'm aware. Sly sank a lot of money into redoing that place a few years back." Artie threw his hands up and leaned back. "So what do we do?"

"We send back an epic prank that'll shut those bastards down. That's what we do."

"Like what?"

I shrugged. "I dunno. I'd have to think." I was silent for several long seconds. "Oh. I got it. I can sneak over there and lace all their alcohol with laxatives, then steal all their toilet paper."

Al lifted his eyes skyward. "Oh, kid. That's just mean! You can't do that."

"Ugh, fine. Oh, I got it! What if we snuck over there after all the late partiers go to bed and flipped their Do Not Disturb signs to Maid Service Requested." Rubbing my hands together, I grinned like a Cheshire cat. "Oooh man. Everyone's gonna be so pissed to be woken up early for maid service."

"I think we need to think of something that doesn't involve messing with the guests," said Artie.

I groaned. "Oh, come on, Artie. You can't tie my hands

behind my back like this. How am I ever supposed to come up with something wicked enough to compete with phallic hedges and chicken crap all over our beaches?! You're gonna have to bend a little."

Artie and Al exchanged a look.

Al shrugged. I could tell he didn't know what to say.

Finally, Artie sighed. "Fine. I'll take the handcuffs off. Just try and think of something that doesn't hurt the guests. Please?"

Excited to have been let loose. I shot him a devilish smile. "I'll do my worst, Artie. I swear I'll make you proud!"

AFTER LEAVING ARTIE'S OFFICE, Al and I headed down to the pool area to supervise the beach and pool cleanup and to try and come up with a suitable prank to really piss off Erika and Sly. As we sat at the swim-up bar, watching half the maintenance crew drag the sand and the other half hose down the concrete around the pool, I found myself getting excited by the possibilities of what we could do to get them back.

With my back and elbows up against the bar, I looked backwards over my shoulder at Manny. "You got any good ideas for pranking the Crystal Point, Manny?" I asked, grabbing my margarita to take a small sip.

Drying glasses with a bar rag, he shrugged. "I could call my cousin. He can get ahold of a truckload of *las cucarachas*. You could put 'em in their food, man."

My eyes brightened at the thought, but when I put my glass back down and looked over at Al, he frowned at me. "Don't even think about that one, kid. You could put the guy out of business with a prank like that."

"They deserve it," I grumbled. "And Artie took the handcuffs off me, you know."

"Yeah, well, human decency still exists."

I sighed and glanced back at Manny again. "Thanks anyway, man. I guess that one's gonna be a no." Just as I turned my head back around, I caught sight of Val getting comfortable on a beach towel covered lounge chair near the pool.

Staring at her, I shook my head. I had an urge to walk over there and just ask her point-blank who she'd been with at two in the morning and why she'd been sneaking around. I looked over at Al. "Hey, Al. How about you and me go for a walk?"

Al looked at me curiously. "What for?"

I stood up and started towards the beach. "For exercise, all right?"

"Exercise?" said Al with a bit of a chuckle. "I did that once when I was younger. I don't know what happened. It didn't seem to take."

I groaned. "Come on."

Al hopped down off his barstool and followed me towards the beach. When we were far enough away from Manny, I looked down at Al. "Look. I just didn't want Manny to hear this. I trust him, but this is sensitive information."

"What is it?" Al looked up at me.

"I didn't sleep very good last night. I guess I had a lot on my mind. So I got up and went out to catch some fresh air."

"*This* is sensitive information?"

"Relax. I'm getting to it. So, I'm sitting there chilling, and it's about two in the morning, and this black car comes pulling up my driveway. About halfway up, it turns its lights off and rolls in the rest of the way and stops at Artie's place."

Al looked surprised. "Artie stayed out until two in the morning?"

"No, not Artie. *Val!*"

"It was Val?!"

I nodded. "Yeah. She got out of the car. She was wearing this skimpy little dress thing, and then she was careful not to slam her door too loud, and when the car backed out and left, she kind of snuck into the house."

"Well, what was she doing out so late?"

"You think I went over there and grilled her?"

Al nodded and looked ahead at the beach. "You tell Artie?"

"No. I told him I was going to be supportive. I didn't think running to tattle that his almost-fiancée was out past curfew was the way to show my support."

"Could you see who was in the car?"

"Nah. They had tinted windows, plus there aren't any streetlights back there. I barely could see the car."

"Huh."

We walked together for a few long seconds before I stopped walking. "So. What should I do?"

"Why are you asking me?"

My arms jerked out from my sides. "Hell if I know. I guess 'cause you're like the Godfather to me. You have all the answers."

Al lifted his bushy brows and sighed. "I don't have all the answers, kid. I wish I did. But I don't."

"Come on, Al. You gotta have an opinion. Should I tell Artie what I saw?"

Al thought about it for a second and then shook his head. "Not yet. Maybe we oughta do a little recon before we concern Artie with it. See if we can't figure out whose car that was, you know? He's got a lot on his plate right now. I don't wanna shake him up if there's no reason to."

"Yeah. Okay. That's a good idea." Even though I agreed with Al, I couldn't think of a single person who could've been in that car with Val that wouldn't shake Artie up. As far as I was concerned, there was never a good reason for your girl to be sneaking back into the house at two a.m.

We walked back down the beach side by side in silence— each of us lost in our own thoughts about the situation. When we got back to the bar, I sat back down again and looked at

Manny. "Hey, Manny. How come you never told me about the Crystal Point Resort down there?"

Manny shrugged. "They're the competition, man. You think I wanna see you go down there? You belong here, with us."

"But remember when I first got to the island, and I asked you where all the chicks were? You could've told me they were just down the beach."

"Yeah. I could've. But I didn't. Artie doesn't like us recommending competitors to our guests, and you were just a guest then."

"Yeah, but I haven't been a guest for a while. They got good-looking women over there."

"We got good-looking women over here," said Al.

I ran a hand around the back of my neck and looked at Al uncomfortably. "I mean, yeah, Evie's hot, Al. But she's taken."

He bumped me with the side of his hand and then pointed at me. "She sure is. You remember that."

I laughed. "I won't forget. Besides, I'm looking for someone a little more age-appropriate."

"The majority of the kids down there are in their twenties. You're thirty-five years old, man. They're too young for you."

"Puh. How old did you say your girlfriend was, Manny?" When he didn't answer, I tipped my head and answered for him. "She's twenty-five. And how old are you?" Once again, his silence forced me to answer for him. "You're thirty-six. Eleven-year age difference and *I'm* too old for those chicks down there?"

Manny swatted their air. "You don't want those kids, Drunk. They're only here for one thing. A good time."

My mouth gaped and I pointed both of my hands at myself. "Are you kidding? Good time's my middle name!"

Al patted me on the shoulder. "Simmer down, Terrence."

I shot him a seething glance.

Manny chuckled. "I thought you were trying to grow up?"

I frowned. "I am growing up. What? Growing up means you're not allowed to have a good time anymore?"

Manny stopped working and put both hands on the bar top, looking at me firmly. "Look. Those guys down there are all wild and crazy. They're doing things their mothers wouldn't approve of."

I stared. "*Exactly!* I like those things, Manny. I *live* for those things."

"Look, Drunk. It's like one big party down there. They stay up all hours of the night raving and drinking and partying and having sex. We're too old for that stuff."

I couldn't believe what I was hearing. Did these people not know me at all?! "You're killing me, Manny. You're absolutely fucking killing me, man."

Al waved a gnarled hand in the air and then cupped the sweaty glass of ice water in front of him. "Oh, knock it off, kid. You just got done cleaning yourself up. We don't need to start all over again with the drinking and the partying. I like you better like this. You can't keep playing it loose."

I groaned. Even though I really didn't want to admit it, Al was right. I *was* trying to do more adulting these days. I had to assume all those kids down there were spending the majority of their vacations blitzed. And while it might be fun for the first couple of days—or weeks—or fine, maybe a month, *two* at the most—the shine on that kind of fun would *definitely* wear off eventually. Who could keep that up for long?

And then a thought hit me.

A smile curved the corners of my mouth. "Oh my God. Guys. I think the perfect prank just hit me."

"Yeah? Whatcha got?" asked Manny.

Clapping my hands together, I laughed a maniacal laugh. "Oh, you'll see!"

9

It was fairly quiet when I left the Seacoast Majestic's pool area late the next afternoon. Relaxing island music followed me down to the beach, where guests clamored around the little white gazebo housing our complimentary snorkeling equipment, paddle boards, and kayaks.

Jesse Coolidge, the twenty-one-year-old Australian surfer Artie had recently hired to man the gazebo, stood in the sand wearing a neoprene wetsuit—the top of which was unzipped and folded down around his hips. He was giving kayaking lessons to a group of sixty-year-old women wearing one-piece swim dresses. The women all giggled like middle-school girls, partly because they were enjoying the time with friends, but mostly because Jesse Coolidge was doing what he was paid to do—be *extra* friendly with the female guests and flaunt his well-defined copper-toned torso.

"Hey, Jesse," I said, giving him a two-fingered wave as I strolled past.

He flipped his long blond hair back to give me a chin-up nod. "Wassup, Drunk."

I passed the lounge chairs where a smattering of guests

reclined, sipping mai tais and margaritas and soaking in the warm Caribbean sun. To my right was Angel's Bay. A couple handfuls of guests frolicked in the water, but aside from that, our beach was fairly empty.

Truth be told, the kind of guests we catered to weren't exactly beach people. They came to the island to relax, enjoy the warm sun, and partake in the food. And on top of that, Artie Balladares's resort was *king* of upselling the many excursions our island boasted. Fishing and sailing expeditions. Four-wheeling jungle adventures. Helicopter rides over the island. Day trips to other nearby islands. Shopping and local sightseeing. Sea turtle or dolphin viewing. The list went on and on. So usually at this time of day, a large majority of our guests were out and about and wouldn't return until it was time for dinner.

I sipped my strawberry-garnished margarita and smiled into the sun as I strolled down the length of the beach that connected the Seacoast Majestic to the Crystal Point and, further down, to Margaritaville. I wore nothing but my fedora and shades and a pair of swim trunks and found myself almost too giddy for my own damn good.

I glanced over to my right. *The Bloody Marauder*, an eighteenth-century pirate ship anchored permanently several dozen yards off the coastline, rocked about with the current. Years ago, a previous Seacoast Majestic owner had had the boat hauled in and anchored out there. At ten o'clock and two o'clock every day, a small excursion left our beach for the ship —giving guests an opportunity to tour it or picnic on it. They raised the pirate flag and guests could "walk the plank" of a real-life vintage pirate ship, children could pretend to fire the cannons, and guests could get their selfies or their family pictures taken. But now *The Bloody Marauder* sat empty, looking like a ghost ship.

I'd never actually gone so far as to walk to the end of our

beach, but when I got there, I discovered that a portion of the island's rugged coastline jutted out into the water, separating our beach from the competitors. So in order to cross, I had to wade out into the water and go around it. When I was back on the sand on the other side, I found a sign that read, *Danger! Guests Not Allowed Past This Point—Crystal Point Resort Management*. I pursed my lips and nodded. So *that* was why we never had any of their guests venture down onto our beach.

Pushing on, I walked down the white sandy beach and began to hear music. It got louder with each step, and when I'd finally made it to the Crystal Point's beach, I almost couldn't believe the party I found. Wild techno pop blared, and the sounds of men and women's laughter, screams, and cheers could barely be heard above the music. There were several beach volleyball games happening, and scantily clad women and bare-chested men were playing frisbee on the sand and screaming in the water as the surf crashed around them. The vibes between the two resorts couldn't *be* any more different.

I wove my way between the thatched palapas along the beach and sipped my margarita coolly, trying to blend in with the rest of the youngsters, but feeling a smidge like the old-timer of the group. But I needed to feel accepted into the fold before I put my plan into motion.

When I finally felt comfortable on the beach, I stopped in front of a row of muscular shirtless dudes who'd made camp on a line of lounge chairs along the water's edge. They all looked like they could play professional football, they were so big, and each one of them held an alcoholic beverage in their hands.

"Hey, fellas," I began, my voice deep and assured. "Anyone here interested in earning an extra hundred big ones?"

The men, all wearing sunglasses, looked up at me in unison.

A blond guy with a tribal armband tattoo and wearing swim trunks featuring a cat eating a slice pizza on the front leaned up on an elbow to look over at me. "Doing what?"

Dropping my now-empty margarita glass in the sand, I crossed in front of him and handed him a flyer from the stack I carried. "It's all in the flyer. It's quick and easy, but it's a limited-time offer and only offered to guests at this resort." I looked down the row at the rest of the men. "Anyone else want one?"

All the guys' hands shot forward. Smiling internally, but fighting to keep a cool exterior, I handed each man a flyer.

"Hey, thanks, man," hollered one of the men as I walked further down the beach.

I looked back at him and waved. "Yeah, no problem."

I walked over to a sand volleyball court next. There were coed teams, and I could tell by their staggered movements and slurred voices they were all feeling more than a little tipsy, but a shade before pass-out drunk. I'd planned it perfectly. Soon everyone would be headed back to their rooms for nap and rally time.

"Hey, guys. Anyone here wanna make an easy hundred bucks?" I hollered, holding up the flyer.

"Doing what?" asked a young woman in a white string bikini. She came running over to me, sideways and barefoot in the sand and tried to pluck the flyer from my hand.

Even though she wore a pink wristband, I lifted it up higher, just out of her reach, and smiled down at her. "You have to be twenty-one."

Pouting, she put her hands on either hip and stared up at me. "I am twenny-one. I jus' had my bir'day," she said, her words coming out in cursive.

I smiled at her and lowered the flyer. "Oh, my bad. Well, then, here you go."

"Thank you s'much." She stared at it for a minute through

her pink-tinted aviator lenses. Then she wrinkled her nose and looked up at me. "Wha's it say?"

I chuckled. "You'd be *perfect* for this. We're conducting a study. All you have to do is to be staying at this resort, be twenty-one or older, and have had four or more drinks today." I smiled at her. "How many have you had?"

"I had seven," she said, but held up four fingers.

"Mia, we had those shots at the bar too, don't forget," hollered one of her friends, who ran over to grab a flyer from me too.

Mia gave me a sloppy grin. "Oh yeah. Shots. I had eleventy-six, then, I guess."

"Hmm," I said, frowning at her. The girl couldn't weigh more than a hundred pounds soaking wet, she was so slim. "Might be time to slow down, huh?"

"Slow down? Not yet." She held up the paper I'd just given to her to show me. "Lookit what I got."

My eyes widened and I nodded indulgently. "Ohh. What is it?"

She shrugged. "I dunno."

Two men that had been on Mia's team came walking over. "What's up, bro?" said one tall, slender, darkly tanned jock.

"Hey, man." I handed him a flyer. "We're doing a study here at the resort. On the effects of alcohol on your body. You can earn a hundred dollars. Interested?"

He looked at me curiously. "Seriously, bro?"

"Yeah. For real." I handed him a flyer. "It's all right there. All you have to do is provide a urine sample to the front desk between three o'clock and four o'clock today and sign the bottom of the form there, giving the hotel consent for your urine to be tested."

"That's it?" When I nodded, he curled his lip. "What are they studying our urine for?"

"Oh, umm," I stammered. I hadn't thought anyone would ask me that. I had to think quick on my feet. I put on my most serious-looking face, and winged it. "To check the correlation between blood alcohol level and the amount of urinal glycolate ribonoids or some bullshit in your body. I think they're trying to invent a drug that lets you drink all day and never get a hangover or something like that."

He seemed satisfied with that answer. "Cool. And then we get a hundred bucks?"

I nodded. "That's it. There are collection cups in all the public restrooms around the beach area and in the lobby." I glanced up to see Al walking out of one of the restrooms on the beach, a smile on his face.

Mission complete.

I smiled to myself. This was going to be fucking epic.

I walked the beach for the next half hour, handing out flyers to anyone with a pink wrist band and who looked even mildly intoxicated. When I'd run out of flyers, I walked over to the edge of the beach, where I found Al waiting for me on a picnic table beneath a palm tree.

"You filled all the restrooms with the sample cups?"

Al's grin lit up his aqua-colored eyes. "Sure did."

"How'd you manage the ladies' room?"

"Let's just say I met a couple of girls that thought I was the cutest thing since the golden doodle." He shrugged. "Their words, not mine. They wanted nothing more than to help out a cute old man such as myself out."

I chuckled. "I don't know what the hell a golden doodle is, but I'll assume it's fucking adorable."

Grinning, Al nodded. "It must be."

I patted him on the shoulder. "Good work, my man." Then I let the howl of laughter I'd been holding back burst out of my mouth. "Hahahaha! Oh my God, Al! This is going to be fucking epic. They're not even gonna know what hit 'em!"

Al laughed too and looked down at his watch. "In about fifteen minutes, they're gonna be inundated with drunk twenty-somethings turning in sloppy urine samples and expecting a hundred big ones. Can you imagine their faces?!"

I couldn't stop laughing. "Oh, I know. Artie's gonna fucking love it."

Al got up off the picnic table bench and beckoned me over to follow him to the golf cart he'd parked up the hill. "Come on. I wanna be in the office when they call!"

10

"MR. BALLADARES, YOU HAVE SOME PEOPLE HERE TO SEE YOU."

Artie shot a look of surprise up at Al and me, who'd been sitting around his office just waiting for the phone to ring. We'd already filled Artie in on the prank we'd pulled, and he'd been pleased as punch. Now, the three of us were just waiting for the fallout.

Artie cleared his throat and looked at the phone curiously. "Who is it, Mari?"

"It's Sly Smallwood from the Crystal Point Resort," she said. "And..." Mari's hand muffled the phone for a second, but we could still hear her ask, "I'm sorry. Who do you have with you today, Mr. Smallwood?"

A female voice piped up. "Erika Wild, head of resort security at the Crystal Point."

"And Erika Wild."

I couldn't stop the grin from spreading across my face. Erika had come for an in-person verbal swashbuckling. I could hardly wait because now, *we* were on top.

"Gimme a second, Mari." Artie pushed the mute button on the phone, and the three of us let out a round of explosive guffaws. I rubbed my hands together excitedly.

Al's eyes widened. "Oh man. I didn't expect them to actually *show up*. I mean, I thought maybe they'd call, but showing up!"

I let out a burst of laughter. "This is *so much better*. We actually get to see their faces!"

"So I should see him?" asked Artie.

"Yes! *We* get to gloat now," I said.

Smiling broadly, Artie nodded. "You can see them in, Mari."

"Yes, sir."

When the phone went dead, Artie suddenly went somber. His hands splayed out over his desk and he tipped his head to the side cautiously. He leaned forward, his office chair groaning. "Alright now, let's just play it cool, fellas."

Cool. I was king of cool. I could do this.

I felt Al reach over and grab my glasses from my hat. When I looked over at him, he'd produced a toothpick out of thin air, he'd put my glasses on, and he'd slouched down in his chair with his arms folded across his stomach.

"Al!"

"Be cool, kid," he said in a gravelly voice.

I fought like hell to rein in the shit-eating grin that covered my face and to extinguish the spark of light in my eyes before the door opened.

By the time Mari opened the door, I'd eliminated all signs of emotion from my face.

"Sly. Come in," boomed Artie from his chair without even the slightest pretense of standing.

Even Al stayed coolly in his seat, forcing me to resist the urge to jump up and greet the guests with a fit of laughter and finger pointing.

It was the first time I'd set eyes on Sly Smallwood, and he wasn't exactly as I'd pictured. He was a tall, somewhat slender fellow with slicked-back silver hair, a black handlebar mustache that curled on both ends, and a tightly manicured salt-and-pepper goatee. He wore rectangular black-rimmed glasses and a charcoal short-sleeved polo shirt tucked into his black chinos. He looked both sinister and smooth. I wanted to ask him if he'd popped out of his mother looking like that because, dare I say it, he looked *sly* as a fox. How she'd managed to name him so aptly, I wasn't completely sure. Maybe he'd just risen to the name's connotations.

Erika hadn't changed much since the day before, only today her blood-red lipstick matched the silk camisole she wore under a black suit. Her eyes still sparkled like emeralds set against dark silk and, as it had the day before also, the stony expression on her face looked like it had been chiseled out of the same lump of coal.

When Mari shut the door behind Erika and Sly, Artie cleared his throat and gestured towards Al and me. "Sly, I'd like you to meet my friend, Al Becker, and my head of security, Daniel Drunk."

Still seated, I gave Sly a casual middle-fingered salute. "Sly. It's a pleasure to finally put a name with an ass—er, excuse me, a face." I winked at Erika. "And Ms. Wild. It's great to see you again. You're looking friendly as never. How've you been? I'd offer you two a place to sit, but well, as you can see, we're out of chairs." I shrugged.

"So *you're* the character Erika told me about," snarled Sly.

I smiled at Erika. "Aww, sweetie. You've been talking about me? How flattering."

But Sly wasn't done with me. He walked towards me wagging his finger in the air. "I've got a *bone* to pick with *you*, son."

Still seated, I held my hands out on either side of myself as if to say, *come at me, bro.* "Sly, man. You sound *pissed*. What's up?" My pun made me smile, and I had to fight the laugh wanting to burst loose.

Sly stopped moving towards me and looked over at Artie.

"You old sonuvabitch. Tell me you didn't just take the training wheels off this kid and let him go rogue over at my resort!"

Artie frowned. "I have no idea what you're talking about, Sly. Is there some kind of problem?"

"You know damn good and well what the problem is. What the hell kind of nonsense was *that*?! I've got a line of kids demanding a hundred bucks for their drunk piss! And you should see my beautiful marble counters. They're covered in a layer of urine because drunk kids apparently don't know how to aim."

That was the final straw. Picturing the front desk girls with their faces drawn up into disgusted grimaces and accepting slimy sample cups was too much. I just couldn't contain myself anymore. I slumped backwards in my seat, my hands covered my stomach and I let out a burst of laughter.

"Ahhhhhahahaha! Gotcha, Smallwood! I guess you *bladder* go clean that up!" As Sly's face reddened, I howled even harder.

Artie, grinning from ear to ear shook his head. "Now, uhh, Sly. About this prank war. Here's the thing. Either *urine* or you're out."

I couldn't believe that Al was the only one of us not laughing. How he managed to keep a straight face, I had no idea. In fact, he shook his head as if he were disappointed in us. "Hey now, fellas. Settle down. Settle down. Maybe this whole prank thing really isn't Sly's cup of *pee*. Oh, I—uh, mean tea," added Al, letting out his own little chuckle.

Artie and I roared with laughter.

"Balladares!" growled Sly. "You know I never did anything to hurt your guests. Guests are off-limits!"

"Haha," laughed Artie. "That's *golden*, Sly. You had two hundred fifty chickens chase my guests off my beach and out of my pool!"

"But you didn't have your guests demanding a hundred dollars for a cup of urine!" snapped Erika from behind him.

I looked at her with a long, patronizing face as she'd done to me the day before. "Oh, sweetie. I'm sorry. Have I somehow managed to *piss* you off?"

She glowered at me, her green eyes mere slits now. "You know what, Drunk? I have a mind to kick your ass."

I jumped to my feet and flicked my nostrils, right thumb, then left thumb, and curled my hands up in a bare-knuckled boxing stance, giving her a shit-eating grin. "I'd sure love to see you try."

She stepped towards me but was stopped by Sly. Unable to touch me, she seethed in my direction.

"All right, all right. I think it's time we all settled down," said Artie. He looked up at his archnemesis. "Maybe it's time we just put this whole prank thing to bed. No one wins in this situation, and if it affects business, I don't want any part of it."

Sly dug his heels in and pointed a finger at Artie. "Oh, no. After the little prank you just pulled? No, no, no. *This* means war."

Artie rolled his eyes. "Oh, for heaven's sake, Sly. It was a practical joke. Can't you take a joke?"

"Not after what you just pulled. You just wait. We're gonna get even with you." With that, Sly strode over to the office door and yanked it open. His finger went up in the air regally. "Don't forget who you're messing with, *Artie Fartie!*" With that, he stormed out.

Erika followed him, pausing in the doorway. "You might have won this battle, but I promise you—the *Crystal Point Resort* will win the war!"

"Hey, Erika," I shouted after her. "You know what? I think you and Sly are the ones that need to grow a pair." I chuckled.

She huffed at me and then stormed out after Sly, slamming the door shut behind her so hard she made the pictures on Artie's walls rattle.

We all stared after them, a little surprised at their outburst. The room was silent for a really long time until finally, Artie expelled an orotund laugh, one fit for an elephant. He laughed so hard that he had to push himself back from his desk and lean back in his seat, his belly shaking like the proverbial bowl full of jelly. Once he got going hard, Al started laughing too, and then I couldn't help myself, I started laughing too. It was one of those contagious laughs where just the sound of the other guy's laughter kept your abs burning and made your cheeks ache. Whether the prank deserved that much energy, I wasn't sure, but it sure felt good to have a little fun for once.

Artie pulled his sweat rag off his desk and used it to blot his eyes. "Ahhhh-hahaha," he cried as the swells of laughter began to ebb. "Oh man, that was funny."

I used my thumbs to blot my own eyes and nodded. "Yeah. I just kept picturing this line of drunk twenty-somethings holding their little yellow cups and Sly and Erika's heads exploding." I chuckled.

"I gotta hand it to you, Drunk—you came up with a good one." He sucked in a deep breath.

"Thank you, Artie. I appreciate that." I smiled at Al. "I'd like to thank my buddy Al here. I couldn't have done it without him."

"Attaboy, Al," said Artie.

Al grinned. "Anything to help the cause."

Artie folded his hands on the desk. "Well, now that that's settled—we need to get down to business."

"What business is that, Artie?" I asked.

"The Carnival festival plans. I think we're gonna have to beef up security. Especially with this prank war going on. I can't have anything unexpected happening."

I help up my hands. "Say no more. I'm on it. I've already got extra help coming in. This place will be a well-guarded machine."

"I think that's well-oiled, kid," said Al.

I lifted a brow at him. "You can oil your machine all you want, Al. But I'll be over here guarding mine."

"Good," said Artie. "Then can we talk about the proposal plans?"

"How're you gonna do it, Artie?" asked Al.

"Oooh, you could rent a helicopter and take her up there and propose in the sky?" I suggested, brightening.

Artie tipped his head to the side and looked at me like I was crazy. "You think me in a helicopter's a good idea?"

I hadn't thought of it like that. "Fair enough. What about synchronized swimming? You know, in the pool?"

Al looked confused. "Synchronized swimming? How's that a proposal?"

"I don't know. You could have someone pop up in the middle with a ring box?"

"But *Artie's* supposed to offer the ring box."

I sighed. "Ugh. Fine. Maybe one brilliant idea a day is all I'm good for. Lemme think on it a little more. You're not in any hurry, are you?"

Artie shook his head. "No. We've got a little time. I'm still mulling over the prenup idea anyway."

"Mulling it over? Artie, what's to mull over?" Al's hands flared out. "It's the responsible thing to do."

"Ahhh, sometimes you just gotta follow your heart. You should know that, Al. I mean, look at us. We made the crazy decision to move down here and start over because something deep inside told us to." Artie poked a finger into the thick flesh covering his heart. "Best decisions are made right here."

"Yeah, well, moving down here was different. There was no one down here waiting to take all our money."

Artie's eyes widened. "You think Val's gonna take all my money? Is that what you're saying?"

I stared at Al, silently bobbing my head and wanting to scream, *Fucking duh. Tell him yes, that's what you're saying. Come on, Al.*

But Al shook his head and looked down at his white New Balance sneakers in a stupor. Then he looked up at Artie.

"Nah. That's not what I'm saying. Look, you've got your love blinders on, I'm afraid. But, in the end, I'm not your father. I'm not gonna tell you what to do, Artie."

"Not his father? *Shit*, Al. You're not my father either, but that doesn't stop you from telling *me* what to do all the time."

Al rolled his eyes at me. "That's because you're an idiot sometimes."

"Thanks, Al."

"My pleasure." He looked at Artie. "Now look. Just don't go rushing into anything and you'll be fine. All right?"

Artie sighed. "Thanks, fellas." He shooed us away with his hands. "Now go. Go. I got stuff to do."

I stood up and walked to the door, helplessly feeling like Artie was going to wind up making a bad decision, but unable to do anything about it.

He pointed at me. "Hey, Drunk."

"Yeah?"

"You better keep a close watch on things. You know? Around the resort. Sly promised to retaliate. Whatever he does, it could be big."

I grinned. Now that I knew it was coming, I could be ready for it. "Don't worry, Artie. I got this."

11

"Hey, Mari." I gave a wave to Mariposa Marrero, who was working behind the check-in counter, when we left Artie's office.

"Good afternoon, Drunk. Mr. Becker," she said, giving us both a big smile.

"Hello, Mari," said Al, pulling up to a stop at the counter. "You're looking lovely as always."

"Thank you." With her eyes chock-full of curiosity, Mari leaned an elbow on the counter and gave each of us a lopsided grin. "Well. Sly Smallwood didn't seem exactly thrilled with the group of you. What happened?"

"Long story," said Al.

"Is it about the prank war he started?"

Chuckling, I shook my head. "Boy, nothing gets past you, does it?"

"Nothing," she said, cutting the air with both hands. "My girls tell me everything that goes down. They have friends, you know. Over at the Crystal Point. I heard you somehow convinced all those kids over there to turn in urine samples at the check-in counter and ask for a hundred dollars."

Al and I exchanged secretive glances.

"I have no idea what you're talking about, Mari," I said, a sly grin pouring across my face.

She reached across the counter to bump me with the back of her hand. "Drunk! You're terrible." She looked at Al. "And you surprise me, Mr. Becker. I can't believe you let Drunk get you involved!"

Al closed his eyes and shook his head. "I also have no idea what you're talking about."

Mariposa giggled. "Well, it's about time we got a little revenge. Did you know that Sly had his gardeners cut the hedges between our two resorts?" Her eyes were wide when she said it.

"Yeah, I heard about that."

"I was here when they did it," said Al, poking his chest. "Sonsaguns should've been arrested for vandalizing the place."

"Why weren't they?" I asked.

"Artie wouldn't involve the police." Al shook his head. "He didn't want to make waves with the new neighbors. Maybe if he would've known things were going to continue, he might've just ended it then."

"Well, I think it's good you finally did something to stand up to them."

I patted the counter and shot her a smile. "Thanks, Mari." Then I looked at Al. "Come on. We've got some things we need to work on. See you, Mari."

Al and I waved goodbye to Mariposa and started towards the front door of the resort.

"So, what do we have to work on?" asked Al, looking up at me.

"That proposal is coming up fast. I think we need to do a little digging on that car I saw here the other night. Let's run down to the guard shack and see if they noticed it coming in. Maybe they can tell us who it is."

"Let's do it."

Caleb Wilson was the guard on duty down at the guard shack. Al pulled his golf cart up to a stop and Caleb walked over to us.

"Hello, Drunk, Mr. Becker," he said, tipping his hat at us.

"Hey, Caleb. Hey, have you ever seen a black Chrysler 300 pass through here?"

"Today?"

I shrugged. "Anytime in the last few weeks."

He frowned. "Not that I can recall specifically."

"I know you and Davis switch shifts at six, but does he ever leave you any notes? Like if he saw anything suspicious for you to be aware of?"

"I'm afraid not."

It would've surprised me if he had, but nonetheless, I was disappointed. I sighed. "Okay. Thanks."

"Sorry I couldn't help."

"It's fine. I'll talk to you later."

Al pressed on the gas and pulled a U-turn in front of the guard shack. "Now what? You wanna call Davis?"

I checked my watch. "I assume he's sleeping right now."

"Oh. Yeah. Well, we could go check the security footage."

"Yeah, I guess we could do that. Let's go."

SEATED in front of my desk back in my office, I pulled the security camera system up on my computer. I didn't have any cameras in the back of the resort, where our cottages were, but I did have footage from the guard shack. I searched the video for the right day and forwarded to the approximate time I'd seen the car. Al and I watched as the black car went through the security checkpoint. The car stopped and Davis went to the window with a clipboard. The two exchanged a word or two and the car took off.

Because it was nighttime, the video was dark and kind of

grainy. There was no way I was making out a license plate, and the face was completely shielded by the tinted windows and mask of darkness. As I'd suspected it would be, the video was absolutely useless.

"Looks like we need to talk to Davis," said Al.

"Yeah, all right. He should be here in a couple of hours. We'll catch him then."

"Well, what do you want to do until he gets here?"

I rolled my head around on my shoulders and then looked over at Al. "I think we should go guard the swim-up bar. What do you think?"

Al chuckled as he pushed himself up off his chair. "I think I'm thirsty too. Let's do it."

12

Davis, the nightshift guard, hadn't turned out to be a whole hell of a lot of help. While he said he remembered seeing the car come through, he didn't have much information to share about it—only that the driver was a Caucasian male with a female passenger and she'd claimed to be a guest in the cottages. When I'd asked what he knew about Val, he admitted he'd heard rumors about her, but he'd never actually seen her. The one bit of information that *had* been interesting was that the same car had come through on multiple occasions in the last few weeks. In fact, he guessed that he'd probably seen it three or four times that he could remember, and they'd all been at random hours in the morning like that.

Thinking that perhaps I'd get lucky and Val would make another late-night walk of shame, I sat out on my front porch, waiting to make a bust. In the end, the stakeout had been for naught. Neither Val nor the car ever showed up. But I did make a decision then and there that I would ask maintenance to install a new camera in the back of the resort.

Despite my late night, I was up early the next morning. I dressed and jogged up to the resort lobby to find Desi, the resort's concierge, already there guiding traffic, booking transportation for guests, and directing the porters.

"Hey, Desi," I said, stopping by the little workstation he had set up in a shaded area off to the side of the lobby's front doors.

"'Ello, Mr. Drunk," he said in his pronounced Caribbean accent. Smiling at me, he showed off his Eddie Murphy–sized gap-toothed smile. "Beautiful day, isn't it?"

"Fucking gorgeous. Hey, Des. Do me a favor?" My eyes skirted the perimeter of the resort's loading area suspiciously. After pranking the Crystal Point the day before, I was on high alert for any shenanigans that might be underway as retribution.

"Anyting, Mr. Drunk."

"Keep an extra close eye on things out here today. I have a feeling something's about to go down."

He looked at me curiously. "Something? Like what do you speak of?"

I shook my head. "I don't know. But I wanna know before it happens, so we can head it off. Got it?"

His wide smile disappeared and his brows knitted together with concern. He leaned into me slightly. "But, Mr. Drunk, how am I to know before something happens if I don't even know what it is that is supposed to happen?"

I patted him on the shoulder. "I think you'll know, Desi. Just be on the lookout." I held my walkie-talkie up. "I got my ear glued to this thing today. Don't be afraid to use it."

"O—okay, Mr. Drunk," he said, nodding like he wasn't sure he understood. "I shall do my best."

"Good man, Desi," I said, pointing at him as I backed away towards the lobby's glass doors. Inside, a blast of cool air countered the humid island heat. My eyes crawled across every square inch of the lobby, making sure everything looked as it should. The usual girls were all at the front desk, dealing with a long line of guests checking out for the day. Gigi Flores, one of the housekeeping staff I'd had a brief, purely physical relationship with prior to Mari deeming her "off-limits," was wheeling a cart into the elevator.

"Hold up, Gigi." I jogged over to her and put a hand on the door.

"You getting on, Drunk?" Her eyes clamped onto mine but then quickly spilled down the length of my body, eying me like a starving man eyes an evening buffet.

"No. I just wanted to chat with you quick."

A flirtatious smile limped across her face. "Yeah?" The singular word managed to come out sounding thirsty, making me chuckle.

I took a step back and held up one defensive hand to clarify my intent. "Business, Gig. Just business."

She tipped her head back slightly, careful not to let the disappointment show on her face. Slightly more hardened now, her jaw clenched. "Oh. What's up?"

"I've got security tightened today. Can you keep me updated if you or any of the girls see or hear anything suspicious?"

Her posture straightened. "Why? What's going on?"

"Don't panic. It's probably nothing. But I know how it works around here. You housekeeping girls get the scoop before anyone else at the resort. So I just wanted to put a bug in your ear. Anything out of the ordinary happens, I want to know about it immediately."

Her eyes narrowed on me. "You get a bomb threat or something you're not telling me?"

My gaze widened. "A bomb threat? Why would you say that?"

"Because you're not saying something. This place isn't going to blow up or anything, is it?"

I chuckled. "I sure as hell hope not. Look, just keep your eyes peeled. Okay? See anything strange, I wanna know about it. See someone that doesn't seem to belong, I wanna know." I took a step back, letting go of the elevator door.

Staring hard at me, she pressed a button inside the elevator. "Yeah. Okay." The doors slid shut, and I turned around to walk across the navy-and-white lobby back to the front doors. I lifted my walkie-talkie to my mouth and held my thumb down on the button.

"Hey, Marcus. Everything good down at the pool?" At my request, Marcus, my night security guard, had come in early to help out down at the pool, considering that I couldn't be in two places at once.

There was nothing for a second, and then he radioed back. "Yeah, Drunk. Everything's clear down here."

"Roger that."

"Al, everything okay on your end?" I said into the walkie-talkie next. I had him hunkered down in my office, watching the security cameras around the resort.

The walkie-talkie made a buzzing sound, then crackled, then finally Al came on. "Drunk. Look out. There's a dime piece comin' in hot on your left."

I turned my head quickly.

"Your other left," barked Al.

I looked the other direction.

"Good morning, Terrence."

I smiled. "Oh, hey, Evie. You're looking extra foxy this morning."

I could hear Al chuckle through the radio just before he let out a catcall. "There's my hot dish!"

"Al sends his regards."

Evie leaned over and shouted at the radio in my hand. "I'm going to put the casserole in at four, Al. Be home for dinner by five."

I held up the radio and pointed at it. "You have to push the button, Evie, or he can't hear you."

She swatted the air. "When you're done playing with your walkie-talkies, tell Al to be home for supper."

I nodded at her. "Will do, ma'am."

I clicked the button when she walked away. "Your wife said dinner's at five, Al."

"Oh good. What are we having?"

"Casserole."

"Casserole? What kind? Is it the tuna one or the chicken one? Because the last time we had the tuna one, it gave me the skidders."

"Shit, I don't know, Al. I didn't ask. Hopefully it's the chicken one."

"Yeah, I hope so too."

"Everything okay up there?"

There was a pause and then Al said, "All this bathroom talk, I might have to make soon."

I rolled my eyes and then spoke into the radio again. "I mean, is everything okay with the resort?"

"Yeah, kid. Nothing to see here. Business as usual."

"Amen to that. 10-4."

Between Marcus and Manny keeping watch down at the pool, all the maintenance men and housekeeping girls on high alert, and Al with eyes in the sky, I felt confident that we had the place on lock. I stood beneath the porte cochere with my arms crossed over my chest like a boss.

For over an hour, I watched the traffic in the circle driveway come and go around me. I watched taxicabs and shuttle busses picking up and dropping off guests. Golf carts prowled the area, and I made sure to verify every face before allowing them to drive down the cobblestone road to the motels and the guest cottages at the end of the driveway. Guests strolled around the grounds, some stopping to ask for directions and others ignoring me completely.

But as I stood there, I felt confident. Everything was in its place. Everything was in order. I was the king and protector of my domain.

"Those bastards aren't gonna catch me sleeping on the job!" I whispered to myself, feeling haughty and in control.

So when, at a little after two in the afternoon, my radio went off and an unexpected, panicked voice muddled through, I was caught a little off guard. "Drunk? Drunk? Is this Drunk?"

I looked down at my walkie-talkie curiously. I almost thought I recognized the voice, but I wasn't quite sure. "Yeah? Who's this?"

"This is, ahh, Jesse Coolidge. Down at the beach," he said. I could hear him panting.

I stared at the radio hard, wondering how in the hell Jesse Coolidge had gotten ahold of a security radio. "Jesse. What's going on, man?"

"Umm. You might wanna get down here, right away, mate. We, uh—got a bit of a problem down here at the beach."

I uncrossed my arms and frowned. "Yeah? What's going on?"

"Two blokes in a little tinny pulled up to our beach a few minutes ago."

"Okay?"

"I was out in the water when they came in. I was teaching this old couple how to use the snorkel equipment."

"I don't give a fuck about your day's schedule, Jesse. Spit it out. What happened?"

"Well—they vandalized the place."

"Vandalized?! What the hell are you talking about?"

"One of the blokes went up to the clubhouse and spray-painted on the side of the building."

"What?!"

"Yeah, mate. While he was doing that, the other one was causing a distraction. He was flippin' over beach chairs and goin' off like a lunatic."

"You're fucking kidding me?"

"Bloody oath, mate," he said, still panting.

I frowned. "Where the hell's Marcus?"

"Out on the beach. They knocked him out cold."

"Marcus got knocked out?!"

"Yeah. I'm on his radio."

"What about Manny? Why didn't *he* call me?"

"He chased after them. He's down by the beach right now. He told me to radio you. You better get down here, mate. Call the coppers or something. The paramedics. We got guests freakin' out down here."

"Well, get them outta there. Send them up to the lobby. I'll be right there."

With my adrenaline now pumping wildly, I was just about to grab a golf cart and fly down there when my brain caught up to me and I stopped short. This was almost all too crazy of a story to believe. How had neither Manny, nor Marcus, nor Al, called me? Just this new kid, that I didn't know a single thing about, had managed to get ahold of me. It wasn't adding up.

As I chuckled to myself, it occurred to me that perhaps *he*'d been compromised by Sly or Erika. Or shoot, maybe he'd been a plant all along! I wondered how much they'd paid him to call me and tell me such a crazy, trumped-up story to get me to leave my post in front of the resort. I shook my head. What an idiot. Now Artie was gonna have to fire the kid, just for making some bullshit up for a couple extra bucks.

I lifted my radio and called Al. "Al, everything good there?"

The radio was silent.

I called him again. "Al. You there?"

Silence.

I frowned. "Al!" I shouted into the walkie.

When a third call went unanswered, a second round of panic set in. I sprinted inside to my office. Bursting through the door, I found Al, with his feet up on my desk, his hands folded in his lap, and his head slung back, snoring softly.

"Al!" I muttered. "What the hell are you doing?"

He startled. "Huh, what?"

"You're sleeping on the job!"

He pulled his feet off my desk and sat up straight. "Oh. Sorry, Drunk, I guess it was nap time. How long have I been out?"

I pulled his chair backwards so I could get a look at the security cameras. "Hell if I know, Al. But we might have a problem." Wiggling my mouse, I woke up my computer and stared at the screen. When I enlarged the camera down at the beach, I was more than a little shocked to see someone down in the sand and people clamoring around him. "Shit!" I breathed almost to myself.

Al removed his glasses and rubbed his eyes. "What's the problem?"

"I think we were just vandalized!" I pointed at the screen, where a man I was pretty sure was Marcus was out cold in the sand, just as Jesse had described.

As I took off towards the door, I hollered back over my shoulder. "Al, call 911. We need the cops and an ambulance down at the beach. And tell them to hurry!"

13

I FLEW OFF MY GOLF CART AND SPRINTED DOWN TO THE BEACH, making it there in seconds with my long legs. Marcus was just coming to when I fell to the sand next to him. "What the fuck happened?"

Gary Wheelan, Ralph the Weasel, and Jesse were all kneeling by Marcus's side.

"I told you, mate. Some blokes in masks showed up on the beach and they knocked him out."

I suddenly felt guilty for not believing Jesse. "I got an ambulance on the way. Marcus. You all right, buddy?"

Marcus blinked a few times as Gary and Jesse helped him to sit up. "I turned around, and that son of a bitch got me right across the jaw. My legs just folded."

Jesse nodded. "He went down like a sack of potatoes," said Jesse, nodding. "I saw it just as I was getting back to the beach."

I looked around. "Where'd they go—the guys that did this?"

"They got back in their tinny and took off!" said Jesse, pointing towards the bay.

Frowning, I looked at Gary and Ralph. "You guys see all of this go down?"

Gary shook his head. "No. We were playing cards in the back of the clubhouse when we heard all the commotion. We just got out here too."

"Shit. Anyone know where Manny went?"

"I told him you wanted him all the guests sent up to the resort lobby," said Jesse, looking back over his shoulder. "There weren't any drivers around, so he took a load of guests up."

My head lolled back on my neck. "Fuck." I looked down at Marcus, whose face looked pale and dazed. "Hey, man. You hang in there. I'm gonna see if I can't chase down those sons-abitches."

Marcus waved me forward. "Yeah, don't worry about me. I'll be fine. Go, go. Get 'em, Drunk."

As I started to leave, Gary shot a hand out to stop me. "I heard someone say they had guns, Drunk. You can't go after them unarmed."

I patted the appendix holster holding Gertie, my Glock 43, and gave Gary a head bob. "Don't worry. I came prepared today." Then I looked at Jesse. "I'm gonna take the dinghy."

"Sure thing, mate. It's got gas in it. But it's probably not gonna be able to catch up to them. The motor's not big enough."

"It's okay," I hollered over my shoulder as I ran towards the end of the beach where the small boat used to ferry guests to and from *The Bloody Marauder* was tethered. "I gotta try!"

Jumping in the boat, I used the little outboard motor to steer me towards the mouth of the bay. My adrenaline pounded as I thought about what had just gone down. Was *this* the retaliation prank? I found it hard to believe that Sly and Erika were such assholes as to have our resort vandalized at *gunpoint* and to knock out a security guard. I mean, that wasn't a *prank*. That was fucking criminal activity.

After navigating around the few remaining guests out swimming in the water, I opened the boat up as fast as the little motor would run me, which Jesse had been right about, wasn't very fast. Water sprayed up around me, providing a cooling mist against my warm skin. I had to keep one hand on my head to keep my hat from flying off and keep the other gripping the tiller. I'd gotten a short ways off from the coast-line when I noticed a small aluminum boat out in the middle of the water. Once I'd set my sights on it, I started full speed towards it.

At some point, I was surprised to notice that I actually seemed to be *gaining* on the boat. It surprised me even *more* when the boat in front of me pulled a one-eighty and headed back in my direction. I tipped my head sideways a tad as I watched it speed full-throttle towards me. Had the *huntee* suddenly become the *hunter*? I pulled Gertie out with my free hand and pulled back on the throttle a little, wondering what in the hell they were doing and having the sudden feeling that perhaps I should turn tail and run back to the shore.

Within seconds, the small speedboat was close enough that I could see two masked men, standing in the boat and aiming guns at me.

My eyes widened.

Fuck.

Why in the *hell* had I thought it was a good idea to chase after them?!

Stopped now, my engine idled. I pulled my walkie from my pocket and prayed I was still within radius. "Uhh, fellas. Mayday. Mayday. This probably wasn't such a great idea. You might wanna send help out here. Over."

"Drop your weapon," shouted one of the masked men.

"Yeah. Alrighty, then." My hands went up on either side of myself and my right hand opened, allowing my gun to clatter to the bottom of the boat. "How ya doing, fellas? What's going on?"

"You following us wasn't a very good idea," growled one of the masked men.

"Me? Following you?" Smiling, I shook my head. "No, no, no. You got it all wrong, fellas. I'm just out for a little boat ride. We musta just been heading in the same direction. I'm going to that island over there. You?"

"You think we're a coupla idiots?" growled the second one, tilting his head so he could see me through the mask holes a little better.

With my hands up by my shoulders, I gave a little shrug. "You want the truth or you want me to lie?"

He cocked his gun.

I nodded. "Lie. Right. No. Most definitely not idiots. In fact, I think you're both very intelligent gentlemen. Good-looking, too. I like those masks. They really bring out the color in your"—I swallowed hard—"guns."

"We gotta message for ya to give Artie," growled the first one, except he forgot to pronounce the *r* in Artie, pronouncing it Autie instead.

"Oh, we're passing notes now. Mmm. Okay?" I said nervously. I patted myself down. "Gee, I left my wide-rule paper at home. You got anything over there I could use?"

"Just tell him he ain't gonna get away wid it."

I frowned. "Do you work for Sly and Erika?"

He pointed his gun at me too. "It ain't nonna yo bidness who we're workin' for." The more I heard his thick accent, the more I decided he sounded very East Coast. Maybe Boston or New York.

I nodded. "Fair enough. Fair enough. Okay. Well, I'll be sure to give him the message. I think it'd mean a little more if he knew *who* was sending it, but—"

"I gotta feelin' he'll figure it out."

"Alrighty, then. I'll move the message along." Anxious to get back to the resort, I moved towards the outboard motor. I'd almost grabbed ahold of the tiller when a shot rang out and a bullet whizzed past my hand and blew a hole in the fucking motor right in front of me. My hand recoiled. I spun around, hugging my hand to my chest, suddenly incredibly thankful it was still attached to my body. "What the actual fuck, man?!"

Each of the men fired again. One bullet struck the motor and another struck the fiberglass hull of the boat.

My eyes widened as the two men continued to pour lead into the tiny tender. Over a dozen shots between the two of them were fired into my boat. Water poured in around my sneakers. I looked up at them. "Are you fucking kidding me? You just told me to deliver a message to Artie. How am I supposed to do that when I'm dead?"

"We didn't kill *you*," said one of them. "We killed ya boat."

The other one chuckled as he climbed into the driver's seat of their boat. "Happy swimmin', asshole."

14

WITH A DOZEN HOLES IN THE SHELL OF MY BOAT AND WATER creeping in around my ankles, I knew it wouldn't take long for the thing to sink right out from underneath me. So I grabbed the walkie-talkie and my gun and jumped overboard. I didn't even watch the boat go down but instead began the long swim back towards land. I struggled in the water for what seemed like hours before an excursion tour boat on a day trip to another island spotted me and picked me up, giving me a ride to shore.

By the time I got back to the resort, the ambulance had already come and gone, and Marcus had been looked over. The EMTs had wanted to take him with them to get checked over, but Marcus had refused, stating he felt fine.

Officer Martinez, the single island cop that had shown up, was still there, interviewing some of the guests down at the beach. According to Marcus, he'd been patrolling the area when a masked man had shown up and started making a scene. He threw over some lounge chairs and railed at the guests. He even went up to the swim-up bar, picked up a barstool and leveled everything on top of the bar. When

Marcus approached the man, gun in hand, someone from behind coldcocked him and that was all Marcus remembered.

It seemed that after everything that had gone down, the fallout was minimal. Because it had happened so fast, there was little information to share. Aside from the spray paint on the side of the clubhouse and a few broken liquor bottles and drink glasses, they'd done minimal damage to the resort. And because the vandals had both been wearing masks, they'd left behind no clues as to their identity. Before he left, I relayed my experience to the officer. He told me I'd been stupid to follow the men, and I'd had to wholeheartedly agree.

Now, with Gary and Ralph flanking me on either side, we stared at the hastily graffiti'd message. In blood-red paint running down the side of the clubhouse's white beach-facing wall, it read *Back Of Artie*.

"Back Of Artie," read Gary aloud. "What's that even supposed to mean?"

"Something wrong with the back of Artie?" asked Ralph, looking over at me and Gary.

Gary's top lip curled. "I mean, he's kinda wide, but other than that…"

"I think that's supposed to say *off*, fellas. Not *of*. Back *Off* Artie." I rolled my eyes.

"But off is spelled with *two f*'s, not one," said Ralph.

"I don't think we're exactly dealing with a couple of brainiacs here." At least they hadn't seemed very intelligent when we'd been out on the water together—although, to their credit, ultimately it had been *I* that looked the fool.

"Back Off Artie?" said Gary. "Someone wants Artie to back off? Back off of what?"

"Yeah, back off of what?" parroted Ralph.

My eyes skipped down the beach towards the Crystal Point Resort. I frowned. "I think I know *exactly* what they want him to back off of."

AFTER TAKING a big swallow of Dr Pepper, I looked up at Artie. "Oh, and the guys in the boat wanted me to give you a message, too." I'd just finished relaying what had transpired down at the beach and was now sitting in Artie's office with him and Al.

Artie looked confused. "*Another* message? What'd they say?"

"They said you aren't gonna get away with it." With narrowed eyes, my head shook angrily. "Fuckers," I muttered under my breath.

Artie frowned. "I just don't understand. Get away with what? Back off what?"

"Obviously this is Sly's way of warning you not to prank him again."

"But this is *his* doing, not mine!" said Artie, his arms extended. "*He's* the one that needs to back off!"

Al, who had been sitting there quietly, looked over at me curiously. "Did you recognize the men in the boat?"

"They were wearing masks. I couldn't see their faces. But I did come right out and ask them if they were working for Sly."

"Well? What'd they say?"

"They said it was none of my business who they were working for. And then they shot me out of my boat."

Artie lifted his brows and nodded. "It's gotta be Sly's retribution. Who else would send me a message like that?"

My head bobbed. "Exactly. It's Sly. I'm sure of it. That son of a bitch." I growled.

Artie gave a little wince like he wasn't completely convinced. "But it just doesn't *seem* like something Sly would do. To knock out a security guard? Shoot you out of a boat? *Scare* all of our guests like that?" He shook his head. "I just can't see Sly going to those lengths all in the name of a prank."

Artie had a point, and truthfully, I'd had the same thought.

It had seemed excessive. I scratched the scruff under my chin and crossed my legs at the ankle.

"You got any other enemies on the island, Artie?"

Artie shook his head. "Aside from Sly, I can't think of a single person that would be upset with me. At least not like that."

I glanced over at Al, wondering if the car we'd been investigating had crossed his mind as it had crossed mine. Maybe it was someone attached to Val that had sent the message.

Al caught my look. With his eyes closed and his lips pursed together, he shook his head at me like he was the fucking Godfather or something. It was his quiet way of telling me now wasn't the time to tell Artie about Val's possible indiscretions.

"Look, kid. Artie's a business owner. Business owners just inherently piss people off from time to time. It's like a law of business."

"Oh really? You owned a Case IH dealership for a hundred years. You ever piss anyone off enough to vandalize your business, knock your security guard old cold, and then shoot your head of security out of a boat?"

Al lifted a shoulder. "Not that I recall. But that's not to say that it didn't happen and I just forgot about it. I'm old. I forget things."

"Yeah, well, I'm pretty sure you'd remember something like that. So I'm gonna go out on a limb here and say it's unlikely this was anything other than a purely personal attack."

There was a knock at the door.

"Come in," Artie's voice boomed.

Gigi Flores's head popped into the doorway. "Hello, Mr. Balladares. Mariposa said Drunk is in here. May I speak with him for a moment?"

I gave a wave from the other side of the room. "What's up, Gig? Everything okay?"

When she saw me, I noticed something in her eyes. Something disconcerting.

I frowned and sat up in my chair. "What is it?"

"Can you come out here? I need to show you something."

"Yeah, of course." I glanced back at Al and Artie as I followed her to the door. "I'll be right back, guys."

In the hallway, Gigi wordlessly grabbed hold of my wrist and tugged me over to the elevator. She pointed at a sign on it. It said "Elevator Out of Order."

I frowned. "There's something wrong with the elevator? Did you call Hector?"

She nodded. "I did, because my cart has been stuck on the fourth floor for the last hour while I waited for the elevators to get fixed."

"What did he say?"

"He said *he* didn't put those signs there."

"Hmm. That's odd."

She sighed and pulled me around the corner of the lobby to the stairwell door. Pulling the door open, she pointed inside. Caution tape had been strung up around the stairs, and there was a red and white caution sign posted that said "Stairways closed for maintenance. Do not enter."

"Hector didn't do this either?"

She shook her head. "He said he didn't. Did you put these here?"

"No. I've been busy down at the beach. We had an incident down there."

She looked concerned. "Yeah, I heard about that. Did they catch the guys that did it yet?"

"I wish they had, but no. Let's not worry about that right now. We need to figure out what's going on here with the elevators."

Gigi shrugged, just as Mariposa came from around the corner to speak with me.

"Drunk, we're having some problems with our door

scanner system. I've had at least a dozen new guests come up to complain their cards aren't working in the doors."

I frowned at her. "You're kidding?"

"Totally serious."

"What floors are you having problems with?"

She shrugged. "There are several of them. Maybe something's wrong with the electrical system. Could that be what's wrong with the elevators?"

"Is the scanner problem just in the main building? Or are we having problems with the motel rooms too?"

"As far as I can tell, it's just the main building."

"What do you know about the elevators?" I asked her. "Do you know who put the signs up?"

"No. I have no idea. The guests are upset, though. They've been having difficulty getting to their rooms."

"Well, then, how have they been getting there?"

"I've been directing them to the stairwell all the way at the back of the building. They're the only ones I'm aware of that aren't under maintenance right now. It would've been nice if Hector could've been a little more strategic with his maintenance stuff so we didn't bother the guests. Maybe you could have a talk with him?"

"I don't understand why the *stairs* would be under maintenance." I looked at the stairwell. "Look, you two keep an eye on things down here. I'm gonna see what's being repaired in the stairwell. When I find out what's going on, I'll let you know."

Gigi nodded. "I'll wait here for you."

At the bottom of the stairs, I tore down the caution tape and then sprinted up the first few flights to find no issues whatsoever. Just a sign and caution tape posted at each level that said the stairs were closed for maintenance. As I continued to find nothing wrong with the stairs, it occurred to me that perhaps *this* was a prank. By the time I got to the seventh floor, not only was I out of breath, but I was also out of patience. I had more than a sneaking suspicion that we'd been had. When I'd gone all the way to the top floor of the building, I exited the stairwell and walked down the hallway to the elevator. Despite the sign, I pressed the button, and in seconds an elevator was there to carry me down to the first floor. I got inside and pressed the lobby button.

When the doors opened and I emerged in the lobby, Gigi and Mari came rushing over to me.

"The elevators work now?!" asked Gigi.

I grimaced. "I don't think they were ever broken."

Gigi shook her head. "I don't get it. Well, then, why were there signs?"

I let out a sigh. "Because I think someone was pulling a prank on us."

"Who would do that?!" cried Gigi.

"That's for me to handle. Look, Gigi. This is what I want you to do. Take the elevator, go to every floor and pull down the signs on the elevators and in the stairwells." Then I looked at Mari. "Mari, you and I are going to figure out what's going on with the key system."

"Okay, I'll go grab a couple keys and tell the girls I'll be right back."

Gigi took off, leaving me to shake my head in wonder. I had to assume the elevator and the stair signs were courtesy of Sly and Erika. So was what had happened down at the beach just supposed to have been a distraction to get me to leave my post? If that was the case, they were seriously disturbed individuals! Criminals, in fact, that deserved to be in jail!

Mari came back holding some room keys. "Okay, I grabbed several for the second floor. We'll try room two fifteen first."

We took the elevator to the second floor and walked down the hall to room 215. Mari scanned the keycard she'd programmed to work, but the little room light flashed red.

"Here, let me try." I took the card from her and inserted the card into the reader, but this time pulled it out slower. The door beeped and a red light lit up.

"See?"

"Well, shit!" I hissed. I tried it again and got the same result. "What number's that one?"

"Two twenty-five."

"Come on." We walked down the hallway to room 225 and the same thing happened. A beep and a red light. "Well, what is going on?!" Looking down the hallway in both directions, I wondered how in the world Sly and Erika had infiltrated our key card system. That was when I noticed something lying on the ground down the opposite hallway. I walked down and picked it up. It was the room number plate for one of the rooms. It had somehow fallen off the door. I stared at it, frowning.

"Hey, Mari. Take a look at this."

Mariposa walked over and looked at the room number plate in my hands. "Yeah?"

"Do these fall off very often?"

She lifted a shoulder. "I've never seen it happen, but that doesn't mean it hasn't. Why?"

I stared at the door in front of me. A small adhesive square indicated where the plate had once been. I turned around and looked at the door behind me. "Were even-numbered rooms always on this side of the hallway?"

Mari stared at the rooms. Tipping her head sideways, she walked back down to the elevator and looked down the hallway, trying to orient her brain to how she was standing in the hotel. Finally, she shook her head.

"No. I think even-numbered rooms are usually on the elevator side and the odd-numbered rooms are across the hall."

I let out a groan before walking back down the hall to room 215 with Mari trailing behind me. "Gimme that key again, would you?"

Mari handed me the key. But instead of inserting it into room 215, I turned around and inserted it into room 216, across the hall. The door beeped and the light turned green, and I was able to open the door.

"Ugh," I groaned. "Bastards switched all the door plates!"

Mari's dark eyes widened. She drew in a breath. "You don't think Sly Smallwood did this, do you?"

"I'm sure he did it. Him and his criminal accomplice. I can't believe they'd stoop so low as to vandalize our property and to assault a guard just to distract me."

"So what are you gonna do?"

I lifted a brow. "Revenge comes to mind."

15

Anger's venom spilled into my veins as I burst into Erika Wild's office. "You evil fucking shitlark. How could you stoop so low?!"

Her eyes swept past me to look at the door I'd just burst through. "I'm sorry. Are we past the knocking phase in our relationship?"

"You took it way too far this time, Wild."

Groaning and with an annoyed look on her face, she leaned back in her seat and folded her hands over her stomach. "Oh, please, Drunk. I thought we were finally on an even playing field. Or am I wrong? Have your testicles suddenly retracted?"

I stared at her—speechless. They didn't *make* women like this where I came from. At least I'd never dealt with them if they did. I didn't even know where to start with someone as morally corrupt and clinically insane as Erika Wild. I shook my head at her.

"Have you been diagnosed as a sociopath, or is it just on your bucket list?"

"Can you be any more dramatic?"

"Eat a dick."

"I'm sorry, you don't look that appetizing. Look, where do

you get off storming into my office and acting like you're suddenly this choirboy?" She rolled her eyes. "Please. You were a willing participant in our little prank war. If you can dish it out, then you better be willing to take it."

I poked a finger into my chest. "First of all, I may not be a choirboy, but I do have ethical boundaries that I wouldn't cross. And second, I wouldn't be a participant if you hadn't released two hundred fifty chickens onto our resort. That kind of prank couldn't go unanswered."

"Oh, God. Not that *again*? You're a broken record, you know that?" Then she lifted a shoulder as if she thought the whole thing amused her. "I thought you seemed bored. I was just trying to liven it up a little over there."

"You crossed a line, Wild." I thought better of that statement and shook my head. "No, let me amend that. You didn't just cross a line, you fucking drove a bulldozer over the line and then set *that* on fire. Get it?"

Erika quirked a brow. "So you *can* be more dramatic. Swell. I didn't realize Sly and I were playing with a bunch of kindergarteners."

"Look, we've got guests that are checking out. They didn't appreciate the chicken prank, they didn't appreciate not being able to use the elevators or the stairs for the last hour, they didn't appreciate not being able to find their rooms, and they *certainly* didn't appreciate the whole scene down at the beach today."

She smiled. "Well, I guess that's what happens when you run a geriatrics resort. They've all forgotten how to take a joke. If you had our clientele, I can assure you—they'd think it was quite a clever prank. Personally, I thought it was hilarious. But to each their own." She lifted her hands and used them to shoo at me. "You can go now. I have work to do."

But she wasn't about to get rid of me that easily. I stared at her, appalled. "Hilarious? What part of knocking out our security guard and spray-painting our building did you find most hilarious? All of that just to pull off a stupid prank?! That's not hilarious, lady. That's fucking maniacal."

Erika's face sobered almost instantly and she leaned forward in her seat. "What did you just say?"

"I said you're fucking maniacal! And now that I think about it, you're also a deranged canker sore that won't fucking go away."

"Not that, you imbecile. What did you say before that?"

I had to pause for a minute because all I could see was red. "Fuck if I know what I just said."

She pointed at me. "You just said something about your security guard getting knocked out and your resort being vandalized."

I stared at her blankly. "Yeah? What's your point?"

"I didn't have anyone assaulted, nor did I have anything to do with vandalism. You can't prove it."

I poked the air. "Bullshit, Wild! We got the little message your guys said to deliver to Artie. And let me tell you, I didn't find it one little bit funny that they shot me out of my fucking boat and left me in the goddamned ocean to die. A shark could've eaten me, thank you very much."

Erika stood up and walked around her desk so that we were face-to-face. Lines creased her forehead and there were no longer any traces of the gloating smile she'd worn only seconds prior. "Drunk, I'm being serious now. I don't have any idea what you're talking about."

That close, I could smell the scent of her hair, like freshly washed linen she smelled so new. I stared hard into her emerald-green eyes, but when I felt like I was being sucked in, I blinked. I knew exactly what she was doing. She was brandishing her sex appeal as some kind of cyanide-laced Kool-Aid. But I wasn't about to drink from her cup of lies.

"Like I believe for a second that you weren't the ones that put the signs on our elevators and closed our stairwells. That had the stench of Sly Smallwood and Erica Wild all over it."

She blanched slightly. "Okay, fine. So I'll claim responsibility for that."

"And switching all our room numbers?"

She cracked a sliver of a smile. "Fine. I'll take responsibility for that too. But those other things—I have no idea what you're talking about. I mean, for heaven's sake, that would be criminal."

I narrowed my eyes at her. "Cut the bullshit. If you didn't order it, then Sly did."

"Listen, Drunk, do you really think we would stoop so low as to cause damage to your resort, assault an employee, and what did you say? Shoot you out of a boat?" A smile tottered around the edges of her mouth.

"Yeah, as a matter of fact, I do think you'd stoop that low."

Erika frowned. "I'm not evil, Drunk. We were just *playing*."

"Who plays like that, Wild? Adults don't do that kind of shit."

Erika walked around her desk and sat back down. "Look, you can think what you want. But I'm being honest. Sly and I didn't do all that other stuff. If you had that happen, then I'm afraid that's a matter for the island police."

"So you expect me to believe that you *just so happened* to pull off your prank at the exact time that I was lured down to the beach by a suspicious incident?"

I could feel her annoyance with me growing. "Look, I don't expect you to believe anything, Drunk. You do you, all right? Now look. I've got work to do and I can't do it with you standing there staring at me. So. Buh-bye."

I couldn't believe the woman was dismissing me like she was queen and I was some kind of servant. But I didn't know what else to say. I couldn't tell if she was fucking with me or not. Had she and Sly been the ones responsible for the vandalism at the beach or not? I honestly couldn't tell. She was so flip about the prank she'd pulled that I believed she was definitely *capable* of the vandalism, but because she was so forthcoming, she also made me believe that maybe she hadn't ordered it. Not knowing if I could believe the woman heightened the frustration I felt. I wanted to punch a fist through something.

"If I find out you're lying…"

She looked up at me, a mocking look on her face. "Then you're gonna what? Tie my shoe laces together? Saran Wrap my toilet seat?" She laughed. "Drunk, there's nothing you can do to me that's going to get that chip off your shoulder. So why don't you just turn around and go?" She shooed me again.

I fucking hated being shooed.

Especially by this smug, psychopathic woman.

I frowned at her. "Don't you fucking shoo me."

She gave me a sly smile and shooed me with her hands again. "I just did."

16

"She fucking shooed me, Artie." I paced his office. "Do you have any idea how much I hate being shooed?"

"Apparently a lot," said Artie, rubbing a hand against the back of his neck. "But you just said she didn't claim responsibility for the attack down at the beach. So at least there's that."

I shook my head. "Just because she said it doesn't mean I believe her. This is war, Artie. Fucking war. You got that?"

"Settle down, kid. If all they did was put some out of order signs on our elevators and switch around our room numbers, I don't think that calls for an all-out war," said Al.

I stopped pacing and stared down at Al. "Oh-ho-ho, that's where you're wrong, Al! It *does* call for war. They have proven that they will stop at nothing to humiliate us. But I have the *perfect* retaliation to stop them in their tracks."

"Look, Drunk. Maybe now's not the best time for retaliation," said Artie.

"What? Why the hell not?!" My face burned. How could Artie just let it all go so easily?

"I'm afraid we have more important matters to deal with right now. The Carnival kickoff is only two days away, which means my proposal is only two days away. I need to put my energy into focusing on those things right now, not this ridiculous feud."

"Oh, come on, Artie!" I cried. "Don't you understand? If we don't respond, they could fuck up your entire proposal! We can't just let sleeping dogs lie! We have to smash 'em in the fucking balls first!"

"Not a very good analogy, kid," said Al.

"Gotta agree with Al on this one, Drunk. Look. I'm not saying we can't answer back, but let's wait until *after* the proposal. All right? I just don't want anything getting in the way of me proposing to Val. I want the day to be perfect for her."

I'd been too busy with the whole prank war thing to even give any thought to Artie's proposal. "You're still going through with it? I thought you didn't even know how you were going to do it."

Artie shot me a devilish smile. "I figured it out, and I've got it all set up."

I groaned. "Seriously?"

"Yes, seriously. Come on, now. Where's that support you promised me?" asked Artie.

I wanted to say, *It flew out the window the minute I found out that Val was stepping out on you,* but one glance at Al made me bite my lip. "Ugh. It's here, Artie. Ignore me. I'm just in a shitty mood because I got shot out of a boat earlier today and no one wants to do a goddamned thing about it. Don't mind me."

"Good. I won't. Now listen, I called my fireworks guy and asked him if he could spell out 'Marry Me Val?' in the fireworks, and he can. It's all set up. At the end of the night, the fireworks will all go off as planned, and then at the end of the show, I'll get down on one knee, and I'll propose to Val. It's gonna blow her socks off!"

I lifted a brow. "Have you practiced that getting down on one knee thing, Artie?" I wasn't *trying* to be an asshole, but the truth of the matter was, Artie was a big dude. His knees were so bad that he took a golf cart whenever he needed to go anywhere on the resort property, and simply walking from his office to the golf cart winded him.

"Drunk!" breathed Al.

But Artie only laughed. "No, no, Al. It's fine. He's right. I'm not in the best shape at the moment. But I promise you both, Val's gonna change all that for me. She's already started cooking for me. No more big buffet dinners for this guy. I can already feel the changes. I'm telling you, Val's the one."

I shrugged. "If you say so, Artie. But what about the prenup? Are you gonna go through with it?"

"I've got time to think on that some more," said Artie. "One thing at a time. Let's get through the proposal before we worry about that. Now look, Drunk. I need to ask you to do me a personal favor."

"What's that, Artie?"

"I want Val to have a nice dress, like one of those fancy Carnival costumes. She's been asking for me to take her shopping in town, but there's just so much going on and I have so much to do to get the resort ready that I don't have time to do it. I want you to take her into town tomorrow and get her whatever she needs to look amazing for the proposal."

I looked at him like he was crazy. "I'm sorry. Did someone tattoo the words personal shopper on my forehead while I was sleeping?"

"Come on, Drunk. I need someone I can trust."

"You don't think Val can handle shopping by herself?"

Artie sighed. "Look, with what happened down at the beach today, and that cryptic message... I'm just not sure what that was about. I don't want her shopping alone. Just in case something happens."

"But why *me*, Artie?! Have Akoni drive her to town and keep an eye on her."

"Because Val knows you. She feels comfortable around you. And I trust you."

"But, Artie, this prank thing—if I'm gone tomorrow, that leaves the resort unguarded."

"They already pranked us. They won't do it again so soon. And we'll just leave it at that."

"I just don't understand that logic! They knocked Marcus out cold, they vandalized your resort, and they shot me out of a fucking boat! Bastards deserve to be in jail!"

"If it was them, then the police will work it out. Look, Drunk, just do me this *one* favor? Take Val into town tomorrow and get her a Carnival outfit and an engagement dress she can change into for the evening. You know what? Let her have a little fun, she deserves it. I'll send my credit card with you. Let her buy whatever she wants."

"Whatever she wants? Artie! She hasn't even said yes yet."

"It doesn't matter, kid," said Al, shaking his head. "Let him spend his money how he wants. He worked hard for it. If he wants to spoil a woman, why do you care?"

My eyes swung over to look at Artie. "I guess I don't care," I said with a sigh. "But if *I* have to go, then Al's coming with us."

Al shook his head. "Oh no. I don't take any woman shopping except my wife. And even that's up for discussion."

"You're gonna make me go *myself*? What kind of friend are you, Al?"

"A smart one. That's what kind." He wagged his finger at me. "You go have fun shopping with Val. When you get back, we'll go have a stiff drink down at the bar. See if we can't get your man card back."

I narrowed my eyes at him. "Gee, thanks, *Al*."

Al tipped his head. "My pleasure."

Suddenly disgusted with my lot in life, I stared at Artie with droopy eyes and a curled lip. I didn't even like being a purse holder for women I *liked* hanging around with. This was going to be a nightmare. I let out an exasperated breath.

"Fine. What time do you want me to take her?"

"I'll tell her to be ready by ten."

"Ugh. Tell her don't be late. The sooner I get it over with, the better."

17

THE NEXT MORNING I SAT OUTSIDE MY COTTAGE IN MY NEW-TO-ME vehicle. A two-year old matte black Ford F-150 Raptor. It was given to me as a sort of thank-you gift after the Jeep Rubicon I'd bought had a helicopter fall out of the sky and smash into it a few weeks back. Frankie had somehow managed to convince the island's governor to reward me for our PGC bust with one of the vehicles they'd impounded, so I'd been given my choice of several different vehicles. The Raptor had impressed me with its big burliness, and as I was six-four, I needed a big vehicle. Plus I'd sworn off flashy colors, so it had seemed the obvious choice.

With one elbow resting in the open window, I drummed my fingers on the steering wheel and stared at Artie's cottage, waiting for Val to make her appearance. It was already ten past ten, and I was annoyed—both with Artie for making me do this and with Val for being late. I adjusted myself in my seat and scratched myself in the sweaty spot beneath Gertie's holster. I'd spent the evening before stewing over the events of the day while giving Gertie a thorough cleaning and drying.

I let out a puff of air and was just about to close up the truck and say fuck it to the whole event when Artie's front door opened and Val emerged looking like a giant banana, if bananas had colossal boobs and wore hats.

She wore four-inch yellow heels and a clingy sunshine-yellow strapless dress that had a big flouncy bow tied between her giant bronzed orbs. Her dark hair was down around her shoulders, and she wore a wide-brimmed yellow hat with pink flowers adorning the crown.

"Good morning, Drunk," she purred when I got out of the truck and walked around it to open the door for her and help hoist her up into the vehicle.

"Hey, Val. We going to Easter Sunday mass before we go shopping or something?"

She giggled, touching her fingers lightly to the base of her throat. "Oh, you are such a funny man. You no like my hat?"

No, I didn't really care for the hat. But I shrugged while walking around the vehicle and climbing in on my side. "Won't it be hard to shop with that thing on your head and in those heels? Maybe you should go put on some sneakers or something. We might have to do a lot walking."

Her eyes widened and she sucked in her breath. "*Sneakers?*" She said the word with a disgusted look on her face like she was repeating a dirty word. "Are you crazy? Sneakers do not go with *thees* dress!"

"You don't have yellow sneakers?" I grinned.

"Do *you* have yellow sneakers?"

Snapping my fingers, I gave her a half-smile. "Shoot. I left mine back in the States. Oh well. You ready to go?"

"Yes." She smoothed out the fine wrinkles on her dress and adjusted her knees so they angled towards me while we drove.

When we were finally off the resort property, Val smiled at me and clasped her hands between her breasts. "Ohhh, I'm so *excited*! I love to shopping. And it is so niiice of you to take me. Artie said you *beg* him to take me."

I had just taken a swig of my soda when she said that, and I nearly sprayed the dark fizzy liquid out across my dash.

Instead, the liquid burned the insides of my nasal passages and made me choke on a cough. When my eyes were done watering and I could speak normally again, I looked over at Val.

"Artie said I begged him to let me take you shopping?"

Her eyes were wide as she nodded up and down exuberantly. "Yes! That is so sweet of you. You know I don't have too many friends, and you want to be my friend!"

I swallowed hard. "Oh. Yeah. That's *totally* why I begged him to let me take you shopping." I rolled my eyes and looked out the driver's-side window. '*Cause that's what I live for. Taking other men's girlfriends clothes shopping.*

But because the broad smile never left Val's face for a second as we drove, I was forced to wrestle with my inner voice. A very large part of me wanted to get to the bottom of the question of who had dropped Val off at two a.m. earlier in the week. But the other voice inside my head, the one that sounded unfortunately like Al's voice, said, *Look at her, kid, sitting over there all excited about the day. How are you gonna ruin her day? Hold your tongue. If you say something, you're only gonna make yourself look like an ass, not her.* My head rolled back on my shoulders. The fact of the matter was, if I pissed Val off at the beginning of the trip by accusing her of something I couldn't back up, she'd likely want to cancel the shopping trip, which would piss Artie off. So, in the end, I bit my tongue. I'd have to be smooth if I wanted to get it out of her.

When we got to the beginning of the shopping district, Val squealed with excitement again. "Ooohh! Where do you want to start?"

I sighed. I had a feeling the day was going to be very painful for one of us, and I knew exactly which one of us it was. I pulled into a parking spot.

"Anywhere you want. Artie said you need a costume for the Carnival festival tomorrow. That's probably going to be the hardest thing to find. Maybe we should get that first."

"Oh, wonderful idea. Do you know where to find that?"

"Yeah. Artie gave me a list of places that might have some costumes."

"This is going to be so much fun!"

When I looked over at the genuine smile on Val's face, I finally felt myself relenting. Having a shitty attitude for the day was only going to make things worse for both of us, and there was no point in making the day more miserable than it needed to be. That was the point that I decided to just relax and give in to Val's over-the-top effervescent personality.

"How about we start with Miss Donna's?" I said, pointing towards the expensive designer boutique that Artie had named first on the list he'd given me. Miss Donna's was located next door to Sapphire Jewelers and just across the street from the Port Bay Harbor, where all the big cruise ships docked when dropping tourists off for day trips of shopping and sightseeing.

The store's oversized front window displayed mannequins wearing brightly colored Carnival costumes, boasting beaded brassieres, huge feathered plumage headpieces, sparkly corsets, and over-the-top ornate accessories. Val's eyes lit up like twin matches when she saw the revealing garments staring back at her.

"Oh my goodness," she purred. "I want everything!"

I chuckled as I followed her inside the little boutique. "I think one Carnival outfit is plenty. When would you ever wear it again?"

She winked at me and held up a particularly revealing two-piece beaded outfit that looked more like uncomfortable lingerie than a costume. "Oh, I *theenk* you can know when I might want to wear *thees* one again."

I grimaced. I wasn't exactly in the mood to picture Val wearing that outfit in the bedroom for Artie. I threw my hands up. "Whatever. I'm sure Artie can afford it."

She clapped her hands together and let out the little high-pitched squeal again. I winced as the shrill sound pierced my eardrums. I glanced up at the woman working the front desk, wondering if they sold ear plugs.

She was an attractive woman about my age with black cornrows that pouffed out at the crown of her head into an afro. She had gold eyeshadow and matching big round hoop earrings, and she wore a long black-and-gold dress. We exchanged appreciative glances before Val linked arms with me.

I let out a little laugh and then felt the need to explain. "My boss's girlfriend." I patted Val's hand now clinging to my elbow.

She nodded as if she didn't believe me, but it wasn't her place to pass judgment.

"Well, let's get started, then. I don't have all day," I said with a sigh. "How about we start over here?" I pointed to the more modest Carnival outfits. The one-piece dresses with the big skirts and the pouffy sleeves. I pulled out a blue dress with yellow fringes around the sleeves and a sharp V cut out of the neckline. It reminded me of something the Chiquita banana lady might wear. "How about this one? We can get you a big hat with fruit on it."

Val looked appalled. "Are you *keeding*? I no wear that clothes. It look like something you grandmother would wear."

I stared at the outfit with one eyebrow cocked. "I can promise you Gam-Gam would've never been caught dead in that. She used to say that breasts were the playthings of the devil. Of course 'Devil' was the nickname she used for my grandfather, but still."

Val ran over to another rack and picked up a sparkly number that barely looked like a set of Band-Aids suspended by strings. "I like *thees* one!"

I sighed. I was pretty sure there was no beating the need for slutty outfits out of Val. "Whatever you like. Go try it on."

After all, Artie had said to get the woman whatever she wanted. Who was I to censor Artie's girlfriend's clothing?

"I try on *thees* one too. Oh! And *thees* one."

I looked back at the woman behind the counter. "Do you have somewhere to sit down? I have a feeling we're gonna be here awhile."

18

"What do you *theenk*?" asked Val, sashaying around in a little circle just outside of the dressing room. She wore a bejeweled top that was basically just two swirly things formed to cup each breast, a matching thong, a bejeweled choker that looked like a torture device of some sort, some kind of crazy peacock-looking crown with matching feathered wings, and her yellow high heels.

By now I was well versed in every square inch of Valentina Carrizo's body. It had been on display in one form or another over the course of the last two hours. It was no secret that she had a smoking hot body (as well a little heart-shaped mole on the underside of her left butt cheek), but each costume seemed to be getting more outlandish, and skimpier, than the last.

I shrugged. "It's okay."

Val sucked in her breath and put her hands on her hips. "Just okay? I no look beautiful?!"

"I mean, you look great, Val. You know that you look great. I'm just not very good at picking out clothes. Especially costume-y things like that." I pointed at her.

She turned around in a circle again, this time stopping so she had her back to me. She moved her arms to spread her wings and looked back at me. "What do you *theenk* of my butt? It look okay?"

I rubbed my fingers against my temples. I was sure there wasn't a single other job in the world that would actually *pay me* to critique my boss's girlfriend's ass. As uncomfortable as being put in that position made me, the truth was, she had a fantastic ass, and I wanted to make her happy. So I stared hard at her butt—you know, to give it a fair *ass*essment. "Wiggle a little bit," I instructed, holding my chin up with my hand and tapping my nose with my forefinger.

She shook her bottom, making her cheeks shake like Jell-O.

"Now can you give it a little twerk?"

Val bumped her butt up in the air like a pro.

"Side to side?"

She gyrated her hips in a fluid Latina sort of way.

"Well, Shakira was right. The hips *don't* lie." I shrugged. "Yeah. Your ass looks great. But now we have to see if you can move around in it." I stood up and walked towards her moving my finger in a little circle. "Spin around."

Giggling, she did as I instructed. "Like *thees*?"

"Yeah, just like that. Okay, now stop. Go that way a little ways, and then I wanna see you walk towards me, like you're a runway model."

"Oooh! Like Victoria Angel!"

"Exactly."

"I practice *thees* at home," she said before turning around and then strutting towards me. Her face in a serious pout, she thrust her chest out, arching her back, her long legs extending gracefully.

"Work it, Val," I said, giving her a wink.

That made her strut even harder.

And then, unbeknownst to either one of us, one of her wings came loose. It floated down behind her, sliding gracefully between her legs and onto the floor right in front of her, but before either one of us noticed it, one of her heels landed on it and her foot slid out from underneath her, like she'd stepped on a banana peel.

"Ahhh!" she screamed, her arms flailing out wide to keep herself from falling.

"Val!" I hollered, darting forward to grab her before she hit the floor.

She fell backwards into my arms. I reached around her and managed to keep her from smashing onto the floor, but when the dust settled and Val was able to get her feet under her again, I realized I'd somehow managed to wind up with two handfuls of Val's breasts in my hands.

Looking down at her breasts in my hands, she giggled. "Oooh, you naughty boy."

"Val?!" said a voice from the counter.

Both my eyes and Val's snapped up to see a tall Asian man in a grey suit, dropping a white lacy piece of lingerie onto the counter.

Val's voice came out breathless, almost in a whisper. "Remy?"

With my hands still clamped to her boobs, I felt her body go rigid against me. She reached up and pulled my hands off of her chest and stumbled forward. "I—I was falling," she said. "He caught me."

I stared at the man curiously. By simply saying her name, he'd somehow managed to turn Val into a completely different person right in front of me—someone who seemed afraid and tense and quite the opposite of the bubbly Val we all knew at the Seacoast Majestic.

He walked over to us. His dark eyes went from Val to me. He pointed at me. "This is him?"

"Remy, please—"

"This is him?!" His voice was louder, and even a little hostile.

Very curious now, I extended my hand to him. "Hey, how's it going? I'm Drunk."

He didn't even so much as look down at my hand. He tipped his head slightly to the side. "Yeah? Well, I'm not." The next thing I knew, Remy's fist decided to make friends with my nose. I knew right away they could never be friends. Mostly because my nose exploded, sending blood splurting all over me and Val and the fancy Carnival costume she wore.

The woman at the counter screamed.

Val screamed. "Remy! No!"

I doubled over, holding my nose, my hand filling with blood. The pain came almost instantly, hit a crescendo and then seemed to make my face painfully numb with prickly bits radiating out into my cheeks, but I was more concerned with the fact that I was bleeding like a stuck pig all over an eight-hundred-dollar costume. I stumbled backwards.

Remy tried to come after me, but Val stepped between us, trying to shove him backwards.

"No, Remy! No!" she bawled.

"You! Get outta here!" the clerk screamed at Remy. "I'm calling the cops!"

"Remy! Don't hurt him!"

"I'm not gonna hurt him. I'm gonna kill him!"

I managed to stand up straight, but immediately staggered straight into a rack of clothes. Dizzy, I could see Val struggling to keep Remy at bay.

I reached under my shirt and pulled out Gertie, pointing it at him. "Get your fucking hands off of her!" I hollered, hoping I sounded scarier than I looked, because I felt like any second I might tip over.

"Remy!" screamed Val. "Go! Just go!"

"The cops are on their way," shouted the clerk, hanging up the phone.

With a gun now aimed at him, Remy wasn't quite so tough. Eyeing me angrily, he took a step backwards. "This isn't over, Val."

"Just go, Remy! Leave us alone!"

He took several more steps backwards and then sirens sounded in the distance. He looked back over his shoulder and then back at us. "I swear to you, Val, this isn't over!" And then he turned tail and ran out of the store.

"Oh my God! Drunk, are you okay?" asked Val, rushing to my side.

I fell sideways into a rack of clothes, toppling it over along with myself. "Yeah, I'm fine." I grimaced, landing hard on the protruding metal arms of the rack, which now dug sharply into my ribs. With tightened breath, I grunted, "No worries. This rack here broke my fall."

THE REST of the time spent at Miss Donna's boutique was a blur. The clerk was not happy at all with the destruction that Remy had caused, and somehow she'd attributed it to Val and me, like it was *our* fault that this guy had come in and punched me in the face! Or that it was *my fault* that my nose had gotten smashed in and had bled all over the place. Could I help it that I was a bleeder?

Once I'd gotten my legs back underneath me and I'd stopped seeing stars, Val and I'd helped the clerk right the racks I'd knocked over and I'd given her Artie's credit card. Not only did Artie pay for the costume that I'd bled all over, he also bought Val two more unbloodied ones, and me a whole new outfit. That squelched any complaints the clerk had about having to wipe blood up off her tile floor.

A cop had shown up. The clerk recounted to him what had happened, and Val and I both gave statements. Val claimed that she didn't know Remy's last name. He was just an acquaintance she'd met once, but couldn't remember where. It was obviously a lie, but I wasn't about to push her to say anything in front of the cops. She and I had the rest of the day together. I figured I would find out more about Remy and whatever was going on with her later when we were alone.

I left the boutique with a trio of garment bags slung over my shoulder—I planned to drop one of them off at a dry cleaners and see if they had anything that might get blood out of feathers. I also left the boutique sporting a brand-new outfit, a swollen red nose, and a throbbing headache. Val clung to my crooked elbow, still fawning over me, and apologizing like crazy.

"It's fine Val, I swear. I'm not gonna die or anything."

"But you look terrible," she said mournfully.

"Thanks," I grunted, unlocking my truck from a few yards down the street.

"You know what I mean," she said with a puffed-out bottom lip as she swatted at my arm playfully.

I opened the back door of my Raptor and tossed the three garment bags inside, then helped Val up into the truck before walking around to get in myself.

I hitched a thumb over my shoulder as I started the engine. "After we drop this stuff off at the cleaners, what do you say we go get some lunch? If we're gonna keep shopping, I need to eat something, and I should probably stop off and buy something for this headache that's eating at me."

Val nodded enthusiastically. "Oh, yes. I am so hungry too! That *ees* a good idea. Where do you want to go?"

I looked over at her as I pulled away from the curb. "How 'bout this? You can pick the place if you can think of somewhere to go that Remy won't make a surprise appearance. And then maybe you can explain what the hell that was all about."

Val kind of shrank a little in her seat but looked up at me, doe-eyed, and batted her press-on lashes. "Oh. Yes. Okay."

19

VAL PICKED MIMI'S SEASIDE CAFÉ, A FANCY LITTLE CHOPHOUSE down along the boardwalk. She said Artie had taken her there once and she'd fallen in love with the view of the water from the outdoor seating deck. Because we hadn't called ahead for reservations, there was a bit of a wait, so I sat contentedly on a bench in the entrance, holding an ice pack to my nose. I'd found it in a convenience store when we'd gone for ibuprofen, and I was already starting to feel a little better.

Val, on the other hand, not one for sitting still, was up, walking around the place, looking everything over thoroughly. Even though my plan had been to interrogate her the second I got her alone at lunch, I appreciated the blissful moment of downtime and the lack of her constant chatter. She was a pleasant enough woman, but she was a handful. She'd been gone about five or six minutes when she came rushing back over to me holding a handful of brochures.

"Look what I find," she said excitedly, waving the colorful pamphlets in my face.

I moved the corner of the ice pack out of my line of vision and tried to focus on it. "What is it?"

"*Ees* island tour. Look at *thees* one. *Thees* one is a night tour.

I always want to go on a night tour, but *ees* too expensive. Maybe I take Artie on *thees* one now."

"You mean maybe Artie can take *you* on it now?" I asked her.

She swatted at me, frowning. "*Ay!* No! I have money."

"Artie's money?"

"I had job before I meet Artie, you know."

"You just said it was too expensive before, but now for some reason it's not too expensive? Gee, what changed in the last few weeks?" I pretended to think hard.

She frowned at me. I could tell I'd pissed her off. She held out her long manicured fingers and began to tick them off. "I no pay rent, I no pay food, I no pay clothes, I no pay electric, I no pay phone, I no pay…"

I held up a hand to stop her now grating voice. "I got it. I got it. You can stop. You have extra money now because *Artie* is covering the bills."

She shook her head at me. "And that is wrong? He ask me *leeve* with him. I take care of him! I cook for him. I do he laundry. I clean he house. I just like he wife. Husbands pay the bills and wife take care of house, no?"

I sighed. When she said it like that, I guessed she had a point. "Whatever."

"Whatever," she muttered, swatting at me in annoyance. "You *theenk* I take advantage of Artie? You just like everyone else at the Seacoast Majestic." She crossed her arms over her chest and pouted.

I sighed. I hadn't meant to make her feel bad. I was just kind of grumpy because I'd just gotten my face smashed in by some ex-john of hers and maybe I was taking my frustration out on her. "I'm sorry, Val. I didn't mean it like it came out. I'm sure you do a good job taking care of Artie."

"I do!" she said emphatically. "I love Artie. And Artie love me."

"But be real, Val. And I don't mean this, like, negatively,

but do you love Artie for Artie, or do you love him for the life he can give you?"

She leaned back against the seat back next to me and sighed. "Look. I know maybe people *theenk* we make odd couple. I young, Artie not so young. I look like *thees*, Artie a *leetle beet* chubby. But Artie has *beeg* heart and I have *beeg* heart. I make Artie happy and he make me happy."

I ran a hand through my messy hair, wishing I'd known in advance that we were going to be eating at a restaurant that didn't allow hats on men. Then I might have fixed my hair. I looked up at her. A million questions swirled through my head, but I had to temper them a little. I didn't want to come off as a complete asshole.

"What about your old life?"

Val looked at me curiously. "What about it?"

I shrugged. "I mean, it can't be easy to just cut everyone from your old life out cold turkey, can it?"

"Turkey? I no understand."

"Like you cut everyone from your old life out suddenly. Like this," I said and snapped my fingers.

She nodded. "I am no going to say *eet* has been easy. But I do my best."

"You gonna tell me about that Remy guy?"

Val sighed and looked away. "I no want to talk about Remy."

"But, Val, he smashed in my nose. I think I should at least have the right to know who he is and *why* in the hell he hit me."

But Val only pressed her lips together.

"Were you dating him or something?"

She shook her head.

"Was he, like—a work colleague?" I suggested as gently as possible.

Val shrugged. "I no want to talk about Remy."

I sighed. "Has Remy ever come to see you before?"

"What do you mean?"

"At the Seacoast Majestic. Has he ever come to the resort to see you."

Her eyes widened as she sucked in her breath. "Oh no. No, no, no." Her finger ticked the air.

"Why do you say it like that?"

"You see what he did to you. Why I would bring him to my new home and ruin my life?"

"Well, has anyone else from your old life ever come to your new home?"

Val looked away. "No."

"No one?"

"I said no."

I scratched the back of my head. "Does Artie know about Remy?"

Her head cranked around, her eyes wide. "No. And you cannot tell him about Remy! I no want him to worry about anything."

"Val! Are you kidding me? I have to tell him! How am I supposed to explain what happened to my nose? It could be fucking broken! I'll probably have a pair of black eyes by tomorrow morning."

She slid over closer to me and hugged my arm. "Please, Drunk. You cannot tell Artie. Tell him you walk into wall or tell him I hit you." She balled her hand in a fist and shook it by my face.

I balked. "I'm not gonna fucking tell Artie that *you* hit me, Val. First off, I do happen to have a reputation to protect here. I don't need all the oldies down at the poker table thinking *you* got the better of *me*. And second, what happened isn't *your* fault. Why would you want Artie to think you assaulted me?!"

"No say that, then. Just say you *heet* the wall with you nose. Okay?"

"No okay!" I said, mocking her cavalier attitude as well as her accent.

"I have to tell Artie, Val. He needs to know there's a psycho on the loose. You heard about what happened down at the pool, didn't you?"

"About the *cheekens*?" asked Val, looking up at me curiously.

"No. Not about the cheekens. About the vandalism," I said, enunciating every syllable. "Those guys who came in off the beach and leveled Manny's bar, spray-painted the clubhouse, knocked out Marcus and then took off in a speedboat."

"Oh, yes. I hear about that, too," she said nodding. "Artie says they wear masks."

"Yeah. I chased after them, you know."

Val's eyes widened. "Really? Oh my goodness, that sound dangerous!"

"Yeah, it probably wasn't the best idea I ever had. They shot holes in my boat."

"You *keedding*!"

"They wanted me to give Artie a message."

Val looked surprised. "Artie no say anything about a message. What is this message?"

"They said to tell him he wasn't going to get away with it."

Val's eyes widened as a hand went to her mouth. "They say that?"

I nodded. "They also spray-painted the words *Back Off Artie* on the side of the clubhouse. Is it possible that those guys had something to do with your past?"

"My past? I—I don't *theenk* so."

"You don't sound very confident."

She thought about it for an extended moment, and then finally she slumped forward with a heavy sigh. In that moment, Val looked older than I'd ever seen her look before. The lines in her face relaxed slightly, as if she'd removed her cheerful mask and replaced it with a mask of worry and regret. Every wrinkle on her face now showed, each line reminding me that she hadn't lived the easiest life.

"*Leesten*, there are a lot of bad people in my past. I no can promise anything. But I promise, if those people are from my past, I no know anything about it. I want past be in past. Maybe some people in my past no like that very much. But is my fault for wanting better life?" Val looked tired, as if it wasn't just the day that had worn her out. "You know, I come to *thees* island to find better life. And help take care of my family. I no come here to do same job I work when we met."

I nodded. I could tell she was being honest. I could see it in her eyes. I patted her on the leg. "I know, Val. I believe you. And of course I don't fault you for wanting a better life and to help your family. I mean, I'm here for a better life too."

"See? We same, you and me." She smiled at me.

I chuckled. "Maybe a little bit."

"Drunk, table for two," said a voice behind us.

"Oh, our table's ready," I said, standing up.

I helped Val to her feet and then decided I needed to squash the topic of Val's previous lifestyle. She wanted to let it go. I needed to just grow the fuck up and let her do it. "Look, I'm sorry for prying, Val. Okay?"

Val gave me a huge smile and then threw her arms around my midsection and buried her head in my chest. Chuckling, I reciprocated the hug and wrapped my arms around her neck, giving her back an awkward little pat.

"Danny?" said a voice behind me. "Is that you?"

I closed my eyes. I would've recognized that voice anywhere.

Fuck.

When I opened them, Francesca Cruz was standing in front of me.

20

"FRANKIE!" MY ARMS FELL FROM VAL'S BODY AND TO MY SIDES almost immediately. I tried to take a step backwards, but Val still clung to my midsection. "Wh-what are you doing here?"

"I had a lunch meeting. What are *you* doing here?"

I cleared my voice and looked down at Val. "Oh. Umm. Artie, umm, asked me to take Val out dress shopping. You remember Val?" I said, gesturing towards the brightly colored woman.

Val pursed her lips as she peeled herself off me. She managed to give Frankie an unenthusiastic little flutter of her fingers. "Hello."

Frankie gave Val a minimal nod as well as a scathing once-over and then turned to look at me. "Since when can you do dress shopping at Mimi's?"

"Well, we just did some shopping, and then we got hungry. Right, Val?" I looked down at her uneasily.

"Yes," she said with a little pouty face.

"And why does your face look like that?!"

My hand went to my swollen nose. "Oh, well, I—uh." I swallowed hard and looked over at Val. I knew she didn't want me telling Artie about Remy, and I guessed that that included leaving Frankie out of it too. "You know, me and this door got into a brutal battle," I said, shooting her a winning smile. "Door one. Drunk zip. What can I say? I'm a natural-born klutz."

Frankie let out a little annoyed puff of air and started towards the door without another word. Like she'd had it with me.

When she left the restaurant, I groaned and shooed Val towards the table seater who was now waiting rather impatiently for us to follow her. "Val, be a sweetie and get us our table? I'll meet you there in a second."

"But I no want sit alone," she said, grabbing onto my arm.

"Val," I said curtly. "Remmmy," I purred under my breath.

Val's shoulders crumpled at the reminder. "Oh-kay," she muttered grumpily. "Fine."

"Thank you."

I didn't even wait for her to disengage from my arm, instead pulling myself out of her grasp before dashing off out the front door towards Frankie. "Frankie! Wait!" I shouted.

She was already across the parking lot when I emerged, making her way towards her little Suzuki Samurai, hidden discreetly behind a van so, of course, I hadn't noticed it when we'd come in.

"Don't talk to me, Danny."

"Frankie. You're being ridiculous. I'm not here *with* Val. Not like that anyway. I'm just doing a favor for Artie."

"It didn't look like you were doing Artie a favor just now."

"Well, no, I mean—I'm sure it didn't *look like*—"

She put a hand on her door handle. "I gotta go, Danny. I need to get back to the office."

"But I haven't seen you in forever. Can't we just talk for a minute? I missed you."

"Well. I've been busy."

"I noticed. Too busy to find time for me?"

She shrugged. "I barely have any time for *Hugo* anymore," she said referring to her Great Dane. "Let alone myself. This new inspector job has me running ragged."

"Aww. Well, that's no fun. You know what they say, all work and no play makes Frankie a dull girl." I reached out and let my hand fall on her shoulder, giving it a playful little squeeze. "How about you hang out with me tomorrow night? We're having this thing at the resort. For Carnival. Artie's putting it on. Come and spend the evening with me? It'll be like a real date. I'll pull out chairs for you and bring you drinks and everything. It'll be like I'm a real gentleman." I gave her a roguish grin.

Frankie sighed. "I wish I could, but I can't. I have to work tomorrow night."

"Do you literally work around the clock now or what?"

Her head bobbed. "I literally work around the clock now. That PGC bust took out more cops than we even realized, and now the workload has tripled. Until things settle down, Danny, I don't really know when we can hang out. I'm sorry."

With my hands on my hips, I leaned forward to look her in the eye. "Did I do something to piss you off?"

"I mean, I'm not real excited to see you out on a date with Val, but—"

I chuckled. "It's totally not a date, Frankie. I swear!" I leaned into her. "I probably shouldn't be telling you this, but Artie's gonna propose to Val at the Carnival thing. He asked me to take her out and get her some new dresses while he gets some preparations made. We both got hungry after spending the morning shopping, so I told her she could pick a spot to have lunch. She picked here."

"Danny. You were *hugging* her."

"Because I said something that made her feel bad and I was trying to apologize."

"With her giant boobs pushed against you?"

I groaned. "Oh, come on. You know Val. That's just how she is."

She rolled her eyes. "Yeah, and I know how you are too."

"Ouch," I said, rubbing the sting from my heart. "Look. I'm being completely honest. I'm not involved with Val. I don't understand why you'd even be mad about that anyway. We don't talk. You don't return my calls or anything. I'm starting to think you're not interested anymore."

She leaned back against the side of her vehicle and crossed her arms in front of her. "That's not it, Danny. I just got the break in my career that I've been waiting for for years. *Finally*. And—I just have to put that first right now."

I groaned. "I think you're overthinking things, Frankie. Lots of people have careers *and* personal lives."

She pursed her lips and opened her car door. "Think what you want. But I gotta get back to work. I have another meeting in a half hour." She got in her car.

Feeling defeated, I took a step back so she could back out of her parking spot. When she had, she stopped and rolled down her window.

"Change your mind about tomorrow?"

She chuckled. "I told you, I have to work tomorrow. I just forgot to tell you that Hernandez told me about the vandalism over at the Seacoast Majestic. I can't believe you didn't tell me."

I smiled at her. "I'd tell you if you'd answer my calls once in a while."

"Everyone all right?" she asked, ignoring my dig.

"Marcus got knocked out, but he's back to normal."

"He said some idiot chased after them and got shot out of their boat."

I gave her a toothy grin and raised my hand to claim ownership. "Idiot here."

Her eyes brightened. "Danny! That was you?"

"You thought we had another idiot at the Seacoast?"

She giggled. "Okay, fine. I'm not surprised. That was a really dumb idea."

"I don't half-ass things, Frankie. You know that. When I fuck things up, I like to fuck them all the way up."

Smiling at me, she put the vehicle in drive. "Bye, Danny."

"Bye, Frankie."

21

THE NEXT MORNING, THE SUN SHONE BRIGHTLY. AS I WALKED along my usual morning path up to the resort I found myself thankful for the low humidity and for the light breeze rustling the treetops and bringing with it the smell of the ocean. Birds warbled, tweeted, and *who-who-whooooed* louder than usual, and in the distance, a rooster, dedicated to waking even the slowest to rise, let out his throaty call. *Er-er-er-er-errrrr!* Lizards filled the corridors, not even pretending to flinch when golf carts drove past, and two stray cats, usually known for just lying in the middle of the road, frolicked in front of the motel rooms, playing with a fallen palm frond. It was as if the island's wildlife were all feeling cheekier than normal, like they could somehow sense the excitement of the day.

Out in front of the lobby, the little circle driveway over-flowed with guests and staff—all of them abuzz, excited about the day's events. Carnival, an event once used to celebrate religious conversion, emancipation, and freedom, now seemed to me to be some kind of cultural mashup of Mardi Gras, Lent, and Independence Day. There would be masquerading, music, food, dancing, and fireworks.

The bulk of the raucous behaviors would take place in a

parade winding through the island streets and culminating in a party downtown. Artie, however, was committed to bringing the flavor of Carnival to the Seacoast Majestic. He wanted his elderly guests to be able to safely enjoy the festivities without having to subject themselves to the sometimes-dangerous celebrations. His guests would get to partake in some of the iconic cultural foods from the safety of the dining room's buffet line, and they'd get to enjoy the sound of the steel drum bands down at the pool or from the comfort of their room's balcony.

Of course, there were those adventurous guests that planned to go into town. Desi was busily arranging transportation for those folks. The resort's busboys unloaded the early shuttle bus riders—those who were just arriving for the long celebratory weekend. Resort employees scurried in all directions, anxiously setting up for the event and making sure everything was exactly as Artie had requested.

Entering the lobby, I stopped at the counter. "G'morning, Mari. Is Artie in his office?"

"No. I just heard he's down at the pool."

I cocked my head slightly. I detected a bit of *something* in her voice. "Why do you say it like that?"

She pursed her lips and leaned in a bit. "From what I hear, he's in a mood this morning."

I wasn't shocked. Artie was easily stressed and knowing that he was proposing by the end of the day, I assumed he was feeling the pressure. "Thanks, Mari. I'll go see what I can do to calm him down."

I caught a ride down to the pool on one of the golf cart shuttles that ran around the resort every fifteen minutes and found Artie in front of the clubhouse, barking orders like I'd never seen him do before. "Caesar, it's not centered. Move it a little more that way, will you?"

From the top of a ladder, Caesar, one of the newer maintenance guys, looked back over his shoulder at Artie. He held the corner of a sign and was just about to attach it to the top of the clubhouse's front porch. "Which way, Mr. Balladares?"

"That way." Artie wagged his hand in the air. "It's not centered. I need it centered."

"Don't worry. I'll center it."

I clapped Artie on the back. "Relax, Artie, just breathe, man. Caesar's got the sign under control. Everything's going to be perfect."

"You don't know that. I only get one shot to make this proposal perfect." Artie looked down at his watch. "When's the extra security going to get here?"

"I don't have them scheduled to come until noon. That gives me plenty of time to get everyone settled before the entertainment arrives." I adjusted the sunglasses on my face, hoping Artie wouldn't see the two shiners hiding behind them or notice that my nose was larger than usual.

"Oh, good." Artie leaned into me and lifted his brows. "And you're keeping a close watch on everything in the meantime, I assume?"

"Of course I am, Artie. Those Crystal Pointers aren't going to get the better of us. Not today, that's for damn sure. This is your day and I'll be on high alert."

"Just remember—no retribution. Not until after I've proposed. Are we clear?"

"Come on, Artie. I'm not a child. You don't have to remind me. I know. I want everything to go good for you and Val too."

"I appreciate that, Drunk. Now. If you'll excuse me. I have to check on the status of the stage I've got Hector setting up for the band."

"Sure. Hey, have you seen Al yet this morning?"

"He's in the clubhouse with the guys."

"Thanks, Artie. I'll let you know when the security team gets here."

As I walked up the clubhouse's front steps, I felt thankful that Artie hadn't said a word about the beating I'd taken the day before. The last thing he needed was to find out that the woman he planned to propose to had friends who would do something like that to one of her new friends. I walked through the Beachgoer restaurant to the back porch to find Al having morning coffee with the guys.

"Hey, fellas, what's cracking?"

"Drunk!" they all said in unison.

"Top o' the mornin', Drunk," said Gary Wheelan, giving me a little salute.

I pulled off my sunglasses and settled them around the brim of my fedora.

"Good Lord," gasped Tony. "What the hell happened to your face?"

I fingered my swollen nose. "Oh, this? Eh, I fucked it up playing Jose Cuervo last night at my place. No big deal."

"Drunk!" breathed Al. "You got drunk last night?"

After lunch the day before, Val and I had continued our shopping spree as Artie wanted her to have an evening dress for the engagement, plus once we'd gotten going, she claimed she needed other resort-appropriate outfits. She'd kept me out the entire afternoon, holding her purse and bags and nodding my head. After I'd brought her back to the resort, I'd run back into town to have my nose looked at. I'd had a sneaking suspicion it was broken. It was already big enough the way it was, and I didn't particularly want it being crooked for the rest of my life too. Once I'd been told it wasn't broken, I'd headed straight home. By then, it was late and the combination of my run-ins with both Remy and Frankie, plus my nearly broken nose, hadn't exactly put me in the best mood for company, so I'd called it a day and holed up in my cottage.

I hadn't told Al about what all had gone down. And I certainly didn't want everyone around the resort knowing I'd been punched in the face by some asshole named Remy.

"Like I said, not a big deal." Playing it off as best I could, I pulled up the last empty seat at the table and looking around nonchalantly. "So. What's happening here?"

Tony shrugged. "I'm just kicking everyone's ass at poker, that's all."

"So nothing out of the ordinary, then?" I asked.

Groans went up around the table.

"Oh, puh-lease," said Al. "He *thinks* he's the king of poker, but we all know the truth, don't we, fellas?"

"Sure do," said Bob. "Tony only wins because he brings the good cards with him."

Several of the guys around the table laughed.

"Oh, shut it, Robert," snapped Tony. He pointed at the man across the table. "That's a bunch of bullshit and you know it."

Smiling, I shook my head. "You guys coming out of your lair this afternoon for the festivities?"

"Hot women in skimpy costumes?" asked Tony, waggling his eyebrows. "Count me in."

"Me too," said Gary, nodding. "Big Ed's coming with us, aren't you, Ed?"

Eddie's eyes widened as if the prospect scared him shitless. "Gary's making me, I guess."

Gary rolled his eyes. "Oh, real punishment—looking at hot women in skimpy costumes."

"What about you three?" I asked, looking at Ralph, Bob, and Elton.

"Meh, their wives won't let them go," said Tony, waving a hand at them.

"You're kidding. Why not? It's going to be fairly tame."

"You *heard* the hot women in skimpy costumes part, didn't you?" asked Ralph. "No, Marge said we have to rearrange the furniture tonight."

I looked at him curiously. "And you'd rather pick rearranging the furniture over hot women in skimpy costumes?"

Ralph looked at me seriously. "Lemme tell you something, kid. You can pick your friends and you can pick your nose, but you can't pick what your wife's gonna let you do on a Friday night."

I laughed and then looked over at Al. "Well, I'm headed up for breakfast. Big day ahead. You wanna join me?"

Al pushed his chair back and tossed his cards down on the table. "Yeah. Let's go."

"Al, didn't you say you ate breakfast already?" asked Gary.

Al shot him a serious look. "You know what my middle name is, Gary?"

Gary shrugged. "James?"

"It's Hungry. You know what Al is short for?"

"Albert?"

"No. Always. Let's go, kid. I'm starved."

22

BEFORE WE WENT TO THE DINING ROOM TO GRAB BREAKFAST, AL and I stopped at the front counter.

"Hey, Mari. Were there any messages for me yesterday?"

"Yes, actually. Just a second." She walked off to grab my messages from the other end of the counter.

When she was gone Al turned to look at me. "So. How was your date yesterday?"

"First of all, it wasn't a date. Second of all, it was horrible."

"Horrible? Really? Val was that bad?"

I sighed. "It wasn't Val that was so bad. She was—well, she was Val. You know how Val is. But one of Val's old work colleagues bumped into me at one of the shops."

"Bumped into *you*? Don't you mean bumped into Val?"

"No. I mean bumped into *me*. His fist mostly bumped into my nose, but whatever."

Al looked up at me. "So you didn't do that getting drunk?"

"No, I didn't do this getting drunk. I got punched in the fucking face. How do you think I got these two shiners? I'm lucky it's not broken," I hissed, trying not to let the girls at the desk overhear. I much preferred everyone at the resort think

I'd done it to myself. Especially since Val didn't want Artie knowing one of her "friends" had done this to me.

Al stared up at the damage that had been inflicted to my face. "But how do you know it's not broken? Maybe we should go have it looked at. It looks sorta crooked."

"Here you go, Drunk," said Mari, handing me a couple of pink message slips.

"Thanks, Mari." I moved away from the counter and Al followed. "In case you hadn't noticed, it looked like that before. And I already had it checked out. It's not broken." I glanced down at the pink slips. "I'm just going to throw these in my office before we eat. Do you mind?"

"No, that's fine." As he followed me through the employee hallway to my office, Al questioned me. "So, who did it?"

"Some guy named Remy. Val wouldn't tell me anything about him."

"You get a last name?"

"Nope."

"You call the cops?"

"I didn't. The store clerk did."

"You tell them who did it?"

"Just that his name was Remy. Val wouldn't tell his last name."

"You tell Artie?"

"Nope." I stopped walking and looked down at Al. "And you can't either. I promised Val I'd keep it to myself."

"You did what?! How could you make a promise like that, kid? Artie needs to know what happened."

"That's what I said, but she begged. I didn't know what else to say."

"Tell me the other guy looks worse than you do."

"I wish I could. He got the jump on me. I had no idea it was coming. All of a sudden my nose is gushing blood and I'm seeing stars. Luckily, I had a gun with me and was able to scare him off. Otherwise, I think I'd be way worse off than I am right now."

Al shook his head. "How is it always *you* that seems to get into these predicaments?"

"Luck, I suppose." Standing in front of my office door, I looked down at the three message slips in my hand. The one on top was from the security company I'd hired confirming the booking I'd made for the extended weekend. The second slip was a note from Hector, our head of maintenance, updating me that he'd gotten the security camera installed in the back of the building like I'd requested.

Al frowned at me.

"What?"

He shrugged. "I don't know. You seem so calm. It's not like you. You got punched in the face and you don't seem to care. Are you growing up?"

Al was right. I should be wanting to find Remy and kick his ass, but ever since Val and I had bumped into Frankie and she'd turned my invitation to the Carnival event down, I'd just kinda been feeling numb. I shrugged.

"It's okay. I took a dose of Fukitol before I left the cottage, so I'm good." I sighed and flipped to the last message in my hand.

I frowned as I read what it said. "What the hell's this?"

Al looked down at it and adjusted his glasses. "Who's it from?"

"Erika Wild."

"What's it say?"

Standing in the middle of the hallway, I read the message. "Surprised we've yet to see retribution. What are you, chicken?"

I flicked the paper in my hand. "See? This is what I'm talking about. They're practically goading us into continuing this prank war. Artie needs to untie my hands."

Al sighed. "Today's not the day for that, kid. It's Artie's big day."

I opened the door to my office, flicked on the light, and walked inside, dropping my messages on my desk. A red box, about the size of a large shoebox, with a lid, was sitting on my desk. I walked around to stand behind my desk so I could read what it said on top.

Deliver to Daniel Drunk.

"Whatcha got there?" asked Al.

"I have no idea. Looks like a present for me."

"Is there a note?"

I looked on either side of the box. "Nope. It just says Deliver to Daniel Drunk." With both hands, I lifted the lid of the box and flipped it backwards. Almost instantaneously, something sprayed up at me, coating my face and neck with some kind of aerosol adhesive. When my fingers went up to feel my face, I dropped the lid, setting off some kind of popping noise, and then I heard an explosion and something white burst forward into my face, like a pillow had exploded in my face.

I could barely see. "What the—!"

"Oh my Lord," breathed Al. He covered his mouth, his eyes wide.

"What?!" I asked, combing my face with my fingers, trying to remove whatever was coating my eyes and cheeks.

"They tarred and feathered you!" He lowered his hand and plucked a white feather off my face. "She made you into a chicken!"

"THAT BEAST!" I ranted as I climbed my front porch steps minutes later. Al followed closely behind me. "I'm gonna get her for this!"

"Look, kid. I know you wanna go over there and have your

revenge, but I don't think now's the time. You gotta look at the big picture!"

"The big picture?! I'll tell you what's big, Al. *Me!* I look like fucking *Big Bird*!"

Thankfully, I'd managed to see only one cleaning girl as I'd snuck out the back of the building. Of course she'd laughed until she'd nearly peed her pants, but Al had brought the cart around and picked me up and driven to my place fast enough that no one else had had to witness my humiliation.

Standing there on my front porch, humiliation and anger burning in the pit of my stomach, I heard a screeching sound.

My brow furrowed. "Wait. What's that?" I asked, holding a hand out to stop Al from talking.

"What's what?"

I cupped my ear. "Do you hear that?"

He frowned. "I don't hear anything."

"Well, then, turn your hearing aids up. I heard a squawking. Like a parr—" And then my mind went to Earnestine. My eyes bulged and I raced inside my house to find Earnestine standing on my kitchen counter, a pile of bird crap around her ankles.

"Well, there you are," I said, relief washing over me. "But look what you did! You made a mess. Do I go to your house and shit all over *your* counter?!"

"*Shit shit shit*," chanted Earnestine, her body bouncing up and down, but her feet remaining glued to the counter.

"Hey, nice mouth," said Al, chiding the bird.

"She doesn't know anything else," I said. Sighing, I looked at Earnestine and shooed her. "Go on now. Go outside. I need to shower."

Her wings flapped when I shooed her, but despite that, Earnestine remained rooted to my counter.

"I said, go!" I roared a little louder this time and shooed her again. I was in no mood to deal with a disobedient parrot.

Once again, Earnestine flapped her wings but didn't go anywhere.

"What the hell?" When her wings had settled, I reached down and wrapped my hands around her and lifted. She squawked when I pulled on her. "Are you fucking kidding me?"

"What's wrong?" asked Al.

"Her feet. They're like glued down or something." Still covered in my own gloppy, gluey, feathery mess, I bent over to look at her little feet. Indeed, they were *actually glued* to my counter. And that was when I saw the little bottle of superglue lying amongst a pile of garbage on my counter. I picked it up and showed it to Al. "Someone superglued my bird to the counter!"

Al looked surprised. "But who would—" He paused then when the answer hit him. "Sly?"

"And Erika!" I growled. "I'm gonna get them for this!"

23

AL STRUGGLED TO KEEP UP WITH MY LONG, EVEN STRIDES. "Drunk, I really don't think this is such a great idea."

"I don't wanna hear it, Al. They superglued my parrot to my kitchen counter. Not to mention what they did to me and to Artie and Marcus. The fuckers are gonna pay."

"But it's Artie's big day."

"What he doesn't know won't hurt him."

"You're not even going to *tell* Artie?!"

I stopped walking and looked down at Al. "You just said it's his big day. *Why* would I bother him with this?"

"Because he's your friend and your boss, and because he owns the place?"

"Look, Artie might own the Seacoast Majestic, but this is personal now. Poor Earnestine's feet must burn after all the chemicals we used to get them unglued."

In fact, Al and I had spent forever Googling tips to remove superglued bird feet from kitchen counters. Unsurprisingly there weren't many tips for that, but I did find that acetone fingernail polish remover worked for removing superglue from kitchen counters. Al had found some of the chemical in Evie's fingernail supply kit, and we'd used Q-tips doused in the stuff to eventually set Earnestine free. Of course, she'd been so hopping mad that she'd cursed us out the entire time, and the second we had her free she'd flown away in a huff, not even bothering to stay long enough for us to check out the condition of her feet.

Now, as we stood there in the sand, it was midafternoon. After setting Earnestine free, Al had left me in my cottage to shower and when I was dressed I'd gone back up to my office to get the security team I'd hired settled in on their assignments, and when I was sure the resort was protected, I'd gone to the kitchen and cooked up a little sweet revenge with the help of Cybil the resort's head cook. As a result, I now carried two five-gallon buckets in either hand, a backpack on my back, and a beach towel around my neck.

Al looked up at me stiffly. "I'm not saying what they did wasn't wrong, kid. It was beyond wrong, but that doesn't change the fact that they could fire back and mess up our event tonight and Artie's engagement plans."

"Look. They're having their own Carnival event over there. They aren't going to have time to come up with something and pull it off yet today. Even if they try, we've got a whole staff of extra security today. We're going to be fine. I'll be on high alert tomorrow. All right?" I turned around and started walking in the sand again. When I'd gone several feet and could tell Al wasn't following I stopped and turned around. "You aren't coming anymore?"

Al swatted the air with his gnarled hand. "Nah. I was only going with you to try and stop you." I could tell by the look on his face that he was disappointed in me.

I walked back over to Al. "Then gimme the posters." I set my buckets down in the sand and snatched the stack of posters I'd had Mari photocopy for me out of Al's hands. I rolled them up into a tube and stuck them into a side pocket on my backpack then squatted down to lift my buckets again. "I'll do this myself."

Al hollered after me. "I want the record to show I told you this was a bad idea."

With my back to Al, I strode away from him towards the Crystal Point Resort's end of the beach. "Duly noted. I'll see you at the swim-up bar in an hour."

JUST BEFORE I got to the Crystal Point's beach, I hid the two buckets as well as my backpack and beach towel in a grove of palm trees. Then I stood back and surveyed the scene. The competing resort had hired a DJ for the day's big event, and there were a few native islanders dressed in Carnival outfits roaming the crowd. Other than that, it was mostly the same as it had been the last time I'd been there. Lots of drinking and laughter. Some of the young crowd danced to the DJ's music while others played sand volleyball or frisbee. Hardly anyone was in the pool, though lots sunbathed on lounge chairs around the pool. The whole place smelled of coconut oil and slightly like pot mixed with sweat.

On a mission, I set about hanging up flyers on every surface I could find. Wearing only swim trunks, my hat, and my sunglasses, I did my best to blend in, dodging the muscular security guard that kept watch around the pool bar and one side of the swimming pool. I kept my hat low on my head, careful not to make eye contact lest I be spotted by a guest that might recognize me from my last prank or by a staff member that might know who I was. I hung the signs in the men's room at eye level above every urinal, and when I was sure there was no one in the women's room, I even managed to sneak in there and tape signs to the inside of every stall.

Once the signs were up, I had time to kill, so I walked over to a shady spot in the trees and copped a squat in the sand next to my supplies. But as I sat there in the sand, thinking and listening to the DJ hyping the crowd, it occurred to me that I needed a bigger voice than just a few signs. So when I saw a waitress wandering around the beach taking drink and food orders, I knew exactly what I needed to do. When she started back towards the resort, I hopped up and rushed over to her.

"Excuse me?"

She smiled at me. "Yes, sir. Can I get you something?"

"Oh, I was just going to let you know the DJ asked me to flag you down. He wants to place a late lunch order or something."

The waitress glanced up at the DJ, busily adjusting his equipment, and nodded. "Of course, sir. I'll go over there right now."

"Thank you."

I snuck closer to the DJ's booth as the waitress approached him. With the music blaring, the two played the "What?!" game for several long seconds, and while he was distracted, I reached over the back of his booth and grabbed his microphone off the folding table.

Then, I snuck back over to my quiet spot in the sand and waited.

At exactly five minutes till two, and with my heart racing, I pulled off my fedora and shades and tugged my backpack onto my lap. Unzipping the bag, I pulled out the Seacoast Majestic's pool man uniform I'd borrowed and quickly slipped into it.

As I stood back up, my heart continued to pound loudly, keeping time with the bass pumping out of the nearby speakers. This was going to be the tricky part. I had to look official and assured. When no one was looking, I snuck around to the pool's maintenance station and grabbed the long telescopic pool skimmer that leaned against the building. Holding that in one hand, I carried one of the buckets with the other.

Then, cool as a cucumber, I strode over to the pool. With the white bucket in one hand and the skimmer in the other hand, I was sure I looked like I belonged there. People danced around me to the techno pop style music, but no one so much as gave me a second look. With a uniform on, I was practically invisible.

Starting in one corner, I began to douse the pool with the bright red dye Cybil and I had prepared. When I'd emptied one bucket and no one had said a word, I returned to my hideout and retrieved the second bucket. I doused the remaining corners of the main pool, and then used the pool skimmer to stir up the water, making it look like I was simply cleaning the pool.

When I'd administered all of the dye, I went back to my hideout, retrieved the microphone, and glanced down at my watch. It was go time.

I waited for the song to end and then tapped on the microphone. "Hello, Crystal Point Resort guests! And welcome to our annual Carnival festivities!" I shouted into the microphone in my best announcer voice.

The whole audience cheered.

I noticed the DJ looking around his booth for his microphone. I had to hurry.

"And now, it's time for the event you've all been waiting for! And this one's only for the sexy people!" I hung on to the word *people* until the crowd all cheered again. "The Crystal Point Resort's tenth annual wet T-shirt contest! So if you're sexy and you know it, *POOL TIME!!*"

I dropped the mic in the sand and headed for cover the second I heard the splashes.

Game.

Over.

24

BRIGHTLY COLORED CHINESE LANTERNS HANGING FROM THE TREES, twinkling white lights wrapped around the clubhouse's porch balusters, and the light of the moon illuminated the pool area that evening. The steel drum band Artie had hired played Calypso-style music on the stage built over the top of the pool while festively costumed dancers strolled the crowd, playing up the event.

Until an hour ago, Val had also been dressed in full costume, carrying on like she was one of the hired dancers, swinging her hips and dancing around while Artie sat on a nearby chair watching, smiling and clapping. Since I'd known him, I was sure I'd never seen him that happy.

I, myself, also smiled. Not because of Val's dancing, or the hot dancers in skimpy costumes, or because of the lively event taking place around me, but because I could still picture the dozens of twenty-something-year-olds with red Kool-Aid-dyed skin rushing to the lobby, and Sly's face when he'd come out of his office and watched in horror as his guests left the resort in droves. Some had simply gone into town to watch the festivities, but more of them had complained that it was the second time the resort had pranked them and they weren't going to wait around for the third time.

Though I did feel some shame for taking the prank quite so far, knowing the dye would wash off eventually made me feel less guilty. When I thought too hard about it, my conscience—which sounded eerily like my mother's voice—told me I was going to hell for that one. I had to remind it that it was Sly and Erika who'd started the prank war in the first place, and it was their fault I'd had to escalate the war because they'd gone so far as to superglue my parrot's feet to my kitchen counter. That prank could've *killed* Earnestine. Never mind the fact that I'd often had thoughts of killing her myself. The point was, I'd never been so cruel as to actually *do it*. And now, I'd grown to sort of like the foul-mouthed bird.

I pushed thoughts of my prank aside and turned to see Val, dressed in a sparkly evening gown, clinging to Artie's arm just a few short yards away. They stood together in the sand looking out at *The Bloody Marauder*, waiting, as everyone was, for the fireworks to start. The dress she now wore was one I'd helped her pick out the day before. It was much more appropriate for a romantic beach and fireworks proposal than her Carnival costume had been. It was long, tight, and sparkly, with a low-cut neckline and an even higher slit along the side, but miraculously, it covered more skin than anything else I'd ever seen her wear.

I spun around on my barstool and plucked a slice of pineapple from the fruit tray sitting on Manny's bar. "So. I wonder when this show is gonna get on the road?"

"Should be any minute now," said Manny.

I turned back around just in time to see Val nuzzle Artie's ear. He looked smug as a cat with a fucking mouse as he held his arm around Val's shoulders. I tipped my head sideways. How was it possible that Artie had found his happily ever after while I continued to be alone?

I turned around again and took a sip of the Carnival punch

Manny had made just for the occasion. The colorful rum drink was refreshingly cool and went down nicely on such a warm, pleasant evening. I wiped the little sweat ring off the counter with my thumb just as the band finished up the song it was playing. The crowd cheered. I saw Artie move the walkie-talkie from his pocket and hold it to his mouth.

I pounded the bar with the bottom of my fists. "Fellas. I think it's happening."

Al waved a triumphant fist in the air. "Go get her, Artie!"

"Should we raise a toast to them?" I asked, holding up my drink.

Al and Manny both raised their glasses with me.

"Let's toast to a flawless, epic proposal."

"Hear, hear!" cheered Al.

I clinked my glass against Manny's, Al's, and Mrs. Al's and then took a swallow just as the first firework boomed off the deck of *The Bloody Marauder* and up into the sky, before crashing into a million colorful sparks. One after the other, the fireworks boomed and whistled. The crowd ate it up, cheering and clapping, making oohing and ahhing sounds.

I could see Val out in front of me, holding her hands to her chest and smiling up at the display of lights. She didn't know what was to come for the grand finale, but she was already in awe of the event—and if I was being honest, even *I* was excited for her.

The fireworks continued one after the other, each one more brilliant than the last. And then there was an extended pause. I glanced over at Al, a wide, dumb smile on my face. "Is this it?"

Al shrugged. "I have no idea."

I looked back at the ship in the middle of Angel's Bay, waiting for the finale. But after an extended pause of silence, nothing happened. I saw Artie lift his radio to his mouth and say something. I pulled my own out of my pocket and turned up the volume.

"What's the problem, John?" I heard Artie say.

"Seems to be a technical glitch," said a gruff, crackly voice in return.

The instant the radio went silent, a lone firework shot off, straying off the beaten path of the previous lines of fire and exploding across the bay, illuminating the darkened horizon. And then the next thing we knew, colorful sparks sprayed off *The Bloody Marauder's* deck like it was one giant Fourth of July sparkler.

Some of the crowd cheered as if they thought it to be part of the show, but I knew better. That wasn't right. I was sure there wasn't any pyrotechnician out there that would fire off sparklers so near unlit fireworks. But before I could give it another thought, rapid-fire booms of fireworks being shot off sounded. All necks in the audience craned upwards, expecting to see the sky light up as it had previously, but this time there was nothing. Instead, a series of fireworks went off on the deck of the ship in rapid succession and then seconds later, an explosion rocked the air, making all eyes squint against the brilliant burst of light on the water.

The Bloody Marauder had exploded into smithereens!

Gasps sucked the air out from around me.

"Oh my God," I whispered, my lungs tight. "What the hell just happened?"

Al put a hand on my arm. "The fireworks man!"

25

Jesse Coolidge, who had been watching the fireworks from his gazebo, and I were the first two to hit the water. With the resort's little tender at the bottom of the Caribbean Sea and the new tender on order, but not here yet, we were forced to swim out to the wreckage in search of John, the pyrotechnician. The last thing I heard before my feet touched the water was Artie hollering after us that he'd call for emergency services.

I swam harder than I'd ever swum before and my shoulders burned by the time I got out to the middle of the bay, where pieces of *The Bloody Marauder*'s wreckage floated around me. "John!" I hollered, my head bobbing up in the inky water and warmed by the fire burning on the water's surface.

"John!" Jesse echoed.

"Over here!" we heard a voice holler back.

The pair of us swam to him. He was lying atop of a splintered piece of the bow, his face smeared with a layer of black soot and his hair matted down over his face.

"Are you all right?" I asked, grabbing hold of the piece of wood he clung to while trying to catch his breath.

John panted. "I had a split second to react when I realized

what was happening. I managed to jump overboard before the ship exploded."

"Are you hurt?" I looked him over.

He reached a hand around and touched the back of his neck. "I got hit in the back by something, but I think I'll be fine."

I glanced over at Jesse. "We need to get him back to shore and get him checked out."

"I'll swim around to the other side and see if his tinny made it through the explosion."

"Thanks, Jesse." Jesse swam away and I looked at John again. "What the hell happened?"

"I've been doing this for thirty years. I've never had anything like this happen before."

"Do you know what caused it, though?"

"Someone tampered with my fireworks."

Hearing the conviction in his voice made my limbs suddenly feel heavy and frozen. I had to remind myself to tread water so I wouldn't become dead weight and sink to the bottom of the bay. "You're sure?"

"As sure as I am that I'm lucky I got off that boat when I did."

"Do you know who tampered with them?"

John's head shook. "I've got no idea. But I could tell they were tampered with. It was obvious. Once I noticed, I decided I couldn't light them. But then the next thing I knew, the sparklers had been set off."

"You didn't set them off?"

"Of course not! It set off a chain reaction. They set off the fuse on the final show, but they weren't set up like I'd had them earlier. They'd been tipped over."

"But you didn't see anyone messing with them?"

"No. They would've had to have snuck on the ship. They were fine before the show. I had everything checked over. Twice."

And then Jesse was back. "The tinny's too damaged to use. We'll have to help you swim back."

"I think I can manage on my own." John shook his head. "In thirty years, I've never had something like this happen. I just can't believe it."

"Come on, John. Let's get you back to shore." As I tugged on the shredded piece of wood, I sent a scathing glance over my shoulder at the lights coming from the Crystal Point Resort.

I'd had all I was going to take. No matter what it took.

I was going to shut the prank war down.

BY THE TIME we got back to shore, Artie had already asked the staff and the team of security guards to move the guests and the party up to the lobby.

So when we got to the beach and the three of us collapsed on the sand to catch our breath, all that remained on the beach were Al, Artie, Val, Gary, and Big Eddie. When I opened my eyes, Artie was looking down at me. "What the hell happened?"

"John said someone messed with the fireworks."

"Who? Who would do that?" asked Artie.

"Artie. Get serious. We know who did it," I said through pants.

Artie's eyes searched the beach, as if the truth were hidden in the palm trees separating our beach from Sly's. "He—he wouldn't!"

"He would."

"Who would?" asked John. "You know who did this?"

"I have a damn good idea," I said, rolling off my back and onto my hands and knees. I climbed to my feet. Sand coated every inch of my hairy legs and feet. I could feel the grit on my face and in my hair. But all I could think about was the people responsible for this vicious crime. Anger heated my insides and propelled me forward. I staggered towards the Crystal Point beach. I wanted to confront them. Make them pay for what they'd done. Not only for nearly *killing* an innocent man and for what they'd done to *The Bloody Marauder*, but for ruining Artie's big moment.

"Drunk!" Artie called after me. "Don't. We'll let the police handle this." I heard the sirens in the distance.

But I kept walking.

"Drunk!"

Anguish lit the fire in my belly, but remorse for what I'd done earlier doused the flame, making me feel overwhelmingly nauseous. Had this been my fault? Would they have done this if I'd never stained their guests' skin red? Was this fair retribution? Their guests' skin would clear in a day and with a soapy shower. But John could've been killed! The famous ship, that part of history, was gone forever. All because of a bully of a man and some stupid prank war?

I wanted to confront Sly Smallwood and Erika Wild. How dare they! I didn't care what I'd done. They were truly psychotic pieces of work. *Criminals!*

And then Jesse was beside me on the beach. "Drunk, Mr. Balladares asked me to stop you."

"Get out of here, Jesse. I'll handle this."

"Drunk, he said to tell you Frankie's on her way."

I stopped walking and looked over at Jesse. He was a tall fellow, making us fairly evenly matched, though I outweighed him by at least thirty pounds. "He said that?"

"Yeah. Who's Frankie?"

Looking ahead towards the Crystal Point, I sighed, then turned and looked back towards our beach. Beneath the moonlight, I could see the wide outline of Artie and, next to him, Al's short, slim frame. Artie was going to be disappointed in me when he found out what I'd done. And Al was going to feed me so full of *I told you so*s, I wouldn't be able to eat for a week. I didn't want to go back and face the music, and yet I wanted to tell Frankie everything they'd done and have her make them pay for their crimes.

I looked over at Jesse. He was still staring at me, wondering how telling me that Frankie was coming had managed to stop me in my tracks. His question lingered between us. *Who's Frankie?*

My shoulders crumpled. It was time to face the music. "Ugh. She's just a friend." I turned around and started back towards home. I waved a hand over my shoulder. "Come on, kid. Let's go."

I waited for Frankie in the circle drive at the top of the hill. The ambulance had beat them there and was already down at the beach tending to John.

When she got out of her car, I rushed to her side immediately, taking her by the arm and pulling her away from the pair of officers that had followed her to the resort. "Finally, you're here."

"I came as fast as I could. Artie said it was an emergency. What happened?"

"We were attacked again," I growled into her ear.

"Attacked! How?"

"Someone blew up Artie's ship, *The Bloody Marauder*. The one in the middle of Angel's Bay."

Frankie turned to stare at me, open-mouthed and wide-eyed. "Someone blew it up?"

"There was a fireworks show. Someone messed with the pyrotechnics."

"Was anyone hurt?"

"John, the pyrotechnician, had to jump overboard, but he wasn't injured. At least not seriously. But he could have been. The paramedics are down at the beach with him already."

"Was he the only person on board?"

"Yeah." I put Frankie into the golf cart I'd driven to the top of the hill in. She waved to the two men following after her like stray puppies, and when I got into the driver's seat, I waited impatiently, drumming my thumbs on the wheel, while they climbed into the back seat of the cart. When the cart lurched forward, she pointed towards the two men.

"Danny, you remember Officer Hernandez? And this is Officer Clarke. Officers, this is Danny Drunk, head of resort security."

"Officer Hernandez and I met earlier in the week. He's supposed to be looking into who shot me out of a boat in the middle of the ocean, but I haven't heard a single peep out of him since. Any news, Hernandez?"

"I looked into it, Mr. Drunk. But there wasn't much to go on. I'm still keeping my ear to the ground."

"Figures," I said, rolling my eyes and focusing on the darkened road in front of me again. I swerved to avoid a slow-moving lizard, making the cart rock from side to side.

Frankie grabbed hold of the handle next to the seat to steady herself. "So do you have any ideas who's been targeting you?"

"I do, as a matter of fact. Fucking Sly Smallwood."

She looked at me curiously. "Sly Smallwood? The name sounds familiar."

"He runs the Crystal Point Resort next door."

"You're sure it was him?"

"As sure as I am of the nose on my face."

"Why do you think it was him?"

"They've been pranking our resort for quite a while now. Between this and the vandalism, I've just about had enough of them." Gritting my teeth, I squeezed the steering wheel tighter making my knuckles go white. "I think it's time you arrested them."

"Them?"

"Yeah. Sly and his accomplice, Erika Wild. She's just as bad if not worse than he is."

Frankie shook her head. "Danny, I can't just arrest them because you want me to. You were a cop, you know that's not how it works. I mean, obviously I can look into it, and we'll interview them and see what they have to say about it. Then we'll go from there. Why don't you start at the beginning? How did this all start?"

"Well, apparently Artie went to school with the guy."

"With Sly? Really? That's coincidental."

"Right? Apparently this guy was a real piece of work in school, and since he's been Artie's neighbor, he's been pulling these pranks on Artie. Like the other day, he let two hundred fifty chickens onto our property."

"Chickens!" Frankie nodded with a little smile. "You told me about it. That night you called."

"The night you hung up on me?" I gave her a side-eyed glance.

She glanced over her shoulder at the police officers in the back and then leaned into me a little, lowering her voice. "Sorry. It was two in the morning. I was asleep!"

"Anyway, he's been pulling all these little pranks. And now suddenly the pranks are getting bigger. I think they did that vandalism down at the beach and shot me out of my boat. Then today, they fucking tar and—" I paused, thinking better of sharing the humiliating tar and feathering story. Maybe Frankie didn't need to know *everything* they'd done. "They superglued Earnestine to my kitchen counter."

"Earnestine? Earnestine your parrot?"

My head bobbed.

"You can't be serious."

"I'm dead fucking serious, Frankie. I had to give her a chemical peel on her feet just to get her unstuck. It was insane. They could have seriously hurt her. And now they blew up our ship and nearly killed a guy. It's getting way out of hand."

"And why exactly you do you think it's *them* doing all of this. Have they left some kind of calling card?"

I poked a finger up into the air. "Ohhhh-ho-ho, I know it's them all right. They've taken responsibility for lots of it. They called to gloat about the chicken prank. And Erika left me a message calling me a chicken, and then next thing I know I'm ta—Earnestine's feet are superglued to my kitchen counter."

"Well, not that they aren't irritating, but they're a little more minor. Knocking your security guard out and blowing up Artie's ship, now *those* I take more seriously. Have they taken responsibility for any of that?"

I frowned. "Not exactly, but it's got their filthy stench smeared all over it!"

"Listen, Danny. People don't exactly go around blowing up other people's ships for no reason. This can't just be a prank. Have you or Artie done anything to piss them off?"

I pressed my lips together. I didn't feel like telling Frankie that I'd turned their guests cherry-punch red. I wasn't in the mood for a lecture.

"Like I said. Artie told me he went to high school with the guy and he was a bully back then. Personally I think Sly's doing all of this just because he's an asshole."

Parked down at the clubhouse now, we all got out of the golf cart and walked down to where the paramedics were putting John on a stretcher, preparing to haul him back up the hill to their rig.

"John, you gonna be all right?" I asked.

One of the paramedics answered for him. "When the boat exploded, some of the pieces struck his head and back. He's got some swelling. We've decided to take him in and have him looked over. We think he'll be just fine, but we didn't want to chance anything."

I patted John on the shoulder. "Get better fast, man. I'm so sorry about what happened."

"In all my years, I've never had that happen before," he said, shaking his head. He was visibly shaken.

"I know, John. I know it's not your fault. You were set up by someone. But don't worry, we'll find out who it was."

"Danny!" hissed Frankie, shooting me a look that said *shut the hell up*.

I pressed my lips together and looked away as the paramedics wheeled John away. Frankie gave a nod towards the two officers that followed us. "Clarke, Hernandez. Follow them up there and see what you can find out from him. I want to know exactly what happened on that ship. I'll see what I can piece together down here."

Officer Clarke nodded. "Will do, Inspector Cruz."

When they were gone, I looked over at Frankie, a smile on my face for the first time since I'd seen her. "Well! Will you listen to that? Inspector Cruz. Impressive, Frankie. Very impressive."

Frankie rolled her eyes. "You thought I was faking all that extra work or something?"

"Some girls are good at that, you know. Faking it." I smiled at her. Then, pressing my fingers to my chest, I took a step backwards, distancing myself from that statement. "Of course I wouldn't know any of them."

"Of course you wouldn't." She shook her head. "Now. We should get on with this. If you're so sure it's Sly Smallwood, I'd still like to get over there this evening and have a talk with them. But first I want to talk to everyone who saw what happened."

We started towards the beach but then stopped short when we noticed everyone that was left standing around the pool wasn't moving. In fact, everyone was stiff as a board and completely silent, all staring off towards the beach. I shot a glance over at Manny, who was leaning against his bar. "What happened now?"

"Mr. Balladares is doing it," he said, giving a nod towards the beach.

"He's what?" I looked out at the beach to see the pair of silhouetted figures alone on the sand. Artie had somehow managed to get down on one knee, and he held an open ring box in the air.

Val stood in front of him, her hands cupping her face. When he finished whatever speech he'd prepared, Val threw her hands up in the air and screamed and then tossed her arms around Artie's shoulders. "Yes! Yes! Yes!" she hollered.

The remaining crowd, Al and Mrs. Al, Manny, Gary, and Eddie all cheered loudly. When I realized what had happened, I clapped too. I was relieved to see that Artie hadn't let Sly ruin his big evening after all.

Artie waved us towards him. He was having problems standing up again. We all rushed him and in seconds had him back on his feet. Val squealed as she stared at the ring on her outstretched hand.

"Congratulations, Artie," said Al, giving his old friend a handshake.

"Yes, congratulations, Artie. I'm very happy for you," said Mrs. Al.

"Thanks, Al, Evie," said Artie, giving them both a nod.

"Real happy for you, pal," said Gary Wheelan.

"Thank you, Gary."

I walked over to Val and held out my hand. "Congratulations, Val. I'm happy for you and Artie."

She squealed, and instead of shaking my hand, she gave me a bear hug. I chuckled, and soon everyone in our little group was accepting a bear hug from Val.

I walked over and shook Artie's hand. "Congratulations, Artie. You actually managed to get it in there after everything. I'm happy for you."

"I wasn't going to let a little boat explosion get in the way of my happiness."

"No, I suppose not." He looked at me curiously then, as if it was the first time he'd seen me all day. "Drunk, what the hell happened to your face? Did that happen when you went out to help John?"

I fingered my swollen nose and darkened eyes. "Oh. This?" I'd worn my sunglasses and hat all day, so I'd been able to hide it from him. I glanced over at Val, who was chatting excitedly with some of the wives, showing off her engagement ring, and then I looked over at Frankie. I swatted the air. "I'm an idiot. I walked into a door yesterday."

"You look like hell."

"Thanks, Artie." Wanting to change the subject, I glanced towards the bay. "So. Too bad about the boat, huh?"

Artie frowned and followed my gaze. "Yes. But I'll deal with that tomorrow. I'm just glad no one got badly hurt."

"I was actually hoping to ask you some questions about it tonight, Mr. Balladares," said Frankie.

"Must we? Tonight? It's incredibly upsetting to have not only the event ruined, but to have it put a damper on my engagement and basically end the Carnival festivities... well, I'd just rather not think of it anymore."

"Danny wanted me to go over and interview Sly yet tonight. Until I've spoken to you about this feud you have going on, I'd rather not speak with Sly."

"Tomorrow's fine with me," said Artie with a nod. "Tonight I'd prefer spending with my new fiancée, if you don't mind."

My mouth gaped. "Artie! You're gonna put this off until tomorrow? That gives Sly time to hide the evidence!"

"As if he hasn't already thought to do that? I don't think one night is going to make much of a difference."

"Don't worry, Mr. Balladares. We'll get what we can from John, and I'll come back tomorrow morning and we can discuss things then."

"My thoughts exactly. So if you'll excuse me, Inspector, I'd like to go celebrate my engagement with my new *fiancée*."

"Be my guest," she said, taking a step back to let Artie pass.

When Artie was gone, my shoulders slumped. "But, Frankie…"

"Danny, please. Mr. Balladares is fine with picking this investigation up tomorrow. We'll take care of it in the morning."

I groaned. I wanted Erika and Sly to pay *now*.

"Besides, he's right. He just got engaged. Let the man have a minute. I mean, how cute are they?" She hugged herself and stared after them.

"Seriously? Now they're cute? Just yesterday you hated Val."

Frankie frowned. "Oh, come on, Danny. Hate's a very strong word. I never *hated* her. I just didn't necessarily care for her fawning all over you. It caught me off guard. That's all."

"So you're saying you were jealous?" The idea of Frankie being jealous made a smile curl the edges of my mouth.

"Not jealous, Danny. Just surprised." She swatted the air. "I'm fine now. I mean, look at them."

I looked over at Artie, who now had his arm around Val. She had her head on his shoulder, and they both looked happier than I'd ever seen them. Al and Evie were snuggling too. It was a beautiful evening, and now romance was suddenly in the air. I had the urge to throw *my* arm over Frankie's shoulder too.

You can think it's cheesy if you want, but I'm not ashamed to admit, I pulled out the yawn move. Lifting both arms up in the air, I yawned and when I lowered them, I let one arm fall around Frankie's shoulders.

She looked over at me, her brows knitted together, and crooked grin on her face. "Smooth, Danny. Smooth." She chuckled.

"Oh, give in. Just once. It won't kill you." With my free

hand, I reached over and pushed her head down on my shoulder.

"Ugh. You're so annoying," she said with a laugh before throwing my arm off her shoulder. "You know I'm working. I just think they're sweet. I can't just watch them for a moment without you putting the moves on me?"

I laughed. "Oh, sweetie. When I put the moves on you, you'll *know*. That wasn't me putting the moves on you."

"Oh yeah? What was it, then?"

"I was just testing the waters."

She smiled. "Yeah? How are they?"

"They've definitely cooled off. But don't worry. I'll find a way to heat them back up again."

27

IT WAS EARLY THE NEXT MORNING WHEN FRANKIE SHOWED UP TO question Artie and Sly Smallwood. She stopped into Artie's office first, bringing with her the statement that her officers had collected from John, the pyrotechnician. Al and Frankie both sat across from Artie's desk, and I stood with my back leaning against a wall as Frankie began her questioning.

"So, Mr. Balladares—"

"Artie. Please. Just Artie is fine."

She smiled at him. "Artie, Danny told me about the 'prank war' so to speak that's been happening between your resort and the resort next door."

"The Crystal Point," he added, nodding.

"Right. Can we just start from the beginning so I have it all straight? How did this all get started and whatnot?"

"Well, Sly and I went to school together. And he always was a bully," said Artie, nodding.

"Did he just have something against you personally, or did he bully others as well?"

"Oh, it wasn't just me. It was just Sly's personality. He bullied others too, but I do think I might have been a favorite of his to pick on."

Frankie nodded as she took notes. "I'm sorry to hear that. And how exactly did the two of you wind up owning neighboring resorts?"

Artie sighed and went on to explain to her what he'd told me. "And I didn't even realize who it was that was next door until, in my very first week of ownership, Sly had his gardeners cut a row of hedges at the entrance of the resort to look like—" Artie paused and glanced up at me as if he didn't want to say it and be rude in front of Frankie.

"Oh, just say it, Artie. Frankie won't be offended."

"To look like what, Artie?" she asked.

Artie cleared his throat and sat up a little higher in his chair. "Well, to look like the male anatomy."

Frankie's eyes widened. "Oh! I see." She scribbled something down in her notes.

"Yes. I had to have that whole row cut back."

"But they were on your side of the property, I assume?"

"They were!"

"And you *know* it was Mr. Smallwood?"

"I do. In fact, he got a good laugh at my expense when he called to gloat about it."

"Artie, did you report this to the police when it happened?"

"I wish I had, but I didn't. I didn't want to rile anything up my first week as owner. Had I known that he was going to keep up with the pranks, I would've certainly put an end to it right then and there and let him know in no uncertain terms that he wasn't going to keep harassing me. Unfortunately, I think my negligence in fighting back may have encouraged him to keep going."

Frankie nodded. "So has he done other things?"

"Tell her about the lobsters," prompted Al.

"Yeah. That one cost you money. I think they should have been prosecuted for that for sure," I added.

"Lobsters?"

Artie sighed and then went on to relay the story about the returned lobsters to Frankie.

"I understand that that whole situation cost you money, but unfortunately, Sly could have probably argued that the whole situation was one big misunderstanding and that he didn't realize it was your delivery."

"Yes, I'm not surprised."

"What else are you sure that he's done?" asked Frankie.

"Well, there were the two hundred fifty chickens he had released on our property," said Artie.

"Danny told me about that. Was there any property damage done?"

"We're still finding chicken crap all over the beach, even now after it's been raked and sifted," I said.

"But that's not property damage, Danny," said Frankie. "I understand it's a mess to clean up, but there probably wasn't a lot you could do to prove that Sly had anything to do with it anyway. But you know he did it?"

"We one-hundred-percent know he did it! Al and I were both here when Sly called Artie to gloat. And then there was the vandalism down at the beach and them shooting me out of my boat. They could've killed me. They could've killed Marcus!"

"That's definitely more concerning," agreed Frankie. "Did they call to gloat about that incident too?" She looked up at Artie.

"No. I haven't gotten a call about that. And Drunk said that Ms. Wild said they had nothing to do with it."

"But she's a nutjob!" I raised my arm to point towards the Crystal Point. "Who believes the word of a fucking nutjob? Not me."

"Kid, simmer down. We're trying to figure this out," said Al.

"Was that all they've done? Aside from the most recent event?"

"As far as we're aware," said Artie.

"Well, there was the elevator and room number prank too, and the Earnestine incident," I said, glancing over at Artie. I hadn't told him about that yet.

"And don't forget, they tarred and feathered you, Drunk!" inserted Al with a raised finger.

I closed my eyes.

"Danny, they tarred and feathered you? You didn't tell me that!"

Opening my eyes, I glanced over at Al. "No. I'd hoped we could keep that little nugget to ourselves."

"How'd they do it?!"

"They booby-trapped his office," said Al. "Left him a little surprise on his desk." Al shook his head as he let out a little chuckle. "Funniest thing I think I've ever seen."

"Thanks, Al."

"I'm sorry, kid, but at this age, you think you've seen it all, and then you see one of your best friends get tarred and feathered and then you find that you can actually say to yourself, nope, I haven't seen it all."

With her brows lowered, Frankie turned and looked at me. "Has the Seacoast Majestic responded to these *pranks* in any way?"

"What do you mean?" asked Artie.

"She wants to know if we've pranked them back," I said.

"Oh, well, we've, uh—" Artie stumbled over his words.

I rubbed a hand over my face and then looked at her. "You didn't really think we wouldn't answer back, did you?"

"I didn't say that. I just want to be prepared so when I go speak with Mr. Smallwood next, I'll know what he's going to say."

"Well, we haven't done any property damage, that's for sure," said Artie.

Frankie nodded. "Good. I'm glad. And you haven't physically hurt anyone, I can assume?"

"I mean, we haven't *hurt* anyone. No," I agreed.

"Well, then, what have you done?"

The room went quiet for several seconds. Frankie looked around at each one of us in turn and then finally she sighed. "Look, I'm not going to arrest you or anything. And you *know* Sly's going to tell me when I go over there. You might as well just fess up now. I'd prefer not to look surprised when I go over there."

"Fine," I sighed. I shot a subtle glance over at Al, but he'd turned around and given me his back. A lot of help he was going to be. "We handed out flyers over there."

"That's all?"

"And we put some little cup—*things*—in all their public bathrooms."

Frankie looked up at me, confused. "Okay. Keep going?"

"The flyers said the Crystal Point Resort was doing a study."

"What kind of study?"

I groaned and tilted my head to look up at the ceiling as I finished. "The effects of alcohol on a urine sample, sort of."

There was quiet for a second as Frankie absorbed that. Then she smiled. "You're telling me that you convinced their guests to give the Crystal Point Resort urine samples? And they fell for it?"

"Well, the flyer said the resort would give them a hundred dollars if they wanted to participate in the study. They just had to bring their sample to the front desk."

Frankie's eyes widened as she clapped a hand over her mouth. "Danny!"

"What?!" I said, shrugging. "They had it coming!"

"Well, yeah, but—" She shook her head, smiling. "Okay. I guess that *was* pretty creative. I take it back."

I couldn't help quirking my own smile. I was thankful that Frankie had a sense of humor. "Thank you."

"And that's all? That's everything you've done in return?"

"That's all we've done!" said Artie with a nod.

"Well—" I ran a hand around my neck uncomfortably. "That's not exactly *all* we've—"

"Drunk!" Artie's head snapped over to look at me in surprise. "That's all I've given permission for!"

"I know, Artie, but after the Earnestine thing, and the tarring and feathering, I could just—"

"I tried to talk him out of it, Artie," said Al.

I looked over at Al curiously. "Did I do something to you, Al?"

"I'm sorry, kid. I did. I told you you shouldn't do it."

I groaned. "You know I had no choice!"

"You did have a choice."

"What'd you do?" growled Artie.

All eyes were on me. "Well, I, uh—" I had to swallow hard as my mouth had gone dry from being put on the spot. "I dyed their swimming pool water red," I said.

Artie's lip curled. "You did what?"

My hands flared out, palms up. "They could've *killed* Earnestine."

But Artie shook his head in confusion. "I don't get it. You dyed their swimming pool water. What's that mean?"

"I dyed it and then I called for a pool party."

"I still don't—"

"It dyed their skin, Artie," said Al.

"Only temporarily. It's like Kool-Aid. It'll wash off with soap. Haven't you ever gotten a Kool-Aid mustache? It's not a big deal."

Artie's eyes grew to the size of limes when the realization of what I'd done sank in. "You stained the *skin* of their guests?! Drunk! How could you!"

"They blew up your ship, Artie! And ruined your proposal! They could've killed someone!"

"But they did that *after* you stained their guests' skin!" Artie's head shook. "They did it *because* you fired first!"

"How can you say that Artie?! I didn't fire first! *They* fired first. They shot me out of a boat!"

"They aren't taking responsibility for that. It could've just been thieves. A completely separate attack!"

"It wasn't, Artie. They sent you a message, remember? It had to have been them. And then they almost killed Earnestine, and they tarred and—"

"I don't give a damn if they plucked Earnestine to feather you with," shouted Artie. "I can't believe you did it after I specifically told you not to ruin my proposal."

"I didn't *try* to ruin your proposal, Artie. I had no idea they'd blow up your boat! I had the whole resort on lockdown."

Artie leaned back in his seat. He couldn't even look at me now. "Anyone else would be fired for this!"

"Fired! Oh, come on, Artie. I didn't start this war. You can't seriously want to fire me."

"Of course I don't seriously want to fire you. But dammit, Drunk. You shouldn't have done it."

I sighed. "Fine. I shouldn't have done it. I'm sorry, Artie. I am. But they've gone too far. Too many times."

Frankie, who had been silent as I'd admitted to what I'd done, sighed. "I'm sorry, Danny, but I have to agree with Artie. I think you went too far too."

"Oh, come on, guys!" I shouted. "It's my *job* to defend our resort. I was only trying to defend the Seacoast Majestic! I was only trying to defend *you*, Artie."

"Look, Artie. I know the kid shouldn't have done it. And he knows it too, but he's right. His heart was in the right place even if his head wasn't."

Finally Al was on my side. "Thank you, Al."

Artie sighed. "I know why he did it. I'm just frustrated that my big proposal got messed up."

Frankie leaned back and smiled at Artie. "Messed up? Artie, I didn't think it got messed up at all! In fact, I admire the fact that you didn't let anything stand in the way of the grand gesture you had planned. You barged right ahead and proposed anyway. I thought it was sweet."

Artie smiled. "Val thought it was sweet too. She's very excited."

"We could tell," said Al.

"I was going to tell you all later down at the clubhouse when all the guys are around, but I guess I'll share now. She's so excited, in fact, that we discussed it last night, and neither one of us wants a long engagement."

"What's that mean?" I asked, looking confused.

"It means they aren't going to wait to get married," said Al with a sigh.

"It means we've already set a date. We're getting married next weekend."

"Next weekend!" I couldn't believe what I was hearing. "But, Artie, that doesn't give you much time to get a prenup drafted."

"Yes. About that. I've come to a decision. There won't be a prenup," said Artie. He held up his hands to stop anyone from arguing with him. "And before any of you say a word, I've given it a lot of thought. It's my decision, not Val's. I trust her. And I want to show her I trust her."

I frowned at him. "Well. I see your decision making has been compromised by your penis."

"Danny!"

"Drunk!"

"I don't want to hear it, you two. I think Artie's making a big mistake by not having a prenup, but only time will tell."

Frankie's face flushed red. Like *I'd* embarrassed her. She tried to change the subject. "But what about a venue, Artie? And food and flowers and a dress? You won't have time to plan a nice wedding. Doesn't Val want a nice wedding?"

"She wants a nice wedding, yes. But we've decided we'll have it here. Down at the beach. The resort's hosted weddings before. It won't be hard to throw together. I've got the best chefs on the island here. We have access to flowers and photographers. She'll get an off-the-rack dress, but she doesn't mind. She said she only wants to be with me."

"I'm sure the wedding will be nice, Artie," said Al.

I shook my head. I couldn't believe what was happening. How had the peace and quiet we'd become accustomed to suddenly disappeared? Nothing seemed to be going right anymore. Suddenly stifling hot, I fluffed my shirt back and forth against my chest. "Is anyone else hot?"

"I'm fine," said Al, looking over at me.

I strode to Artie's door. "I'm not. I'm sorry, but I need some air. Excuse me."

28

I WAS SITTING BEHIND THE WHEEL OF AL'S GOLF CART WHEN Frankie emerged a half hour later. Absorbed in scanning her notes, she didn't even notice when I pulled up beside her.

"Well, hello, Officer Cruz. Need a lift?"

She smiled when she saw me. "Oh, Danny! You scared me. I was just on my way over to speak to Mr. Smallwood, but I've got my car."

"It's not far. Why don't you let me drive you? It'll give us a chance to talk about everything."

"Isn't this Al's cart?"

I grinned mischievously at her. "Sometimes, when I'm a good boy, Dad lets me take the car out for a spin."

She laughed and walked around to the passenger side to jump in. "Then why's he letting you take it today? From the way Artie reacted in there, it doesn't sound like you've been a good boy at all."

I put the cart in drive and we cruised down the driveway. "Eh, Artie's forgiving me. He wouldn't be that mad if it wasn't for the proposal getting messed up. And you saw him. He's already almost done being pissed."

"You've just got everyone here wrapped around your little finger, don't you?"

I shrugged. "Only Al, Mrs. Al, Artie, Mariposa, Gary and the rest of the fellas, and pretty much the whole staff."

"Isn't that everyone?"

"Not everyone."

"Who's not?"

"You're not." We exchanged a look.

Frankie sighed and watched the scenery pass by as I drove towards the guard shack. "You're not pushy or anything, are you?"

"I prefer to call it persistent. It's part of my charm, I suppose."

"Or the reason people think you're a pain in the ass."

"That too." We drove quietly for a minute before I looked over at her. "So you liked Artie's big grand gesture, huh?"

Seemingly pleased to take the focus off us for a second, she nodded. "I did. It was pretty romantic. I'm happy for them. You should be happy for them too."

"I *am* happy for them. I'm just worried that without some protection, she's gonna take him for all he's worth."

"Let Artie worry about that. He's a smart man."

"Even smart men do stupid things."

"Like you? I can't believe you dyed their swimming pool water."

I chuckled. "It'll wash off! I tested it on myself. It came off with soap and a little scrubbing. It's not that big of a deal."

"Obviously, it must've been a really big deal to Mr. Small-wood, if he responded by blowing up your ship."

We pulled up to the front door of the Crystal Point Resort, and I pulled over. "Can I go in with you? I wanna know what Sly has to say about everything."

"Is that the real reason you wanted to drive me over here?"

I stared at her hard. How did the woman *not* know how I

felt about her? "Seriously, Frankie? Of course not. I just wanted to visit with you. Seeing Sly would only be a bonus."

She shook her head. "No. I think you'll hinder me getting to the bottom of all of this. You stay out here."

"Ugh, come on, Frankie. Please?"

"No. Now I mean it, Danny. You stay here. We'll talk when I'm done."

Frankie gave me a warning glare as she went inside, leaving me outside to sit and stew over everything that had happened as of late. I thought about her comment about making a grand gesture. Maybe all it would take for me and Frankie to happen was for me to make some kind of grand gesture. Lost in a daydream, I almost didn't notice when a familiar person walked by.

"Drunk? What the bloody hell are you doing here?" asked Erika Wild.

I sat back and folded my arms over my chest. "Well, hello, Satan. I'm surprised you're out this time of day. Doesn't the sun burn the skin of your people?"

"Eat a bag of pretzels or something? It seems you're extra salty this morning." She cocked her head sideways towards my resort. "Having difficulties over at the Seacoast Geriatric?"

My temperature seemed to rise steadily as I looked at her. "You know damn good and well what my problem is today. And let me tell you, we're not taking this one lying down."

"Oh, really? But I thought that was how you dealt with all the women you came across."

"Ha!" I pursed my lips. "You're the exception to that rule, Wild. I wouldn't lie down with you if you were the last woman on Earth."

She shook her head haughtily. "Don't flatter yourself. I'd never give you the chance. I'm much too smart for the likes of you, Drunk. And besides, I prefer my men with a full set of testicles."

I had to suck in a deep breath to keep from lurching out of

Al's cart and taking her over my knee. If my mother had taught me anything in life, aside from not budging in front of old people in line at the airport, it was never to put my hands on a woman. So I kept my hands closely guarded by my sides. I didn't want to be tempted.

"You really are something, you know that? I really hope you get thrown in the jail cell alongside your asshat of a boss."

"Jail cell? You really think the police would get excited about the little bit of jolly fun we've been having with one another?"

"Jolly fun? You think everything that you've done is *fun*?! Do you think it's *fun* that you almost killed our pyrotechnician last night? Because where I come from, they call that attempted murder."

"Attempted murder? Are you quite insane?" She rolled her eyes. "Oh, yes, you are insane as a matter of fact. You turned most of our female guests red yesterday. You know that little stunt sent over half of our guests packing."

"Good! You deserved it!"

"So if you want to talk about someone sitting in a jail cell, I think you should be talking about yourself. I'm sure that's some kind of arrestable offense."

I pretended to think about it for a minute. "Hmm. When was the last time I read about anyone getting arrested for making an extra-large batch of Kool-Aid?" I tapped a finger on my chin.

"Pool water Kool-Aid? Now there's some bullshit if I've ever heard any."

"Oh, come now, Erika. You should be very familiar with bullshit. It pours out of your mouth constantly."

She looked around. "You know, I think perhaps I should have you thrown off resort property for loitering."

"I wonder how the police inspector inside will like coming out and finding her ride gone."

"Police inspector? What are you talking about?"

"Are your ears plugged, Wild? I told you already. She's here investigating the attempted murder of John, the pyrotechnician."

She was quiet for a second and then looked at me curiously. "What the bloody hell are you talking about? What pyrotechnician?"

"The one you tried to kill last night."

"Who *I* tried to kill last night? I'm sorry, but the only person I *wanted* to kill last night was you, but unfortunately, here you stand. I don't know anyone around here named John."

"Oh. I see. Did you think I was going to be on the ship, then? Is that what happened. You didn't think we'd hire someone to do the fireworks?"

"This is about the fireworks on the ship last night?"

"Duh."

She rolled her eyes. "Your use of the English language astounds me, Drunk."

"Yeah, well. Your use of that face shocks the hell out of me."

"You *look* like an adult. But you *act* like a child. Now look. If all of this is you implying that *we* blew up your ship, then I'm afraid you're sorely mistaken."

"Like I believe that?"

"Believe it. Don't believe it. I don't quite care what you believe. But haven't we claimed responsibility for everything else that we've had a hand in?"

"No. You haven't claimed responsibility for knocking out our security guard, vandalizing us, and then shooting me out of a boat."

"That's because we didn't *do* that, you fool."

"You didn't claim responsibility for either of those things not because you didn't do them but because those are both things you can get arrested for and you're scrambling to save your asses. Well, I tell you what, you're not going to get away with it. Inspector Cruz is on the job now and she won't let you."

"I heard my name," said Frankie, coming out of the resort finally.

"Oh, there she is. Inspector Cruz, I'd like you to meet the head of resort security here. This is Erika Wild. She's the one that's aided Sly Smallwood in all of the pranks they've perpetrated on the Seacoast Majestic."

"Ms. Wild," said Frankie, giving her a nod. "Perfect timing. I just finished interviewing your boss. I wonder if I might have a few minutes with you?"

"Well, I have a meeting in twenty min—"

"I won't take long."

Erika looked over at me, fire seething behind her emerald eyes. With gritted teeth, she nodded. "Fine. This way. We can use my office."

As the two of them walked away, I couldn't stop the grin from spreading across my face. If anyone was going to get to the bottom of things, it was Francesca Cruz. Hopefully she'd have two more feathers in her cap soon, one for Erika Wild and the other for Sly Smallwood.

"Nah, Frankie said they've clammed up tight," I said, punching the air.

"Well surely they've got to be able to find *something* to tie them to the explosion." Artie had calmed down considerably while I was gone, and now he sat behind his desk, shaking his head. "They need to pay for what they've done."

"Now you're thinking, Artie."

"Look, Drunk, I'm sorry I yelled at you. Especially in front of Frankie. I was just upset because I specifically asked you not to do anything yesterday to jeopardize the day."

"I know you did, Artie. And I'm sorry I had to go behind

your back. I wouldn't have usually, but I didn't want to ruin your big day. I'll be sure to keep you in the loop from here on out, I swear."

"I appreciate that Drunk. And I appreciate you helping me sort all of this out. I just wish Frankie would've gotten something out of Sly and Erika."

"That makes two of us," I agreed, nodding.

There was silence as Al, Artie, and I all sat around, each thinking about the recent events and wondering what to do next. Finally, Al broke the silence. "So what are you going to do about *The Bloody Marauder*, Artie?"

"What can I do?" asked Artie with a shrug. "It was blown to bits. What wasn't blown to pieces is at the bottom of Angel's Bay."

"You know, when they find Sly guilty, he should really have to pay to have a new ship brought in and anchored there. Guests really liked the ship. It was a big draw," said Al.

"I know they did. And I agree. He *will* have to pay for it. You know, that's where Sly feels the pain. In the pocketbook."

I looked over at Artie and frowned. "If that's the case, then maybe we've been playing this game with Sly all wrong."

"What do you mean?" asked Artie.

"He's been firing punches and we've been counterpunching. But that doesn't seem to be working. All that's happening is we're both getting hit. Maybe instead of punching, we need to get creative. Hit him where it *really* hurts."

"Uh, Drunk. That's illegal in boxing," said Al.

"I meant *financially*, Al," I said with a smile. "We need to think of a way to hurt Sly's bottom line."

Artie nodded. "I have to agree. If the police can't stop him, then that may be the only way to finally put a stop to his pranks once and for all."

"Okay. Then now's the time to put on our thinking caps and see if we can't come up with a way to hurt his bottom line."

29

EARLY THE NEXT EVENING, I STARED AT MY REFLECTION IN THE mirror while smashing a glob of sticky pomade between the pads of my fingers. Tipping my head from side to side I ran the grease through my long dark hair, then poked and prodded until my hair was perfectly coiffed and rose inches above my forehead.

Hey. If it worked for David Beckham, who was I to argue? He was, after all, married to the spiciest of the Spices.

I rinsed my fingers under my bathroom sink, then dried them on a bath towel I'd slung over the shower rod. Adjusting the collar on my pink button-down shirt dotted with palm trees and flamingos, I turned around and smiled at Al, who leaned against the wall behind me.

"Well? What do you think?"

With his upper lip curled, Al stared up at my hair. He gave me a look somewhere between stupefied and offended.

But then, that was the look he always gave me.

Now, mind you, it was a rare occasion that my hair made an appearance. Usually I hid the unruly mess under a hat, mostly because I was too lazy for anything more than a wash and wear. But today I needed something more. Today I had to look good.

You know what? Scratch good.

I had to look a-*fucking*-mazing, all right? I had to look so good that even Mother Teresa herself would wanna lay one on me.

Al scratched the liver-spotted skin on top of his bald head. "I'm not sure what you're going for there. You *trying* to look like a member of a boy band?"

Frowning at him, I dropped my chin and lifted a brow. "I don't know. Are you *trying* to score a role in *Grumpy Old Men 3*?"

He shrugged and waved a hand in the air. "Eh, fine. What do I know about fashion?"

I turned around and stared at myself in the mirror one more time, moving my head from left to right, right to left, like a boxer avoiding a hit. Maybe I did look a little like one of those Jonas Timberlake Bieber brothers, but *fuck*, they always got the girl. Right?

I ran a hand against my smooth, baby-soft chin. I'd shaved, though if I didn't get going, I'd surely be sporting the early stages of fine grit sandpaper around my jaw by the time my plan was put into action.

"I don't look that bad, do I?"

Al shook his head and let out an age-worn breath. "It ain't that, kid."

Through the mirror, I stared at him. "It ain't what?"

"Look," he muttered, "I'm tired of standing." Without so much as another word, he turned and shuffled away midconversation.

I gave myself one more look in the mirror. Satisfied that there was little else I could do to make myself look any better, I flipped off the light and followed Al out into the living room to find him already seated on one of my rattan chairs.

Earnestine was finally back, tapping about on my kitchen counter, chattering to herself.

I looked over at Al. "Okay, you gonna explain what your problem is, or are we gonna play the married game where I spend the whole fucking night trying to *guess* what your problem is?"

Pausing a beat before looking up at me, Al shook his head. "Look, I'm just gonna come out and say it. I think this is a bad idea."

"Rawck! Bad idea, bad idea."

"Bad idea?" From a side table, I picked up the bouquet of exotic flowers I'd procured for the evening. "These flowers cost me seventy-five bucks. I've got a box of imported chocolates in the kitchen and a two-hundred-dollar bottle of champagne chilling in the fridge. How's this a bad idea?"

With narrowed eyes, Al considered me for a long second. Then he sat back in his chair and crossed his arms over his chest. "You, Mr. Cheapskate, spent two hundred and seventy-five dollars on a bottle of champagne and some flowers? The last time we went to lunch together, you refused to split the tab because I got a milkshake with my lunch and you didn't."

With my lips pressed together and my eyes wide, my head bobbled like A-Rod on a New York City cabby's dash. I wanted to say, yes, of course I'd spent that much. But lying to Al was like lying to my father. Even though there was no way either of them could *prove* that I was lying, I just knew somehow, some way, they knew the truth. I let out a puff of air.

"Ugh. Oh fine. The flowers were on sale." I put them back down on the side table. "But the girl told me they were *originally* seventy-five."

Al swirled one arthritic finger in the direction of my kitchen. "And the champagne?"

I stared at him through narrowed eyes. "Are you *always* this nosy?"

Al lifted his bushy white brows and let out a sigh. "Look,

kid, I really think you should listen to me. Have I ever steered you wrong before?"

The truth of the matter was, I couldn't think of a single time that Al Becker had steered me wrong since the day I'd met him. But he was also eighty-seven years old. What did he know about dating in the twenty-first century?

"Look, Al, I get that you think it's a risky move. But how can this be a bad idea? Frankie all but said she wanted me to make a grand gesture for her. I've finally cleaned myself up. *This* is what I've been working towards. *Now* I get the girl."

Al adjusted the floral pillow behind his back and shot me a staunch look. "That's not how it works, kid."

"Yeah? Then tell me how it works, sensei."

Al sighed. "Look, I don't know how it *works*. I just know how it *doesn't work*. You're trying too hard. Frankie asked you to be patient with her. I don't think *this* is you being patient."

But I was too excited to listen to him. "Look, buddy, you worry too much. This is gonna be great. I'm gonna have Frankie locked down by the end of the day."

"You sure that's what you want?"

"Of course I'm sure that's what I want."

"You do realize that by locking *her* down, you're locking yourself down too?"

Smiling, I gave my head a slow, deliberate shake. "I don't know what to tell you, Al. Frankie's worth it."

Al let his head fall. Slowly, he shook it from side to side. "All I'm saying is, it's not the right time, Drunk. But, look. We all gotta learn stuff the hard way. You do it your way. Just don't say I didn't warn you."

30

Nervous energy bubbled through my veins while pterodactyls took flight in my stomach. Even though I didn't feel like I had it together on the inside, I thought I did a pretty good job of keeping a cool veneer.

"Hey, thanks, fellas. I really appreciate all the help here."

Rico Cruz, one of Frankie's brothers, patted me on the shoulder. "It's the least we could do, man."

"Yeah, Drunk. We owe you a lot. You got our sister out of the dungeon finally," agreed his brother Diego.

"Listen, she earned that promotion herself. Frankie's one amazing woman."

Diego flashed me his palms. "Don't get me wrong. I know my sister's badass, but you helped get rid of her boss. There was no way she was moving up the ladder with that *pendejo* in charge."

"Yeah, man. I'm thankful we got Gibson out too."

With her brothers' help, we'd decked out their smallest charter boat. We'd scattered rose petals across the deck. There were candles. Soft music. Dinner. The bottle of champagne I'd dropped twenty-nine ninety-five on sat in a bucket on the table next to the chocolates. Plus there was a fifth of tequila in the mini-fridge. I held the bouquet of flowers in my arms. I felt ready. It was time to take my friendship with Francesca Cruz to a whole new level.

The sex would just be a bonus.

I swallowed hard and tipped my head forward. Several dozen yards up the gangway in front of me, Miguel, another of Frankie's six brothers, came out of the King's Bay Marina office and started towards us. Beto and Solo Cruz followed behind him. When they were within earshot, I hollered at Miguel. "She coming?" My heart was in my throat. If Frankie didn't come—all of this would have been for naught.

He nodded. "Yeah. I felt bad lying to her, though. She sounded freaked out when I told her we needed the police down here ASAP."

"Don't think of it as a *lie*, Miguel. Think of it as a means to an ends." I smiled. "I'm about to make your sister *very* happy."

"After all of this," said Beto, "you *better* make our sister happy."

"My brother's right," said Solo. "We're giving you the benefit of the doubt here. You mess up, and that's it. We don't take kindly to people hurting our little sister."

"Come on, Solo. You know I'd never hurt Frankie. I fell hard for the woman."

"You aren't the first to do that, Drunk," said Rico. "Frankie's a good woman."

"I know she is. But haven't I proven myself by now?"

Everyone turned to look at Solo, who let out a heavy sigh. We'd had our share of run-ins, but ultimately, I knew how he felt about me. I knew I'd finally secured his blessing to date his sister.

"You have," he said stiffly. "Just don't mess it up."

I grinned from ear to ear. "Oh, don't worry. I don't intend to mess this up at all." I let out a breath of relief. I felt like everything was finally in place. I was finally ready to commit to exclusively dating their sister. I knew Frankie liked me. Her brothers liked me. Everything was good at my job at the resort. Life was good. "Okay. Does everyone know the plan?"

"It's not rocket science, Drunk," said Rico, chuckling. "We got this. You just worry about what you're going to say when she gets here. She'll be here any minute."

The realization that it was actually go time and Frankie was on her way made my stomach feel worse—some weird combination of needing to vomit and shit at the same time.

"Fuck," I breathed, nodding at them. "You better go get in your places."

Rico backhanded his brother's arm. "Come on, D. We're at the top. Let's go."

Diego and Rico took off up the boardwalk first. Their job was to meet Frankie at her car and escort her down to Miguel, who would walk her down to Beto. Beto would take her to Solo and Solo would hand her off to me on the boat, a silent blessing. Then Frankie and I would sail away together for an evening of romance.

It was perfect.

As I stood, holding the flowers I'd bought her, I thought about all the things I wanted to say to Frankie. How she was everything I wanted in a woman. Intelligent. Kind. Sweet. Sexy. Spicy. The whole package. The more I thought, the more nervous I felt myself getting. I took a couple of deep breaths and let them out slowly. I needed to relax. I shook my head. I never got this nervous when it came to women. I wasn't sure what the fuck was going on. It wasn't like I was proposing to the woman or something.

Finally, I heard shouts from the mouth of the trail.

She was here.

Adrenaline spiked my blood, making me feel light-headed and dizzy. I swallowed hard and wished that I'd taken a couple shots of tequila before going through with this. I glanced backwards at the boat. It floated peacefully on top of the glassy water. The air was calm—warm, but not hot. Coquis sang in the trees, providing a symphony just below the low whisper of music on the boat. The sun had just begun to set, but it was still early. I wanted to have plenty of time with Frankie. If things went well, it would be our first night *together*. And I could hardly wait.

As I heard her voice carry down towards the water, I turned to look for her. I imagined her brothers holding her elbows, helping her glide gracefully down the path to the water. But when they came into sight, she didn't seem to be gliding exactly. In fact, it looked more like she was feverishly running.

I furrowed my brows. Diego and Rico trailed after her, hollering. Not only was Frankie running, her face was set in a grimace, and she had one hand on the weapon on her hip.

"Miguel, where is he? Which boat is he trying to steal?" she hollered as she barreled down the path towards Miguel. Her eyes scanned the waterline.

Miguel held up two hands to slow his sister. "Panchita!" he hollered. "Slow down."

"Did he get away?" she asked as she whizzed past him.

"Panchita," hollered Beto as she closed in on him. "It's not what you think."

But she flew past him without stopping.

Solo tried to stand in her way, blocking her. "Whoa, whoa, whoa. Slow your roll, sis," he said.

She stopped running when she saw me standing at the end of the pier, and her head cocked sideways. Solo let go of her, and she slowly walked towards me. By now all of the Cruz brothers stood together in a group, watching as she walked curiously in my direction.

It was go time.

"Hi, Frankie," I said, a nervous grin easing up the sides of my mouth.

"Danny, what's going on? They called you too?"

"No. I, uh. I—" I swallowed hard. "I called them, actually. There was no boat thief."

"No boat thief?" She turned and looked back at her brothers in confusion. "But Miguel said his—"

"I asked Miguel to call you."

"You asked him to call me? But there was no thief?"

"No. The only thief here is me." Smiling, I took one step towards her and extended the flowers towards her. "I came to steal your heart." I refused to look over her shoulder at her brothers because I knew they were probably restraining their laughter at my cheesy line, but I didn't care.

Frankie stared down at the flowers I held, which she'd yet to take. "I don't get it, Danny. What's going on?"

"Here, these are for you."

She frowned. "You had my brothers call me down here in the middle of work, told me a thief had stolen one of their boats, and all just so you could give me flowers?"

I chuckled as I took hold of one of her hands while I kept the bouquet in my other hand. "No, silly. It wasn't just for that. I called you down here because I planned an evening for us. Your brothers helped me." I gave a glance over my shoulder. "We're taking the boat out."

"What do you mean, *we're* taking the boat out?" Her brows knitted together as she frowned.

"Don't you get it, Frankie? I'm asking you out. I'm making a grand romantic overture," I added proudly.

Frankie's head jerked back slightly. She was quiet for several long seconds as she took in everything around her from the boat, to her brothers, to the flowers I carried, to me.

"You and my idiot brothers did all of this just to get me down here so you could ask me on a date?"

The smile on my face evaporated. Something in her voice told me this wasn't a *good* thing that I'd done. Perhaps it was her calling her brothers idiots, I wasn't sure. I cleared my throat. "I mean, yeah?"

"Danny!" she breathed. "I was *at work*."

"I know, but you don't understand, I—"

"No, *you* don't understand. I got *promoted*, Danny. I'm a *detective* now. I'm not sitting around getting someone's coffee and opening their mail. I'm actually working on my own cases already. *Big cases*."

"I know, and I'm so proud of you," I said, flashing her a smile.

"Danny, you can't just make plans for me and call me out of work and expect me to swoon."

I frowned. I hadn't really thought of it like that before. Heat flushed my face. "Oh, I guess I wasn't thinking."

"No, you *weren't* thinking."

"I-I'm sorry, Frankie, I—"

Frankie spun around then to face her brothers. "And I can't believe that all of *you* aided and abetted this ridiculously dumb idea. Did *no one* think this was a dumb idea to pull me out of work and *lie* to me to get me to come running down here?"

Miguel tentatively lifted a hand. "I didn't like lying to you, Panchita. I told Drunk—"

"Well, if you didn't like it, then you shouldn't have *done* it!" she railed.

"But, Frankie," I inserted. "I was trying to be *romantic*. You told Artie you appreciated his big grand gesture. I'm ready to take our relationship to the next level."

"Well, good for you, Danny. But just because *you're* ready for that doesn't mean that *I'm* ready for that."

I pulled my head back. "Frankie, you said it yourself. You thought what Artie did was romantic, so I—"

"You thought because I said what Artie did for Val was sweet that I wanted you to override everything else I'd told you and plan some big romantic gesture and sweep me off my feet?"

With big eyes, I pouted. "Well—I mean—yeah."

Throwing her head back, she let out a guttural groan. "Ugh, Danny! What the hell? That's not *you*. You're not that guy."

"What guy?"

"The guy that gets all soft and mushy and buys flowers and chocolates and wine and stuff," she shouted. "The guy that drags me out of *work* when I'm in the middle of a handful of big cases. That's why I liked you in the first place, because *you* were one of the few men in my life to *get me*. To get that my career comes first. I asked you to be patient. How's this being patient?"

My heart froze. The clouds of confusion were finally parting for me. I'd done bad. *Real bad*. Al had been right.

Fuck.

I hated it when Al was right. But I hated it more when I was wrong.

"Look, Frankie. I'm really sorry. I thought I was doing something good here. I—"

"Danny, you don't get it. I'm *finally* getting somewhere in my career. *Finally*. It's taken me *years*, but I'm getting somewhere. I don't have time to be dating right now. I don't have time for romantic boat rides and flowers. And I *especially* don't have time for a man who thinks that it's acceptable to pull me out of *work* to wine and dine me!"

Behind her, Frankie's brothers all stared at us. Rico winced as I took my verbal beating courtesy of his sister. Diego tried to suppress laughter, apparently thinking me getting my ass handed to me was funny. Miguel looked completely embarrassed by the whole situation, and Solo and Beto looked like they wanted to rip my head off for pissing their sister off and getting them involved in it.

"You're absolutely right, I shouldn't have—" I put the flowers in her arms and, surrendering, held my hands up. "I'm sorry."

"No. You shouldn't have." She shoved the flowers back in my arms.

The push caused me to stumble backwards, and the back of my heel caught on a dock cleat. The next thing I knew, my originally-priced-at-seventy-five-dollars flowers went sailing through the air as my arms flailed. And in one huge splash, I landed in the cool harbor water.

I sputtered up to the surface for air. Water dripped from my once perfectly coiffed hair onto my nose as Frankie looked down over the dock at me. She shook her head. Whether it was a look of disappointment or anger or sadness or all three on her face, I wasn't exactly sure. She let out a sigh.

"It's not our time, Danny. And I don't know if it will *ever* be our time. I'm going back to work. Don't ever pull something like this again."

31

CRADLING MY HEAD IN MY HANDS AS I SAT DOWN AT THE Seacoast Majestic's swim-up bar a couple hours later, I grunted at the bartender, "Hit me again, Manny." A plucky steel drum version of *Under the Sea* played on the bar's speakers, trying to cheer me up, but I refused to so much as tap my toe. I was far too miserable.

"Look, kid, I don't wanna say I told you so, but—"

I swiveled around to stare at Al. The twinkle lights hanging from the thatched roof of the bar shone around his head in the darkness, making his bald head shine like the roof of a freshly washed car. "Then don' say it." My tongue was heavy and thick and didn't move right in my mouth.

Al turned his own chair so he wasn't looking at me anymore. He took a sip of his beer. Putting the bottle down on the bar, he shrugged. "But I *did* tell you." He shook his head sadly. "You should've listened. I might be an old man, Drunk, but I know what I'm talking about."

"Manny, can you kindly tell Al to shut it?"

Manny let out an almost inaudible groan. "Oh, come on, Drunk. It's not Mr. Becker's fault you got shot down."

"I know. But it'll make me feel better."

"No, it won't. It'll make you feel worse. But here." Manny slid another shot of tequila across the bar. "This'll dull the pain a little more."

"Thanks." I lifted the shot glass to my lips and threw back the clear liquid. Pursing my lips as the biting liquid went down, I shook my head. Even in my drunk stupor, I was still in shock. "I don't understand, guys. What am I supposed to do now?"

"You move on. That's what you do now," said Al.

I looked at him. "But you don' unnerstand. She was my endgame. Without her, what've I been working towards?"

Manny sighed and leaned over the bar on one elbow, looking me squarely in the eyes. "Nah, man. You got it all wrong. *She* wasn't the endgame. *Women* aren't the endgame. You live on a fucking Caribbean island, Drunk. You got a great job. You got good friends." He stood up straight then and held his arms out and shook them in the air. "*This* is the endgame."

I closed my eyes and sighed. When I opened them, Manny was leaning across the counter again, staring at me.

"Look, Drunk. I don't get it. You're a good-looking guy, and you got game. Women love you. Why you wanna end it all and hook up with *one* woman?"

I rolled the end of my shot glass around on the bar. It wasn't that I'd been convinced that I needed to *marry* Frankie or anything. I wasn't that far gone, but I *had* somehow convinced myself that cleaning up my act meant that I'd *won* her. Like she was my prize. How could've I been so stupid?

"I don't know, Manny."

He poured me another shot of tequila.

I downed it and slid the shot glass back over to him. I wanted another.

That was enough to send Al swiveling back around again. "Oh, for crying out loud, kid. Pull it together. You're being ridiculous. You got shot down. Do you know how many men get shot down?"

I shrugged. It didn't matter. I generally wasn't one of those men. Of course, I didn't generally try very hard. I didn't have to. Manny was right, I was a good-looking guy. Women generally came on to me. And I rarely met a woman that I wanted to try very hard to get. So to actually get shot down by another woman so soon after Pam—it stung. It felt like *I* was doing something wrong. Like *I* was the broken one.

"A *lot* of men get shot down. I think I might've even got shot down once." Al paused for a moment and frowned. "To be honest, I don't really remember it happening. But I'm old and that's the point, you know? It really doesn't matter in the grand scheme of things."

"Jeez, Al. It just hurts. *Fuck.* Can't you be a little nicer?"

"I'm your friend, kid. Not your mother. Now the way I see it, I think this is more about your wounded pride than it is about Francesca."

"No, it's not," I insisted. "You didn't see her face, Al. She's pissed at me. She was one of my best friends."

"Fine. She was your friend. If she's a real friend, then she'll forgive you."

I shook my head insistently. "No, she won't. I treated her like all the guys down at the station have ever treated her. Like because she's a woman, her job doesn't matter. What the hell was I thinking? I knew better than that! Why didn't you stop me, Al?"

Al's watery blue-green eyes widened. "Stop you? I tried to stop you. You wouldn't listen to me!"

"Well, obviously you didn't try hard enough." I took another shot of tequila.

Al's hand shot out and he took hold of the shot glass and sent it sliding across the bar. Then he pounded his fist down on the bar. "Quit feeding this guy's pity party, Manny!" Then he looked at me sternly. "Now look, you need to snap out of this, Drunk. Like I told you before you left on this cockamamie mission, it was *too soon*."

I let my head fall into my hands again. My hat fell off onto the bar, and I massaged my scalp with the pads of my fingers. I didn't know how to fix the problem. I was annoyed at myself for two reasons. First, I felt like I'd put all my eggs in one basket, and after Pam, I'd sort of promised myself I'd never do that again. And second, I felt like I'd humiliated myself. Not only in front of Frankie, but also in front of her brothers. It'd take forever to live that shit down. All I wanted to do was to get drunk and maybe find another woman to help dull the pain of losing Frankie.

I looked up and nodded at Al. "Fine. It was too soon. You were right. Is that what you wanna hear?"

"It's a start," said Al, nodding.

"Good." I tapped the bar with my fingers. "Now gimme another drink, Manny. I'm gonna drink until someone around here looks hot."

"Good Lord," sighed Al, rolling his eyes. "Of all days to wear my good shirt. Manny, you gotta quit serving this kid. At the rate he's tossing 'em back, it'll be me he's hitting on soon."

Manny looked at me cautiously, like he agreed with Al. "Look, Drunk, I hate to cut a man off when he's wallowing in self-pity, but I don't think I like the sound of that."

I threw my hands up in the air. "Ahh, you two. You're just the same—always trying to ruin a man's good time. Fine. I'll go drink somewhere else, then." I stood up off the bar and realized my legs weren't quite as steady as I thought they'd be. My knees and ankles buckled at the same time, and I tipped sideways, crashing into a pole holding a speaker. I held out my hands. "Oh, excuse me, sir," I said to the pole as I got back on my feet.

Al palmed his forehead. "Come on, kid. I'm taking you home."

"But you're not hot yet," I mumbled. "And you're not my type. I like my dates younger and female."

"You're not exactly my type either, kid. I like my dates

sober. Now come on. I'm giving you a ride to your place and you can sleep this off."

But my feet and pelvis had other plans. They propelled me forward, like I was the dead guy walking around in the movie *Weekend at Bernie's*. I stumbled down off the concrete and into the sand. I wasn't completely sure if I'd come to the bar with shoes, but now the sand slid through my toes and made me stumble a little. I ran straight into a hammock suspended between two trees, and it threw me backwards onto my ass.

"Shit," I breathed. I rolled onto all fours and managed to get back on my feet. Walking around the trees, I headed down for the beach.

"For crying out loud, kid. Where you going?" I heard Al yell after me.

"I'm going where the women are hot!" I hollered back.

My pelvis aimed itself like a pointed arrow at the Crystal Point Resort. It was as if my brain had quit working for the evening and Little Drunk had taken over. I'd gotten to the first pair of lounge chairs along our beach when I saw a ghostly figure appear out of the darkness.

I stopped walking and stared, wondering if it were a mirage or really a person. I rubbed my eyes with my fists, and when I removed them, I saw her white halter dress glowing against the backdrop of her dark skin, making it seem as if only the dress were floating in the air towards me. My breath caught in the back of my throat, and my eyes bulged as I watched the figure come towards me. Long, slender legs poked out of the skirt's short hem and moved gracefully through the sand. My eyes traveled upwards, around the hips, to the breasts and bare shoulders. And then the face appeared from out of the shadows, and I realized it was none other than Erika Wild.

She was out of uniform, and for a second, I thought my eyes were playing tricks on me. The Erika Wild I knew didn't look like that. The Erika Wild I knew was cold and hard, and any small amount of sex appeal I'd seen in her when I first met her had completely vanished when I'd gotten to know her true personality. I rubbed my eyes again as she came towards me.

"Wild? Is that you?" I asked her.

"Well, it isn't Sly Smallwood, now is it?" she asked.

Yup. It was her all right. Smart-ass and all. "What the hell are you doing here?" I muttered. But instead of focusing on her face, my eyes trailed down to her body and those legs! I had to admit she had phenomenal legs. They were long and slender, and the way they moved...

Uncontrollably, my head tipped sideways slightly, watching them move towards me. They looked graceful and sexy. My mind wandered to how they'd look sprawled out across the sheets of my bed. Who knew she'd actually been hiding a female frame behind those boring business suits?

"I'm up here, Drunk. Hello," she said, breaking my daydream.

My slow-moving, highly intoxicated eyes slid up her body to look her in the face. "What are you doin' here?"

"I just came to check out the view over here without that bloody ship standing in the way anymore." Barefoot, she turned in the sand and propped her hands up on her hips, and stared at the horizon.

I stared at her side profile hard. The straps of her halter dress cut across her chest and tied behind her head. Standing there with her hands on her hips like that, her dress puckered slightly, giving me a clear shot of the sides of her breasts. They were deeply tanned without a hint of a tan line. They weren't overly large, but they looked firm, and with no bra to hold them up, they seemed to manage just fine on their own, thank you very much. Blood flowed south as the cogs in my brain chugged along slowly.

When I looked up at her face, she was looking at me. "What are you looking at?"

I swallowed hard, trying to moisten my suddenly dry mouth. "You're a girl," I whispered.

"I prefer woman, but yes," she sighed. "I do possess female DNA. You're just now figuring that out?"

"I never really thought about it? You just looked like a bitch before," I said. I hadn't really intended it to come out as an insult, but it was the first thing that popped into my head, and the alcohol seemed to be controlling my words and body now.

Her eyes narrowed and her lips puckered. "Are you drunk?"

Smiling, I ticked a finger in the air at her. "Oh no. I'm not playing that game again. I already answered that question once. Yes. I'm Drunk. *Mr.* Drunk to you." My head bounced once and I pointed at myself and then I poked my finger into her chest, in a little spot of her dress where a triangle had been removed from the fabric revealing a small bit of cleavage. "An' you're Wild. Haha. Drunk an' Wild. Sounds like a spring break porno, doesn't it?"

She looked down at my finger pressed between her cleavage and then tipped her head sideways as she swatted it away. "You *are* drunk. Good Lord. I didn't think you could be any more of an asshole, but now I see you can. Just add alcohol and stir."

"You know what? You're wound too tight. When's the last time you got laid?"

"I don't know. When's the last time you got your ass kicked?"

My eyes rolled back in my head a little as I gave that thought a second. "Mmm, Thursday."

Her dark hair swayed as she shook her head. "I don't know what women see in you. I really don't."

I grinned lasciviously. "I can show you if you want. But not out here. Artie frowns on that—*Sex on the Beach is a drink, Drunk, not a hobby*," I said, mocking the lecture Artie had given me once after a housekeeper and I had gotten frisky on the beach late one evening when we thought we were alone. But that was not long after I'd gotten to the island. I was a better man now. I took hold of her hand. "Come on. We can go back to my place."

She groaned and pulled her hand out of my grasp. "How does anyone take you seriously around here?"

I frowned at her. "You thought I's jokin'? I'm totally serious. You needa get laid and I needa distraction. Is a win-win. We can hate each other again tomorrow."

"You think me sleeping with you is a win for me? Maybe it's a win for you, but it's certainly not a win for me."

I ignored the disgusted look she gave me. None of this was making any sense to my drunken brain. "Then why'd you come over here to my beach lookin' like that if you didn't wanna sleep with me?" My eyes narrowed and I wagged my finger in her face. "Wait a minute. Did you come over here to pull another prank on us?"

"I did not. I came to check out the damages. You know, after the last prank you pulled on us, we had about half our guests check out. Things are really slow over there right now, thanks to you. There's hardly anyone left."

I popped my hat off my head, curled it around in the air, and took a deep bow. "My pleasure, m'lady."

"Well, at least you got what you deserved. Your pirate ship is gone now. Serves you right."

I poked the air. *Finally an admission!* "Ah-ha! I knew you did it!"

"As if I'd admit to you if I did. You're really not very good at this game, Drunk. And the truth of the matter is, you'll never win the war."

"Oh, we'll win all right. In fact, I already won."

"Have you?"

I nodded, grinning from ear to ear. "Only *one* of us has to sleep with you tonight, an' I'll give ya a clue—it's not this guy right here."

32

Hungover as hell, I stumbled into the lobby the next morning. It was the Mondayest Monday I'd ever Mondayed. Noises felt more pronounced than usual and made my head feel like a thinned eggshell with spiderwebbed cracks precariously close to splitting open. Even in the building with my sunglasses on, the lights still managed to hurt my head. I walked cautiously, as if I were walking barefoot across a path of Legos. And when I stepped in front of Mari's half of the counter on my way to the back offices, she hollered at me, making me shrink.

"Mr. Balladares isn't in his office this morning, Drunk."

I stopped walking and pivoted. With raised shoulders, I hissed over the noise of the lobby. "Shhh!" Through squinted eyes, I looked up at her. "Where's he at?"

"The conference room."

I frowned. "The conference room? What for?"

"It's become the headquarters."

"Headquarters? Headquarters for what?"

She grinned. "You'll see."

I turned in the other direction and headed across the lobby and down the hall to the conference room. It was the large room we rented out when people were having events or parties. For so early on a Monday morning, I was surprised to see both doors wide open and people coming and going like a busy beehive. I was sure I hadn't seen any events on the calendar for the day.

"Artie? What's going on?" I said as I rounded the corner.

I stopped in the doorway and my mouth fell open. Booths had been set up around the room, each one manned by a person or a pair of people. The booths were all wedding-themed. One featured mannequins wearing penguin suits, another few were set up with wedding cakes and samples, another had flower arrangements, centerpieces, and bouquets, and in one corner of the room, an entire wedding dress shop appeared to have been set up, complete with a dressing room and a little platform in front of trifold mirrors.

Val was there already, dressed in pink and wearing heels and another funny hat. Artie was there too, busily directing traffic and chatting with everyone that stopped to ask him a question.

Val caught sight of me first and gasped before rushing over to hook my elbow with her arm. "Good morning, Drunk!" she purred.

"Hey, Val," I said gruffly. "What's all this?"

"Isn't it wonderful?" she asked brightly. "Artie did *thees* for me!"

I stared at everything around the room in confusion. "But what is it?"

"It *ees* a wedding fair!"

"What's a wedding fair?"

She giggled. "All of these people *breeng* they wedding ideas and I get *peeck* what I like!"

"I'm surprised you're up so early!" boomed Artie when he saw me. He walked over to me and clapped me on the shoulder, making me wince. "Al said you had a hell of a night."

"Earnestine," I grunted, as if that explained it all. The bird had woken me up the second the sun was up, and ever since I'd unglued her feet from my kitchen counter, she'd seemed more attached to me than usual. It was as if her way of thanking me for saving her was to annoy the hell out of me until I died.

"Ah. Well, now that you're here, maybe you can help us pick out some things for the wedding. We have to pick out a cake and flowers and centerpieces and my tuxedo…"

Holding up my hands to stop him, I frowned. "You got the wrong guy for this stuff. I couldn't pick out a tuxedo if it walked up and jumped on my body." Shaking my head, I looked around the room. "I don't understand, Artie. You literally just proposed on Friday. It's Monday. How the hell did you get all these people to show up with such short notice?"

"It's called planning, Drunk. I've been planning this since I decided to propose."

"*Eeesn't* he so good to me?" asked Val, grinning at her future husband brightly as she left my arm to cling to his.

Artie patted her hand. "That's because my little love muffin deserves the best!"

I rolled my eyes. I felt like shit, both because I was hungover and because Frankie had rebuffed my overtures. And now I had to watch these two fawn over each other like a couple of love-struck teenagers. "Well, I'll let you guys get to work."

Artie held out a hand to stop me. "Well, wait, wait. Al said that Erika Wild paid a visit to our beach last night. What did she want?"

"Who *ees* Erika Wild?" asked Val, frowning.

"She's Sly Smallwood's head of resort security," explained Artie patiently.

"Ohh, yes!" She nodded. "I remember."

"Yeah, well, I think she just came over here to gloat about blowing up our ship."

Artie shook his head. "The nerve! I can't believe there's nothing Francesca can do to prosecute them."

"I know. Unless some new evidence comes to light, unfortunately, I feel like they're just going to get away with it."

Artie frowned. "Well, like we said the other day. The only way to hit Sly Smallwood is to hit him where it hurts. We'll think of something."

Val winced. "Ooh, isn't that a *leetle* bit bad?"

Artie and I both chuckled at the same time.

He patted Val's hand again. "I mean his pocketbook, sweetheart."

"Oh! Yes!" she said, nodding. Then she sucked in her breath and lifted her brows. "Oh! Maybe you should make him pay for his guests go do something."

I frowned. "Do something? What do you mean? Like what?"

She shrugged. "I don't know. Like go on boat trip or something. You know, they have overnight trips. I have the brochure in my purse." She let go of Artie and turned around. Her round bottom swayed as she walked briskly across the tile floor, her heels making little chattering clicks.

Artie and I exchanged a look as ideas began to spin through my head. "That's actually not a bad idea, Artie."

"You think you could make that happen?"

"I think I could."

Val came back over and handed me the brochure she'd picked up when we'd gone out to lunch a few days prior. "See? *Ees* very expensive to do *thees* trip. Send all of his guest, but make the small penis man pay the bill."

I lifted my brows. "The small penis man?"

Artie glanced at Val and cleared his throat. "Val seems to know that his name isn't far from the truth. But we don't talk about how she knows that, do we, dear?"

Val's brows lifted, forcing her eyes open wider. She pretended to zip her lips together.

"I see." I looked down at the brochure. "Well, this might just work. I'll see what I can do with this. Thanks, Val. Good idea."

She smiled broadly. "I have lots of good ideas, right, baby?"

"That you do, sweetheart. That you do."

AL WAS with me when I finally made the call later that afternoon after I'd had plenty of time to think about how to do it.

"And Artie doesn't mind you doing this?"

"It was practically his idea! Actually it was Val's idea, so if it fails, this one's on her," I said, grinning. I pointed at the brochure Al now held in his hands. "It's one fifty a person and includes dinner, drinks, a small stateroom on the boat and an evening under the stars cruising around the nearby islands. Even if they're at half capacity over there after the Kool-Aid stunt, they're still gonna be eating a huge chunk of change if we send them all."

"They won't *all* go," said Al, adjusting his glasses so he could scan the pictures.

"The cruise ship is big enough. It could probably hold them all. Wouldn't you and Evie go on a free overnight cruise if Artie offered it to all the guests?"

"Well, yes, I'm sure we would."

My head bobbed. "See? They'll do it. Who wouldn't?"

"Maybe you're right. Okay. It's worth giving a try. Give 'em a call."

I rubbed my hands together and blew into them before picking up the phone, letting out a nervous breath, and then dialing. I put it on speakerphone so Al could hear the conversation too.

"Paradise Isle Tours. Denise speaking."

"Hello, Denise. I was wondering if I could speak with

someone about reserving a block of rooms on one of your night tours this week."

"I can help you with that. How many rooms?"

"Well, that's the thing. I don't know exactly how many I have just yet, but it could amount to filling up your ship."

There was a pause. "Sir, our capacity is seven hundred fifty passengers. Are you saying you'd have seven hundred fifty guests?"

I chuckled. Surely Sly's capacity wasn't that high at the moment. "No, I'm sure it won't be that many. Let me explain to you what I'd like to do."

"Go ahead, sir."

"Well, my name is Sly Smallwood. I'm the owner of the Crystal Point Resort."

"Oh, yes, Mr. Smallwood. I'm familiar with your resort."

I looked up at Al, and we exchanged sinister smiles. "Yes. Well, here's the situation. We had a mishap at our resort the other day and I'm afraid we upset many of our guests. I feel just horrible about the situation, and I'd like to make it up to them by offering them a free overnight trip on your cruise ship."

"I see. You realize our fees are one hundred fifty dollars per passenger, sir?"

"Yes. I was hoping that perhaps we could negotiate a lower rate since I may be booking several hundred guests." I had to sound legit, after all. What tycoon businessman would book a whole block of rooms on a cruise ship without negotiating the price?

"Sir, for a block of ten rooms reserved, we offer a fifteen percent discount, and for a block of twenty or more rooms reserved, we offer a twenty percent discount."

"I was thinking more along the line of a hundred or more rooms. Is twenty percent the best discount you can offer?"

"Do you mind if I put you on hold for a moment? I'll have to speak with my boss."

"Oh, absolutely."

"Thank you, sir." The phone clicked, and I looked up at Al.

"She's buying it!" I said excitedly.

"Hook, line and sinker!"

I pounded the air with my fists, excited to be doing something constructive with my time. It was a minute or so later that she came back on the phone. "My boss said if you have a hundred bookings, he'd do it for one hundred per person."

My eyes widened. "Fabulous! Well, would you like me to have my guests book directly through you, or would you prefer that I get all their information and then send that to you?"

"We prefer to book our guests directly, sir. We have different menus available, and we do like to discuss that on the phone."

We went on to discuss the booking details and I was thrilled to discover that there were plenty of rooms available for the next day.

"Tomorrow it is. And then you'll just bill me with the final charges?"

"We do prefer a deposit to hold the rooms and payment in advance, sir."

"Yes, I wondered if that wouldn't be a problem. The only thing is, we don't know how many we'll be booking until the day of. Would it be possible in this case just to invoice me after the trip?"

"I'll have to get approval for that from my boss, sir."

"I can hold."

"Very well, sir. Just a moment."

She put me on hold and I held my breath, looking over at Al.

"Final test," said Al.

"Final test."

"This is evil, you know."

"I know. But he blew up a hundred-year-old pirate ship

and is gonna get off scot-free. Do you have any idea how much that boat had to cost?"

Al nodded.

The woman came back on the phone. "Sir, I've gotten that approved. I think we're all set."

"Wonderful. Well, I'll get my staff on letting our guests know about the offer immediately. You should probably start getting calls very soon."

"We'll be prepared."

"Very good. Thank you, Denise. You've been a real help today."

"Thank you for your business. You have a nice day, sir."

I smiled from ear to ear. "Oh, you as well. I know I certainly will!"

33

It turned out to be quite the undertaking, creating the promotional materials needed to pull off such a big prank, then getting them to Sly's guests without his knowledge. In fact, I spent the entire rest of Monday working on it. I could only hope that his guests had taken the bait.

So when Tuesday evening rolled around, I made a quick trip over to the Crystal Point Resort beach just to see how many of their guests hadn't gone on the cruise. It tickled me pink to see that their beach was literally a ghost land.

Tuesday evening, I returned to my cottage giddier than a baby in a barrel of tits. I practically danced around my cottage, talking to Earnestine. "We did it, we did it, we did it!"

That's when there was a knock at my door.

I glanced over at my clock. It was late—too late for Al to be out and about. And then my heart jumped for a second. Maybe it was Frankie! Maybe she'd changed her mind, decided she'd overreacted the other day and was there to make up with me. I rushed to open the door to see a woman on the other side, but not the woman I'd been hoping for.

"Wild!"

"Drunk."

I frowned at her. "What the hell are you doing here?"

Wearing only a short pink satin robe belted around the waist, she pushed past me into my cottage and held up one of the brochures for the night cruise, fanning it in the air. "What the bloody hell is this?"

Earnestine let out a wild squawk and flew off towards my bedroom, likely scared away by the evil witch that had just joined our midst.

A sly grin quirked the corner of my mouth. "Huh. I don't know, what is it?" Feigning ignorance, I plucked it out of her hands.

"You know exactly what it is."

"Do I?"

"Sly's livid, you know."

"I would be too if I had such a small penis that someone actually *named* me Smallwood."

"That's going to cost him a pretty penny."

"Well, then, I guess he should've thought of that before sending all those people on a cruise."

"*We* didn't send them on a cruise. *You* sent them on a cruise."

"Once again, Ms. Wild, I have no idea what you're talking about." I smiled at her. "Now, if you'll excuse me. I was just retiring for the evening. So. Buh-bye." Holding the door open, I shooed her out the door as she'd shooed me in the past. It felt good to be on the shooing end of the stick.

"I'll stay, thank you," she said curtly.

Standing there in only a pair of athletic shorts, I sighed. I didn't want her to stay. I wanted to continue with the private party I'd been enjoying. "Whaddaya want, Wild?"

She walked over to me, pulled the door from my hand and slammed it shut. "I wanted to have a little chat."

"Yeah? About what?"

"Didn't your mother ever teach you you're supposed to invite visitors in for tea?"

"My mother died giving birth to me, you heartless monster, and I'm American. We don't drink tea."

"Whatever alcohol you have is fine." She wiggled her hands in the direction of my kitchen as if I were her personal servant. Then she moseyed over to my sofa and sat down. "Rugged little place you've got here, by the way."

"We can't all have new and improved like the Crystal Point. And listen, I don't drink, so unfortunately I don't have anything to offer you."

"Bullocks," she said. "You were drunk the other night."

"I'm Drunk every night." I smiled at her.

"Yes, well, you were highly intoxicated when I last saw you."

"Was I? Huh. I guess I don't remember."

"You were. And you were quite insistent on taking me to your bedroom."

"What a man won't do when he's had a few too many to drink. Even the bottom of the barrel isn't too good for him."

"Sobering up seems to have made even more of an asshole of you."

I gave her a tight smile, my lips pulling tautly around my teeth. "Thank you."

"Now, that drink?"

"I'm sorry. I thought you said you were leaving."

"I just got here. I'm parched. It was a long walk."

I sighed and got up and went to the kitchen, wishing I'd mixed up a pitcher of arsenic-laced lemonade earlier in the day. If only I'd have known I'd be having company. I opened the fridge and pulled out a bottle of beer. "I've only got beer."

"That'll do quite nicely, thank you."

Groaning, I pulled out two bottles. If I was going to be dealing with this woman, I needed to have a little alcohol in my system as well. I opened both bottles and walked to the living room, handing her one.

"Thank you." As she took the beer I handed her, she

crossed one of her long legs over the other, forcing me to notice how her skirt rode clear up to her lady bits when she sat. I averted my eyes. I might've had lingering memories of her breasts from a few days before, but I certainly wouldn't commit the smoothness of the inside of her thighs to my memory as well. She was the enemy, and I refused to cross enemy lines!

I stood next to the chair and took a swig of my beer.

"Well, aren't you going to sit down so we can talk like civilized people?"

"You won't be here long. I'll stand."

She narrowed her eyes. "What's the matter? Are you scared of me?"

I quirked a brow. "Scared of *you*? Of course I am. You're a nutjob. Nutjobs are loose cannons. I have no idea when you might explode. I don't need to be all up in that shit when it does."

She chuckled. "I don't even think you realize how funny you are."

"Oh, I know how funny I am. It's part of my charm."

"I don't know that I'd call you charming."

"Why not? Other women do."

"Other women have obviously never met an *actually* charming fellow, then."

"Are you like this with all the men? I assume that's why you're single. Either that or you're just lousy in bed."

"I can assure you I'm neither. You just seem to bring out the worst in me."

"Ditto. Are you done with that beer yet? It's past my bedtime." I looked down at my empty wrist.

"What's the rush? You have another woman coming?"

"Wouldn't you like to know?"

"Sit. I won't explode on you, if that's what you're thinking."

Rolling my eyes, I walked around the chair and plopped

down. "I'm sitting because my legs are tired, not because you told me to."

"You're so obstinate, aren't you? I bet you were a ball of fun for your mother. She didn't *actually* die when you were born, did she?"

"Don't talk about my mother."

"Oooh. A momma's boy. Why am I not surprised?"

"What do you want, Wild?"

She shrugged and took a draw of her beer, then leaned back, switching legs and giving me a clear shot of her nether regions. "I wanted to compliment you on your most recent prank. I thought it was quite brilliant."

I paused my bottle midway up and dropped it back down. "I'm sorry, you what?"

"I thought it was quite brilliant. You're smarter than I gave you credit for."

I stuck a finger in my ear and wiggled it, then, switching my beer to my free hand, repeated the gesture with my other ear. "I'm sorry. You might have to repeat that because I thought I heard you say I'm smarter than you gave me credit for."

She rolled her eyes. "Oh, get over yourself."

"Since when are you giving *me* compliments?"

"What can I say? It was well deserved. Just don't tell Sly I said that. He's quite pissed that you cost him such a fortune. Of course he'll try and get it out of you if he can."

I looked her up and down, wondering if somehow she wore a wire in that skimpy getup of hers. "Once again, I don't know what you're talking about." Unnerved now because I didn't understand the rules of the game we were now playing, I stood up and walked my beer up to my kitchen. "Well. It really is late, and I—" I turned around to see that somehow she'd stealthily stood and walked over to me. If she'd been just a smidge taller, we'd now be standing nose to nose.

"You have to get off to bed?" She tipped her head slightly sideways. Her arms hung limply by her sides.

I tried to take a little step back, but my kitchen counter backed me up. "Yes." My voice came out gruff. I didn't understand what was happening.

"Well. Then maybe we should get you ready for bed." She hooked her fingers in the waistband of my athletic shorts and tugged them down. They fell to the floor around my feet in a puddle, leaving me standing there with only my boxer briefs restraining me.

I swallowed hard and put my hands up on either side of myself, like I'd just been told to stick 'em up. I didn't understand her game at all. Was she going to try and get me for improper touching or something? Was that the prank? "What are you doing?"

"I'm getting you ready for bed." She hooked her fingers in the waistband of my remaining article of clothing.

I lowered one of my hands and grabbed the elastic. "Please don't. I'm not sure what you think you're doing, but I'm not about to get arrested for touching you or raping you or something. I'm not that stupid."

She laughed. "Is that what you think this is about?"

I stared down at her, wide-eyed. "Umm. Yes?"

She smiled. "Never start a sentence with umm. It makes you sound stupid."

"Umm. Thanks?"

That made her laugh. That was when she unleashed her pink satin robe. It fell to the floor in a puddle around her feet, letting me see that she only wore a little pink teddy that barely covered the bottom of her butt.

"Really, Wild. What are you doing here?"

"You invited me to your bedroom the other night. Are you trying to tell me the invitation doesn't stand anymore?"

Little Drunk was telling me in no uncertain terms that the invitation most certainly *did* stand. "I was drunk."

"So it doesn't stand?"

There was something standing all right.

I stared down at her as she brushed one of the satin spaghetti straps off of her shoulder. It fell to her elbow and exposed the top of her left breast. My eyes widened.

Holy shit.

"Well, now." I swallowed hard. "I mean. I just don't know that I understand your sudden change in heart."

She put her hands around my waist then, but they quickly slid around front and up my bare-skinned torso. "I don't know. I guess your offer tempted me."

"But it didn't tempt you the other night. What changed?"

She reached across her right shoulder and pushed the other spaghetti string off of her shoulder and her nightgown dropped to the floor. She was now completely naked in front of me.

Definitely not wearing a wire.

"Well. I guess your new prank kind of turned me on."

"It did?"

She nodded as her hands slid around my pecs and onto my shoulders. "It told me that maybe you had some fight in you after all."

"Oh." My skin flashed hot. "So you're saying you want me to take you to bed, then?"

She grinned. "What gave it away?" Palms up, she put her hands out on either side of herself and gave a little spin in front of me. "Is it because I'm standing naked in front of you in the middle of your living room?"

I took a hard swallow. "Maybe?"

"Well. Then I guess you got me." She stopped moving and put her hands on her hips. "You want me?"

Words I never thought I'd hear Erika Wild ask.

And my response seemed even more unlikely.

Oh God, did I.

I took a step towards her and pushed my mouth onto hers.

It wasn't one of those soft romantic kisses. Not even close. It was heated and backed by little more than contempt and anger. But she fought back with just as much fervor. I leaned over, scooped her up, and carried her back to my bedroom, then tossed her onto my bed.

"You sure about this?"

When her head bobbed, I dropped my underwear.

"Well," she breathed, her eyes widening. "I guess I was wrong. You've got quite a dandy pair of balls after all."

34

I woke up with a smile on my face. Sunlight streamed in through my open window and birds chirped happily outside. Surprisingly, Earnestine had skipped my morning wakeup call, allowing me to sleep in, something I was extremely thankful for as the night before had been a wild ride that had lasted well into the early-morning hours.

I went to roll over onto my side but discovered I couldn't move. My arms and legs were both tied to my bedposts. As if attached to springs, my eyes shot open. I discovered the other side of the bed was empty and Erika Wild already gone. Shocked, I lay completely silent for a moment, wondering if maybe she was in the bathroom and coming back to take advantage of me, but when I heard no noises after a few long moments, I realized she must've snuck out at some point.

"Shit," I muttered, looking up at my tied wrists. I gave a tug and found that they hadn't been tied tightly. I was able to slip my hands out of the bindings with little trouble. When I'd pulled all the ties off, I noticed a note on the bedside table.

Drunk, I was going to invite you to breakfast, but I saw that you were all tied up. XX Erika.

Lying back, I chuckled. I thought about the evening, and

the shock I'd felt over finding her scantily clad self in my doorway the night before. I thought about how much more shocked I'd been when she'd stripped in front of me. And then even further, how shocked I'd been when I'd discovered how amazing she was in bed. It had been a good night. And if she wasn't the enemy, I might've actually looked forward to having a rendezvous like that again sometime. But as it stood, she *was* the enemy.

I lay there for another minute, basking in the afterglow of fornication before I heard the sound of sirens in the distance. I lay their comfortably, listening to them whine for a while, but after a while, I realized that they seemed to be growing closer. I rolled onto my side, wishing I could fall back asleep again, but found the sirens too annoying to allow it.

My phone rang.

I closed my eyes and a little groan escaped the back of my throat. It was too earlier to be bothered by anyone. I was barely awake and had yet to have any caffeine. I rolled onto my back and looked at my phone on the nightstand. It rang again.

I reached out and picked it up, half expecting to see my mother's picture on the screen with the words Momma Drunk printed across her forehead. But it was Artie.

Fuck, it's work.

I stared at his name for a long second debating on whether or not to answer. And then I thought about the sirens that seemed to have landed not so far away.

"Drunk here," I grumbled into the phone, my voice bristly and gruff.

"Drunk, it's Artie. You're gonna want to get over here right away."

"What happened?"

"I can't talk about it on the phone. Just get over here right away. No time for a shower."

The phone went dead before I could ask any more questions.

I rolled onto my back and closed my eyes. Why did I have a feeling this was going to be a really bad day?

I smelled the smoke even before I'd stepped foot out of my cottage. It poured in through the open windows and was the first thing I caught a whiff of when I left my bedroom to go into the kitchen for a soda. My oversized nose prodded the air, searching for more scented clues. It wasn't a campfire. At least I was fairly confident of that.

The smell of smoke combined with the sound of sirens and Artie's phone call poured a chilling sense of fear into my veins. I was afraid of what I'd find when I left the protected confines of my cottage. It took me less than two minutes from Artie's call before I was dressed and out the door. I went in through the back entrance, something I rarely did. I always preferred to go around the building and come in through the lobby so I could get the feel of the day, say my good mornings, and check on everything. But today was different, I knew right away. Getting there fast was my only priority.

Going in through the back, I was thankful to see the building still standing. No fire in the employee hallway, that much was sure. I stuck my head in Artie's office to find it empty. The door to my office was closed, but I opened the door and flipped on the light anyway.

Empty.

No fire.

Swishing my lips to the side, I adjusted my hat, took a drink of my soda and walked down the hallway and out to the lobby. It was surprisingly quiet. I frowned. Well, what the hell was going on? Where were all the guests and the staff?

I walked around a pillar and looked towards the front doors to see a crowd standing beneath the porte cochere just outside the lobby's front doors in the circle driveway. The doors slid open when they caught me in their range, and the sound of sirens poured in along with a puff of smoke.

What the—?

I rushed outside.

"Drunk!" shouted Gary Wheelan, standing with some of the geriatric squad at the top of the cobblestone hill. He waved me over to him. Al and Evelyn Becker stood in front of him, and Big Eddie and Ralph stood on the other side of them.

Walkie over to them, my eyes followed every other onlookers. But I could only see smoke between us and the pool area and the driveway.

"What's going on? Where's Artie?"

"Drunk!" said Al, smiling up at me. "Thank God you're all right."

Mrs. Al wrapped an arm around my waist in a side hug and patted my stomach. "There you are. We were so worried."

I squeezed her back. "Yeah. I'm fine. What's going on?"

"There's a fire!" said Ralph.

"That's usually where smoke comes from, Weaz. Where's it at? The clubhouse?" Just saying the word, panic gripped me, wondering if perhaps that had been the newest prank. Had Erika set fire to our clubhouse after leaving my place early in the morning? Was that why she'd coerced me into bed?

"No, not the clubhouse," said Al. "It's further down. Next door."

"Next door?" I frowned. "You mean the Crystal Point?"

Gary, Eddie, Ralph, and Al all nodded.

"The Crystal Point!" My eyes shot open wider as if my caffeine had suddenly kicked in.

"I'm afraid so," said Al. "Artie's trying to find out more right now. Maybe you should go find him."

"Oh, but be careful, Terrence. We don't want anything happening to you."

I patted Mrs. Al on the shoulder as she squeezed me tightly

around the middle again like a worried mother. "I'll be fine, Evie. But Al's right. I should go find Artie."

Al took a step forward. "I can come with you."

His wife looked up at me sharply. Worry filled her eyes.

"No, Al. You stay here with Evie. Has anyone seen Val?"

"I haven't," said Al. He looked back at the rest of the group. "Have any of you?"

Everyone shook their heads.

"Artie would want someone to make sure she's safe and sound. Al, why don't you go check on her, and I'll go find Artie and see if there's anything I should be doing. Okay?"

Al nodded. "Of course."

"I'll go with you, dear," said Mrs. Al.

Once we had that decided, I took off through the crowd of onlookers down the hill. The closer I got to the guard shack, the thicker the smoke got. And then a puff of air coming in off the bay blew apart the smoke for a split second, allowing me to see the Crystal Point through a grove of burning palm trees. The main building was completely engulfed in flames. I took off on a run towards it then, wondering where in the hell Artie was.

I crossed the expanse of grass behind the employee parking lot, passing the low shrubs that Sly Smallwood had once cut to look like male genitalia, and found the fire trucks, police cars, and paramedics in the parking lot. Firemen worked hard to put out the blaze, their hoses blowing up huge rolls of smoke. Across the parking lot, I could see Sly Smallwood and Erika Wild speaking with a pair of police officers. My eyes searched the crowd for Artie but failed to find him.

Very few guests were outside, and I was almost immediately reminded about the prank I'd played on them the day before. The reason that Erika had come to see me was to compliment me on the ingenuity of my prank. But had it perhaps inadvertently saved hundreds of people's lives? Had the fire started in the night when they were all there, would there have been too many casualties to count? Questions filled my brain.

And then I saw a familiar face in the crowd.

Frankie!

I pushed through the firefighters and the police to be by her side. She was speaking with someone animatedly. Afraid of being too pushy with her once again, I waited until they were done speaking. "Frankie!"

"Danny? What are you doing over here?"

"Are you kidding? The neighbor's place is on fire. I have to know what's going on. What happened?"

"We aren't exactly sure yet. Is everything okay over at the Seacoast?"

I glanced backwards over my shoulder, not that I could see anything, the view was entirely obscured by billowing smoke. "Yeah. We're fine over there. Just getting the smoke from the fire."

"You should probably keep your guests inside until we get the fire put out. Or even evacuate them."

"Artie won't want to evacuate." I nodded towards the Crystal Point Resort. "I hope everyone got out in time?"

"We think we have the building cleared."

"Thank God."

"Yeah. Mr. Smallwood said that the majority of his guests were out on some kind of night cruise. Courtesy of you, I hear?"

Like a deer caught in the headlights, my eyes widened and my mouth gaped a little as I shook my head. "I have no idea what you're talking about."

"Danny. Don't lie to me. You're not good at it. I can see right through it."

I swallowed hard. "Can we talk about this another time?"

She pulled on my arm then.

Hard.

Tugging me over so that we were behind the fire trucks and

away from the biggest part of the chaos, she hissed, "Danny." She looked deeply into my eyes. "Tell me you didn't do this."

"I didn't do this!"

She stared long and hard at me, like she was trying to see through to my soul. "If I find out you did…"

I held both hands up. "I swear, Frankie. I'd never burn down their building."

That was when I caught sight of Artie, lingering in a golf cart in the middle of the parking lot. "Artie!" I breathed, thankful to see that he was all right. "Frankie. Can we talk about this later?"

"Danny…"

I sidestepped her and rushed over to the golf cart. "Artie. There you are. I've been looking all over for you. What are you doing over here?"

"Just assessing the damage," he said, shaking his head. "This is terrible. I mean. I know we both hated the guy, but I never would've wished for his resort to burn to the ground. It was a beautiful resort."

"Yeah. I agree," I said, nodding. "I'm in shock."

"Me too."

"There he is!" shouted Sly Smallwood, coming between a row of fire trucks to point at Artie. His face was set in a stony snarl. "Arrest him! Arrest that man! He's the one that burned down my building!"

35

Artie sucked in his breath as he stared in shock at Sly. "Me?! I didn't burn down your building! I'd never!"

"Officers, I know this is the man responsible! And this is his accomplice. He's probably the one who did the dirty work. Arrest them both!"

Frankie, who'd overheard the accusation, spun around and rushed over to join the conversation. "What proof do you have, Mr. Smallwood?"

"I don't need proof! I know they did it!"

She looked at him, her eyes merely thin slits. "Without proof, then, how do you know they did it?"

"Their resort has been pulling mean-spirited pranks on my resort for the last few weeks. I think this is the last straw in everything they've done."

"*Our* resort has been pulling mean-spirited pranks!" I repeated, shocked that he'd spin it like that. "That's bullshit. Smallwood started all of this."

"Ah-ha! So you admit it!" he snapped, pointing at me.

"I don't admit anything! I'm only saying that any pranks that were pulled were done only *after* you pulled a prank. But we didn't do this!" I looked at Frankie, my eyes pleading for her to believe me. "Come on, Frankie. Tell me you don't believe this guy."

She looked at Sly. "Mr. Smallwood. We *will* get to the bottom of this and find out how this happened. But without proof that Mr. Balladares and Mr. Drunk were involved in this, I don't think it's appropriate for accusations to be thrown around for something of this magnitude. This could have easily been accidental."

But Sly shook his head and pointed his finger at us. "Oh, no. This was all the Seacoast Majestic. They think we burned down their ship. This is retribution for that, only we didn't do that."

I rolled my eyes. "Oh, isn't that rich. You most certainly *did* do that."

Erika Wild, appeared from between the fire trucks then. She saw the group of us arguing and walked over to stand next to her boss.

"Tell them what you know, Erika," said Sly, looking her up and down.

Erika looked around the group, her eyes landing on me. "What specifically would you like to know?"

"They think we were responsible for burning down their boat. Don't they?"

Without moving her dark eyes off me, Erika nodded. "Yes. They do think that. It's true."

I pursed my lips.

"And tell them what they did to our guests!" he insisted, bringing his pointed finger down like a sledgehammer.

"*Someone* sent all of our guests on a night cruise. So they'd be gone overnight," said Erika, quirking a brow.

Frankie looked at me. I knew she was starting to believe them. I could tell by the appalled look on her face.

"I believe that this fire was ordered by Artie Balladares, but that his henchman here was the one to execute the plan!" railed Sly.

I shook my head. "I swear to you, Frankie. I did not do this. And I know Artie didn't have anything to do with it either."

Artie's head bobbed. "Drunk is absolutely correct. I would never do anything like this. You're the one that blows up ships! This is *your* style. Not mine."

"I didn't blow up your damned ship!" Sly's face was red as he hollered.

Frankie looked at me then. "I don't want to have to ask you this, Danny, but where were you in the wee hours of the morning?"

"Obviously I was home sleeping!" I said.

She nodded sadly. "And without anyone to vouch for you…"

Erika's voice suddenly piped up. Her hand went up too. "I can vouch for him."

Frankie's eyes snapped over to look at Erika. Shock filled them. "I'm sorry. What?"

"I can vouch for him. There's no way he started the fire."

Frankie's head tilted slightly to one side. "And you know this how?"

"Because I was with him. I was the one to spot the fire on my way back home this morning. I'm the one that called it in."

Frankie's mouth gaped. She looked like someone had just punched her in the stomach.

I held my breath then as I stared at her. My pulse thundered in my ears.

Fuuuuuck.

This was bad.

Very, very bad.

Even though Frankie's rejection had been brutal and quite absolute, jumping into bed with another woman so quickly surely wasn't a good look for me. I wanted to explain to her that I'd been seduced. Possibly even tricked! Maybe this had all been part of Erika's evil plan somehow. My mind raced, trying to figure out how I was going to spin my way out of this, but there were too many people around to do it all now. And Erika was staring at me hard. I couldn't read her thoughts. Was that a look of victory on her face? Or a look of desire? Hatred? Lust? I was confused and nauseous all at once.

"*You* were at Danny's place this morning?"

Erika nodded.

Sly looked at Erika in shock. "What were you doing over there?"

"I had personal business to discuss," she said, lifting her shoulder.

"What kind of personal business?" pressed Frankie.

"The kind that's *personal*." Erika didn't even *pretend* to look embarrassed.

Frankie looked to me, searching for answers. "Care to expand on that at all, Mr. Drunk?"

Mr. Drunk.

Not a good sign.

"Yeah, Drunk. What was she doing at your place?" demanded Artie.

"Well." I swallowed hard. I felt like I was in a hole and the dirt walls were crumbling in around me, threatening to bury me alive if I wasn't careful. "Ms. Wild stopped over. *Not* at my request…" I glanced over at Frankie. "…to, umm, have a word with me about their guests going on some evening cruise. She seemed to think I had something to do with it. *Which I didn't.*" Fine, it was a lie. But was I *really* supposed to admit that I'd been responsible for that after what had just transpired?

Erika rolled her eyes. "Whatever, Drunk. You did too. We both know it."

Ignoring her, I continued. "And then she, uh…" I didn't think I could say it.

"And then we slept together. Okay? Look. I get that I slept with the enemy, but we were both consenting adults. It happened. I'm not proud of it." She looked over at Sly, who stared at her in shock, and tossed her hands up. "I don't know what you want me to say. It was a weak moment."

If Frankie's eyeballs hadn't been attached to the insides of her head by nerves and whatnot, I was pretty sure they would've easily popped out, they opened that wide when Erika admitted that we'd slept together. "I see. Is that correct, Mr. Drunk?"

"Well, it didn't go down *exactly* like she just described it, but…"

"But you did sleep together?" pressed Frankie.

"I mean, she came on to *me*…"

"And you just couldn't turn her down, huh?" Frankie's head shook as she scribbled something down in her notebook. I was pretty sure it was just a distraction because she couldn't look me in the eyes.

"Drunk!" Artie looked shocked. "Sleeping with the enemy. I can't believe it."

My brows peaked. "Can we all just get to the point of why we're here? I have an alibi. Okay? I didn't do this. Artie didn't do this."

Frankie let out a little noise, but turned her attention to Artie. "Do you have anyone who can vouch for *your* whereabouts this morning?"

Artie looked at me.

"Val should be able to, right, Artie?"

He cleared his throat and then kind of nodded. "Oh yeah. Umm, I suppose she can."

I stared at him hard, wishing I could read his mind and know why he was hemming and hawing about Val vouching for him, and then silently I had to wonder if he had something to do with the fire after all.

But if Frankie noticed Artie being suspicious, she didn't say it. She nodded her head at him. "Good. All right, well, of course I'll have to verify that, but Mr. Smallwood, I think it's safe to say you've got it wrong. I'm sure this will turn out to be some kind of kitchen fire or something like that. So let's wait for the facts before we go spreading rumors, shall we?"

Sly narrowed his eyes on Artie. "Just because henchman number one was preoccupied"—he shot an angry look at Erika —"doesn't mean henchman number two didn't step up to the plate."

"Who's henchman number two?" asked Frankie.

"Like I know?!" spouted Sly. "He's got all kinds of employees. Check them all out for alibis. One of them did this, and I'm not going to rest until the truth comes out!"

36

ARTIE AND I SAT IN FRONT OF FRANKIE'S DESK DOWN AT THE police station the next day. As I already knew, she'd moved up in the world and now she had her very own office as opposed to a cubicle in the middle of the building like she'd previously had. She also had a window that faced a side street and a door that could block out the noise of the station behind us.

Frankie sat behind her desk, looking grim. After the fire and the admission from Erika that we'd slept together, she'd not taken any of my calls for the rest of the day. Instead, the next morning when I'd gotten out of the shower, I had a voice-mail from her instructing me to meet her down at the police station and to bring Artie. Of course I'd agreed, but Artie hadn't been very excited, and now the three of us stared at each other.

"I've got some news about the fire," said Frankie finally. She'd barely made eye contact with me since we'd been there, looking at me only once when I'd come in and then after that not at all.

Artie sat in his chair, wringing his hands. I knew he was worried about them trying to pin the fire on him, even though he swore up and down he had nothing to hide and hadn't had any "second henchman" set the fire. He didn't even know who a second henchman would be.

"What's the news?"

Frankie sighed and looked down at her desk. "The deputy fire chief is reporting that the fire *is* believed to be arson. Mr. Smallwood was right about that."

"But who would do something like that?" asked Artie, shaking his head.

"Well, that's what I wanted to talk to the two of you about. Deputy Fire Chief Malone believes an accelerant was used and a box of matches was discovered on the property. It was partially burned, but the fire didn't completely destroy it."

I looked at her curiously, unsure of where she was going with that information. "Okay? So why does that make you want to talk to us?"

She pulled a zipped baggie out of her desk drawer and laid it on her desk. In the baggie was the charred remains of a box of matches. In one corner you could make out the end of the business from where they'd originated: "—*jestic.*"

"Do those look familiar?"

Artie and I both stared down at the little box. It was one of those little amenities we gave away to our guests. A box of matches. A shoe polish kit. A pen and little pad of paper. Branded Andes mints. Not only were they in all the rooms, but Artie even had a small bowl of matches and mints on his desk. Which I was keenly aware of because the mints were chocolate, and I stole them often.

Fuck.

"Well, yes, of course they look familiar. We do offer those as a giveaway to our guests, but certainly..."

"Deputy Fire Chief Malone thinks they may have been used to start the fire."

"But anyone could've gotten ahold of those, Frankie. You know that."

She refused to make eye contact with me. "I'm aware of

that. I also checked with the cruise ship company that Sly's guests were sent to prior to the fire. I was able to trace the incoming call that made the reservation back to you, Mr. Drunk."

"Come on, Frankie. It's Danny. Please don't do this."

"I find it very suspicious that not only did your resort ensure that the majority of Mr. Smallwood's guests would not be on site the evening of the fire, but also that you were both upset that there was little we could do to prove that they were the ones responsible for the loss of *The Bloody Marauder*. And now I discover that your matches were found at the scene of the crime. I have to be honest. This isn't looking good for you."

"Oh my God," breathed Artie, leaning forward slightly. His breathing was labored, making him wheeze.

"Frankie, you know we wouldn't do that."

"I thought I knew you, Mr. Drunk, but apparently I don't know you as well as I thought I did."

"Look, Frankie. Please don't do this. You—"

"It's Inspector Cruz to you, Mr. Drunk."

My head rolled back on my shoulders. "Fine. Inspector Cruz, look, I'm sorry for what happened between me and Erika, but—"

"Keep this discussion related to the case, please, Mr. Drunk."

She was killing me. If Artie hadn't been there, I might have done something uncharacteristically Drunk and begged for her to listen, but he was, which, thankfully, probably kept my man card firmly tucked in my wallet where it belonged. "Ugh, fine. All I wanted to say is that I hope you know Artie wouldn't do this. Okay?"

"We'll be making a conclusion based on fact, but, Artie, I called you down here so I could tell you in person that as of right now, you are a person of interest in this case. Don't leave the island."

Artie's mouth gaped. "But my wedding is coming up this weekend. I planned to take Val on a short honeymoon after—"

"I'm sorry, but if we don't get this case wrapped up by then, you may have to honeymoon on the island."

I couldn't believe it was happening. And *now* of all times. It was almost all too convenient. Putting my hands on the desk, I pushed myself up. "I'm not letting this get any further. I'm going to prove to you that Artie didn't do this."

"And how exactly are you going to do that, Mr. Drunk?"

"Quit calling me, Mr. Drunk. You know I hate it. It's Danny to you. And you know I can do it, Fran—Inspector Cruz. I can and I *will* clear Artie Balladares's good name."

37

After dropping Artie off at the Seacoast Majestic lobby, I drove over to my place to park the Raptor. Al was waiting for me in his golf cart.

"So what's going on? What did Francesca want?" asked Al as I climbed aboard.

"You mean Inspector Cruz? Oh, just to tell Artie that he's officially been named as a person of interest in the case."

Al covered his mouth with his hand. "You're not serious."

"Oh, I'm serious all right. This is bad, Al. This is really, really bad. We have to do something to help him."

"Whatever we can do!"

"Well, for starters, I think we need to work on Artie's alibi. If we can prove he was at his house with Val when the fire started, there's no way Frankie can keep him as a person of interest. Maybe we should go talk to Val and get her to go down to the station and give a statement. I'm sure Frankie's already planning to contact her, but we should—"

Al cut me off. "It's not gonna do any good, kid."

"What's not?"

"Val can't be Artie's alibi."

I turned to look at Al. "What? Why not?"

"You remember when you went looking for Artie and you asked me to go check on Val?"

"Yeah?"

"She wasn't there."

I frowned. "Where?"

"At Artie's place."

"Well, then, where was she?"

Al shrugged. "I have no idea. She just wasn't there."

"But she might have just gotten up early and went to breakfast or something."

"I don't think so. I looked all over the resort for her. I went to the dining room, the clubhouse, the pool, the beach. I looked everywhere."

Remembering the whole wedding thing I'd been in several days before, I nodded. "Did you check the conference room? They have this wedding thing set up in there. I'm sure she—"

"I checked there too, kid. She wasn't there. I don't think she was anywhere on resort property unless she was in one of the hotel rooms."

"But she might've been here when the fire started. We don't know?"

"We can talk to her, but I find it unlikely that she's going to be much help."

I took my hat off and put it in my lap, then leaned back against the seat and fisted my hair, groaning. Why did everything always have to be so difficult? "Shit," I breathed before sitting up and putting my hat back on.

"Maybe we should find out where she was?" said Al.

"Yeah, okay. While we're still here, I'll go see if she's home."

"Good idea. I'll wait here."

I hopped out of the golf cart and walked over to Artie's place and knocked on the door. I waited and waited, but she never came to the door. Sighing, I went back over to the golf cart. "I guess we'll catch her later."

Al nodded. "Hey, didn't you say that you had a new camera installed back here?"

My eyes went up to look around the area in search of the camera. I pointed to one attached to the eve of Artie's cottage, then I turned around and saw that Hector had attached one to the eve of my cottage as well. "Looks like we've got two of them."

"That oughta prove that Artie was home when the fire started."

"Al, you're a genius! I could kiss you!"

Al swatted the air. "Kiss me and I'll lay you out flatter than piss on a platter."

I rolled my eyes and leaned back against my seat, pulling my long arms back to fold my fingers behind my head. "Jeez, cowboy, don't squat with your spurs on."

"Don't squat with your spurs on? What's that supposed to mean?"

"I don't know. Relax? Take a chillaxative?"

Al groaned as he drove us up to the resort. "We really gotta work on your pearls of wisdom, kid. You sound like an idiot."

"Thank you, Al. And as a side note, I think your filter has officially worn off."

"Meh, my filter rubbed off thirty years ago. It's one of the perks of being a card-carrying member of the AARP. You can say whatever the hell you want and not give a shit anymore."

"I was born with that perk. They gave free passes out to anyone born with the last name Drunk."

Al chuckled. "For good reason. Come on, kid. Let's go prove Artie didn't start that fire."

WE STARTED the video with me leaving my cottage the morning of the fire and rewound from there. Surprisingly, we discovered that Artie had actually left his place way earlier that morning. Much earlier than when the fire had been reported.

"I wonder why he didn't tell us that," said Al.

"Maybe he thinks we'll think he did it?"

"I'd never think that of Artie, not even if I saw him light the match himself."

"Well, maybe he's more concerned with what the police think than what you or I think."

"Your girlfriend didn't ask you for this security footage, did she?" asked Al, rubbing a hand across his smooth-shaven chin.

"First of all, Frankie would punch you in the nads for calling her that, and second of all, no. She didn't ask for any security footage."

"Good. Well, whatever you do, don't go volunteering this. It doesn't help Artie's case."

"No, it really doesn't." I leaned forward and gave the mouse a little wiggle. "You wanna go back and even further and see where Ms. Carrizo was during the fire?"

"Might as well, since we're here." Al leaned forward too so he could get a better look at the screen.

Without knowing what time she'd left, it was harder to pin Val's whereabouts down, but after a little rewinding and fast forwarding, we discovered that a little after midnight, a car, barely visible in the dark on the security camera, had picked her up.

I had to squint and get closer to the screen. "Does that look like a Chrysler 300 to you?"

Al lifted his chin and looked down his nose and the bottom of his glasses at the screen. "Sure does."

"Well, I guess this proves your suspicion. Val wasn't on resort property the morning of the fire," I said.

"It doesn't prove that at all. All it proves is that she wasn't in her cottage the morning of the fire," said Al, holding up a finger. "There's a difference."

"What's the difference?"

"The difference is that this video doesn't clear her either."

Al had a very good point. "So now what?"

"Now? Now I think we need to go start our own fire investigation."

"You wanna go over to the Crystal Point?"

"I think going back to the scene of the crime is where all good detectives start. Don't you, kid?"

"When I meet a good detective, I'll let you know. Until then, I'll take your word for it. Let's make like a bird and get the flock outta here."

38

DESPITE THE FACT THAT THE SMOKE HAD CLEARED AND THE FIRE trucks were long gone, the thick smell of smoke still clung to the air, making my nose sting and my eyes water. Nearby trees were covered in a layer of black soot, as were the building's still-standing brick walls. The pitched roof that I'd admired so much on my first visit to the Crystal Point had caved in, and now, through the wide-open entrance, we could see the charred remains crumbled inside the previously grand lobby.

The resort's entrance had been taped off as a crime scene, but as we pulled the golf cart to a stop in front of the building, Sly Smallwood and Erika Wild came walking around the side of the building.

Sly's eyes widened when he saw us parked in front of his burned-down resort. Immediately he came towards us, yelling and pointing fingers. "You get off my property, you sonovabitch arsonist! Look at what you did! I sure hope you're happy! You've ruined me!"

"We didn't do it, Sly!" I hollered back at him.

"You did too! The police will prove it. You're all going to jail for this!"

When Sly reached out to try and grab ahold of my arm, Al

hit the gas and the golf cart lurched forward. Sly chugged along, trying to keep up and yank me out at the same time, but when Al got the cart up to a steady clip, Sly was forced to let go. Al steered the cart in a figure eight around the parking lot, weaving around lampposts and the few parked cars in the lot, Sly chasing after us the whole time.

I turned around to yell backwards at him. "Erika knows we didn't do it," I hollered when we passed by her, standing in front of their resort, watching her boss chase a golf cart.

"I know *you* didn't do it," she hollered back. "I don't know your supreme leader didn't do it."

"Oh, come on, Erika. You do too."

"I really don't," she said with a flip shrug.

"Get out of here!" barked Sly, still chasing after us, but slowing down and now getting winded. Even though he was in much better shape than both Al and Artie, he was just as old if not older and was beginning to breathe heavily.

"Come on, Al. The only thing we're doing is making me dizzy and helping Sly lose his breath. We're not gonna get any investigating done with these guys down here. Let's go grab lunch and we'll see what we can do after that."

"Lunch sounds good to me."

WITH PLATES FULL OF FOOD, Al and I took seats in the dining room's outdoor eating area. I always found it was a good place to clear my head and think, and today of all days, I needed to think.

"I don't even understand how it got this far," I said, shaking my head.

"What part?" asked Al.

"What part?! The whole part! The prank war. The fact that Sly's resort burned to the ground. The fact that he's blaming it on Artie. The fact that—"

"That you slept with Erika Wild?"

I glanced up at Al sheepishly. "You have to remind me?"

"I just don't understand, kid. What the hell were you thinking? Last I heard, you hated the woman."

I tossed my fork down onto my plate. It made a loud clinking noise, making a nearby pigeon look up at me curiously. I leaned back in my seat and groaned. "Ugh! That's just it. I *do* hate the woman. And now Frankie hates me."

"Well, then, why'd you sleep with her?"

"I don't know, Al. Why do men do stupid stuff at all?"

"Because sometimes they *think* with the wrong parts of their body."

"You know, I didn't go in search of her. I want you to know that right now. I didn't hunt *her* down. She hunted me down."

"Sure she did."

I leaned forward. "She did!"

"Whatever you say, kid."

"Al, come on. You gotta believe me."

"Why do I gotta believe you? It doesn't matter a hill of beans to me."

"Liar. I know you. It bothers you that I slept with her."

Al lifted a shoulder rather noncommittally. "What you do is your business. I just thought you were smarter than that."

I just thought you were smarter than that. It was like getting a lecture from my dad. Dads say that kind of shit to guilt you into feeling like crap about yourself. If he'd just said "that was a stupid thing you did," I'd have preferred it. Because then I could've just agreed with him and moved on. But now it was like I'd disappointed him or something.

"I *am* smarter than that. But *she* came over to my place. And she was wearing this little—*thing*." Using my fingers, I drew the outline of her nighty against my chest. "And it was short. And she kept crossing her legs and she—" I leaned in across the table, widening my eyes, and hissed the rest at Al. "She was wearing lingerie, Al."

Al's eyebrows shot up with interest, but he didn't say anything.

"I mean, what was I supposed to do? When a woman comes to your house wearing only lingerie, are you just supposed to send her *home*?!"

Al quietly blotted the corners of his mouth with his napkin and then laid it in his lap. "Well," he said, drawing out the word. "I suppose it depends on who that woman is."

"Really?" I stared at him hard. I wanted to call bullshit, but I knew I couldn't play that game with Al. He'd win. "Aside from Evie, have you ever found another woman attractive?"

"Of course I have."

"Fine. Name one."

"Well, I always thought Sophia Loren was a foxy dame. I think it was the red hair. You know, Evie had red hair once upon a time."

My chin jerked back. "Really? Evie was a redhead? I never would've guessed."

That comment made Al smile and wag his finger. "Ahh. There's a lot you never would've guessed about my Evie."

"Okay, well, let's say you were home alone one evening and Sophia Loren came over to your place wearing only lingerie. Then she undresses you. All the while, you haven't laid a hand on her, mind you. Then she starts to rub her hands all over you, and then she tells you she wants you to take her to bed. What would *you* have done?"

"That's easy. I would've sent her home."

"Bullshit," I snorted.

"I'm a married man, kid. I love my wife."

"But you weren't married at the time. You and Evie were only kind of seeing each other, and in fact, she'd just shot you down when you asked her out."

Al tapped his finger on his chin then. "Well, then, it's a moot point."

I stared at him incredulously. "How's it a moot point?!"

He shrugged. "Sophia Loren wouldn't have known where I lived back then. That situation could've never happened."

I palmed my forehead. "Oh my God, Al. It's a hypothetical question! I'm just trying to show you how tempted you would've been in that situation."

"Well, hypothetically speaking, if Sophia Loren *had* come over to my house before I married Evie, she still wouldn't have gotten very far with me."

Now I didn't believe anything coming out of Al's mouth. "Sure, Al."

"No, I'm serious. Before I married Evie, I lived with my folks on the farm. My mother would've stopped her cold. She had four brothers and raised six sons. She was a tough old broad. She didn't tolerate much." He chuckled.

"You're unreal. You know that?" I picked up a piece of bacon and bit half of it off, pointing the rest of it at Al. "*You* know what I mean. I was tempted, and honestly Frankie doesn't want me. I didn't do anything wrong."

"Well, maybe not, but *Erika Wild*? I didn't think you'd want to give her the satisfaction."

"Honestly? I wasn't exactly worried about *her* satisfaction." I quirked a smile. "Not to say she *wasn't* satisfied. It just wasn't priority for me."

Al threw his hands up. "Okay. Time to change the subject."

"You lobbed that one up at me!"

"My mistake." Al stuck his finger in his ear and wiggled it. "Sometimes there are things in life you just can't *unhear*. That's one of those things."

I laughed. "Fine. So let's talk about Artie and how we're going to get him out of this situation."

"I think the only way we're getting Artie out of the situation is if we figure out who *actually* set fire to the Crystal Point Resort," said Al.

"Frankie's on the case. She'll figure it out."

"Kid. You said it yourself—they have evidence tying Artie

to the fire. He's got a motive. He has no alibi. It doesn't look good. I'm gonna be real here. I think whoever set that fire is trying to frame him."

"But who would want to frame *Artie*?"

Al shrugged. "That's what we have to find out."

"Artie lives a pretty quiet life. But when you think about it, what's the only thing that's changed in his life recently?"

"Val, obviously."

"Right. And if Artie gets sent away to prison for arson, but he marries Val before he's convicted, who stands to gain his fortune while he's in the big house?"

"Val, obviously."

I pointed at Al. "Bingo. I think after lunch, our priority is finding Valentina Carrizo. We've got a few questions to ask her."

39

After lunch, Al and I split up. Evie needed help fixing her vacuum cleaner, and I wanted to go back over to Artie's place one more time to check for Val. We both agreed if she wasn't there, we'd have to go back to my office after lunch and see if we couldn't spot her on a security camera.

Standing on Artie's front porch, I knocked. When no one came to the door, I knocked again. This time, I was sure I heard something inside. I moved to the big picture window next to the door and cupped my hands to peer inside. My eyes scanned the living room but came up empty. I went back to the door and knocked again.

"Come on, Val, I know you're in there. It's Drunk. I need to talk to you. It's important."

I heard another noise inside, but still no one came to the door. I knew it wasn't Artie. I'd just seen him up at the resort. It had to be Val inside.

I tried the door and found it locked. Glancing around behind me, I lifted my hat off and pulled out the bobby pins I kept inside the hat band. Glancing around one more time, I knelt in front of Artie's door and set about picking the lock. When the door popped open, I stuck my head inside.

"Val! I know you're in here!" I hollered.

I heard noises in the kitchen, but still, Val didn't answer.

Putting the pins back in the band of my hat and my hat back on my head, I went inside, feeling slightly guilty that I'd just broken into Artie's house, but not too guilty. I was, after all, trying to keep him out of prison for arson. I was sure he'd forgive me for the break-in.

This time, I was quiet as I moved through the living room and dining room to the back of the house, where the kitchen was. I heard a whistle and then tapping. Crooking my head sideways, I paused for a second and listened.

"*Whee-ooo, whee-ooo, whee-ooo,*" went the high-pitched whistle, mocking the sounds of sirens. Then, "*Rawck, pretty bird, pretty bird. Rawck! Fuck you, motherfucker!*"

I rolled my eyes and went to the kitchen. Pausing in the doorway, I propped both hands on my hips. "Earnestine!"

"*Rawck!*" She hopped around, startled, and pulled her head down into her neck like she was a turtle. She was standing on Artie's kitchen counter, and there was an open sleeve of crackers broken around her feet.

"Busted. How'd you get in here?" I looked around and saw the back patio door to the swimming pool was left ajar. "Ahh. I see. I don't think Artie would appreciate you eating his crackers. I think you better go."

"*Rawck! Fuck you, motherfucker!*" she screeched.

"Yeah. Back at you, asshole," I said, lifting her off the counter and taking her outside to the pool. I put her on the little table next to Artie's grill beside a can of lighter fluid and went back inside, making sure to shut the door tightly so she couldn't get back in. Then I went in search of Val.

"Val? You here? It's Drunk."

I poked my head into Artie's room and found that housekeeping had been there already. The room was neat and tidy and the bed was made up, but there was no sign of Val. I poked my head into the room across the hall to discover a mess of a room. Dresses, shoes, and hats littered the floor. The vanity top was covered with makeup and jewelry. Surprised, I glanced backwards at the bed. The bedsheets were strewn around, the pillows with a clear indentation of a head. Clearly, Val was sleeping in that room.

That fact came as a shock to me. *They weren't sleeping together?!*

I went back into Artie's room and poked my head into the master bathroom and discovered it as neat and tidy as his bedroom, but no Val. Then I went to the bathroom down the hall, and while it wasn't as messy as Val's bedroom, it was clear that she was using the hall bathroom, not the master bathroom.

"Huh, that's weird," I said to the room. I nodded, though, thinking how much easier it would be for Val to have snuck in and out if she had her own room. I wondered how I'd broach the subject with Artie. I couldn't very well tell him I'd broken into his house and knew that they weren't sharing a bedroom.

I walked to the front of the house and peered out the window. I didn't want to go outside and get busted by Val, or Artie for that matter. But when I didn't see either of them out front, I let myself out, careful to lock the door before leaving.

Just as I started down the front steps, I noticed a dark car coming down the little gravel drive. I recognized the car's grille almost immediately. It was the same Chrysler 300 that had dropped Val off in the middle of the night and recently picked her up. It seemed to speed up the closer it got, but my feet remained glued to the sidewalk in front of Artie's place. If Val was going to emerge, I wanted to be able to confront her about her whereabouts the morning of the fire.

The car pulled to a stop in front of Artie's house. The windows were darkly tinted, so I couldn't see anyone inside. But then two doors opened and two men stepped out. The driver was a bald black guy with a beard I wouldn't be caught dead in, and the passenger was a skinny white kid, all tatted up around the neck. I didn't recognize either of them, but they both walked right over to me without so much as a pause, like they knew me or something.

"You got Val in there?" I asked, puffing out my chest.

But neither of them spoke. Instead, the one that had come out of the passenger side of the car tossed a gunny sack over my head, knocking my hat off, while the other one grabbed me around the middle, pinning my arms to my body. The next thing I knew, a plastic zip tie had encircled my wrists, and my hands were locked behind my back.

"What the fuck?!" I hollered, my pulse accelerating as I tried to kick and get my arms free.

Despite my struggle, the two men were able to get me around to the back of the vehicle, and it only took them a few seconds to fold my lanky body into the trunk. And then I heard the trunk door slam shut, and everything went completely pitch black.

Fuuuuck.

40

THE CAR TORE OUT OF ARTIE'S DRIVEWAY AT BREAKNECK SPEED, bouncing me around the trunk like a metal ball inside a pinball machine. Despite the fact that Chrysler 300s had fairly large trunks, I still felt like I was stuck in a sardine can. I had to lie with my long legs pressed up against my chest, and with my arms pinned behind my back, I found it difficult to take in deep breaths. In normal tightly confined spaces, I wasn't claustrophobic, but in this situation, with a bag over my head, inside a dark trunk, with my hands tied behind my back, and forced to take tiny shallow breaths, I found I had to force myself to relax so I could breathe at all.

Without the use of my arms, I struggled in vain to get the burlap bag off my head and torso. Music blared from the car's speakers, making it impossible to hear anything going on in the front of the car or outside.

At one point, I had to stop and give myself a little pep talk.

You got this, Drunk. You've been in many difficult situations before. Just relax. You'll find a way out of here. Relax!

When I finally allowed my limbs and shoulders to go slack, I found myself able to think a little more clearly. I discovered that if I wriggled down an inch or two and lifted my head, using it to press the bag back, I gathered a little slack and the bag moved up my body a little bit. So on and on I went, feeling the bag inching its way up my torso like a snake shedding its skin. Finally it was over my head. Even though it was still a small dark space, I could breathe better without the hot, rough material pressing against my nose and mouth.

Once I was free, I rolled onto my side and hunted for what I knew should be there—a glow-in-the-dark T-shaped emergency trunk release. They were standard now on cars this new. My eyes scanned the dark walls in confusion.

It has to be here.

When the car braked, I felt around for it as best as I could, then suddenly they'd take off again and I'd struggle not to be tossed around. Finally, I felt where I was sure a trunk release latch should be on the inside of the trunk lid, but all I felt was a broken cable. I was sure that the latch had been intentionally disabled. I wished I had my gun on me so I could've shot my way out of the trunk, and so I had something to protect myself when I finally was let out.

The combination of the hot trunk, the lack of air, and the sudden stopping and starting and the unexpected turns made for quite the nauseating ride. By the time the car came to an actual stop where I felt the engine shut off and the music go dead, I was ready to hurl.

But instead of letting me out immediately, I heard two car doors slam and then nothing.

"Let me outta here, you fuck boys!" I hollered, pounding on the inside lid of the trunk. I was met by only a deafening silence.

So with no clue how long I might be stuck in the cramped space, I fought the urge to vomit with everything I had. I swallowed hard several times and focused on my breathing.

Frustrated and nauseous, I continued to search for a way

out of the trunk, but found nothing. At some point, the sweltering heat and the combined nausea overwhelmed me and I couldn't take it anymore. I emptied my innards of the huge lunch I'd just had with Al in the furthest corner of the trunk, then tried to scoot away from the nasty-smelling remnants.

I was pretty sure I was just about to pass out from the smell and lack of oxygen when finally, after what seemed like an eternity, I heard a noise and then voices coming towards me. My heart sped up, and I tried to prepare myself for whatever I was about to face. The thought crossed my mind that I might be killed the second the trunk opened.

"So ya just took him?" said one of the guys, his rough voice muffled by the trunk's lid.

"We thought it'd be easier that way."

"Ah you stupid? That's not easier. Now we gotta figga out what to do with him."

The trunk popped open, letting light into the otherwise dark place. I squinted so hard into the light that my eyes went closed, but just before they closed, I managed to catch sight of three men and three guns all staring down at me.

So this is how it ends. I kept my eyes pinched shut. Waiting for the moment when my head exploded, I said my final goodbyes.

Bye, Mom.

Later, Pops.

Love you both.

Mikey, Al, Frankie, it's been real. It's been fun. But it hasn't been real fun. Just kidding. I love you all.

"Oh my God, it stinks in there," said one of the voices.

"You fuckin' puked in my cah, you sonavabitch? Ya gonna clean that up, ya little bastard. Ya fuckin' morons let'm puke in my cah."

"How was we s'posed to know he was pukin' in ya car? We was up there."

With the trunk now open and fresh air raining in on me, I realized that I recognized the voices. I cracked one eye open and peered up at the men. They were all standing up straight now, their guns more relaxed, and they were looking at each other instead of me.

"Hey," I shouted up at them. "You're the motherfuckers who shot me outta my boat last week."

The two men who'd grabbed me from Artie's front porch exchanged a wide-eyed look. I hadn't seen their faces that day because they'd been wearing masks, but their East Coast accents had been strong. I was sure it was them.

The stoutest of the three men, a dark-haired Vinnie-looking guy, pointed his gun down at me. "What'd you just say?"

"You heard me. You're the motherfucking asshats who shot me outta my boat last week and made me swim to shore. I'd recognize your voices anywhere."

"Get'm outta the cah," barked Vinnie, keeping his gun trained on me.

The two on either side of him jumped when he said so. The one on the right, a slicked-back blond anemic-looking guy with pock-marked skin and a neck covered in tattoos, grabbed me by the arm first. The one on the left, a black fellow with no hair on top of his head but an afro beneath his chin, as if his hair had slipped off his head and fallen under his face and he'd forgotten to pull it back up, grabbed my legs and pulled them out.

When they'd managed to get me out of the trunk and stand me up straight I stared at the black guy. I wanted to ask him if he was part Amish or something with that ridiculous beard, but as he had his gun pointed at my brains, I restrained myself.

"So whadda we do wid'm?" asked the tatted-up blond guy.

"Let's put him in the back," said Vinnie, cocking his head towards the back of the building.

"Or you could lemme go. I mean, either way, it's cool," I added with a shrug.

"Get movin'!" He kicked me in the back of the leg, making my knee buckle.

"Fuck! You don't have to be a dick about it. Jeez. I'm going, I'm going." As I started walking, I realized I was in an autogarage of some type. There were three vehicles in the garage, but otherwise, not much else.

They took me to the back of the garage, where there was a door that led into a small room. The top half of the door was glass, but it was so grimy and filthy that it was just as opaque as the wooden bottom. The room itself was empty, with the exception of a single metal swivel chair with a padded seat and a metal shelf up against one wall.

I was pretty sure that at one time, the room's walls had been blue, but now they looked brown. The padded top of the rolling chair, which looked like it had been white once in its life, was also brown and looked like someone had taken a shit on it and then smeared it all over and left it to dry.

"Siddown," hollered Blondie, the words one long drawn-out phrase.

I stared at the chair in horror. I'd rather put a campfire out with my face than to sit on that chair. "On the chair?"

"No, you asshole. On the fuckin' throne over there. Yeah, on the chair."

I turned around to face him again. "I'll just stand if you don't mind."

"Sit down!" shouted the Amish guy, shoving me by the shoulder onto the filthy chair.

My face curled into a disgusted wince as the Amish guy and Blondie set about tying me to the chair. "You dig this thing out from beneath a porta-potty or something?"

"This place was an auto garage once," said the Amish guy.

"So you're saying the mechanics used this as their shitter?"

"It's just grease."

"Sure it is. I'd wash my hands before I ate anything if I were you."

"Shut up."

Wearing shorts, I tried to keep my bare legs from touching the metal parts of the chair. "You might not have a problem with germs, but some of us are allergic. I'd take some hand sanitizer if you've got any. Preferably a forty-gallon bucket. I'll just dip my whole body in it when we're done here."

When Blondie and Amish guy were done tying me up, they stood up and looked at the doorway, where Vinnie stood supervising.

"Now what should we do?" Blondie asked him.

"I'll have to talk to the boss and tell'm what a coupla fuckin' idiots he's got workin' for him."

I glanced over at Blondie, whose head now hung slightly. Vinnie's words had wounded his pride.

"Hey, cheer up, pal. I think you're doing a real bang-up job." I figured making friends with the people who had the power to kill me couldn't be all bad.

Blondie pointed his gun at me as he snarled, "Shut up."

"What I'm sensing here is a little displaced anger," I said with a knowing nod. "Tell me about your life as a child. Were your parents absent? Or is it just Vinnie that's got you bent?"

"Vinnie?" said Blondie, jerking his head back. "Who the hell is Vinnie?"

I bobbed my head in the direction of the stout, dark-haired guy who I'd named Vinnie in my head. "That guy."

Vinnie frowned. "Vinnie? My name ain't Vinnie, it's Cholly."

"Cholly?" I wrinkled my nose. "The fuck kind of name is Cholly? Jolly Cholly?"

"Not Cholly. *Cholly*." He said it slower and louder the second time, as if that made it better.

"That's what I said. Cholly."

"Whatsamatta with ya? Ya can't talk right? His name's Cholly," said Blondie.

I stared blankly at the men, then I looked around the empty room. "You got anyone around here who speaks English?"

The black Amish guy rolled his eyes. "His name's Charlie, smart-ass."

"*Ohhhh, Charrrrlie,*" I said, emphasizing the r. "Like Charlie Brown."

"No, not like Cholly Brown, you fuckin' moron. Like Cholly Chaplin," said the Vinnie/Cholly guy.

I shook my head. "What's the difference?"

"One's a fuckin' cahtoon character, ya idiot. I ain't no fuckin' cahtoon, wiseass."

"First I'm an idiot and then I'm a wiseass? Isn't that kind of an oxymoron?"

"Hey!" Blondie shouted, pointing his finger in my face. "Watch who you callin' an oxy-whatchamacallit."

"I wasn't—" In that moment, I wished stupidity was painful to the owner and not the receiver. I shook my head. "Never mind."

But Charlie was looking at me, one eyebrow cocked up curiously. "So *you're* Autie." He shook his head. "Why didn't ya tell us that on the boat? When we told ya to give yaself a message?"

I looked at him in confusion. "What do you mean?" Then I looked at the other guys. "I'm not Artie."

"O' course ya Autie. We saw ya comin' outta ya house," said Blondie.

"I was coming out of *Artie's* house, yes. I was looking for someone. That doesn't make me Artie."

"O' course it does," he argued.

"No, you fucking morons. Me coming outta Artie's house doesn't make me Artie any more than you coming out of a Chinese restaurant makes you Chinese."

The three of them turned to stare at one another, as if their shared brain needed to reset the network connection before they could figure out what to do next. Charlie motioned for his two accomplices to step back to have a word with him.

This gave me my first quiet minute to process all the information I'd received. And for the first time, I was able to put two and two together. These were the asshats that had shot me out of my boat. Which meant they were the ones that had vandalized the Seacoast Majestic and knocked out Marcus. Perhaps they'd been responsible for blowing up *The Bloody Marauder* too. And if they'd done that, then it wasn't too far-fetched to think that *they* might also be the people responsible for the fire over at the Crystal Point Resort.

"Hey," I said, giving a nod towards them and breaking up their little private conversation. "You're the guys that fucked with the fireworks too, aren't you? You blew up our ship."

The Amish guy and Charlie both practically got whiplash as their necks snapped looking over at Blondie. The simple gesture practically *admitted* to me that *he'd* been the culprit. I couldn't fucking believe it. Now I *had* to find out who they were working for. There was no possible way that one of these three was the *brains* of this ridiculous operation, plus Charlie had mentioned talking to the boss only a minute ago.

But Blondie wasn't going to accept responsibility. He stuck his chin out obstinately. "You ain't gonna pin me for nuttin'."

"You did the Crystal Point fire too, didn't you?" I nodded at him knowingly.

"Ya better shut ya fuckin' mouth before I shut it for ya," he snapped.

"I wanna speak with your boss. We have business to discuss." I said it to them firmly and then turned my head and stuck my nose up in the air, like that was all I had to say.

In my peripheral vision, I could see Charlie, Blondie, and the Amish guy staring at me.

I could tell I'd stumped them.

Charlie pointed at me. "You betta not go anywhere."

I looked down at the chair I was tied to. "The fuck you think I'm gonna go?"

He nodded his head as if to say *damn straight*, then spun on his heel and headed out the door. Amish guy and Blondie followed closely behind. Blondie slammed the door shut, making the glass rattle in its frame and leaving me alone in the small office tied to the shitty chair.

41

With the Bostonians gone, I stood up, holding the filthy chair to my ass, and walked over to the half-glass door. I tried peering out the window, but it was too dirty to see through. I winced as I tried to get a shoulder up against the window to clean it off. With my shoulder pressed to the glass, I squatted up and down several times. Then I squatted low and looked through the glass. All I'd managed to do was smear the glass. I opened my mouth and breathed on the window, then quickly used my shoulder again. It was better. I repeated the process two more times until I could finally see out the window.

The black Chrysler 300 that had picked me up was parked there, as was a silver Lexus and a black Denali. There were three overhead doors whose windows had been papered and a regular door with papered windows, but I could see light filtering in through and around the paper. I couldn't see anyone in the garage.

All I knew in that moment was, I had to get to that door.

I turned around, giving my back to the door, stood on my tiptoes, and with one solid twist hit the glass with the legs of the chair. I didn't put enough muscle behind the hit, because the chair only managed to bounce off the door, making my body rattle and the zip ties dig into my wrists. I winced. Gathering my breath and all my strength, I twisted again and unwound. This time, I shattered the glass.

With my hands still holding the chair to my ass, I turned sideways and struggled, but managed, to get the knob turned and the door opened. Knowing I probably only had a few seconds before I was made, I hobbled towards the exterior door. I'd gotten about three-quarters of the way when I heard a voice behind me.

"Make another move and it'll be your last."

Closing my eyes, I froze.

Fucking fuck fuck fuck.

"Now turn around. Slowly."

Letting out a sigh of frustration, I turned around to come face-to-face with none other than my old pal Remy. Flanking him on both sides were his merry band of misfits, each of them holding guns on me.

"Remy?"

"Mr. Balladares. We meet again." Remy's hands rolled over one another just in front of his stomach, as if he were just itching to hit me again.

"Mr. Balladares?" I said, making a face. And in that moment everything came together. He thought I was Artie too. That was why he'd hit me that day at the clothing store! He'd thought I was Val's new man!

"He says he's not *Autie*," said Charlie. "But we caught'm coming outta Val's new place."

"Yeah, well, *lying* is precisely what liars are known for, now isn't it, Charles?"

I thought about trying to convince him that I was telling the truth, but then I thought maybe I'd find out more information if he thought I was Artie. I had to know if he'd been the one to burn down the Crystal Point Resort. That would make sense now—if this were all about Val. Maybe Remy wanted to frame Artie to get him out of the picture.

The thought gave me a moment's pause. If he wanted Artie out of the picture so bad, and he thought *I* was Artie, then wouldn't it stand to reason that me might want me dead? I swallowed hard.

"You want us to kill'm, boss?" asked Blondie.

"Oh, come on now, you don't want me *dead*. What good am I to you dead?" I asked.

"What good are you to us alive?" he retorted.

My brows went up. "Shit. I don't know. I'm pretty good at jokes. Knock knock."

Blondie smiled. "Who's there?"

"Little old lady."

"Little old lady who?" he repeated.

I sniggered.

Blondie frowned at me. "What's so funny?"

"I didn't know you could yodel."

Charlie laughed. "Ha. He got you, Denny."

I frowned and looked at Blondie. "Wait. Your name's Denny? And you're Remy and Cholly?" I looked over at the black Amish guy. "What are you? Larry? Billy? Bobby?"

"Nah. He's Ennis," said Denny.

I nodded. "Ah. *Ennis*. Of course. I really should've guessed."

"Are you guys done? Can we get down to business now?" asked Remy.

"Oh, sorry, boss," said Charlie. "You want us to kill'm now?"

I let my head fall back on my shoulders and my mouth gaped open. "Ugh. There we go with *that* again. That's so *unoriginal*." I lifted my head and looked at Remy. "Can't we start with like a civilized conversation first?"

Remy bobbed his head towards the concrete floor. "Have a seat."

Hoping it would buy me a minute or more, I took a seat on my chair.

"What would you like to talk about? How you stole my girl?"

"So Val's your girl, huh?" My head bobbed as my lips pursed. "I wondered."

His face burned red. "She didn't tell you about me?"

I lifted a shoulder. "Meh, we don't like to talk much about her days *in the business*."

"Ah. So she hasn't told you that she was my best girl?"

"Best girl as in your girlfriend, or best girl as in best—"

"She made me the most money, let's just leave it at that."

I looked at him then. "Ahh. So you were her pimp?"

"Who in the hell did you think I was? Her father?"

"I don't know. An ex-boyfriend. An ex-john. I wasn't sure, to be honest."

Charlie and the guys chuckled.

"Remy don't date no hoes," said Charlie.

And suddenly, out of nowhere in particular, I didn't like the fact that Charlie had just referred to Valentina Carrizo as a ho. And then it hit me how Artie had felt about me referring to Val as a hooker or a prostitute. It dehumanized her, and Val didn't seem to deserve that. Hearing someone else look at her as an object and not a person—it jumped up and punched me in the gut. I'd been an asshole.

"Let's not call her that, shall we, fellas?"

Charlie laughed. "And why the hell not? That's what she is."

"Not anymore."

"Once a ho, always a ho."

I gritted my teeth. "I mean it. Val's a good girl. I don't appreciate you calling her that."

"Oh yeah? And whatchu gonna do about it?" Charlie walked right up to me and gave me a smack across the jaw with the back of his hand.

My head snapped sideways. Gritting my teeth, I looked up

at Charlie, my mouth set in a grimace. "How about you untie me and try that again?"

"How 'bout I *don't* untie you and just do it again anyways?" he snapped, pulling his hand back to hit me again.

"Down, Charles," said Remy smoothly.

Charlie's hand hung in the air. "But, boss…"

"Why don't the three of you go check on things out front for me?"

With narrowed eyes, Charlie looked back down at me again. I could see it in his eyes that he badly wanted to finish that hit. But he did as instructed, backing up without another word. He turned and walked towards a grey metal side door. "Let's go, fellas."

After the three of them filed out and the heavy door closed behind them, Remy sighed. "Oh my goodness. It is *so* hard to find good help. Of course, I'm sure you know that, owning a business and all as well."

"Yeah, I hear ya. You should meet my head of resort security. He's a real smart-ass. Anyway, as your guys were telling me, I've got Denny to thank for my boat exploding then?"

Remy's lips pressed together into a tight line and his head crooked slightly to the side. "They told you that?"

I nodded.

"Idiots." He sighed. "I heard through the grapevine that you were planning to propose to Val that night. I couldn't let that happen."

I frowned. "How the hell'd you hear that?"

He considered me for a second and then shrugged. "It's actually a funny thing. Your fireworks guy mentioned it to his barber, who just happened to be one of Val's better customers. He came running right over to me asking me if it was true that Val was getting married."

"Ahh. That makes sense," I said, nodding.

"You know, I'm not going to let you do it."

"What's that?"

"Marry her. She's mine and she always will be mine. I'd hoped I could just scare you off, but it looks like I'm going to have to come up with a more permanent solution to our little problem."

"*Val* doesn't seem to think she's yours. And that's what matters. Even if you kill me right here today, Val's leaving your little business. She wants out. She wants a better life. And don't you think she deserves that?"

"Val deserves whatever I give her, and that's that. She owes me a lot, you know. I brought her here. From Colombia. She has me to thank for that."

"I tell you what, Rem. Why don't you let *me* pay off whatever it is that she owes you, then the two of you call it even?"

Remy laughed. "Oh, you're funny, Artie." He pointed at me. "Can I call you Artie?" Without waiting for me to respond, he kept going. "In my line of business, it doesn't work like that. Her debt can't be paid off that easily."

"I have a lot of money."

"Yes. I'm sure you do," he mused, tapping his chin lightly as if he were briefly debating if he wouldn't be willing to sell her to me.

"We could work something out."

"No. I don't think we could. I think I'll just take back what's mine."

"By killing me?"

"It makes the most sense, don't you think?"

"Not really. I think your other plan was better."

He frowned at me. "What other plan?"

"The one where you frame me for arson and send me up the river."

42

Remy stared at me hard. Tipping his head to the side, he seemed to give my words some careful consideration. "I think the idea definitely has merit."

"I'm sure you do. That's why you did it."

His mouth curled into a devious grin. "Did it?"

"Oh, no need to play coy with me. Your boys admitted it." It was a lie, but I had to feel him out. I couldn't read him. "It was a brilliant plan, really."

After a long pause, he finally threw his hands up, frowning. "I'm sorry. I'd love to play along, but I'm too curious. I honestly have no idea what you're talking about. What did my boys admit to?"

"Obviously, burning down the Crystal Point Resort."

His face registered only a complete and utter lack of awareness. I could see it in his eyes. He literally had *no idea* what I was talking about.

"That *was* you, wasn't it?"

"I heard about the fire," he said, frowning. "Val mentioned it, but she didn't tell me that you were suspected of burning it down."

My eyes narrowed. "So you *are* still in contact with Val."

A dark shadow passed over Remy's face. "Of course I am," he snapped. "I told you. She'll always be mine."

"But you're saying that you had *nothing* to do with the fire?"

"Unfortunately, I did not. Thought it would've been brilliant, and perhaps I should've taken credit for it, I did not have involvement," he chuckled. "I don't know why my guys would've admitted to doing that. It must've been some kind of misunderstanding."

I nodded. "Speaking of misunderstandings, I think there's something else you should know."

Closing his eyes, Remy held his hands up as if to stop me. "If it's about how much you love Val and she's turned your world upside down, save it. I don't want to hear about it. Okay?"

"Yeah, no. It's not about that. In fact, the truth of the matter is, Val's not even my girl."

Remy's left brow quirked up in the middle. "Look, just because my guys in there are about as gullible as they come doesn't mean their idiocy rubbed off on me. All right? I'm the boss for a reason. You don't just propose to a hooker for shits and giggles."

"No, I'm serious. I didn't propose."

He wagged a finger at me, smiling. "You know, if it hadn't been for one of my girls just happening to see the announcement in the newspaper this morning, I might actually believe you."

"I don't know what to say. I think you should believe me."

"She showed it to me," he said frowning. "I know you and Val are planning to marry. And like I said, Artie, I just can't let that happen." He pulled a gun out that had been holstered under his suit jacket and pointed it down at my face.

"But that's just it, Rem. I already told you. I'm. Not. Artie."

Smiling, he shook his head. "You really think I buy your bullshit?"

I squinched my eyes shut and looked at him out of the corner of one eye. "It's the truth, Remy."

He gave his gun a little bounce. "You know, it's offensive how stupid you think I am. I *saw* you and Val together shopping. And my guys got you coming out of your house. I *know* you're Artie."

"Look. Unless you *witnessed* me coming outta Artie's momma's vajayjay, I'm afraid you're wrong. I'm a *friend* and *employee* of Artie's. I live next door to him and Val. Your friends just happened to catch me coming out of Artie's place today because I was looking for Val."

"But you were shopping with her the other day."

"As a favor to Artie. He asked me to take her shopping for an engagement dress. He was planning to propose, and he asked for my help. Look, if you'll remember, before you punched my face, I introduced myself to you."

Remy frowned at me, like he was trying to recall what I'd said before he'd punched me. "Yeah, as Artie."

"No. I said, 'Hey, how's it going. I'm Drunk.' You said, 'Yeah, well, I'm not,' and then you punched me and almost broke my nose."

Remy stared at me for a long moment and then nodded. "I do remember you saying you were drunk. But what's that got to do with anything?"

"My *name* is Drunk. Danny Drunk."

Remy laughed. "Sure it is."

"I'm serious. I'm not Artie."

Remy stared at me then, not sure what to believe. He shook his head and pointed his gun at me again. "Nah. You're just pulling my chain."

My head rolled back on my shoulders. "I'm dead-ass serious. Look, my wallet's in my truck back at the Seacoast Majestic or I'd show you. You said you saw Artie's engagement announcement in the paper. I assume there wasn't a picture, but does that mean you get the paper here?"

"Yeah, out front."

I had to think back to what day it was that Al had seen my picture in the paper. "It was the Sunday before last." My head bobbed. "Grab the Sunday paper. My picture's in it. There's a story about me."

"You were in the paper? For what?"

"You can read all about it when you see it. Then you'll know I'm telling you the truth."

"I think it'd just be easier to kill you."

"Then you'd be killing the wrong guy, and Artie would still be out there. Okay? Would you just go look for the fucking paper!"

"Ugh. You're really turning into a pain in my ass."

"Same. Just go look."

He moved to the door and pulled it open, putting his foot between the door and the jamb to keep it propped open. Then he stuck his head inside. "Charles!"

Seconds later. "Yeah, boss?"

"Go get me the stack of newspapers in my office. They're on the floor under my desk."

"All of 'em, boss?"

"Yeah, just grab the whole stack and bring it here."

"Sure thing, boss."

Remy and I stared at each other while we waited for Charlie to bring the papers in. Minutes later, he appeared with a big cardboard box. Charlie had thrown all the papers in haphazardly, and they stuck out in every direction.

"Sorry, boss, I couldn't find anything to put 'em in."

Remy groaned as he looked down at the mess. "You got 'em out of order, Charles. I just wanted you to carry them out here to me like they were. You couldn't just do that, could you?"

Scratching the back of his head, Charlie looked down at the mess blankly. "Oh. Uh. Sorry, boss. I didn't know whatcha—"

"It's fine, Charles. I got it. You can go back up front now."

Charlie slipped away with a nod before his boss could say anything else.

Remy squatted down to rifle through the box.

I watched him for a whole minute before I cleared my throat. "You know, if you untied me I could help you find it. It'd be faster that way."

He sighed. I could tell he didn't like that idea, but he also didn't like not knowing the truth about who he was about to kill. He reached out to spin me around. Then he cut my zip ties with a pocket knife and spun me back around again.

Thankful as hell to finally have my hands free, I pulled my hands together to rub my sore wrists.

"No funny business."

"Yeah, yeah." Even though I badly wanted to punch the guy in his smug face for having punched me days prior, he was the one with the gun, not me. I needed to restrain myself for the time being.

The two of us worked quietly, rifling through the papers until finally I found the right one. "Ah. Got it." I flipped through the pages until I found the picture of myself in my fedora and shades. I showed it to him. "See? That's me. Daniel Drunk."

Remy snatched the paper from my hand and read the article. *"Newest Islander Takes Down the PGC."* He looked at me then, eyes wide. "Holy shit, that was *you*?"

I shrugged.

He kept reading. *"Officer Drunk of the Kansas City, Missouri Police Department..."* He looked at me again. "You're a police officer?"

I rolled my eyes. *"Was* a police officer. Back in the States. I'm not anymore."

"So you're really not Artie, then?"

"That's what I told you."

His eyes widened as he stared back down at the paper. He scanned the rest of the article and then looked up at me again.

"There's a lot of guys who want you dead for bringing down the PGC."

I swallowed hard, hoping that Remy wasn't one of those guys. "Oh yeah?"

He nodded. "I had a lot of clients in the PGC."

I swallowed hard. "Oh yeah?"

"Yeah. Most of them are in jail now."

Fuck.

"Huh. Well, sorry about that, I guess." I lifted my hands in an awkward shrug.

"I should fucking kill you myself." He pointed his gun at me again.

I smiled at him, holding my hands up on either side of myself. "You really don't have to do that. I wouldn't hold it against you if you just let me go."

Remy laughed. "You know, the more I think about it, you're actually more valuable to me alive."

I lifted one hand to my chin in a thoughtful position and gave it a little rub, nodding. "I like the sound of that. Keep talking."

"I bet you could fetch a pretty penny for those wanting to get some revenge."

Panic froze my limbs. "I'm sorry. What?"

He nodded. "Yeah. You know. I think that's what we'll do. If I put the word out I've got *Officer Danny Drunk* here, I bet there will be a bidding war over who gets to be the one to kill him."

"Uh-huh. Uh-huh," I said, nodding. "*Or*—just hear me out —or, I could round up some cash to give you *instead* of you selling me to one of them."

Remy grinned. "Nah. I think I like my idea better." He opened the door to the front and hollered inside again. "Charles! Get me John Oakley on the phone. I got something he might want!"

43

REMY AND THE BOSTONIAN MISFITS (SOUNDS LIKE A SWEET NAME for a band name, doesn't it?) spent the rest of the afternoon working out a plan to sell me to John Oakley, some guy who apparently had a major bone to pick with me. When they finally got the go-ahead to make the handoff, Remy ordered Charlie to load me back up into the Chrysler 300.

I made a face as the memory of my purge session took hold of me. "Can't we take one of these other cars?"

Remy frowned at me. "What's it to you which car we take?"

"Ah, he made a mess in the back of Cholly's car, boss," said Denny.

"A mess?"

"Yeah, sonovabitch tossed his cookies," said Charlie. "Smells like the inside of a dumpster back there. I can't drive it until I hose it out or sumpin'."

Remy glanced over at me and then pulled his keys out of his pocket and tossed them to Charlie. "Fine. Take my car." He pointed at Charlie. "But you put a scratch on it and I'll have your ass in a sling."

"I got it, boss. I'll be careful, don't worry," said Charlie. He nodded towards the silver Lexus parked on the end. "Boys, put him in the back. I'll be right there."

Remy gave me a little salute before Denny and Ennis dragged me away. "It's been real, Officer Drunk. You have a great day now. It's about to be your last."

Denny and Ennis forced me into the trunk of Remy's car, folding my body in like an accordion.

Suffering with my legs up by my chin, I whined. "Oh, come on, guys. My body don't bend like this. Can't I just sit in the backseat?"

"No! And you puke in the boss's car and I'll shoot you. Got it?" snarled Denny, pressing the cold muzzle of his gun to my forehead.

"Yeah, yeah. I got it. I got it. Jeez."

He slammed the trunk on me and then I heard Charlie's voice.

"Get in the cah, fellas. I ain't got all day. Let's go."

As the car began to move, my eyes immediately began to look for a way out. I couldn't let myself get handed over to John Oakley. I didn't know him, but I was already sure I didn't like him.

And then I saw it.

The T-shaped latch on the inside of the trunk lid, glowing in the dark like a fucking beacon of hope.

I knew what it did. I only had to find the right time to pull it and hope that it worked.

I had no idea how far we were going. John Oakley could be up the street or he could be on the other side of the island, but I didn't want to take the chance. I'd plan that I didn't have a lot of time. I needed to get out sooner rather than later, yet far enough away from Remy's place that I wouldn't be busted.

And as much as it would've been easier to escape when the car was stopped at a light or something, I knew they were more likely to feel my weight fall out of the trunk and I'd be dead within seconds. I had to do it when the car was moving so if they did feel me, I'd have at least a few seconds to get away before they got out of the car and could chase after me.

So as soon as I felt them accelerate, I pulled the latch. The trunk popped open, but I held it from popping up too high into their rearview mirror and alerting them that I'd opened it. I peered out at the street. There was a car behind us with a female driver. If I rolled out now, she'd hit me for sure.

I waved at the car, trying to get the driver's attention, but the woman was talking animatedly on her phone, oblivious to my hand sticking out of the trunk. We drove through an intersection and she took a right.

Now's your chance!

I kicked out one leg and then the other and then closed my eyes. I knew it was going to hurt like hell and probably tear off some skin, but I was pretty sure a bullet to the skull and whatever beating or mutilation John Oakley had in store for me would hurt much worse. So I sucked in a deep breath and pushed myself out of the trunk.

I rolled out of the vehicle in a lump, rolled twice, and when I came to a stop, I was staring at the back end of the Lexus as it drove away. Charlie and the boys didn't stop despite the fact that the lid had popped up.

And now there was only one thing on my mind.

I had to run like hell.

With my pulse racing and my knees and elbows burning from the gravel-covered road rash I didn't have time to inspect, I climbed to my feet and took off, running in a dead sprint to the nearest alley. With no idea how long it would be before Charlie noticed the trunk open, I couldn't afford to hesitate. I kept running, with no idea where to go. I had no phone, no wallet, and no idea exactly where I was. So I kept running until I came to a run-down little strip mall in a shitty part of town. I ran inside a little rent-to-own furniture store and up to the counter. An old man working behind the desk looked up at me.

"Can I use your phone?" My breathing was labored and my arms and knees were bloodied from the fall.

He stood up immediately and pointed towards the door. "Get outta here before I call the cops!"

My eyes widened. "Yes! Please. Call 'em! It's an emergency."

The man looked like he was going to kick me out again but then pursed his lips and picked up the receiver of his landline phone and dialed.

I gave him a huge smile and clapped my hands together. "Oh, thank you. Ask for Inspector Francesca Cruz. Please. Tell her it's an emergency and she needs to get here right away."

He didn't say a word to me but waited with one eye glued to me until the police answered. He told the officer who answered the phone that a man had burst into his building and he wanted Inspector Francesca Cruz to come right away. Then he hung up and pointed at the door. "You'll have to wait outside."

With my hands up, I backed away from his counter, nodding. "I understand. Will do! Thank you for calling. You probably just saved my life."

The man gave me a chin-up nod but didn't say anything else.

I went outside and hid, crouching behind a dumpster in the alley until I heard the sirens.

I poked my head around the corner to see that sure enough, it was Frankie. I breathed a sigh of relief and stood up just as she got out of her car.

"Danny?" Frankie looked shocked when she saw me come around the corner, bloodied and bruised. "What happened to you?"

"It's a really long story, but oh my God, I'm so glad to see you. Can you gimme a ride back to the Seacoast?"

She frowned at me. "Late for a hot date?"

My eyes shifted around the neighborhood nervously.

"Look, Frankie, can we talk about this in the car? I'm in a little bit of danger right now, and I'd prefer to get outta here before someone decides to put a bullet in my head."

Annoyed, but obviously concerned, Frankie looked around before climbing back into the driver's seat. "Yeah. Get in the car."

44

"So what's going on, Danny? What happened to you?"

As we drove, I kept a close watch on her car's side mirror and shot furtive glances down back alleys, keeping a watch out for the silver Lexus. "It's kind of a long story."

"Well, if I'm driving you back to the Seacoast, I suppose we have time for a long story."

I sighed. "Some guys grabbed me earlier today. They thought I was Artie."

"Artie!" Frankie looked over at me.

"Yeah. It was Val's old pimp, Remy. The guy who gave me that shiner the other day."

"Ah. I knew something was up with that. But I don't understand. Why did the guy think you were Artie?"

"Just a misunderstanding. But then it occurred to me that maybe they were the ones responsible for burning down Sly Smallwood's resort."

"What?"

"They were the ones that shot me out of my boat and set our ship on fire."

Frankie looked over at me in shock. "How in the world do you know that?"

"Shockingly, I got them to admit it."

"You seriously expect me to believe that they just came out and admitted it to you?"

I held up three fingers in a Boy Scout salute. "Swear. It wasn't that hard. I recognized the voices of the guys who shot me out of my boat. I took a leap and told them I knew it was them that set the ship on fire and they basically admitted it."

With her mouth gaping open, she shook her head. "I'm shocked."

I gave a little shrug and glanced in the side mirror again. "Meh, don't be. They aren't the sharpest peckers in the peter patch. I tried to get them to admit to burning down the Crystal Point too, but I don't think they did it."

"Why not? If they're responsible for the boat explosion and the vandalism, why wouldn't you think they started the fire?"

I squinted. "I don't know. I could just tell, I guess. I think I'm pretty good at reading people. When I said something about it to Remy, he honestly had no recognition in his face at all."

"So, if these guys had you, how'd you manage to escape?"

"They were going to sell me to some guy named John Oakley. Apparently he's got a bone to pick with me for taking down the PGC."

"Sell you to John Oakley!" Frankie looked stunned.

"Yeah. Know him?"

"He's a small-time insurance agent. We didn't have him on our list of names to take down. I'll look into it."

Even though she had her air conditioning on in the car, I rolled down my window. I felt a little unable to breathe. "Good. Look into this Remy character too, if you would."

"Yeah, I'll add him to my growing list of things to investigate."

I looked over at her, dead serious now. "I mean it, Frankie. He can't be on the back burner. This guy would've killed me if he didn't think he could make a couple bucks off me. I'm worried about Artie. He's not safe while that guy's on the loose."

Frankie sighed. "I'll put him at the top of my list."

"Thank you."

She shook her head as she stared at the road ahead of us. "Sergeant Gibson let so much slide when he was in charge. It's like Paradise Isle was the Wild Wild West for quite a long time. Getting it whipped into shape is going to take me some time."

Putting my elbow on the windowsill, I looked over at Frankie. "You don't have to do it all yourself. You know that, right?"

"I know that."

"Do you?"

"What's that supposed to mean?"

The warm island air blew my hair, drying the sweat that had made it damp when I'd run. "It just means you're allowed to have a life, Frankie. It's not *just* about work."

She shook her head. "Oh, no you don't."

"No I don't what?"

"We're not going back to that. We're not going to talk about me and you. There is no me and you. Not after the you and Erika thing."

"Oh, come on, Frankie. There is no me and Erika thing."

Frankie gave me a tight smile. "That's not true, Mr. Drunk, and you know it."

"Oh, now we're gonna start with the formalities again. Frankie, don't be like that. Please?"

"Inspector Cruz."

"Ugh." My head fell back on the headrest. I looked out the window and then looked at her again. "You know, *Frankie*, I don't know what you want from me. You shot me down cold. *Cold.* Pushed me in the fucking harbor cold."

"That was an accident."

I held a finger up in the air at her. "Pushed me in the *fucking* harbor cold. You don't wanna date me, but then you don't want other people dating me either? It doesn't work like that, Frankie. If we're not dating, I'm free to do whatever I want."

"Obviously."

"Please, don't *obviously* me."

"Look, Danny, you slept with another woman like five seconds after I turned you down. Obviously whatever feelings you had for me didn't run very deep if you were able to do that."

I threw my hands up. "Look. I don't know how deep my feelings went for you, Frankie. We've never even been on a date before! How am I supposed to know how I feel about you? All I know is that I liked you and I wanted to date you. I don't feel that way about very many women. But you didn't want any part of that, so when a beautiful woman came over to my place late at night wearing little to nothing and *begged* me to sleep with her—"

Frankie let out a little puff and rolled her eyes. "Begged? Oh, please—"

"Yes, *begged*! When a beautiful woman *begged* me to sleep with her, I relented. I would *never* do that if I was in a relationship with you, but we aren't *in* a relationship. You made that perfectly clear the other day."

"No, we're not," she said stiffly, staring out the window ahead of her.

"Exactly. So I don't understand how you can be mad at me."

"Who said I was mad?"

I stared at her hard. Why did women have to be so damn infuriating? *Who said I was mad?* Umm, I don't know. Your expression. Your attitude. Your demeanor. The tone of your voice. The way you're driving the damned car... pick one. I wanted to yell all of that at her, but I resisted.

Instead I swallowed it all back and with clenched teeth muttered, "Gut feeling."

"Fine. You know what my gut is telling me?"

"What, Frankie? What is your gut telling you?"

"It's telling me that it's very odd that you and Artie sent all those people from the Crystal Point Resort out on a night cruise and the next morning the resort burned to the ground."

I puffed air out my nose and shook my head softly. So we were done talking about us. She'd made it very clear.

Point taken.

"It was just a prank, Frankie. I swear to you. We didn't have anything to do with the fire."

"Maybe you didn't. But maybe Artie did. Ever think of that?"

"Artie didn't do it."

"You don't know that, Danny. Maybe he set this whole thing up and kept you in the dark. You gotta admit, that night cruise was awfully convenient."

"Artie would never. Besides, it wasn't even his idea to send all those people out on the night cruise."

"Yeah? It was your idea?"

"No, as a matter of fact. It was *Val's* idea." Just saying the words aloud made it all resonate in my mind.

Val.

Val was the one coming and going at weird hours. The hooker with the heart of gold that was still working for her pimp even though Artie had said that she'd left that all behind her. And she wasn't even sleeping with Artie. She had been missing the morning of the fire. And it had been *Val's* idea to get all those people out of the resort. *Val.* What if *she* was the one that had set Artie up? The thought had occurred to me before, and now I couldn't readily remember why I'd dismissed the idea!

Maybe this was all *Val's* doing?

But Frankie couldn't hear all the thoughts rushing through my mind then. She just kept chattering right on along. "Oh, Val!" said Frankie, nodding. "As if Artie couldn't have planted the idea in her head? I don't think that would've been very hard."

Staring off into the distance, I shook my head. "No. I was there when Val got the brochure. It was her idea. I'm sure of it." I glanced up the road. "Look, Frankie. Can you step on it? There's someone at the resort I need to speak with."

45

When Frankie turned into the Seacoast Majestic's driveway, the first thing I noticed was Gary Wheelan's Land Cruiser pulled up to a stop in front of the guard shack. I leaned forward to stare out Frankie's window at it as we pulled up.

"That's Gary's Land Cruiser. He hardly ever leaves the resort. I wonder where he's going."

Frankie pulled to a stop next to the vehicle. From the window we could see Gary behind the wheel wearing what appeared to be a tactical uniform. His face was smudged with grease or something, and he wore a tactical military bullet-proof vest with a handgun strapped to his chest.

Al was in the passenger seat holding a walkie-talkie and also wearing a tactical military vest with a camo hard hat dwarfing his head. In the back seat, Big Eddie, who looked like he'd just shit his shorts, was sandwiched between Ralph and Bob, who also wore bulletproof vests. Ralph had a rifle propped up on his lap and lying across one shoulder. They were all looking into the guard shack, speaking with Wilson.

"Is that Al in there?" Frankie asked incredulously.

I stared at them all hard, wondering what in the actual fuck they thought they were doing looking like the geriatric SWAT team. "Yeah. What the hell are they up to? Give the horn a blast, would you?"

Frankie gave a little *bup-bup* on her horn, and all necks in the FJ40 snapped around to look at us.

All five sets of eyes immediately widened. Gary and Ralph both rolled down their windows, and Al scooted over to lean across Gary's lap to look at me.

"What the hell is going on here? Is it stripper day down at the women's senior citizen center or something?"

"Drunk!" said Gary. "You're here!"

"Well, I'm sure as hell not anywhere else."

"We were just going out to look for you," Al shouted over Gary's lap.

"No shit?"

"Where you been?" asked Ralph.

"Long story." I frowned at the vehicle full of old men. "I don't understand. Why were you heading out dressed like a military brigade?"

"Because you got Drunknapped!" said Al. "We were gonna rescue you."

"Drunknapped?" A dumb smile made my mouth gape open. "How the hell'd you guys know that?"

"Al found your hat in front of Artie's house," said Gary.

"When I found the hat and you were nowhere to be found, I got worried. So I went to your office and checked the security tapes. I saw those two guys throw you in their trunk!" said Al.

Marveling, I shook my head. "Get outta here. *You* knew how to use my security software?"

"Well, Big Eddie had to help," said Al, hooking a thumb over his shoulder at the small man in the backseat.

Giving me a little flutter of his fingers, Eddie crooked an uncomfortable smile.

"Wow. I'm impressed, fellas." I suddenly felt both grateful for having such good friends and relieved that I'd stopped them before they'd gone out looking like that.

"I figured if you could do it, it couldn't be rocket surgery," said Al, giving me a little wink.

I rolled my eyes. "Thanks, Al."

"My pleasure. But I'm sure glad to see you got away."

"Me too. Thankfully Frankie picked me up."

"We all owe you one, little lady," said Ralph, giving her a smile.

"*You* don't owe me anything," said Frankie with a chuckle. She crooked her thumb over her shoulder at me. "This one, though—this one owes me a lot. But don't worry, I'm keeping score."

I smiled at them all. I was still in awe that they were willing to go to such great lengths to save me. "You guys were seriously gonna try and find me?"

"Of course we were," said Ralph. He patted his rifle. "We were ready for anything."

"I see that."

Gary frowned and looked over his shoulder at the rest of the guys. "So now who're we supposed to shoot?" He pulled the CZ 75 SP-01 Shadow out of the holster on his vest. "I just got this cutie. I was looking forward to finally getting to see what she's got."

I'd only heard about his new handgun a time or twenty in the last couple of weeks since he'd gotten it. He'd shown it to me once. It was a 9mm semiautomatic with an 18 double-stack magazine he'd custom-ordered from the Czech Republic and one badass of a weapon, way more than a retired security guard on a tropical island needed for casual protection.

I held up a steadying hand. "Simmer down there, Gunslinger. Trust me, it's better this way. You don't wanna hurt yourself."

As the guys all started chatting amongst themselves, Frankie looked over at me. "Look, Danny, I gotta get back to the station. I have a lot of work to do. I'll drop you off here so you can play with your friends."

I nodded and leaned over to give Frankie a quick kiss on the cheek. "Thanks for everything, Frankie. I appreciate all your help, as always." I climbed out of the vehicle and looked back inside the open window. "I know you're mad at me, but let's keep in touch, okay?"

She nodded. "I'll let you know when I find out anything about this Remy character."

"Thanks. I appreciate it."

The boys all waved at her as she pulled ahead and turned around to leave.

I held a finger up to the guys. "Gimme a second, fellas. I need to talk to Wilson." I walked around the vehicle to the guard shack, where Wilson was settling back into his chair.

The second he saw me, he stood up. "Drunk."

"Hey, Wilson. Listen, there are three specific vehicles that I need you to refuse entry without my permission. Okay?"

"Sure thing." He grabbed a notepad and pen from his counter and handed it to me.

I wrote down a description of the three vehicles I'd seen in Remy's garage. "But be careful. The men driving these vehicles are all armed and extremely dangerous. All right? You see them, you call the cops."

Wilson, also armed, was extremely somber when he nodded. He took his job very seriously. "Yes, sir. I'll be on high alert."

"Thank you."

I walked around the vehicle to Gary's open window and looked inside. "So. Did you guys seriously think you were going to be able to find me?"

"We had to try, Drunk. We couldn't just leave you hung out to dry!" said Gary.

I patted him on the shoulder. "Well, I appreciate that a lot. You have no idea, fellas."

"So how'd you manage to get away?" hollered Bob.

"And do you know who took you?" asked Eddie. "Y-you don't think they'll come *here* looking for you, do you?"

"If they do, we'll be ready," said Gary, patting his gun.

"Like I said, fellas. It's a really long story."

Ralph scooted away from the door. "Get in, get in. You can tell us all about it on the way back to Gary's."

I sighed. I was going to have to be strategic in the information I shared with the guys. Even though I now suspected Val of setting the fire, I wanted to speak to her before I spread a rumor I couldn't take back.

I climbed into the vehicle, forcing Ralph to shove over and Eddie to have to practically climb on Bob's lap. I stared across the back seat at them. Not only did Ralph have a rifle across his lap, but he also had a pistol strapped to his chest, as did Eddie and Bob. I shook my head. I couldn't believe these guys. They'd actually given Eddie a fucking gun.

"So what's the story?" asked Ralph the second his door slammed shut.

As Gary pulled a U-turn to head back down to his cottage I began. "For starters, the guys that nabbed me were working for a guy named Remy."

"Remy? What did he want *you* for?" asked Gary, looking back at me in his rearview mirror.

"They didn't exactly want *me*. They thought I was Artie."

"Artie?!" The voices in the car were unanimous in their shock.

"Why'd they think you were Artie?" asked Bob. "You don't look a thing like him."

"I actually met Remy the other day. You guys remember when Artie asked me to take Val into town shopping?"

"I remember. You came back the next day with that shiner," said Ralph, nodding.

"Yeah, well, that was courtesy of Remy. I didn't realize it then, but he thought I was Artie that day."

"No kiddin'," said Ralph. Then, as if his memory had just

kicked in, he snapped his fingers in the air. "Hey. You said you got that panda eye playing Jose Cuervo over at your place."

I groaned. "I lied, Weaz. That was a fucking lie."

"Drunk!" said Gary, his eyes snapping up to his mirror again. "You lied to us?"

"Guys, we're veering off track here. You're missing the main point of my story. Remy thought I was Artie. And then when his goons grabbed me earlier, I was coming out of Artie's house. I'd been looking for Val, and I guess they just assumed I was Artie then too."

"But that doesn't make any sense. What would they want with Artie?" asked Gary.

My eyes skirted the vehicle. "Look, fellas. I need you to be discreet here. Can I count on all of you to keep this between the six of us?"

"Of course you can, Drunk," said Gary.

All the rest of the heads in the vehicle bobbed.

"Fine. Remy is sort of—Val's old employer."

"Employer?" said Al, his bushy brows knitted together. "But I thought Val was a—" His head bobbed then, as his mouth formed a little O. "Ohhh."

When I saw the answer register on Al's face, I nodded. "Yeah. So, Remy's not very happy about Val leaving the business to marry Artie."

"So if you *had* been Artie, what were they going to do with you?" asked Eddie.

"I'm pretty sure if I *had* been Artie, I would've been fitted for a nice pair of concrete shoes."

"Concrete shoes?!" Eddie sucked in his breath. "You mean they were going to *kill* Artie?"

"I'm sure of it. In fact, I think with the wedding coming up fast, Artie's in a hell of a lot of danger until Frankie can find Remy and his little gang and get them behind bars."

"Does she think she can?" asked Gary.

"She's sure as hell gonna give it her best shot. I gave her as much information as I had about them."

Gary's eyes darted up to look in the rearview mirror. "Well, then, you know what this means, fellas?"

"That we're going to let the police handle it while we go finish our card game?" asked Eddie, his eyes hopeful.

"No. It means we're on active around-the-clock security detail for Artie until this Remy character is caught!"

Eddie's head fell into his hands.

Gary pulled his vehicle to a stop in front of his Pepto-Bismol-pink cottage and turned off the engine.

"I think that's a good idea," I said. "While you guys keep an eye on Artie, I need to have a word with Val and see what she knows about this Remy guy. I'm hoping she can give me an address I can give to Frankie."

"Great idea," said Gary.

"You want me to come with you, Drunk?" asked Al, looking back over his shoulder.

"I'd rather you help the guys keep a watch on Artie. I need to have a heart-to-heart with Valentina Carrizo, and I think it'll work best if I'm alone."

46

I found Val down at the beach just as the sun was beginning to set over Angel's Bay. The air was still warm, and the light, bouncy sound of Caribbean music followed me from the swim-up bar down to the water, where the dry rustle of palm trees and the soft sound of the water ebbing against the sand met me. A tranquil, salty breeze fanned my face and brought me the first sense of peace I'd had all day, reminding me that it was good to still be alive.

It had been a long, painful day and yet there was still more I wanted to accomplish before I hung up my fedora for the evening. I'd showered and changed into clean clothes, and now the skin on my knees and the palms of my hands burned and my legs felt stiff as I walked through the sand with a drink in one hand and one of Trinity's famous chicken wraps in the other.

As Manny had promised, Val was seated on a lounge chair only a few yards away from the water's edge. She wore only an orangey-red one-piece bathing suit—probably the first one-piece I'd even seen Val wear, though it might as well have been a two-piece for as much skin as it showed. The sides were cut up high over her hip bones, and the neckline plunged down to her navel, and the sides seemed barely able to contain her voluptuous assets. She had one deeply tanned leg propped up on her lounge chair and a beach towel folded up behind her head. Her eyes were closed, but since there were no more rays with which to tan, I could only assume that she'd fallen asleep.

Shoving the last half of my wrap into my mouth to hold, I pulled up a lounge chair and slid it over in the sand next to her and sat down. "Hey, Val," I said before taking a big bite out of my wrap.

Val opened one eye and turned her head to look at me. "*Hola*, Drunk. What are you doing here?"

"Oh, just grabbing a bite to eat. I saw you down here and thought I'd come say hello."

"Oh, that is so niiice," she purred, shooting me a megawatt Val smile.

"You want a drink?" I offered her my blended margarita.

"No, thank you."

I shrugged and washed down my bite with a big gulp of the pink slush. Pain immediately shot through the back of my throat and up my nose, settling at the base of my forehead between my eyes. "Shit," I breathed, pinching my nose and bearing down to stop the brain freeze.

"Put you tongue on the roof of you mouth," said Val.

I pressed my tongue upwards and when I felt the pain starting to recede, I took a bite of my grilled wrap, hoping the warmth would help ease my suffering. When I felt better, I nodded. "Damn, I hate those things. Thanks for the tip."

"No problem. When I was a *leetle* girl, my sister and I used to buy *raspados* after we go swimming. It is like—how you call it? Ice in a cup with the color syrup?"

"Like a snow cone?"

Val lit up. "Yes! Like a snow cone. It was so delicious, but it always give me the pain there." She tapped her forehead. "My mother tell me put my tongue on roof of my mouth and it stop. I never forgot."

I nodded as I chewed, and I realized that aside from what she'd done for a living before coming to live with Artie, I really didn't know very much about Valentina Carrizo. "Is your mother still living in Colombia?"

"Oh no," she said, shaking her head. "My mother die a few years before I come here. She was very young."

"Oh, I'm sorry. How'd she die?"

"She have the cancer in the breast," she said quietly. "But we don't know until it was too late."

"Wow. I'm really sorry to hear that."

She nodded and then looked at me. "You know, these are no real." She cupped both breasts.

I gave her a crooked smile and lifted my brows. "You don't say?"

She gave me a tight smile. "After my mother die, my sister and I have the tests."

"The tests?"

"You know, if I will get breast cancer like my mother."

I nodded like I knew what she was talking about. "Oh, right."

"The doctor say I have the thing that say I get cancer someday."

"You're kidding?"

She shook her head. "No. My sister no get it. Just me. So I have the surgery and they take the old ones and I get new improve ones."

I stared at her a little. I didn't know what to say to that. It had never occurred to me that Val's augmented breasts had been done because of her health. I'd just assumed that she'd done it purely for the curves and, if I were being honest, because I assumed she *wanted* them for her line of work. And now I felt like an asshole because Val had just opened up to me about something *real* and *private* in her life, and the only reason I was even talking to her was because I wanted to find out if she'd framed Artie for the fire and ask her how to find Remy.

I swallowed hard and nodded at her. "Well, the new ones look nice. Real nice."

She smiled at me. "*Muchas gracias*." She gave me a little wink. "I think so too." She sat up in her seat and swiveled around so her feet were flat on the sand. "Well, maybe I go home. I no realize it getting so late. Artie probably ready eat supper with me."

"Can we talk for a second before you rush off?" I asked, putting my margarita down in the sand. Condensation rolled off the sides of the glass, landing in the sand and curdling the grains around the base.

"Talk? Sure?" said Val with a curious shrug. "What you would like talk about?"

"Well, can I just be honest with you?"

"Yes, of course."

"Remember that guy that punched me at Miss Donna's the other day?"

Val's face fell. "Oh, yes. I remember."

"His name was Remy, right?"

Val's head bobbed, her eyes wide.

"You didn't tell me much about him then. I was wondering if you could tell me more about him now?"

Her eyes skipped across the sand and then finally rested on the tops of her bare knees. Absentmindedly, she brushed off some sand and then drew a little line in the sand with her toe. "I don't know too much."

"You probably know more than you think. Can you tell me again how you know him?"

"I *deedn't* tell you how I know him," she said.

"Yes, I know that. And so now I'm asking."

She puffed a little bit of air out her nose and stood up. "I no want talk about Remy."

I grabbed her by the wrist and pulled her back down. She looked me straight in the face, her face long, like she was surprised I'd been so bold with her. "Yeah, I get that. But I do.

Because here's the thing, Val. Remy, with the help of Boston Charlie, Denny, and Ennis, kidnapped me today."

At the sound of all of their names, Val's eyes widened. "What?" Then, almost as quickly as she'd shown surprise, it disappeared from her face and she shook her head. "I have no idea what you are talking about."

"Val."

She shrugged. "I no understand. Kidnap? What kidnap?"

"They stole me, Val. Grabbed me right out in front of the cottages. Shoved me in a trunk and pointed a gun at my face."

She stared at me then. Her fingers went to her mouth and her long red nails crawled around the edges of her lips. "Oh my God. Are you okay? They didn't hurt you?"

"They tried to," I said. "But it takes a lot to hurt me."

"What do they say?" she asked, her eyes full of obvious fear.

"About what?"

She shrugged. "I don't know. Anything?"

"They told me a lot, actually."

Like a deer in the headlights now, her face went ashen.

"Remy told me who he is to you."

Val's eyes closed for a split second. When she opened them, I could see her backbone stiffening ever so slightly. "Drunk. Please. You can no tell Artie about Remy. Artie agree with me. The past stay the past."

Even though I didn't believe that line for a second, that was not the biggest fish I had to fry at the moment. If only her commitment to Artie *was* the biggest problem, life might actually be easier. "Val, I don't think you realize something. They didn't kidnap me just to beat me up. They kidnapped me because they thought *I* was Artie."

"What?!"

"They wanted to kill him."

"Oh my God," she breathed, covering her open mouth with her hand.

"Yeah. And I don't think Remy's going to give up until he's done it either. He doesn't want the wedding to happen. Artie's life is in danger."

Val looked down at her hands, which now trembled in her lap. "Yes. I know. I trying to stop Remy, but he no *leesten* to me."

I looked her in the eye. "Trying to stop him. What do you mean? How?"

But she couldn't hold my gaze and instead looked away. "I no can tell you."

I grabbed her chin and forced her to look at me. "Yeah, you can, Val. Look, now's not the time to clam up on me. I need to know everything you know if I'm gonna save Artie."

She pressed her lips together.

"Val. Does this have anything to do with Charlie and the boys picking you up and dropping you off at random hours of the night."

Her eyes shot up to meet mine. I saw the glimmer of fear in them. She was afraid. Afraid of what I knew, and afraid of what I might tell Artie. "What?!"

"I know you've been leaving with them at night. And I know you aren't sleeping in Artie's room. So my question is, does Artie know that you've been sneaking in and out at random hours?"

Val sucked in her breath and then retracted her long legs. She spun around so that her back was to me. Within a second, her shoulders were shaking.

Fuck.

I was not equipped to deal with a crying, emotional woman. It just wasn't in my wheelhouse. When I was dating Pam and she cried about something, my instinct was just to give her whatever she wanted to make the crying stop.

Now, my head rolled backwards on my shoulders. I didn't know what to think. Was she emotional because she felt guilty or because she'd been busted or because she was genuinely upset about the situation?

I just didn't know.

Lifting my head, I stood up and walked around the lounge chair to sit on the other side of her so we were once again facing each other. "Look, Val, I don't know exactly what's going on, but I've got a pretty good idea. Have you gone back to working again? Is that it?"

Her head was in her hands, and when I said that, her shoulders shook harder.

Sighing, I reached out and put a hand on her shoulder. "Oh, come on, Val. Talk to me. I'm here for Artie. And if you're *really* here for Artie too, like you say you are, then you should talk to me too."

Val looked back over her shoulder at the pool area and then she looked at me. Her dark, glossy eyes shone in the moonlight. "Okay. I tell you what I know. But no here. We go somewhere private."

"Fine. Why don't you put some clothes on and then come over to my place? We can talk there."

With her lips mashed together, Val gave me a muted nod. I handed her the scrunched-up napkin Trinity had given me with my sandwich and she pressed it to her eyes right away. "I be there soon."

47

IT WAS OVER FORTY-FIVE MINUTES LATER WHEN VAL KNOCKED ON my cottage door. She'd gone back to her place and showered and changed. Her long brown hair was now bound up in a bun on top of her head, and she wore a short sleeveless dress that wrapped around her and was held together with an over-sized pin at her hips. It was low-cut as usual, but thankfully much less revealing than the bathing suit she'd been in down at the beach.

"Hey, Val," I said when I opened the door.

"Drunk." Her usual supersized personality was much more subdued now. When I opened the door for her, her eyes shifted to the floor and she walked in with her hands clasped in front of herself, like she was attending a funeral or something.

"You want something to drink? Water, soda, beer, shot of tequila?"

"No, thank you. I meeting Artie in the lobby for dinner in a few minutes."

"Okay, well, have a seat."

"Thank you." She sat down on my rattan sofa and I sat across from her. She seemed nervous, unsure of what to do with her hands when she sat. This was a very different

Valentina Carrizo than I was used to. Usually she was so flamboyant and self-assured that I almost didn't know what to do with this new quiet, awkward version.

"So. Since Artie is waiting for you, I'll cut right to the chase. There are a few reasons I wanted to speak with you, Val, but the first and main reason is I need to understand how I can keep Artie safe from your old pal Remy."

"I really have no idea how you can—"

I held up a hand to stop her. "Remy's guys admitted that they were the ones who blew up *The Bloody Marauder*."

Her eyes widened, but she let me keep talking.

"They also were the ones that vandalized our beach. They were the ones that knocked out Marcus and sank my boat in the water."

Tears welled up in her eyes and her face flushed bright red, but she didn't make a move. Instead she just pressed her lips together and fought her emotions.

"Now, I understand parts of what's been going on around here lately, but I certainly don't understand everything," I added. "One of the things I want to talk about is you sneaking out of the resort at odd hours. First of all, does Artie know you've been doing that?"

Her glossy eyes couldn't meet mine, and her head merely shook.

He didn't know.

Just fucking great.

"I see. And how are you able to pull that off?"

She shrugged. "I tell him I no want to share a room until after the wedding."

"And Artie was okay with that arrangement?"

"He say we have something now look forward to."

"But you're *sleeping* together, right?"

She looked at me and frowned.

My head bobbed. "Fine. None of my business. I get it.

Okay, so is what's going on with you and Remy what I assume it to be? You're still working for him?"

Val let out a big breath of air. "It is no what you think."

"Really? So you're not working for Remy?"

Val's head dropped. "No, I am, but—"

I couldn't believe that she was still hooking. I shook my head. "Val! Artie thinks that's all in the past! If he knew you were still—"

"You don't understand, Drunk. I *deedn't* have a choice. Remy tell me he will kill Artie if I won't do what he want. I *deedn't* want to do it…" Fat tears rolled down her cheeks now.

"It doesn't matter if you wanted to do it or not. Artie's going to be crushed when he finds out." I got up and walked to the kitchen to get her a paper towel and to give myself a second to catch my breath. This was such a nightmare.

When I returned, she pressed the towel to her eyes and tried to keep her makeup from smearing. Then she looked up at me. "But you no understand. I *deedn't* do it, Drunk." She swallowed hard and looked up at me, her eyes pleading for me to believe her. "I hire someone else to do it for me."

My head snapped up in shock. "What?"

She nodded. "I couldn't do it. I hire a girl I know to take my place. She pretend she is me."

"But I saw Charlie and the boys picking you up!"

"Yes, I know. They take me to the hotel, but another girl meet me there and she take my place."

"You're kidding?"

Val's head shook. "No. But Remy doesn't know. And you cannot tell him, Drunk. Please!"

"I would never tell him. But, Val! If he finds out, he could kill you *and* Artie."

Val's head bobbed. "I know." Then she began to sob. "But I don't know what else to do! He say he will kill Artie if I don't do what he tell me to do."

"Val, you have to tell me everything you know about

Remy's operation. I'll get the police over there *right now* and have him arrested so he can't hurt you or Artie."

She blotted her cheeks and dried her nose. "You don't understand. He have more people on the island. If Remy go to jail, he will have *them* kill Artie, and if he knows I am the one that told the police, he will kill me too."

Groaning, I dropped my head into my hands. This was all worse than I'd thought it was going to be. "Val, I have something very serious to ask you, and I need you to be honest with me."

Her head bobbed.

"Where were you the morning of the fire at the Crystal Point?"

Val frowned and sat up straighter. "I was here."

I shook my head. "Val, I know you weren't in your cottage. I know Remy's guys picked you up in the middle of the night again and you hadn't gotten back to your cottage yet that morning."

She looked down at her hands while I continued.

"Is it possible you were over at the Crystal Point that morning?"

Val's face wrinkled into a confused pout. "Why I be there?"

"I don't know. Maybe you started that fire."

Her eyes widened. "You theenk I start the fire?!"

I shrugged. "I really don't know, to be honest. That's why I'm asking."

"Why I would start the fire?"

"To frame Artie, maybe."

"What frame means?"

"So the police will think Artie did it and then he will go to jail."

Her eyes burst open wide as if she'd been slapped. She looked at me in horror. "Why I would want Artie in jail?"

"If Artie goes to jail after you get married, then you get all his money while he's gone."

"You theenk I want Artie go to jail?!"

"I don't know, Val. It's what I'm trying to figure out."

Val stood up and looked down at me. "How you could think that?!"

"Val, I—"

"I love Artie!"

"I mean, you say you do, but—"

Val's hands were on her hips. "I do!" Her tears were dried up now and her face was redder than I'd ever seen it before. "I *deedn't* start that fire."

"But it was your idea to send all those people on that night cruise. The police are suspicious about that."

"My idea!" Wide-eyed and frazzled, Val sucked in her breath before railing at me in Spanish. On and on she went, and for once I was thankful I understood very little of the language. I did, however, know some choice curse words, and I was sure that those had been lavishly sprinkled in during her tirade. When she was done, she stormed away, slamming the door to my cottage behind her.

I stared after her, scratching my head. "Well. That was fun."

48

"GOOD MORNING, DRUNK, MR. BALLADARES IS EXPECTING YOU IN his office," hollered Mariposa Marrero across the hustle and bustle in the lobby the next morning.

I walked over to the counter, dodging the event planners and their crew that were there a day early, already decorating for Val and Artie's big day. "Thanks, Mari," I said, leaning on the counter. I shook my head. "Wow. So this wedding is really going to happen, huh?"

"Looks that way. You doubted it?"

I shrugged. "I had my concerns."

"But they're settled now?"

"Not really," I admitted, giving her a tight smile. In fact, my concerns were far from settled. I'd slept on everything Val had said, and to say that I wasn't convinced she was telling the truth was an understatement. *Someone* had set that fire. I was fairly confident that Remy and his men hadn't done it. And though the police thought he had, I felt sure that Artie hadn't done it either. But *Val* was the common denominator. "Mari, what do you think of Val?"

"Of Ms. Carrizo?"

"Yeah."

With her lips pressed together tightly, Mari sucked air in through her nose, forcing her chest to puff up. As she worked that question over in her brain, she slowly released the air. "Ms. Carrizo is a big personality."

"Yes, she definitely is. What else do you think of her?"

"I don't know her well enough to think much more."

"Yeah, I suppose," I said on the back end of a sigh. "You said Artie's in his office?"

"Yes. He's been waiting for you."

"Okay." I walked slowly to Artie's office, lost in thought. The second I closed the door behind me, Artie pounced as if he'd been lying in wait.

"How dare you, Drunk! I can't believe what you did!" he roared.

I glanced over at Al, who shook his head sadly, as if even *he* was upset with me too. I frowned. "I'm sorry. You're going to have to be more specific. What did I do?"

Artie swiped at the air. "Oh, knock it off."

"No, I'm serious. What did I do now?"

"Val told me what you said to her last night, Drunk. I can't believe you accused my future wife of setting the fire over at the Crystal Point."

My mouth hung open for a long moment. I was shocked to hear that Val had actually *told* Artie. I had sensitive information about *her* that I could share, but I didn't think she'd want that. "Well, the truth is, Artie…"

"Al already told me about Remy."

My eyes snapped over to look at Al. I couldn't believe it. "Al!"

"I had to, kid. Artie wanted to fire you after Val came crying to him last night."

"Fire me!" This had gotten out of hand fast. "Artie! I'm only trying to keep you safe."

"Well, you'll have to find another way to keep me safe, Drunk. I can't have you harassing my future wife like that.

She's just been a mess since you spoke to her last night. For crying out loud, tomorrow's our wedding!"

"But, Artie! If Al told you about Remy, then surely you understand—"

Artie held up his flattened palm. "What I understand is that you came back yesterday understandably upset because someone in Val's past thought you were me and wanted to hurt me. I get that. And I appreciate that you, Al, and the rest of the boys want to keep me safe, but Val also wants me to be safe. She would never do anything to hurt me. She especially wouldn't *frame* me for arson! She's just not like that."

"But you don't know everything about her, Artie. You haven't known her long enough to know all of the ins and outs of Valentina Carrizo."

Al let out an extremely tired-sounding sigh. "Look, kid, I don't think you wanna press your luck with Artie right now. He's pretty worked up."

"Press my luck? Artie, do you not understand I got kidnapped and beat up yesterday because your fiancée's *pimp* thought I was you? I was almost *killed*. And if the idiots Remy's got working for him had half a brain to split, *you* would be *dead right now*."

"But that doesn't mean you have the right to attack Val!" argued Artie.

I held up a hand as if to say *I'm not finished*. "On top of that, someone is trying to frame you for arson and I'm trying to figure out who *and* I have to make sure you're alive long enough to get married tomorrow. How the *hell* am I pressing my luck? I'd say you should be thanking your lucky stars you've got me on your side!"

Artie started to say something, but I'd heard enough. I stormed out the door, slamming it shut behind me, and walked down to my office and slammed that door too, just for good measure. I hoped that Artie could hear the walls rattle from his office. As I sat there behind my desk stewing over our conversation and the wedding that was coming, my phone rang.

I pulled it out of my pocket and looked down at it, surprised to see that it was Frankie.

"Frankie, what's up?"

"Hi, Danny. I've got some news on the arson investigation."

"Yeah? Whatcha got?"

"Unfortunately, you're not going to like what I have to tell you."

My heart dropped. "Just tell me."

"It's looking more and more like Artie did it."

"What? How?"

"Well, a couple of things. I hadn't wanted to mention it before until I was sure, but there was a witness who admitted to seeing Artie at the Crystal Point just before the fire began."

"What? There's no way! He never mentioned it to me…"

I could almost hear Frankie jeering on the other end of the phone. "Danny, why would he? That would be practically admitting to his own crimes."

"Frankie—"

"I'm not finished. Forensics just came back with a fingerprint discovered on the book of matches discovered at the crime scene. We got a partial match on Artie."

"He owns the resort, Frankie! Is it a shock his fingerprints were on a box of matches that came from his resort? There's no way Artie did it, Frankie!" My mind reeled. I didn't believe for a second that Artie had done it.

"I don't know what to tell you, Drunk. It was *his* fingerprint. *His* matches. *His* employee chased all the guests out of his resort. And not only does he not have an alibi, but we have a *witness* that puts him at the scene of the crime right before the fire."

"Who? Who was your witness?" I demanded, my voice getting louder on the phone.

"I can't tell you who. All I can tell you was it was an employee."

"Was it Erika? Because it wouldn't shock me for a second if she's lying just to make Artie look guilty! Her and her boss think he did it. But someone's setting him up! Isn't it obvious?"

"It wasn't Erika. Look, Danny, I shouldn't have told you this, but I thought you should know."

"Frankie, you can't be serious. You should be building a case for his innocence, not his guilt!"

"Danny, I haven't found evidence or witnesses of anyone else that would've started the fire."

"Well, keep looking, because I know it wasn't Artie. And I'm going to prove it myself if I have to!"

"Look, Danny, I know how you are, and I know you like to get yourself wrapped up in these cases, but you really need to leave it up to the professionals."

I grimaced. "You know, Frankie, the other day I forgot for a *split second* that you had big dreams and aspirations. Now I think the shoe's on the other foot. You seem to have suddenly forgotten that you can't keep Danny Drunk from doing what needs to be done. I'll call you when I have something to share." With that, I hung up the phone. I was more determined than ever to bring whoever was framing Artie to justice.

Fired up, I jumped to my feet and marched out my door and back to Artie's office, where I burst inside. Al and Artie were talking, but they both stopped and looked up at me when I walked in.

"Drunk!" said Artie, surprised to see me back again so soon.

"Someone saw you over at the Crystal Point the morning of the fire, Artie."

"What?!"

"They have a witness."

Artie's eyes shifted over to look at Al. "They couldn't possibly."

"It was an employee. An employee saw you over there."

Artie's face paled.

I stared at him hard. "Artie. Tell me you weren't over there."

"I, uh—wasn't…"

"*Artie*," I growled, digging into my lowest register as if to threaten the truth out of him. If I was going to go to all the trouble to defend him, the least he could do was to tell me the truth.

His head dropped and he stared at his desk for a long moment. Finally, he looked up at me and Al and nodded. "Oh, all right. I did go over there."

"Artie!" said Al in surprise.

I was glad to know that Al hadn't known either. At least *he* hadn't been keeping secrets from me. "I can't believe it! And you didn't tell me?!"

Artie held up his hands to steady both of us. "I didn't *do* anything while I was over there. I'd just drove the golf cart over there, but before I had a chance to do anything, I noticed the fire and I rushed right back here."

"But someone *saw* you!"

He rubbed his squishy fingers against his temples. "Yes, I got that part."

"Why in the hell would you go over there?!"

"Well, I had a call from Ms. Wild. She wanted to speak with me."

I frowned at him. "What?"

"Early that morning. She called and requested a meeting."

"And it didn't occur to you to tell the police?!" Had hell frozen over and everyone turned to a bunch of fucking idiots?!

"I didn't mention it at first because I didn't want to put myself at the scene of the fire. I knew Sly would want to blame me. And then when I actually became a person of interest, there was no way I could tell anyone that I'd been there. I'd *really* look guilty."

"Artie. Artie. Artie." I shook my head. This was just horrible. "I can't believe it. You could've told *me and Al*. At least then there wouldn't be any surprises."

"Okay, fine. In retrospect I should've confided in the two of you. I just didn't want you to think I'd done anything unscrupulous."

"Artie, we know you. *I* know you. I've known you for years. I know you wouldn't commit arson."

Artie's head bobbed as he looked down at his desk.

"Well, now the police know you were there. And *you* weren't the one to tell them. Do you have any idea how guilty that makes you look now?"

Artie sighed. "Oh, I have a pretty good idea."

"So explain it to me. What did you do when you got there. Don't leave anything out!"

"Well, there really isn't anything to tell. I pulled into their parking lot, I noticed the fire had already started, and I rushed right back over here."

"Did you even call the fire department when you saw the fire?" asked Al.

"No. I saw an employee out front talking on the cell phone. I was sure he was on the phone with emergency services. I figured if I called too, then my number would be associated with the fire and then they'd know I'd been there!"

I looked at Artie with interest. "Wait a minute. You *saw* an employee? That was probably who reported you to the police. Do you know who it was?"

"I don't. I don't know any of Sly's employees. It was a young man in uniform."

"What kind of uniform? What did the man look like?"

Artie's hands went up. "I didn't get a very good look at his face. He wore a red shirt and khaki pants. He was black. Curly hair. Young. Maybe in his twenties."

"And you think that's who saw you?"

"Had to have been. I didn't see anyone else there."

Al shook his head. "I can't believe you didn't tell us this before. That employee could've been the one that started the fire, Artie!"

"Al's right. He could've been a disgruntled employee or something."

Artie's mouth opened. "I hadn't thought of that. I just assumed he'd shown up to work and discovered the fire."

"Well, it's possible that he did. But maybe not." I shook my head. "Look, Al and I will look into it. What about Erika? Have the two of you spoken about what it was that she wanted at the meeting she invited you to?"

Artie shook his head. "No. After the fire, she never called to set up a new meeting. But I'm not surprised. They have bigger problems now that their main building has burned down. Plus I've got the wedding to worry about."

I groaned. "Ugh. We'll find out more about that, too. Something sounds fishy. And now I wonder if maybe Erika Wild knows more than she let on to the police." I went to the door. "You coming with me, Al?"

Al stood up and hobbled towards me. "Of course I am. But what about Artie's safety?"

"Get the geriatric squad to keep watch on him. While you're arranging that, I need to go have a word with Mari. Artie, tell Val not to leave the resort property. In fact, it might be a good idea if you keep her over here while you're not at home, so Gary and the guys can keep an eye on her." When Artie nodded, I looked down at my watch and then at Al. "Meet me at my place in fifteen?"

Al gave me a little salute. "Got it."

49

"I can't believe you confronted Val like that, kid." Al gave me the side eye as he drove us over to the Crystal Point. We were hoping Sly and Erika wouldn't be there this time and we'd actually be able to do a little under-the-radar investigation. "What were you thinking? You had to know she was going to go straight to Artie."

My hands splayed out in front of myself. "How was I supposed to know she was going to take it so badly?"

"You didn't think accusing a woman of arson might set her off? I thought you considered yourself some kind of ladies' man. Isn't that sort of like Ladies Ed 101?"

"Look, Al. I honestly thought she was guilty. If she was guilty, then why would it set her off?"

"Because women get set off by everything."

"Yeah, I see what you're saying." My head bobbed as my eyes narrowed. "Okay, point taken. I didn't mean to piss her off, just so we're clear."

"You thought she'd take it as a compliment, did ya?"

"That she'd be smart enough to pull something like that off? Yeah, I'd say that could be looked at as complimentary."

Al shook his head. "You're too much, kid. You really have a way of pissing people off, don't you?"

I shrugged. "What can I say? I can't make everyone happy, Al. I'm not nachos."

We drove in silence for the next minute until we pulled into the Crystal Point parking lot. "Ah shit. Someone's here." I pointed at a beat-up four-door Mitsubishi Lancer parked right in front of the building. "Think that's Sly's car?"

Al shook his head. "I can almost guarantee you Sly Smallwood does not drive a car like that."

He had a point. The car rivaled the piece-of-shit Acura I'd driven back in the States, not something the owner of a multi-million-dollar resort would drive. "Erika, maybe?"

"I don't know what she drives," said Al. "But I really doubt that's it."

After my abduction the day before, and with Remy still on the loose, I wasn't chancing anything. I whipped out Gertie and climbed out of the golf cart. "I'll go in and see who it is. Why don't you stay out here? Just in case it's a looter or something."

Despite my suggestion, Al climbed out of the golf cart too. "It's not a looter."

"You don't know that. Or it could be whoever set the fire come back to make sure they covered their tracks."

"In broad daylight? Doubtful." He beckoned for me to follow him as he walked up to the building. "Come on, kid. And do me a favor? Put that thing away before you hurt yourself."

I frowned as I followed after Al. "Says the guy who felt safe in a car with Big Eddie packing."

Without even turning around, Al swatted the air behind him. "Meh, it was a BB gun pistol. You really think we'd give Big Eddie a real gun? The guy's scared of spiders, women, and everything in between."

Inside, everything was black. It no longer looked like the

amazingly epic grand resort it had been. There were fallen beams, loose wires dangling from the ceiling and melted things around the room. The only thing that hadn't completely melted into something unrecognizable was the stone front counter, which still remained standing.

I cupped my hands to my mouth. "Hello?" I hollered. "Anyone here?"

Al and I were silent as we listened for a response, hearing nothing in return. We walked further into the building when we heard the sound of something scraping down a hallway. Following the sound of the noises, we discovered a man in Erika Wild's office.

"Hello?" I said.

The man looked up. "Oh. Hello."

He was a rotund white guy in his late fifties or early sixties. He had a bad combover and wore a brown suit and tie and clear-framed aviator glasses that I was pretty sure he'd stolen from the eighties. He didn't *look* like a looter. He looked like a used car salesman from Hoboken.

Al and I exchanged a look. I had to assert control of the situation before he did. I walked over to him and shook his hand. "I'm Daniel Holmes and this is my friend Alfred Sherlock. We're inspectors with the Paradise Isle Royal Police Force. And you are?"

The man shook my hand and nodded. "How you doing? Leonard Waterman."

"Mr. Waterman, I don't have notes in my file that permission has been granted for you to be on the premises," I said in my most serious tone.

Leonard cleared his throat. "I'm actually working at the request of the Atlantic Insurance Limited firm. I'm a private arson investigator."

"Oh, I see," I said, nodding. I looked at Al. "Why do we not have that in our notes, Mr. Sherlock?"

Al's eyes got big as he shrugged.

"Uh-huh. Well. This is the resort's security office," I said to Leonard. "The fire didn't start in here. Do you mind explaining to me what you're doing in this room?"

He cleared his throat. "Yes. Well, as I'm sure you're aware, records show that the security officer, a Ms. Wild, disabled the security camera system prior to the fire starting. I'm checking to see what's left of her computer setup, but I see that whatever was left after the fire has already been removed by your office."

My heart raced. *Erika* disabled the security camera before the fire. *What?!* I nodded. "Yes, of course it was. It could be evidence. Now, tell me, exactly how *you* were made aware that she disabled the security system if you don't have access to her computer system?"

He lowered his brows. "Well, I requested a copy of the report from the security system contracted by the resort. They're required by law to turn it over to AIL upon request. I assume your office requested a copy of that report also?"

Al nodded. "Of course we have the report. Mr. Holmes just didn't realize that you'd have been given a copy of it too. I'm sure he wanted to make sure there wasn't some kind of breach of information. Right, Mr. Holmes?"

I gave Al and Leonard both a stiff smile. "Yup, my partner nailed it all right. I hate snitches. Fucking rat bastards. You know what they say, snitches get stitches."

Al rolled his eyes.

Leonard looked slightly confused, but nodded. "Oh, I see."

Widening my stance, I put my hands on my hips. "What I'm wondering is how there even *was* a report if Ms. Wild's computer was destroyed in the fire?"

Leonard's head flinched back slightly. "Well, obviously we pulled it off the cloud."

I frowned. "I'm sorry, you pulled it off what?"

Leonard looked over at Al like he knew what the fuck pulling it off the cloud meant any more than I did. Apparently

Al's vacant expression made him not so sure. "You guys *do* know what the cloud is, right? The security system here backs up to it."

"Oh, the *cloud*!" I said, throwing my hands up in the air. "Of course I know what the cloud is. I thought you said *clown*. I was like, what the fuck is this guy talking about?" I chuckled. "Oh, yeah. The *cloud*. Sure. Yeah. Don't all security systems back up that way these days?"

"Well, it is *the law*," he said, lifting his brows and nodding. "But you guys should know. Now, if you don't mind, I'd like to continue with my investigation. And you're welcome to check, but I did file a request to be on site today with your office."

"I'm sure you did. We actually didn't check into the office this morning," I said, giving him a tight smile. "We wanted to get an early jump on our investigation. But by all means, continue, continue."

Leonard gave Al and me a tight-lipped smile before giving us his back.

"Come on, Mr. Sherlock," I said, jerking my head sideways. "Let's let Mr. Waterman finish his work."

Outside, Al and I stopped in front of the golf cart.

"Al. Why in the hell would Erika have disabled the security system right before the fire?"

Al lifted his arms in a shrug. "Beats me. If I had to guess, though…"

"You'd guess that she was involved?"

Al nodded slowly. "I'd have to."

I shook my head. Had I been played? Was that it? Had Erika really come over to my place the night before the fire to seduce me and then somehow set Artie up to take the fall for the fire? But why? Why would she want Sly's resort burned down? I didn't understand. "Al, I think it might be time we have a conversation with Erika Wild."

My phone rang.

"Drunk here."

"Drunk it's Mari. I got that information you requested."

"Perfect."

50

ACCORDING TO THE ADDRESS MARI GAVE ME, KINGSTON JAMESON lived in a small shack in a seedy area of Paradise Isle's oldest residential area. Like many of the houses around it, the grass was high and weeds spouted up around the foundation's perimeter. Like a tooth dangling by only a bit of root, a shutter hung off the front window by one hinge. The window itself was shattered and a baseball lay out on the street. Baby doll strollers and dump trucks were tipped over in the tall grass, and two rusted bicycles, one with an unhooked chain, leaned up against the porch railing.

Screams and loud voices poured from the broken window, and before we'd even gotten to the porch, the front door burst open and a young boy raced out, followed by another. They didn't even pause, but instead ran around us and out into the street, where one seemed intent on punishing the other.

Al and I looked at each other uncomfortably as we approached the house. Equally unsure if it was the right address and debating silently if whether what we were doing was such a good idea. I sucked up a deep breath and knocked on the frame of the wide-open door.

"Come in," yelled a distinctly Caribbean voice.

I stepped in first and found a black man of about twenty-five to thirty sitting in a recliner looking at the television set. He looked up at me when I entered and gave me a nod.

I pointed at him. "Mr. Jameson?"

"Kingston is fine. You'll be the famous *Mista* Drunk?"

I smiled at him. "I don't know about famous, but, yes, I'm Drunk. This is my friend Al."

"'Tis nice to meet ya both. Have a seat."

Al and I took a seat on a sofa next to his chair. Kingston lowered his feet and sat forward in his chair. "What I can do ya for?"

I sucked in a deep breath and then nodded. "Well, I won't waste your time and beat around the bush, but I hear that you think you saw the owner of our resort coming out of the Crystal Point right before the fire started."

"I don't be thinkin'. I know what I saw."

"You really saw Artie coming out of the resort?" asked Al.

"I wouldn't say it if it weren't true."

I looked at him curiously. "Because he told us he never went inside."

The man lifted his shoulders. "I saw what I saw."

"Okay, well, can you tell us *exactly* what you saw?"

"I pulled into the parking lot. I saw Mr. Balladares coming out of the resort. That's it."

"That's all you saw?"

"That's all I saw."

"What about the rest of the staff? Why didn't anyone else see him?"

"The rest of the staff had the morning off because all the guests were gone."

"Then why were you even there?"

He shrugged and gave me kind of a stout look. "I was told to be there."

"Why?"

"Just because there wasn't anyone to wait on hand and foot don't mean there wasn't other work to be done."

"Okay, so you got there and you saw what exactly?"

"I saw Mr. Balladares leaving, and not long after that, I saw the fire. I called it in."

"But I thought Ms. Wild called it in," I said, crooking my head.

"Maybe she called it in as well, I couldn't tell you."

"Kingston, who told you to come to work that morning?" asked Al.

"Ms. Wild asked me to."

"Does she usually assign your work schedule?" he continued.

"No, not usually."

"Then why would you take orders from her?" I asked.

"It's not the first time she's given me orders. She just don't usually do it."

I glanced over at Al. This was looking more and more fishy by the second. "Kingston, are you absolutely *certain* you saw *Artie Balladares* coming out of the resort and not just driving by in his golf cart?"

He shrugged. "What's the difference?"

I stared at him hard. "Are you kidding? The difference is huge! The difference is my boss could go to jail for starting that fire, and I *know* he didn't do it. If the cops are relying on *your word* that he was coming out of the resort, it means an innocent man could be held responsible for something that someone else did!"

Kingston pressed his lips together and gave a nonchalant shrug. "'Tis not my problem."

I narrowed my eyes. His somewhat cavalier attitude made my Spidey senses tingle. "If you're lying, then it *is* your problem. Because I'm going to find out the truth."

"'Tis my truth. I can't help it if you don't believe me."

I scooted forward in my seat. "Kingston. Just out of curiosity, did someone pay you to tell your truth?"

"Are you callin' me a liar, Mr. Drunk?"

"I'm not calling you anything. I'm just asking."

"I think maybe you should go now." He stood up then.

"But we weren't finished asking questions."

"Oh, I think we are finished here. Don't you?"

I curled my lip. "Not really."

"Have a nice day, gentlemen."

Al stood up too. "Come on, Drunk. Let's go."

"But, Al, we..."

"We got what we needed. He told us his story. It's not going to change. Now let's go."

Kingston shot us a sly smile as we walked out his front door. "Thanks for visiting now."

I hated that shit-eating grin, and it was then I knew for sure that something suspicious was up.

"THE EVIDENCE IS STARTING to stack up against Ms. Erika Wild," I said as I drove Al and I back to the Seacoast Majestic.

Al nodded. "I can't say I'm surprised. What I can say is that I'm surprised that you fell for it."

I looked over at Al in shock. "That I fell for her—Al! I told you what happened there. She seduced me!"

"Because you let her! You should've been on your toes. Especially after everything that happened with Mack. You do remember what happened with Mack, don't you?" Al held up his stiffened pinky finger as proof.

I gave his hand a shove. "Put that thing away. You *always* have to bring that up, don't you?"

"I don't have to bring it up. It doesn't go down, remember? I can't bend it anymore. Thanks to you and Mack."

I rolled my eyes. "Listen, I *was* on my toes this time. She just got around me somehow."

"Well, that's what I'm saying. I'm surprised you allowed it."

I groaned and jammed the palm of my hand into the steering wheel. "Do you really think she's capable of burning down Sly's building and then framing Artie for it?"

"You do remember the woman we're talking about, don't you?"

"Yes, I do, Al. Okay, fine. She's capable. But I don't understand *why*. *Why* would she do it?"

"I'm sure she's got a motive that we just don't know about," said Al. "Maybe we need to lay out what we know."

"Well, we know that she called Artie in for a meeting that morning and she called Kingston Jameson into work and he just *happened* to see Artie leaving the resort."

Al wagged a finger in the air. "Very convenient. It's also convenient that she left your place the morning of the fire just in time to see the place burning up."

"*And* the part that gets me. She *shut off the security system* prior to the fire. Who shuts off their security system?"

"A guilty person," said Al, nodding.

"Exactly." I shook my head. "Ugh. We need to have to have a conversation with her."

"Do you know how to get ahold of her?"

"I'm sure Mari can find out for me. She figured out who'd seen Artie and how to get ahold of him."

"So what do we do in the meantime? Artie's wedding is *tomorrow*. Between her and Remy, how are we supposed to keep everything from going off without a hitch?"

I smiled at him. "I've got it. You just gave me a brilliant idea, Al. You know what they say. Keep your friends close and your enemies closer."

Al chuckled and patted me on the arm. "Haha, *finally*, kid. You got one right."

51

"Come on, Frankie. Just look into it for me?"

"Well, of course I'll look into it. I'd love for Artie to be innocent just as much as you would, but I wouldn't hold your breath that anything will come of it."

It was the next morning, and though I'd called and left her a message the day before asking her to look into the claim Leonard Waterman had made about Erika shutting off the security cameras before the fire, Frankie was only now getting back to me.

With my phone on the bathroom counter and Frankie on speakerphone, I looked at myself in the mirror as we spoke, adjusting the aqua-and-white flower boutonniere that Val, by way of Artie, was forcing me to wear for their beach wedding. I twisted it, trying to get it straight on the front of my white button-down shirt. "Here's the deal. Erika Wild had something to do with the fire. I'm sure of it. She shut off the security camera system. She was the one that *told* Artie to go over to the resort because she wanted to speak with him, which placed him at the scene of the crime, and she was the one that ordered Kingston Jameson, your *star witness*, to show up at work after everyone else had been dismissed just so he'd be there to witness Artie being there when the fire started."

"She didn't tell *me* that she'd invited Artie over that morning," said Frankie. I detected a bit of annoyance in her voice.

"Well, of course she wouldn't, now would she? Do guilty people admit their crimes to the police? No. No, they don't!"

"Well, as far as that goes, Artie didn't tell me anything about going over there that morning either. That would've been great information to have."

"I agree. Which is exactly why I'm telling you!"

"If what you're saying is true, it does raise a red flag for me as well."

"A big red flag."

"Drunk, come on. We gotta go!" hollered Al from the living room.

"Was that Al?"

"Yeah. I gotta go, Frankie. Big day here. Artie's wedding."

"Oh, wow. This week went by fast. Are you in the wedding?"

"I'm one of his groomsmen, yeah. Can't say I'm overly excited about it, but all I wanna do is to make sure that Artie stays safe until he says 'I do.'"

"You don't think this Remy guy can get to him after he says 'I do'? Will he suddenly have a protective shield around him then?"

I chuckled. "No, but if he's going to try anything, I just feel like it'll be *before* the nuptials, that's all. Anyway, I've got security on high alert today, and I've arranged personal security for Artie too."

"Oooh, personal security, huh?"

"Yeah. Call me if you hear anything on that report. I'll have my phone on me all day. Okay?"

"Will do, Danny."

"Bye, Frankie."

I pressed the red button on my phone and walked into the

living room. Al was there wearing the same white button-down shirt and sand-colored linen vest and pants outfit that I wore, except Al wore a matching sand-colored fedora with a black hatband.

"Is she coming to the wedding?" he asked, looking up at me.

"Not unless Val and Artie invited her, and I highly doubt they did."

Al handed me my own matching fedora. "You didn't invite Frankie! Drunk! It would've been the perfect excuse for you to—"

I held up a hand to stop him. "Uh. I've already got a date."

Al frowned while I put the hat on, looking at my reflection in a picture hanging on a wall.

"You do? Anyone I know?"

Just then, there was a knock at my front door.

I smiled at Al. "Oh, speak of the devil—*literally*," I added under my breath, "I think my date's here now." I walked to the door while Al hobbled around in a slow circle.

I gave a low bow just before opening the door. "Al, may I present to you, my date!"

Erika Wild stood on the other side of the door wearing a long aqua sundress and a smile. "Hello, Drunk."

"Erika. Come on in. So glad you could make it work with your schedule last-minute."

"Well, as you're quite aware, my job burned down recently. My schedule happens to be pretty wide open right now."

I smiled at her. "Touché."

"I must say, though, I *was* a little surprised to get your call. I thought maybe after the whole fire incident, we'd not be on such jolly terms."

I leaned forward and kissed her on the cheek. Though the gesture sickened me to no end, I still reached around to squeeze her ass and then whispered in her ear, "Are you kidding? After that night you gave me? How could we not be on good terms?"

Looking me squarely in the eye, she lifted a brow, no doubt curious regarding my change in attitude towards her.

Closing the door behind her, I gestured towards Al. "Erika, have you met my friend Al Becker?"

She walked in and extended a hand to Al. "I think we've been in each other's presence before, but we've not been properly introduced. Hello, Mr. Becker. Erika Wild."

"Ms. Wild, it's a pleasure," said Al, giving her a tight smile.

I shot him a look that clearly read *liar* but kept a smile plastered to my face as well. Taking her hand in mine, I lifted hers up high, giving her a little spin. Her dress spun around her ankles and her hair bounced lightly across her shoulders. "Well! For such short notice, I must say, you managed to look incredibly hot. Of course that goes without saying."

She gave an easy laugh. "That's very kind of you. And since we're being kind, I might say you're very easy on the eyes as well."

Al let out a little old man grump and then proceeded towards the open door. "Come on. We better get going or we'll be late."

"You're walking Val down the aisle, Al. The wedding can't start without you. You're essentially the belle of the ball."

"I think Val might disagree with you on that one, kid. But come on. I promised Artie we'd be there to help him get ready."

Al was already halfway to his golf cart when I gave a stiff butler's bow to let Erika go next.

"After you, m'lady."

Let the games begin.

52

AT THE FAR END OF THE BEACH, A SMALL TENT HAD BEEN SET UP, close enough to the venue but out of sight of the wedding guests. Val and the rest of the bridal party were dressing in the clubhouse, but Artie wanted a place for him and his groomsmen to be able to hang out and keep cool while waiting for the wedding to begin. He'd even had maintenance install a portable air conditioning unit inside the tent to keep Artie from completely sweating through his cream-colored linen suit.

Inside the tent, the air conditioner hummed noisily. All of the guys were present and accounted for. They all wore bullet-proof vests, all compliments of Gary's military arsenal. Everyone except for Eddie and Elton was packing. Gary, who'd been assigned as the head of Artie's security detail, had barely left his side since I'd returned from my visit to Remy's camp. He'd even gone so far as to sleep on Artie's couch, though I'd offered to do it.

As Artie's oldest and most trusted ally, Al had been selected to walk Val down the aisle, as her own father lived in Colombia and wasn't able to attend the nuptials. She'd originally wanted me to do it, but after I'd accused of her arson, she'd somehow managed to take offense and had withdrawn her request.

Go figure.

And with Val opting to have only a maid of honor, and Al giving away the bride, that had left *one* groomsman position up for grabs. Artie'd almost played eeny, meeny, miny, moe to select which one of his friends would get the high honor, but he'd hated the idea of offending any of them, so he'd punted on picking and offered me the highest honor of the day.

While I didn't *love* wearing a vest and button-down shirt, I hadn't minded being his best man for three reasons. One, it was Artie, and I wanted to do whatever made him happy. Two, I got a snappy new fedora out of the deal. And three, if I was standing next to him at the altar, I could keep a very close watch on him during the wedding. Just in case anything were to go down.

"You know, it's not too late to back out," I said, giving his white satin bow tie a little jiggle.

Artie rolled his eyes. "Oh, for Pete's sake, Drunk. Are you gonna be like this all day?"

"Be like what? I just didn't want you to think that if you'd changed your mind, it was too late. It's not too late until you say 'I do.'"

"Well, that's happening in T-minus seventy-five minutes," he said, checking his watch.

"Exactly. There's time."

"Oh, forget about the kid," said Al, swatting the air next to me. "He doesn't know what being in love is all about."

"Thanks, Al. I *do* happen to know what being in love is all about. I'm just doing my job as best man."

Al hobbled around in a circle and leaned back to look up at me. "Are you kidding? That's not what the best man's job is."

"Sure it is. It's to make sure the groom doesn't make the biggest mistake of his life."

"No, it's not," said Gary Wheelan. "I've been in my fair

share of weddings. Your job, plain and simple, is to hold on to the rings."

My eyes widened, panic filling my face as I patted myself down. "The rings? I'm supposed to hold on to the rings?"

"Tell me you didn't lose the rings," said Artie, groaning.

"Did you give them to me?"

Artie's face grew completely somber. "Yes, I gave them to you. Last night at dinner. Tell me you're not serious?"

Everyone in the tent stopped moving and looked at me.

I'd held out as long as I could. I cracked a smile and pulled the rings out of my breast pocket. "Ahhh haha. Gotcha. Oh, come on, Artie. I might be irresponsible, negligent, a pain in your ass, and quite frankly, a jerk at times, but—I'm not a bad best man."

"Oh, thank God," said Al, holding a hand to his heart. "I was starting to think I was going to have to beat you silly before the day was over."

I laughed. "Guess you'll have to save that beating for another day, huh, Al?"

"I guess."

Mariposa's head poked into the tent. "Mr. Balladares, sorry to bother you, but guests are starting to arrive already. They're so early! What should we do with them?"

I clapped Artie on the shoulder. "It's your day, old man. Lemme handle this."

"I appreciate that, Drunk."

"No problem. I'll be right back." I followed Mari out of the tent. Erika was there, seated in one of the white wooden folding chairs on the beach. I'd invited her to be early because not only did I want to keep her close in case she had any pranks in mind, but I also wanted an opportunity to feel her out a little about her involvement in the fire situation. But once the three of us had shown up on the beach, Al and I'd been whisked away to go with the rest of the wedding party and I'd had to leave her sitting alone.

"Where are they?" I asked, looking around for any new guests.

"Akoni brought them up from the parking lot and I've got them waiting in the lobby right now. Artie had said to bring them down to the beach, but it's so early. The wedding doesn't start for more than an hour."

I looked down at my watch. "Yeah, you're right. It is quite a while to have guests seated out here in the sun. By the time Artie walks down the aisle, this place'll smell worse than a men's locker room on cardio day."

"So what should I do with them all? We've already got two couples here, and I just sent Akoni down to pick up someone else that just arrived."

"Keep them in the lobby. Offer them all drinks. Complimentary, of course, whatever they'd like. You can start seating a half hour prior to the wedding. How about that?"

Mari smiled at me and squeezed my arms. "Perfect. You should be a wedding planner."

"Ha, I don't know about that. My idea of a nice wedding would be no guests in front of a justice of the peace. Why make everyone in the world show up in fancy clothes just for you to say 'I do'? I'd rather they just sent me a postcard from the honeymoon."

Mari giggled. "I stand corrected. Okay, I better go before someone sneaks off down here."

"Thanks, Mari." When she'd gone, I glanced over my shoulder at Erika, who'd been watching me. When she saw me look at her, she gave me a little wiggle of her fingers. Giving her an easy smile, I walked over to her. I had a few minutes. Maybe that was enough time to get something out of her.

"Hey," I said, sliding into a seat next to her.

"Hey."

I squeezed her knee. "Sorry I left you all alone out here. I didn't realize I wasn't going to get to spend the time with you before the wedding."

"It's fine. You're the best man. You've got duties, I understand."

"Getting warm out here? You could go into the clubhouse and have a drink. It's all on Artie, of course."

She gave me a relaxed smile as she adjusted the length of her dress to expose her thighs. "It's okay. I don't get to sit out in the sun much, being in the office all day. I'll chalk it up to working on my tan."

I stared at her long, slender legs. They looked pretty sun-kissed already to me. "You sure?"

"Absolutely. So what's going on over there?" she asked, thumbing the area of the beach I'd just come from.

"Artie's got a tent set up. All the guys are in there. We're just getting him ready. You know, psyching him up for the big event."

"He needs to be psyched up to marry her?"

I chuckled. "Okay. Fine. If you must know, he's trying to psych *me* up to marry her."

Erika looked at me in surprise. "You don't like the bride?"

"Oh, no. I like her. I just don't know if I completely trust her."

"Really? Why's that?"

I shrugged. "For a minute I thought maybe she was responsible for the fire." I watched Erika's face closely for signs of anything. Surprise. Shock. Relief. But all that registered was curiosity.

"*Really?* Why did you think that?"

"Oh, kind of a long story. But I'm working on it." I leaned back and yawned, pulling the clichéd move of letting my arm fall over the back of her chair. "You know, while I've got you here, I was wondering if I could ask you a question. About that morning?"

She lifted a shoulder and then leaned back against my arm. "Shoot."

I gave her bare thigh a little squeeze. "Great. Well—"

Someone cleared their throat behind us. "Uh-hum."

Looking back over my shoulder, I saw Frankie Cruz standing behind us with her hands on her hips looking down at me sharply.

My heart froze, like I was a little kid with my hand caught in the cookie jar. "Frankie!" I leapt to my feet.

"Danny," she said curtly.

My heart pattered against my chest. "Frankie, you remember Erika Wild?"

"Of course I do. Ms. Wild," said Frankie, giving Erika a semi-polite, but also semi-poisonous nod.

"Ms. Cruz," answered Erika with just as coarsely civil of a nod as she'd received.

"Danny, may I have a word with you?"

I looked down at Erika. "Do you mind?"

"No. Go, go. The wedding starts in an hour, right?"

"Just over an hour," I said, nodding.

"Well, maybe I'll just go use the ladies' room and then grab a drink on my way back to keep me cool."

"That sounds like a great idea."

Erika stood and walked down the aisle in the opposite direction so she wouldn't have to walk past Frankie.

When she was gone, Frankie turned her dark eyes on me. "What is *she* doing here?"

I pursed my lips into a tight, uncomfortable smile. "Oh. Umm, I invited her."

"*You* invited her? To Artie's wedding?! What's he think of that?"

"Well, she's sort of my date, and I don't think he knows yet."

"Your date? You invited Erika Wild to be your date? I thought you suspected her of starting the fire?"

"Shhh," I hissed, looking over my shoulder to make sure Erika was completely out of earshot. "I *do* think that, but *she* doesn't know that."

Frankie glanced backwards at Erika, who was almost to the clubhouse, then looked back at me again. "I don't understand, Danny. *Why* in the *world* would you invite her to be your date to Artie's wedding if you suspect her of trying to frame him for the fire?!"

"Look, Frankie, the moral of the story is to keep your friends close, but your enemies closer. I don't trust Erika Wild any more than I trust Val. I didn't want her to find some way to ruin Artie's wedding, and I thought maybe I'd find a minute to get a little intel out of her, which was what I was doing before you showed up."

Frankie's posture straightened slightly. "Oh. Well, I'm sorry. It appeared cozier than that to me."

"Appearances can be deceiving."

She rolled her eyes. "Okay. Fine, it wasn't cozy. Whatever you say."

I looked at her curiously then. "So. What are you doing here? Did Artie invite you to the wedding?"

"No. I got my hands on that report you spoke of. The security company had already sent it over, but it got buried in my email."

A sudden burst of excitement buoyed my heart. I beamed at her. "You found it?!"

"I did."

"Well, why didn't you call?"

She sighed. "I've *tried* calling. For the last hour. You don't answer your phone!"

I frowned at her and patted myself down. "But I didn't even hear my phone ring." And that was when it hit me. Al had been in such a hurry for us to leave that after hanging up Frankie's call earlier, I'd left the phone on the counter in my bathroom. When I realized my error, I groaned. "Oh, sorry, Frankie. I think I forgot my phone in my cottage."

She nodded. "Yeah. And I knew you were waiting for the

information and I had a minute to spare, so I thought I'd run the report over to you so you could look at it yourself."

"You brought it with you?"

She pulled a folded sheet of paper from her pocket and handed it to me. "Yes. And I think you'll be happy to see that the arson inspector was correct. Erika *did*, in fact, disable the security system prior to the fire."

Bright-eyed, I snapped the paper out of Frankie's hands and unfolded it. My eyes scanned the page to see a spreadsheet printout of timestamps, passcodes, and actions taken.

Frankie pointed at the last line on the page. "There's the last entry. The morning of the fire."

"System disabled," I read. "But how do we know it was Erika and not someone else at the Crystal Point?"

"That passcode." She pointed to the top of the page where there was a key. It listed passcodes and their respective owners. "That's Erika's unique passcode."

I shook my head in disbelief. In my hands, I held physical proof of my suspicions! I couldn't wait to have it out with Ms. Erika Wild and make her *admit* what she'd done! I folded the paper and then threw my arms around Frankie's shoulders. "You have no idea what this means to me, Frankie. Thank you!"

"Oh, I do know what it means. It means I've got another person to add to my persons of interest list."

I wagged the paper in the air. "As far as I'm concerned, you can take Artie *off* that list right now. Erika's your man! Or *woman*, I guess. Look, Frankie, I have to go up to the clubhouse and confront Erika before the wedding. Can you keep an eye on things down here? I've got security at all the entrances, but you never know when someone can slip past. I don't wanna leave Artie unattended."

Frankie shook her head. "Danny, you can't confront Erika now. Artie's wedding is about to start. It'll cause a scene."

I began to walk backwards in the sand towards the clubhouse. "I can't wait, Frankie. The best wedding present ever would be to tell Artie he's been cleared as a suspect and Val too. I have to do this. For Artie!"

"Danny!" she hollered after me.

"Artie's in the tent down the beach. Al and the other fellas are in there with him, so I'm sure he's fine, but *please* keep an eye on him. I'll be back soon."

"But—"

"Thank you, Frankie!"

53

I passed Jesse Coolidge as he was coming out of the clubhouse. He'd been asked to help out at the wedding and was carrying a big bucket of ice that I assumed he was taking to the swim-up bar.

"Hey, Jesse."

"G'day, Drunk," he said, giving me his broad smile. "Beautiful day for a wedding, eh?"

"Perfect. Hey, you seen a tall, dark-haired woman in a long blue dress?"

"The woman from the other resort?"

"Yeah, Ms. Wild. You seen her?"

He hooked his thumb over his shoulder. "Right through there."

"Thanks, man."

As I walked through The Beachcomber restaurant, I saw Erika emerging from the bathroom. I grabbed her by the elbow and, without a word, dragged her into the dance hall next door. "You're coming with me," I hissed in her ear.

She stumbled along next to me as I pulled her. "What the bloody hell do you think you're doing?"

"You and I need to have a serious conversation."

She jerked her arm out of my grasp. "I can walk on my own, thank you. What do you want?"

Inside the dance hall, I let go of her elbow and shut both sets of French doors.

She stood staring at me as I did. "What in the hell is this about?"

I walked right up to her, flicked open the paper Frankie had given me, and shoved it in her face. "I'll tell you what this is about. *This* is what it's about."

Frowning, Erika pulled the paper out of my hands and scanned it. She shook her head. "I don't understand. Where did you get this?"

I smiled haughtily at her. "I had Frankie get me a copy of it. Do you know what it is?"

"I'm not a bloody idiot. It's a copy of the security log for the Crystal Point."

"Ha*ha*!" I gloated. "It *is* a copy of the security log for the Crystal Point! And can you tell what it says?"

"I'm not *blind*, Drunk. I *can* read," she snapped.

I wagged my finger at her as I began to circle around her. "You know, I *knew* there was something suspicious about the night you came to my cottage and threw yourself at me."

"*Threw* myself at you?! Don't be daft. I didn't *throw* myself at you."

"Au contraire," I said, smiling at her. "You *did* throw yourself at me. You undressed right in front of me. *You* threw yourself at *me*."

Erika remained quiet but rolled her eyes in what I assumed to be silent protest.

"And I knew there had to be a reason. And then there was the fire, but I couldn't quite put my finger on it then. How did *you* sleeping with me play into the *fire*? And now I know."

She crossed her arms over her chest and pursed her lips. "Do you?"

"I do! Because here's the thing—I recently discovered that

not *only* did you disable the security system the morning of the fire, but you *also* requested that Artie come to the Crystal Point Resort that morning to meet you."

"Did I?"

"Yes. And further, you requested that Kingston Jameson also be there that morning at the same time so that he'd *just happen to see* Artie leaving the resort when the fire broke out. And then you went as far as sleeping with *me* in order to provide an alibi for yourself that morning."

A little haughty snort escaped her as she threw her nose up into the air. "You're delusional, Drunk."

"Am I?" I waved the paper in her face. "This report was the physical proof I needed for the cops to investigate each and every claim I just laid out for you. You're officially a person of interest in this case. And it won't be long before they speak with Artie and Kingston Jameson, and then *you* will be where you belong, behind bars."

Her eyes narrowed as she seethed in my direction. "You think so, do you?"

Gloating, my head bobbed. "I do. And you thought you were going to get away with it because you knew your computer would be melted by the fire, deleting the entire security system's log. What *didn't* occur to you was that these days it's all backed up to the cloud." I thought about it for a split second and then added a brief synopsis of my most recent research. "The cloud is like a backup for your—"

"I know what the bloody cloud is, Drunk!"

"Oh, okay. Well, as I was saying, what didn't occur to you is that it didn't matter if your computer burned to a crisp, the records are all safe and sound floating around in the sky."

Erika rolled her eyes. "Oh my God. You don't really think that's what the cloud is, do you?"

I shrugged. "It was metaphorical."

"Sure it was." Erika crumpled the security report and

tossed it over her shoulder. "There are just a few little holes in your story, Drunk."

"Are there? Please. Do tell."

"Well, for starters, I'm not stupid. I'm completely aware that my security system backs up to the cloud. I'm the head of resort security. You really think I wouldn't know how my own system works?"

I took pause for a second, and frowned.

"Only *an idiot* wouldn't know that it backed up to the cloud." Then she looked at me out of the corner of her eye. "Wait. You *did* know it backs up to the cloud, didn't you? It's mandatory due to the threat of natural disasters where we live."

I mean, I knew *now* that the security system backed up to the cloud. That was all that mattered. Right?

"I mean, duh? I know that," I said, giving her the stink-eye.

"Well, then, do you really think I'd be so daft as to disable the system using my own passcode, knowing full well that the police would be able to download a report?"

I frowned at her, feeling slightly speechless for once.

"And another thing. I didn't *call* Artie to set up a meeting with him. I don't know whom he spoke to, but it certainly wasn't me. I also didn't ask Kingston Jameson to come to work that day. It's not my job to make his work schedule, so why would *I* request that he come in on a morning that all the rest of the staff were given off because of a prank that *you* pulled?"

I frowned at her. "I don't know. I don't know your life," I said with a snort.

"No. You don't. But I can tell you this, I did not start that fire."

"Don't lie, Erika. I've got the proof."

"You have nothing but a bad case of idiocy. Look, what possible reason would I have to want my job to be burned to the ground?"

"I don't know. Because Sly's an asshole boss and you know it."

She rolled her eyes. "You haven't a clue what you're talking about. Sly's been a brilliant boss. This has been one of the best jobs I've ever had in my life. The pay is good. I'm the *head* of my department. I work at a bloody beach resort day in and day out. Aside from having to deal with Sly's occasional juvenile antics, I love my job."

I shook my head in confusion. "Well, then, why would you want to burn it down?!"

"I didn't want to burn it down! That's what I'm trying to tell you!" She shook her head when she saw me staring at her in disbelief. "Look, I was *with you* before the fire started. How could I have possibly started it myself? It had already begun when I started back over to the resort."

"That's what you *say*."

"That's what I say because it's the *truth*. The fire investigation confirms the time the fire started." Exasperated, she let out a little grunt and then walked over to pick up the paper she'd tossed to reexamine it. A smile spread across her face when she held it back up again. "Look. Look at the time stamp of this entry. This was stamped at four o'clock in the morning. I was with you at four o'clock in the morning. I was nowhere near the Crystal Point. So how could I have disabled the security system?"

I stared down at the time stamp. I hadn't even noticed that. I'd seen her passcode and that was it. "But I don't understand. How could it say that your passcode was used if you didn't use it?"

Erika sighed. "Obviously someone got ahold of my user passcode and logged in to the system as me."

"But who would have access to that?"

"Well, Sly, of course." She shook her head. "I don't know who else could've gotten it."

I stewed on that for a long moment. "Sly. Sly wouldn't intentionally burn his own building down, would he?"

Erika strode over to a chair in the corner and sat down. "I have absolutely no idea, but I can't believe you invited me here to accuse *me* of starting that fire. You're really something, you know that?"

I began to pace the floor as the idea of Sly starting the fire himself took flight in my mind. "You know, if Sly did it, it might be the ultimate prank. Burn his building down and frame Artie for the crime?"

"Sly wouldn't do that," she said.

"I don't know. He might actually be *that* demented."

Erika sat quietly thinking about it while I paced the room, wondering if anyone would be that crazy to burn down their own multimillion-dollar resort. Finally, she piped up. "He wouldn't do it for a prank. But he might do it for other reasons."

I stopped walking and looked back at her. "What other reasons?"

She sighed and rolled her eyes. "I really shouldn't tell you this."

"Erika! Tell me!"

"I'm still quite angry you brought me here as your date just so you could accuse me of setting the fire."

I rushed over to where she sat on a chair and got down on one knee so I could look her squarely in the eye. "I'm sorry, Erika. You looked guilty. I don't know what else you want me to say. I'm trying to get to the bottom of this! You of all people should understand that!" I took her by the arms. "If you know something, you have to tell me. This affects you too."

She sighed. "Well, he wouldn't like me knowing this, or telling you for that matter, but Sly Smallwood is in debt up to his ears."

I stared up at her in surprise. "What?!"

She nodded. "He renovated the resort a few years back and

had to take out some massive loans in order to do it, and unfortunately it hasn't paid off. Our client base is all young people, but young people don't have a lot of money. We've tried catering to all ages, but middle-aged families and older people don't like going to a resort where it's all kids, drinking, and parties. They go to quiet places, like the Seacoast Majestic."

"But you guys always made fun of that!"

Erika lifted a shoulder. "It was Sly. He was jealous."

"You're kidding? He seemed to gloat all the time."

"Well, I mean, he's proud of his resort, yes. And I'm not saying he did it. I'm just saying I happened to know he's deep in debt."

"So you think maybe he did it for the insurance payout?"

"I wouldn't rule it out completely."

"Why didn't you tell the police any of this?!"

Erika's eyes widened. "Are you mad? It never occurred to me that Sly would've done something so vile. But then again, I also didn't know that someone had logged in to the security system using my code. And I didn't know that Kingston Jameson is claiming that I told him to come to work, or that Artie thinks I wanted to have a meeting with him."

"It sounds to me like you were supposed to be the backup plan if framing Artie fell through." And then a thought hit me. I sucked in my breath. "Do you think Sly started the whole prank war, just to get Artie riled up enough to fight back? Just so he could show that Artie had a motive to want to burn down his resort?"

Erika's chin jerked back. "Well, that sounds incredibly demented. Much more demented than I'd give Sly credit for."

"Since when do we give Sly Smallwood credit for anything? He's a nutjob."

"Look, Sly's still my boss, so I'm not going to say anything like that, but he's not exactly the most level-headed guy. I'll give you that."

"Thank you," I said, my hands punctuating the air grandly.

"So now what? You suspect Sly might have done it himself. There's no way you'll be able to trace it back to him if he did. He's a very smart man. I'm sure he's covered his tracks well."

I shook my head. "I don't know, but I've gotta figure something out. I can't let the cops pin this on Artie."

"Or me!" added Erika.

"Fine, or you. *If* all of this is to be believed."

She rolled her eyes. "I told you. I was with you when whoever it was used my passcode to disable the security system. But it certainly wasn't me."

I looked at her curiously then. "Would you be willing to do me a big favor if it meant clearing your name?"

"If it meant clearing my name? Of course, absolutely. What do you want me to do?"

"I want you to call Smallwood."

"Call Sly? What good would that do? He'd never admit it to me even if he did it."

"Maybe not. But if he did it and he thinks that we have proof?"

"He'd want to get his hands on it."

"Exactly. And with Artie's wedding going on, what if the proof we have is conveniently unguarded?"

Erika nodded, finally picking up what I was putting down. "He'd come looking to steal it."

"Bingo."

Erika pulled her phone out of her purse. "Where should I tell him you hid the evidence?"

"In the tent down at the beach. Frankie should still be on resort property. I'm going to go find her and have her guard the tent while Artie and I are at the altar. If Sly shows up looking for it, then I think we've found our man."

Erika shook her head at me, a smile playing around her lips.

"What?"

"You," she said with a soft chuckle.

"Me? What about me?"

"You never struck me as being that smart, and then out of nowhere you do something like this and you amaze me. That's all."

"Thanks? I think."

She laughed. "You're welcome." She picked up her phone and dialed Sly. "Now. If you'll excuse me, I have a phone call to make."

54

AFTER WHAT SEEMED LIKE AN ETERNITY, THE PIPED-IN ORGAN music finally began, pouring through the canvas tent and filling the small space with the sounds of wedding.

Gary and the rest of the security detail had already gone to take their seats in the crowd. Al was in the clubhouse, waiting to walk Val down the aisle, leaving only me and Artie in the tent.

I patted Artie's arm, giving it a little squeeze. "Sounds like it's finally time. You good?"

Artie straightened his jacket and let out a big lungful of air in one robust burst. "Yes, I think so."

"Nervous?"

"No, no, of course not."

"Good. Well, you look great."

"Thank you, Drunk. And thanks for keeping watch for me today. I'm glad to know that nothing bad happened after all."

"Day's not over, Artie."

"True enough, true enough. But it looks like I'll make it to the altar after all."

I thought about telling Artie all the new information I'd gotten from Erika. About Sly and his possible role in the fire.

But then I felt like I'd be forced to tell him about the plan Erika and I had concocted—that while he was getting married, we hoped that Sly would slip in and show his hand.

But I couldn't do that.

Not only didn't I want Artie to ruin things somehow by giving the plan away, I also didn't want to plant the seed in his head. He was supposed to be getting married, not worrying about Sly sneaking into his tent and/or pranking him yet again. No, that was for me, Erika, and Frankie to handle, and of course Gertie, whom I'd brought along holstered under my vest.

But I did feel a sudden innate sense of urgency about getting Artie out of the tent and up to the altar. I knew as soon as Frankie saw me leave, she'd slip away from the wedding to guard the tent and keep a watch out for Sly.

I walked to the canvas doorway. "All right, well, we better get up there. We can't have you late for your own wedding."

"No, no, we can't," agreed Artie in a booming voice.

Giving him one last tight smile. I reached forward and pulled back the tent flap but was startled to discover someone standing on the other side.

"Sly!" I said, sucking in my breath.

"Leaving so soon?" he asked smoothly as he whipped a pistol out of his jacket pocket, aiming it at us.

My heart dropped.

Shit.

It wasn't supposed to happen like this.

I closed my eyes briefly, my shoulders slumping forward.

"Sly!" exclaimed Artie. "What the hell are you doing at my wedding? And what's with the gun?"

"Oh, I think you know what I'm doing here, Artie." Sly gave the gun a little wiggle. "Get back inside."

Artie and I took a few steps backwards and Sly stepped forward, shutting the tent's flap behind him. I pointed at the canvas walls. "Sly, there are over a hundred people out there.

You're not going to get away with this. If you shoot us, they'll hear you."

Artie's eyes flared open wide. "Shoot us?! Why in the hell would he shoot us?!"

"Why else? To keep you quiet," said Sly. "I never thought it would come down to this, honestly. But you surprised me, Artie."

"*I* surprised *you*? How? What did I do? I didn't burn down your resort. I hope you know that. I would never!"

"Well, obviously we both know that you didn't," said Sly.

"Well, then, what are you doing here? I'm supposed to be getting married right now! Don't tell me this is another one of your pranks. I'm sick and tired of the pranks, Sly. You've been pulling them since grade school and I'm over it!"

"Another of my pranks? Don't you get it, *Artie Fartie*? There *are* no more pranks. This is it. The final chapter in our saga."

"I have no idea what you're talking about." Artie turned to me. "Drunk, do you know what he's talking about?"

I rubbed a hand around the back of my neck. "I do, Artie. I was going to tell you *after* the wedding. But…"

Sly looked surprised. "Are you trying to tell me that my old pal Artie doesn't know the truth? Erika said he knew."

"No. Only I knew."

Sly sighed. "Well, regardless. Artie would've found out soon enough. So you can blame all of this on Drunk, Artie. If he hadn't gone poking around in my business and had just let you take the fall like you were supposed to, then I could've collected the insurance money and gotten on with my life, and you could've gotten married today."

"And gone to jail in a few months!" I argued.

"At least he'd have gone to jail a happy married man," said Sly with a devilish smile.

Artie, swiped both hands in front of him, slicing the air.

"I'm sorry. Back up a minute. Are you saying that *you* started the fire?!"

Sly looked at Artie curiously. "Well, yes. And shockingly, your idiot security guard managed to figure it out." He looked at me like I stank to high heaven and shook his head. "I'm not sure how he did it, but I hear you've got some evidence in this very tent. I'm afraid I'm going to have to ask you to turn whatever it is over to me." He held out his hand.

Artie looked shocked as he turned to me. "Evidence? What evidence?"

Sly wagged the gun at us while holding out his free hand to us. "Well, come on, then, hand it over! We haven't got all day."

I grinned at Sly. "Unfortunately, I can't really do that. You see, your *confession* just now and your presence are all the evidence I needed."

Sly took a step back. "What?"

"You see, I really wasn't *sure* that you'd set that fire. Not until you showed up here, anyway."

"Drunk! You planned all of this?" asked Artie.

"Not exactly. Sly wasn't supposed to show up looking for the fake evidence until you and I were standing at the altar." I sighed. "I guess it didn't go *exactly* as I'd planned."

"I'd say not!"

Sly grinned an evil smile. "Well, it's going exactly as *I've* planned. Neither of you have any evidence. So all I need to do is *kill* you and then my secret remains safe."

"Not exactly," I said, shaking my head. "We're not the only ones that think you did it."

Sly's head bobbed. "Yes. Obviously Erika has her suspicions as well. I'll have to handle that."

"She's none too thrilled about the fact that you were planning to frame her if Artie didn't work out."

"Well, every good plan needs a solid backup plan," said Sly proudly.

"I just don't understand any of this," said Artie, shaking his head. "Why in the world would you want to burn down your own resort? You just remodeled it a few years back. It was beautiful!"

"Yes, well, beauty costs a pretty penny, and unfortunately I wasn't recouping my investment at the rate I needed to be. Damn kids and their all-inclusive. They were going to drink me out of business at the rate they were going!"

"But you catered to kids!"

"Only because you had the market cornered on the seniors. Now *they're* the ones with the *real* money. Give them an early buffet line and free putt-putt and they're thrilled! Kids want everything *new* and *hip*. I'll tell you something. New and hip don't come cheap!"

Artie lifted a shoulder. "Well, I don't know if catering to the senior clientele is as easy as that, but they definitely don't need state-of-the-art to be satisfied."

"Exactly. I thought renovating would bring in the older crowd, but it didn't. The two groups are like oil and water. They just don't mix, no matter what I've tried."

"So that's why you've been pranking me all this time? You were goading me into a prank war so I'd look like the biggest suspect?"

Sly sighed. "Yes, and it seemed like you were never going to take the bait. But this last prank was *perfect*! You got all of my guests out of the resort, which made it easy for me to give all the staff the morning off. All I had to do was have a friend of mine make a few phone calls to invite you to the property the morning of the fire and to place a few matches and voilà! You're the prime suspect. It really wasn't that difficult. And to be honest, I *am* a little shocked that this idiot that you employ figured it out!"

I frowned at Sly. "Well, fuck you very much."

"My pleasure," he said with a grin. "Now, where were we?

Oh, yes! I was saying goodbye." Sly pulled back the hammer on his pistol and aimed it Artie.

"Not so fast!" I slid my hand into my vest and whipped Gertie out, aiming her at Sly.

His gun went from pointing at Artie to pointing at me. "Drop it."

"You drop it."

"No, you drop it."

"Oh, for heaven's sake. Put the guns away!" said Artie.

"Sorry, Artie. I can't do that." I frowned, wishing I'd had time to run back to my cottage to grab my cell phone so I could call Frankie. I knew she was only a few yards away, waiting for us to emerge before coming to the tent.

"Me either. Now, I suggest you put that down or I'll be forced to shoot Artie first," said Sly, pointing the gun at Artie again.

Before I could get in another word, the front flap of the tent was thrown open and another group of familiar faces filed inside.

"Remy!" I said in shock, my eyes flitting from him to Boston Cholly to Ennis to Denny. Each of them carried a gun.

"Well, well, well. I see I'm late to the party. What do we have going on in here?" asked Remy, smiling from ear to ear.

I gave a hard swallow as I eyed all the guns now pointed at all my vitals, and suddenly I felt slightly outnumbered. "What the hell are you doing here?" I demanded, swiveling to aim Gertie at him instead of Sly.

"Who's this?" asked Artie, frowning.

I grimaced. How could I tell Artie that this was his soon-to-be wife's ex-pimp come to kill him before he could marry her?

Thankfully, Remy answered before I could. "I'm a guest of the bride's. And you are?"

"Artie Balladares."

Remy's eyes widened. "*You're* Val's fiancé?"

Artie's head jerked back on his neck as if Remy's shock had offended him. "I am. And just who the hell are you?"

"Artie, this is Remy," I said in a low voice.

"Remy?" His head snapped over to look at the snappily dressed Asian man. "Val's old pimp Remy?"

"The one and only," I said, my head bouncing sadly.

Remy looked surprised. "You've heard of me?"

"Of course I have," said Artie. "You think I'm an idiot? What the hell are you doing at my wedding? I know Val didn't invite you."

Remy twisted his gun hand slightly. "Obviously I'm here to ensure you don't make it to the altar, but I see someone else has a problem with you marrying Val as well." He looked over at Sly. "And you are?"

"I'm Sly."

"Yes, aren't we all?" said Remy with an evil grin. "And what do you want with these two?"

"None of your business," snapped Sly.

Remy turned his gun on Sly. "Oh, but I think it *is* my business."

Sly swallowed hard. I could see that for the first time, he was also genuinely concerned with how this awkward Mexican standoff we'd suddenly entered into might shake out. "They know too much about something," was all he muttered.

"Too much about what?"

Sly pressed his lips together tightly, silently refusing to speak.

Remy looked at me, his smile had turned into a snarl. "Too much about what?"

"He owns the resort next door. He burned it down and tried to frame Artie."

That made the smile return to Remy's face. "Ahhh. *You're* the one that started that fire. So you're an arsonist."

Sly took a nervous step backwards towards the flap at the back of the tent. "Look, if you're planning to kill these two, then it saves me a couple of bullets, so I'll tell you what. I'll just skedaddle on outta here and get out of your way."

Remy's arm went up, aiming his weapon at Sly. "Oh, now, hold on. Wait just a moment. Sly, was it?"

Sly froze.

"We can't have you going anywhere and tattling on what's going on in here, can we, fellas?"

"No way, boss," said Boston Cholly, turning his gun on Sly, accidentally crossing over Remy's arm in the process. "Want me to kill 'em for ya?"

Sly pushed away the muzzle of Charlie's gun and looked over his shoulder at Charlie. "Do you mind?"

"Oh, sorry, boss." Charlie's gun pointed at Artie now.

His eyes shot open wide, and both of Artie's hands went up.

Remy sighed and, closing his eyes, rubbed one side of his temples. When he opened them, he looked around the crowded tent. "Okay, so let me get all this straight." He looked at Sly. "You want to kill them because they know you burned down your resort."

Sly gave a solemn nod.

"I see." He looked at me. "And you want to kill him because he framed your boss?"

I shrugged. "No. I just want to kill him because he wants to kill me. My original plan was to get him arrested, but I see that's probably not happening now."

"Agreed, that plan's not happening." He looked at his guys. "But we came here to kill both of you. And now it looks like we'll have to kill this guy too, just so he can't talk. Have we gotten everything sorted out?"

"Not quite everything," said yet another voice as the tent flap opened up. "Freeze!"

55

"AL! GARY!" I SAID AS THE TWO MEN PUSHED THROUGH THE FLAP to join us in the already full tent.

Al shuffled in holding Gary's old-fashioned-looking little snub-nosed .38 Special.

Gary the Gunslinger was right behind him brandishing his brand-new 9mm. He pointed it at the group.

"What the hell is this?" shouted Remy as Bob and Ralph the Weasel filed in through the tent's back door, both of them holding handguns as well.

"We've got you surrounded," said Gary. "Drop your weapons."

"Like hell," growled Sly. "I don't know where in the hell you feeble old farts came from, but you better get the hell outta here before one of you gets hurt."

Ralph shoved the muzzle of his gun into Sly's back. "Nah, I don't think so. You heard what my buddy said. Drop your weapon."

And *that*, my friends, was when all hell broke loose.

Because before Sly could drop his gun, Boston Charlie fired a shot meant for Ralph, but instead hit Sly in the shoulder. As Sly crumpled to the ground, Remy turned to fire at Artie. But

Gary and I were faster and fired several rounds at him before Remy could get a single shot off. He reeled back against the blood-splattered tent wall.

Al pointed his gun at Ennis's back. "Drop it. Or you'll end up like your boss, because I just happen to have a twitchy trigger finger." And then as an aside, Al added, "Although according to my doctor, that's perfectly normal for a man of my age."

Ennis opened his hand and his gun clattered to the ground.

But Boston Charlie wasn't going down without a fight. Something inside me told me was going for Artie next, and just as I saw him raise his gun, I threw my body over Artie and tackled him to the ground. On the way down, the shot whizzed past me.

Covering Artie's body with my own, I heard yet another gunshot. My eyes pinched shut as I heard someone behind me make an "*oof*" sound. I was afraid to open them and see who had been hit, scared it might be Al. But when I opened them, I found Charlie sprawled against the back of the tent with a bullet hole between his eyes. I looked up to see Gary looking amorously at his 9mm, nodding his head and smiling.

Without even being prompted, Denny, the last one standing, dropped his gun and surrendered, holding his hands up on either side of himself. "Don't shoot!"

And then Frankie's head was inside the tent, followed closely by Erika. "We heard the gunshots! I've got all the guests evacuating to the clubhouse. What the hell's going on in here?" asked Frankie. Her eyes went wide as she took in the carnage and the blood on the walls of the tent.

"Just a little Mexican standoff. Nothing we couldn't handle," I said, breathing heavily. "We've got your arsonist," I said, pointing at Sly, who was writhing around on the ground with a bullet wound to the shoulder.

"What?" Frankie gasped in surprise.

"Sly! It *was* you? You bastard!" hollered Erika. "You tried to frame *me* for the fire!"

"At least it didn't work," I said, crawling to my feet. When I was up, I reached back down and held a hand out to Artie to pull him up.

"And now he's going to get what he deserves," said Artie.

Erika looked down at her boss. Intense anger made her green eyes glow. "But I *trusted* him. Sly, I *defended* you, you dodgy wanker. And then you stabbed me in the back!"

"I had good reason," said Sly, wincing through the pain as he said it.

"No, you didn't. You got greedy. You wanted an insurance payout. And now you're going to pay the price." Erika looked over at me. "Drunk, are you all right?"

"Oh yeah. I'm fine. None of this is mine," I said, gesturing to the blood splattered all over me. "You okay, Artie?"

Artie looked himself over. His cheeks were flushed, his face dripped with sweat, and he had blood splatter on his suit. Otherwise he appeared all right. "I—I think so."

"For God's sake! Can someone *please* call me an ambulance," begged Sly as he writhed around on the ground, favoring his right arm. "I'm dying here!"

"You're not dying, Sly," said Frankie. "But I've already got emergency personnel on the way. They should be here shortly." Looking at me, she nodded her head towards Remy and Boston Charlie. "What's the story with these guys?"

I pointed at Remy, who was lying in a puddle of blood on the floor of the tent. "That one there is the elusive Remy."

"I wondered," she said, nodding.

"As I thought he might, he came here to try to kill Artie before he could marry Val. But thanks to my friends here, we stopped him."

Gary, Al, Ralph, and Bob all beamed proudly.

Frankie cocked her head backwards towards the rest of them. "And these are his guys?"

"Yeah. That one with the spot for a third eye is Charlie. This is Ennis and Denny. They've graciously decided to surrender."

"Danny, I need to step out and get some cuffs from my car for these two. Can you keep an eye on them for me?"

"With the help of my military brigade, it looks like we've got it covered."

But Gary held up a hand to stop her. "No need for cuffs, ma'am. We've got enough cuffs here to go around."

Frankie looked surprised as Gary held up a pair of handcuffs. Al, Ralph, and Bob all followed suit, holding up their own pair. She nodded as sirens sounded in the background. "Oh. Well, then, very good. I'll take care of this, but someone probably needs to go direct the medical team down here. And someone needs to go talk to the bride."

"Thanks, Frankie. I'll take care of Val," I said.

"She's probably freaking out right now, wondering what's happened to me. Not to mention all of our guests," said Artie. I could see the anxiety practically spilling out of him.

I held my hands out calmly. "Artie, relax. Take a deep breath. I'll handle everything." I looked over at Al. "Al. Can you take care of Artie? Calm him down? Maybe see what you can do about the blood all over him?"

Al nodded. "I got it under control. You go do damage control out there."

"Thank you." I tugged on Erika's arm. "Come on. We should get out of their way. Give them some space to work."

Outside the tent, a breeze pushed past my face, cooling me, and for the first time I realized how tight my body had been in there. I took a moment to inhale a deep breath and then I sighed. I looked down at my shirt. "Oh, geez. I can't go out there like this. Val'll lose it when sees all the blood."

Erika stopped walking and turned around. She sighed. "Here, lemme help you take it off."

Before I could even refuse her offer, her hands were on my

vest, unbuttoning it. She pushed it back over my shoulders and then began to unbutton my white shirt.

"Well, I can do that," I mumbled, but her fingers worked quickly and easily. Faster than my thick fingers could have.

"I don't mind helping," she said softly. "You might've saved my life in there."

"We *did* save your life in there," I said. "Sly said it himself —he was going after you next to make sure you didn't talk."

When she got to the end of the buttons, she yanked my shirt tails out of my pants and quickly finished off the buttons. She pushed it back over my shoulders just as Frankie emerged from the tent.

Frankie froze, staring at the two of us.

My eyes widened. "She was, uh, just helping me off with my bloody shirt."

Frankie rolled her eyes. "I see that."

I smiled at Erika but took a step back into more neutral territory. "Thanks. I can take it from here." I pulled my shirt off completely and tossed it onto the sand. "Get them all cuffed up in there?"

"Yeah, I was just going to go get the med team. You want to tell me exactly what all went down in there?"

"I—"

Before I could start my story, Jesse Coolidge came through the trees. "Everything all right, mate? The bride's havin' a bit of a fit in there."

I smiled at him, thankful for the interruption. "Oh, yeah, gosh. I better go, Frankie. I'll give you the whole story and all those pesky details later. Okay? First I need to go talk to Val and assure her that Artie's not dead."

I started backing away, heading towards the beach wedding area. I pointed at her as I walked. "Just know that not only did Sly admit to starting the fire, but he came here to kill both Artie and me to cover up what he did. So go ahead and add attempted murder to his list of crimes."

"Danny!"

"I gotta go, Frankie. You've got a big mess inside that tent to deal with, and I've got a bride to deal with. We'll talk soon." I spun around then, thankful to jog away and leave that mess behind me.

"Val!"

The bride stood at the edge of the pavement, looking off towards the beach. Tears streamed down her face. Evie held on to her, trying to comfort her as best she could, but Val was hysterical.

When she saw me coming, Val hollered out through her tears. "Drunk! Where *ees* my Artie?!"

"He's back there. In his tent. Calm down, Val. Artie's okay."

"He *ees*?" she asked, her eyes brightening. "Remy no kill him?"

"Remy no kill him," I said, smiling.

Val sucked in her breath and then launched herself at me, throwing her arms around my neck. "Oh my God, I was so scared! I hear the guns and I know right away it was Remy!"

"It was Sly too," I said.

Her eyes widened as she sucked in her breath. "What?"

I nodded. "We found out that *he* was the one that burned down the Crystal Point and tried to frame Artie."

Val slapped her hands over her mouth. "Oh my God."

Evie put her hand on my arm gently. "Terrence, but what about the gunshots we heard? Al was headed down there. Tell me my Al's all right."

I put my hand over hers and gave it a squeeze. "Al's fine too, Evie. Actually, it was Al and the guys that saved the day. They came in guns blazing." I smiled at her. "You should've seen him, Evie. He was a real Clint Eastwood."

Evie wiggled her brows. "Did he tell you I had a thing for Clint Eastwood?"

"And he had a thing for Sophia Loren? I heard."

She laughed.

"Nobody get hurt?" asked Val.

"Sly got shot. But he's alive." I let out a breath. I didn't know how Val would feel about the rest of it. Would she be devastated about the news? Remy had, after all, been her boss. I took her by the hands. "And Charlie's dead."

Her eyes widened.

"Denny and Ennis are fine."

"And Remy?" I could see her holding her breath.

"Val. Remy's dead," I said softly.

She slapped her hands over her mouth. As the news slowly began to sink in, her eyes filled with tears.

I grimaced and looked over at Evie, unsure of what to say. Finally, I put out a feeler. "I'm sorry?"

She let out a little squeaking noise as the tears rolled down her cheeks.

"Breathe, sweetheart. Remember, you must breathe," said Evie, quietly squeezing her arm.

Val nodded and drew in a deep breath. When she let it out, she found she almost couldn't get the words out. "You mean I am free?"

"Free?"

"Of Remy. He is gone?" She smiled from behind her tears.

"Yeah, he's gone all right," I said with a nod.

She squealed. "I am free!"

"Oh, I thought maybe you were going to be sad."

"Sad? No way, Jose! I so angry with Remy! He say he going to kill my Artie! Now I no have to worry anymore. I am so happy!" She threw her arms around my shoulders again and squeezed me tightly. "*Gracias*, Drunk. *Muchas gracias!*"

I pulled my head back and looked at her out of the corner of my eye. "Does this mean you forgive me for accusing you of setting the fire?"

"Yes! I *forgeeve* you!"

"Good."

When she finally let go of me, she looked up at me. "So I am still getting married?"

"Of course you are, if you want to be getting married. Of course there's a crime scene over there that Frankie has to deal with now, so, it might be a little while before we can get started again." I looked down at Evie. "Al was going to help Artie with his clothes. He got a little, uh, *schmutz* on his outfit with all the activity."

Evie's eyes widened. "Al doesn't know a thing about getting schmutz out of anything. If we've got plenty of time, then I think maybe we're just better off running and getting Artie a different suit. Maybe I'll go give Al a hand picking something out."

"I think that would be helpful. I'll stay here with Val."

Evie took off, leaving Val and me alone. Though she radiated happiness, her mascara was smeared all down her cheeks, and I knew she wouldn't want to get married looking like that. "Val, it's going to be a while before the police get this all sorted out. How about I drive you back to your cottage so you can freshen up? I'm afraid your makeup is a little smeared."

She giggled. "It is okay. I have makeup in the clubhouse. But the guests—"

I held up a hand. "Say no more. I'll take care of the guests. You just go get back in the clubhouse and relax and get cleaned up. Okay?"

She squeezed my arm. "Thank you, Drunk. Thank you so much. You save my Artie and you save the wedding."

"My pleasure." I leaned forward and planted a kiss on her cheek. "It's the least I could do after how happy you've made one of my best friends."

When she was gone, I took a deep breath. Then I turned to address the crowd of guests wandering around the pool and clubhouse area. "Attention, wedding guests! As you are probably aware, we've had a little setback." I held my hands out. "But don't worry, the groom is just fine. It is, however, going to take us a little while to get things rolling again. So, if you don't mind waiting, we'd like to invite everyone into the clubhouse for a little pre-wedding party. How's that sound? Open bar, on Artie!"

Cheers went up all around.

56

"If anyone has any objections as to why these two should not be wed in holy matrimony, please speak now or forever hold your peace."

Standing up for Artie, I glanced out into the crowd. I caught Al and the geriatric squad all looking over at me to see if I was going to object. And when I noticed Artie send a glance backwards at me, I opened my mouth and sucked in a deep breath like I had something to say. When the guys in the crowd all slid their hands into their vests as if they were going to stop me with whatever force they had available, I closed my mouth and let out the breath I'd just sucked in, grinning to myself that I'd psyched them out. I mean, even if I *did* object to the wedding, I wasn't that big of an asshole as to make yet another scene on Artie's big day.

When nothing came out of my mouth, all the guys relaxed. When Artie turned back around to face the officiant with a smile on his face, I shot Al a wink and the wedding continued.

"Since there are no objections, then by the power of your love and commitment and the power vested in me, it is with great pleasure that I now pronounce you man and wife! You may kiss your bride."

Before Artie could make a move, Val launched forward, laying a kiss on her new husband that brought hoots from the audience, followed by applause and laughter.

"Ladies and gentlemen, family and friends, it is my great pleasure to present to you, Mr. and Mrs. Valentina and Artie Balladares!" said the man officiating the wedding.

Artie took hold of Val's hand and lifted it into the air. "My beautiful bride, ladies and gentlemen!"

Val giggled as cheers went up across the beach and the organ music started back up again. Keeping hold of her hand, Artie and Val turned and walked down the aisle sprinkled with pink and aqua flower petals.

After everything that had happened, the wedding turned out perfectly. Artie had been granted his wish—to marry Valentina Carrizo. And without Remy or Sly there or the threat of a looming unwarranted arrest, he was able to say "I do" stress-free.

The newlyweds made their way to the pool area, where cocktail tables had been set up around the pool and a little live band was nestled in the corner. When Artie and Val's feet hit the concrete, the band kicked into action, and Artie spun Val around for their first dance as husband and wife.

As the wedding guests flooded the area from the beach, Al, Evie, Erika and I all made our way to the walk-up side of the swim-up bar to grab drinks before the line got too long.

"Well, they actually did it," said Al, leaning onto the bar.

Manny slid two of the couple's signature wedding drinks across the counter to Al and Evie. For Evie, Val's pale pink gin spritzer served in a tall glass and garnished with a bit of lemon peel and a hot pink flower, and for Al, a tumbler of Artie's old-fashioned, served over ice and garnished with a strip of orange peel. There was a cocktail table full of the signature drinks up in the clubhouse, and Manny would be serving them well into the evening.

"Yeah, they did," I agreed. I glanced over to watch Artie

spinning Val across the dance floor, and I had to admit he looked younger than I'd ever seen him before. Val seemed to pull something out of him that no one else could. Maybe everything had unfolded as it was supposed to.

"After everything, it really turned out to be a beautiful wedding," said Evie, taking a sip of her drink.

"And they look so happy together," said Erika.

I lifted another pair of drinks off the counter and handed Erika the pink gin spritzer. "For you, m'lady."

She smiled at me. "Thank you."

After the ruckus on the beach earlier in the day, Frankie had taken down everyone's statements and then left with the rest of the emergency personnel that had shown up to haul everyone away. Remy and Charlie's bodies were taken away in body bags while Denny and Ennis were handcuffed and thrown in the back of a cruiser. Sly left in an ambulance, cursing Artie the whole way and promising to get even someday. Of course Frankie told him that arson and attempted murder on the island carried a hefty sentence and he probably wouldn't be getting even anytime before his hundredth birthday.

Despite the lengthy commotion, Erika had decided to stick around and be my date for the wedding. Of course, originally I'd only asked her to be my date when I'd thought she was the arsonist and I'd hoped to get intel out of her. Now that things had changed and I had no intel to get out of her, I wasn't exactly sure how I felt about the woman. While it was true that she *hadn't* framed Artie for the fire, she'd still been responsible for some of the pranks around the resort, like tarring and feathering me and gluing Earnestine to my kitchen counter, so I couldn't exactly just grant her amnesty and make her my new best friend.

But we *had* slept together since all of our initial problems, so I was pretty sure Erika thought it was water under the bridge at this point. I, however, wasn't so sure. I still felt like I had to keep my guard up around the woman, and that wasn't exactly the best feeling to have about your date.

The band stopped playing and people around the pool area began clinking their glasses almost immediately. The clinking didn't stop until Artie leaned forward and kissed his new bride. Cheers went up again and someone handed the couple a drink.

Artie held it up. "I'd like to start this party off with a toast!"

Around the room, drinks went up into the air.

"First of all, I'd like to thank every one of you that made it here today. I'd like to thank all of my employees for putting this shindig together so quickly. And I want to especially thank my dear friends for being here for me today and honestly, saving my life. Without you—well, without you guys, I'd be dead right now and we'd have nothing to toast."

The crowd chuckled.

"But mostly, I'd like to raise my glass to this beautiful woman right here. She's made me young again, and I can't wait to spend the rest of my life growing younger every year with her by my side."

A collective *awwww* filled the salty beach air.

"To Val. The woman of my dreams. The spring in my step. And the new queen of the Seacoast Majestic. I'm so lucky to have found you."

"Hear, hear!" went the cheers.

Val giggled through tears. She leaned over and planted a kiss on her husband's cheek. Then she held up her own glass. "To my new husband. Artie, you have given me *everytheeng* I want in a man. You are kind. You are sweet and loving. You make me smile all the time. And you make me feel like the prettiest girl in the world. I love you, baby."

Cheers went up again. Val held her hands up, holding her pink drink in one as if she weren't done. "And I have a wedding present for the groom."

The pool area fell silent as everyone looked at her again.

Even Artie looked at her curiously. "Oh, sweetie. You didn't have to get me anything."

She smiled. "Yes, I did. Now. I don't know what to get my husband who have *everytheeng* he want, but I want to get *thees* for you." She pulled something from the cleavage of her dress. It was a long tube of paper, rolled up and tied with a little pink ribbon. She handed it to Artie.

Artie frowned as he took the tube and unrolled it. "What is it?"

"It *ees* marriage papers. I sign it today."

"Papers?"

Her brow furrowed. "How you say it? Prenup?"

"Prenup? Val! I told you we didn't need to—"

Val pressed a finger to Artie's lips to quiet him. "I know what you say," she said with a smile. Then she winked at him. "But I no want you to take my money."

The crowd laughed.

Even Artie chuckled.

Smiling, Val continued, "I appreciate that you trust me, to marry with no papers. But I want prove to you, and every one of you friends, that I marry you because I love you. No because I want to take you money."

Wow. Smooth move, Val, I thought, shaking my head. She'd managed to shock me, and I was sure she'd shocked Artie. I glanced over at Al.

Lifting his brows, he smiled at me and nodded, like he'd expected that to happen all along, what had *I* been worried about?

"But *I* knew why you were marrying me," said Artie.

Val lifted a shoulder. "But maybe you friends not so convince."

"Well, you certainly didn't have to prove anything to my friends!"

"But I want to. Now. You just need sign." She produced a

pen from the depths of her cleavage, like she wore a magical brassiere beneath her dress, and handed it to Artie.

"Sweetheart, I don't want to—"

"Sign," she ordered, holding the pen up to him strictly.

Artie and all the guests chuckled. "Okay, okay."

A nearby guest bent slightly, crooking at the waist to give Artie a hard surface to use. He gave a quick glance at what he was signing and then scrawled his signature at the bottom of the short document. Then he rolled it up and handed it to Val.

"There. Thank you, sweetheart. I love you."

"I love you too. Now kiss me, husband," she said, pulling him in for a big wet one.

The crowd cheered and the band fired up once again.

57

IT WAS MONDAY MORNING, AND ARTIE AND VAL WERE GONE ON their honeymoon. As Artie's second-in-command, I'd been tasked with keeping the place running while he was gone, and since the resort pretty much ran itself, I was down at the pool playing miniature golf with the guys.

Eddie was up to swing. He pulled his club back to give the ball a whack and sent it flying over the course and into the resort's pool.

All the men groaned.

"Oh, come on, Big Ed," said Ralph. "The balls go in the monkey's mouth, not in the pool."

I laughed. "Oh, come on, fellas. It takes a lot of balls to golf the way Eddie does. Cut him a break." I put a hand to the side of my mouth and winked at Trinity, who was working behind me at the snack bar. "A *lot* of balls."

She laughed.

"Hey, Drunk, since you're the boss today, can I leave early?" Trinity hollered over at me.

My face sobered up. "Oh. What time?"

"Can ya think of a better time than now?" she laughed.

I pointed at her and my smile returned. "Good one. Nah, if I'm stuck working, we're all stuck working."

She bobbed her head towards the miniature golf course. "I don't know that I'd call what you're doin' workin', though."

"What? I'm making sure the golf equipment is all in order." She rolled her eyes. "Hard job."

"*Someone's* gotta do it," I quipped, turning around to watch Gary take his shot next.

"Huh-ummm," I heard a voice clear behind me.

"Fine, Trin. You can play next round, how's that?" I said, looking over my shoulder. But it wasn't Trinity clearing her throat behind me. It was Erika Wild. I stared at her for a moment, a bit dumbfounded.

Even though we'd had a pleasant enough evening the night of Artie and Val's wedding, I didn't think I'd see much of her anymore. That evening, we'd danced together until the festivities wound down, but when she'd suggested we go back to my place, I'd taken a step back and told her maybe we just needed to go our separate ways. I hadn't wanted to wake up tied to the bed again, even if it did sound like a pleasant way to part ways.

I turned around, apparently missing Gary's shot as all the guys booed. I suspected he'd sunk the shot and the boos were simply due to jealousy. I looked Erika up and down. She was wearing one of her suits again. And her heels. Her hair was loose around her shoulders, and she wore her blood-red lipstick. She looked like she was headed back for a day at the office.

"Ahh, Wild? What are you doing here? Can't get enough of me?"

She clicked her heels together, straightened her spine, and gave me a little salute. "Actually, I'm reporting for duty, sir."

With a dumb smile still plastered to my face, my head tipped slightly. "I'm sorry. You're what?"

"Reporting for duty? It means I'm here to work."

"Yeah, I know what that means. But what does that *mean*?"

She quirked a brow as she looked at me curiously. "You know. First day on the job. *Primer día de trabajo,*" she added with a smile.

"First of all, I don't speak Spanish."

She pointed at me. "But you do speak English?"

"Not British English."

"American English?"

My hand teeter-tottered back and forth in the air. "Meh. Apparently that's questionable. You see, I still don't get what you're doing here."

"Drunk, didn't Artie tell you? He hired me."

My eyes nearly bugged out of my head. "I'm sorry. Artie did what?!"

She chuckled. "Before he left. He hired me."

"As what?! Resident smart-ass? Because we already have one of those," I said, thumbing my chest. "And I don't think having more than one is a very good idea."

"He hired me to be the new activities director."

I frowned at her, confused. "But we don't have an *old* activities director. That position doesn't even exist."

She shrugged. "It does now."

"Artie *made up* a position for you? Why would he do that?"

"I don't know. I guess he was grateful to me for helping you clear his name, and he knew I was out of a job. He said something about good help being hard to find. And he mentioned that he might like to buy Sly's resort so he can expand."

"I don't understand. So he just *hired you*? Without even checking your references or anything?"

"Sly was a reference."

"Sly was a criminal!"

"He was still a reference. And I did a good job when I worked for him."

"You *glued* my parrot's feet to my kitchen counter!"

395

"Because Sly *told* me to. I have a very good work ethic."

"What's going on over here?" asked Al, hobbling over to my side.

I pointed at Erika. "Erika is trying to get me to believe that Artie *hired* her before he left for his honeymoon."

"He did. She's the new activities director. Welcome aboard, Ms. Wild."

I stared down at Al, stunned.

She smiled at Al. "Thank you, Mr. Becker. I appreciate the warm welcome from *someone*."

"You *knew* about this, Al?"

Al scratched his chin. "Oh, uh, yeah. Artie mentioned it before he left on his honeymoon."

"You're telling me you knew about this since he left and you didn't tell me?"

Al swatted the air. "I didn't wanna ruin your weekend, kid." He pointed at me. "You're welcome."

I stared at the two of them with my mouth gaping wide. I had to *work* with this woman now? What the hell was Artie doing to me?

Erika reached a hand out and pushed my jaw up to close my mouth. "Now. Do you have anyone that can help me with unloading my car?"

My eyes swiveled to look at her. "What do you mean, unload your car? What's in your car?"

"Well, my stuff of course."

"Your stuff? What stuff?"

"Duh? My suitcases and my TV. And my cat, Juno. I thought Americans were smarter than this," she said to Al.

"Most of us are," he said.

I shook my head. "I'm sorry. I really don't understand what's going on here. Why do you have your cat in your car?"

"Erika's moving into the cottage next door to you, kid."

My head swiveled to stare at her. "She's what?!"

"I was living on Sly's property before. But now that I'm not working for him anymore, I had to move. Artie said he had a place for me."

"Oh no," I said, crossing my fingers in the air. "No, no, no. No. This is not happening."

"Oh, it's happening." Erika grinned at me. "We're gonna be neighbors."

"Nuh-uh."

"We can have movie nights and popcorn parties."

"This isn't happening."

She put a finger on her chin and frowned. "How does Earnestine feel about cats?"

I grabbed Al's shoulder. "Al. Please. Tell me this is another prank."

"It ain't a prank, kid." He patted my hand and then shoved it off his shoulder and addressed Erika. "I'll get Hector and Caesar to help you move in," said Al, waddling away. "You can pull your car around to the back."

"Al, don't!"

"Sorry, kid," he threw back over his shoulders. "Artie's orders."

"Ugh!" I groaned, unable to believe this was seriously happening.

Erika grinned at me from ear to ear. "You and me are going to have so much fun. I can tell already!"

HEY THERE, IT'S ZANE...

I'm the author of this book. I've got a huge favor to ask of you. If you even remotely enjoyed Drunk, Al, and their predicament, I'd be honored if you left a review on Amazon. I'd love to see this book reach more readers, and one way to do that is to have a whole bunch of feedback from readers like you that liked it.

Leaving reviews also tells me that you want more books in the series or want to read more about certain characters. Or, I guess, conversely, if you didn't like it, it tells me to either try harder or not to give up my day job.

So, thanks in advance. I appreciate the time you took to read my book, and I wish you nothing but the best!

Zane

MANNY'S CARNIVAL RUM PUNCH RECIPE

8 oz chilled cranberry juice
8 oz chilled orange juice
8 oz chilled pineapple juice
4 oz Bacardi 8 Dark Rum
4 oz Bacardi White Rum
2 oz Amaretto Disaronno

Mix all ingredients together in a large pitcher and pour over ice in a punch glass.

Pineapple wedges, orange slices, and maraschino cherries make a nice garnish.

Enjoy!

ALSO BY ZANE MITCHELL

If you'd like to notified when new books in the series are released, then consider joining my newsletter.

I swear I won't spam you, I'm really not that ambitious.

I'll only send out an email when I write a new book or have something to give away that I think you might like.

So what is that?

A couple emails a year?

You can handle that, can't you?

Go to www.zanemitchell.com/news to signup!

ABOUT ZANE

I grew up on a sheep farm in the Midwest. I was an only child, raised on Indiana Jones, Star Wars, and the Dukes of Hazzard. My dad was a fresh-water fish biologist and worked on the Missouri River. My mom was a teacher when I was young, and then became the principal of my school around the time I started taking an interest in beer. My grandpa, much like Al in my Drunk in Paradise series, actually owned a Case IH dealership, and I thought the world of him and my grandma.

I've been married twice. I'd say the first was a mistake, but that marriage gave me my four kids. Marriage numero dos came with two pre-made kids. So yeah, we're paying for Christmas presents for six and college for three. So buy my next book, *please*. I'd say that was a joke, but jeez. College is expensive.

In a former life, I was a newspaper columnist, and I actually went to journalism school but eventually dropped out. I did go back to school and eventually got a teaching degree, but let's face facts. I sucked at being a teacher. I was just as much of a kid as the kids were.

The love of my life and I live in the Midwest. We go about our boring lives just like you do. We parent lots of teenagers and twenty-something-year-olds. We watch superhero movies and Dateline on TV. We're a little obsessive in our love for the Kansas City Chiefs. We take yearly visits to the Caribbean because hey, tax deductible. And now, I write books - sort of a life long dream, to be honest.

So thanks for reading. You have no idea how cool I think it

is, that you picked *my* book out of all of the choices you had to read and you made it to the end. You rock. Don't ever let anyone tell you otherwise.

Zane

Oh. P.S. I don't do Tweets. Or Insta. I do have Facebook and a website. www.zanemitchell.com. You're welcome to come over and hangout. BYOB.

Made in the USA
Columbia, SC
27 May 2021